NOT QUITE A WIFE

**Center Point
Large Print**

Also by Mary Jo Putney and available from
Center Point Large Print:

The Lost Lords series
  Nowhere Near Respectable
  No Longer a Gentleman
  Sometimes a Rogue

**This Large Print Book carries the
Seal of Approval of N.A.V.H.**

NOT QUITE A WIFE

Mary Jo Putney

CENTER POINT LARGE PRINT
THORNDIKE, MAINE

This Center Point Large Print edition
is published in the year 2014 by arrangement with
Kensington Publishing Corp.

Copyright © 2014 by Mary Jo Putney.

All rights reserved.

The text of this Large Print edition is unabridged.
In other aspects, this book may vary
from the original edition.
Printed in the United States of America
on permanent paper.
Set in 16-point Times New Roman type.

ISBN: 978-1-62899-326-4

Library of Congress Cataloging-in-Publication Data

Putney, Mary Jo.
  Not quite a wife / Mary Jo Putney. — Center Point Large Print edition.
      pages ; cm.
  Summary: "Laurel Herbert married James, Lord Kirkland, as an
innocent young girl. When she saw him perform an act of shocking
violence, she declared she never wanted to see him again. Now, ten
years later, a chance encounter with him turns passionate, with
consequences that cannot be ignored"—Provided by publisher.
  ISBN 978-1-62899-326-4 (library binding : alk. paper)
  1. Large type books. I. Title.
PS3566.U83N68 2014
813′.54—dc23
                                                    2014030599

To PandaMax,
the leader of the pack.
And to all the generous rescuers who
help animals in distress
find better lives.

Acknowledgments

To my friend, fellow author, and ER nurse, Laurie Kingery, for still more valuable medical information!

And, of course, the Cauldron and the Wenches and my most excellent agent, Robin Rue.

Chapter 1

James, Lord Kirkland, owned a shipping fleet and half a fashionable London gaming house, and was a darkly effective spymaster in the shadow war between Britain and Napoleon's France. He was seldom self-indulgent . . .

. . . except when his business took him to the port city of Bristol, as it had done today. He met with the captain of his ship, deciphered the letter the captain had brought, and gave it to a courier to carry back to London with all due haste. Then he dismissed his assistant, saying that he preferred to walk back to the inn where they were staying.

The late spring afternoon sunshine and warmth made his words plausible, though rain, ice, or snow wouldn't have stopped him. For these brief minutes, he wouldn't think about his business, or his covert work, or the possible undesirable outcomes to various plans, or potentially lethal threats to his agents. Instead, he'd remember, and grieve for, what he'd lost.

The day had warmed up considerably while he conducted his business on shipboard. If he were private, he'd strip off his coat and hat and work in his shirtsleeves. Ah, well, he'd be back at the inn soon enough.

Now he tormented himself with the knowledge

that she lived only a few streets away. He savored the bittersweet thought that in minutes he could knock on her door.

She might open it herself—she was never one for ceremony—and they'd be face to face again. Would her lustrous bronze hair have darkened? Would her misty sea eyes be blue or gray?

His mouth twisted at the knowledge that her expressive eyes would be gray with anger and disappointment when she saw him. Which was why he wouldn't turn down the street that led to her home. She'd said she never wanted to see him again, and he'd sworn that she wouldn't.

Sometimes his sophist's mind played with that. He'd promised she wouldn't see him, but did that mean that he could look at her if he remained unseen? But looking would never be enough. . . .

He cut off his line of thought, for that way madness lay.

Damn, but it was hot today! He wrenched at his neck cloth, feeling suffocated. Only then, as he lurched against the wall of the building beside him, did he realize that he was having a malaria attack. He seldom had them these days, but sometimes, usually at the most inconvenient possible moment, the fever would flare up again.

He must return to his inn, where he had Jesuit's bark to tame the fever. The inn couldn't be more than ten minutes' walk away. Head spinning, he turned down an alley that would take him in that direction.

Halfway down he stopped, not recognizing the buildings at the other end. This wasn't right, he must have walked farther than he'd realized. He turned uncertainly and started to retrace his steps.

Dizzy, he halted to lean against the wall, grateful for the cool brick against his sweating forehead. The inn. The *inn!* What was the name? The *Ship?* The *Ostrich?* Dammit, *what was the name?* He'd stayed there often.

He pushed himself upright and started again toward the alley entrance, one hand skimming the wall for balance, but after a dozen steps he folded to his knees, gasping for breath. He needed to get to a safe place. The inn, or back to his ship, which would still be in the harbor.

The light darkened and he saw two men approaching down the alley. *"Please,"* he said raggedly. "I need help. . . ."

"Well, lookee here," a crude West Country voice said. "A pigeon for the plucking. Drunk as a lord, he be."

"Mebbe he is a lord," his companion cackled. "Look at them clothes! I wager he has a heavy purse. That coat'll be worth a pretty penny, too."

Kirkland swore to himself. Ordinarily he could handle two clumsy louts without even breathing hard, but at the moment, an alley cat could take him down.

11

Even so, his trained reflexes kicked in when a rough hand grabbed his arm and dragged him to his feet so the man could yank at his coat. Kirkland wrenched free and kicked the fellow's knee, sending his assailant staggering.

"Bugger!" the man swore, enraged. "You'll be sorry for that!"

They came at him together, snarling the filthiest oaths imaginable. Kirkland managed to land a few blows, but he was quickly knocked to the ground. A booted foot swung viciously toward his head. He tried to roll away, but the wall prevented him from getting clear. The boot grazed his skull, and merciful darkness descended.

Infirmary hours were over for the day, and Laurel Herbert luxuriated in the quiet. Not many people had come seeking treatment that afternoon. That was fortunate since Daniel was away and Laurel was no physician, though she'd learned a great deal through working in the infirmary for years.

Betsy Rivers, her assistant, was away visiting her ailing grandmother, so Laurel had the house to herself for the night. Such delicious peace!

She made a cup of tea, releasing her hair from its knot as the tea steeped. When the drink was ready, she carried the gently fragrant cup upstairs to the music room, where her piano, a magnificent Broadwood, awaited.

Also waiting was her gray tomcat, Shadow. He

looked up from the chair where he'd been snoozing, blinked his golden eyes, then tucked his nose under his tail again. He was very easy company, which suited her mood.

Laurel settled on the bench and put the tea aside to cool. What to play? She was learning a new Mozart piece, but since she was tired, her fingers drifted into her favorite Beethoven sonata. Music was food for the soul, and she loved the serene power of the piece even though it carried too many memories.

She had just finished the Adagio movement when she heard the knocker hammering on the infirmary door. She smiled ruefully and took a large swallow of tea before setting the cup aside to head downstairs. She should have known that peace and quiet were not guaranteed. The Herbert Infirmary never refused anyone, and since she lived upstairs and was the only one here this evening, the duty was hers.

In the interest of dignity, she tied a simple knot in her long hair. It would slide out soon, but while it lasted, she'd look more mature and responsible.

She opened the door to find two stevedores from the port who attended services at her brother's chapel. Between them they carried an unconscious man wearing only drawers and a torn, bloody shirt, his limp arms slung over their shoulders.

"Sorry, Miss Herbert," the taller man, Potter, said. "We found this fellow beaten bad in an alley and figgered you'd see to him."

"And so I will. You were right to bring him here." Laurel stepped back so they could move past her. The injured man's head was hanging and dark hair obscured his face, but he looked fit and healthy, which always helped in recovery.

As they carried him to the nearest examination room, Larkin said worriedly, "He's got a fever, poor sod. Not the pox, is it?"

"I see no signs of smallpox," Laurel said reassuringly. "Fevers have many causes."

The examination room had good natural light and a wide, padded table standing in the middle. Built-in cabinets held instruments, bandages, linens, and other supplies.

The stevedores laid the man down with surprising gentleness and rolled him onto his back. Laurel frowned as she scanned the damage. Bruises and lacerations aplenty, but no massive bleeding, no obviously broken bones, and his breathing was good.

If there wasn't a serious head injury . . . Her gaze moved to his face. Strong, even features, high cheekbones . . . She gasped, icy weakness washing through her.

"You know him, miss?" Potter asked.

She struggled for control, and was surprised how calm her voice sounded. "He's . . . Lord Kirkland.

A friend of the family. He and my brother were schoolmates."

Larkin scratched his head. "If he be a lord, someun' will be looking for him. Was he comin' to visit you?"

"He has a shipping company, so likely he's in Bristol on business," she said, still unnaturally calm. "He had swamp fever as a boy and sometimes it flares up again. If that's the case this time, there's no risk to you for your good deed."

Potter asked, "Do you need help with the fellow, Miss Herbert?"

Guessing that they wanted to get home for their supper, she shook her head. "No, I'll examine Lord Kirkland to see how serious his injuries are. If he needs a surgeon, I'll send someone from Zion House to bring one." She managed a smile. "Mr. Potter, Mr. Larkin—you have been true good Samaritans today."

Pleased by her praise, they ducked their heads bashfully and left. Laurel latched the door behind them, then leaned back against it, shaking. Could she have been wrong in her identification? She'd been seeing shadows of James Kirkland in other men for years.

No, she would recognize him at midnight in a coal mine. Steeling herself, she returned to the examination room to tend his injuries. He looked oddly vulnerable lying there. Young. Not as enigmatic and formidable as he loomed in her memory.

15

James, Lord Kirkland. Rich beyond imagining, onetime best friend to her brother, the most dangerous man she'd ever met.

James, the husband she'd left ten long years ago.

Chapter 2

Kirkland struggled through agonizing darkness, knowing it was a fever attack. His dreams of Laurel were always most vivid when his body burned. Then she seemed real enough to touch. Memories of her flooded through him with hypnotic intensity.

If he lived to be a hundred, he'd never forget the night they met. Laurel's older brother, Daniel Herbert, had been a student at the Westerfield Academy a class behind Kirkland. Daniel hadn't been sent there for bad behavior—he'd been a paragon of courtesy and discipline.

But his parents worried that he was too religious. A proper English gentleman should be a man of faith, but too much faith was—unseemly.

Worse, Daniel was drawn to reformist sects like the Methodists, and his parents saw no reason why society needed reforming. They'd sent their son to Lady Agnes Westerfield on the assumption that a duke's daughter would ensure that her students had a good Church of England upbringing.

They'd been right, to a point. Students had to attend weekly chapel services, but they weren't required to hold any particular set of beliefs. Lady Agnes Westerfield, who had traveled widely, believed that the Church of England was not the only path to heaven.

Kirkland and Daniel Herbert had become friends when they discovered a mutual passion for discussing ethics, morals, and philosophy to a depth that sent other students fleeing. Daniel's views were more religious and spiritual while Kirkland leaned toward philosophers like Locke and Voltaire. Their conclusions about justice and morals were often the same, but the paths they took there were different.

Their stimulating discussions continued for years as they moved from the Westerfield Academy to Oxford. Kirkland had just finished at Balliol when Daniel invited him to visit the Herbert family home near Bristol.

Slowed by muddy roads, the two of them had arrived late at Belmond Manor, after the household had retired. Daniel showed Kirkland to a guest room, then went yawning to bed.

Though the room was comfortable, Kirkland had trouble falling to sleep. He was tossing and turning when he heard music. A pianist was playing Beethoven in the room below his bedchamber. He loved music and was competent on the piano, but whoever played downstairs was extraordinary.

Kirkland was cursed with curiosity, so he donned slippers and a banyan and followed the enchanting music. Downstairs he opened the door to the music room—and saw Laurel Herbert for the first time.

She sat on the other side of the piano, her delicate features illuminated by a branch of candles. Her face and fair coloring emphasized her resemblance to Daniel, and she was so beautiful that she hurt his heart. She didn't have the flamboyant appearance of a girl who could enter a room and draw every eye. Yet when he looked at her, he couldn't look away.

She glanced up as the door opened. Her wide-set eyes were a misty blue gray and the heavy braid of hair falling over her shoulder had the lustrous warmth of polished bronze.

As their gazes met, powerful energy sparked between them like silent lightning. Every fiber in his body came alive.

For the space of a dozen heartbeats, her hands stilled on the keyboard as her eyes widened. Then she rose and circled around the piano to greet him. Though he knew she was not yet eighteen, she had a quiet self-possession that was rare at any age.

"You must be Daniel's friend, Lord Kirkland." She smiled and offered her hand. She was tall and graceful as a fawn. "Welcome to Belmond Manor, my lord."

"Call me James." As he took her hand and met her steady gaze, warmth and peace flowed through him, touching places in his soul that had been numb his whole life. Warmth and openness were the very essence of Laurel Herbert, and as he tightened his clasp on her hand, he knew with absurd certainty that he would love this woman till the day he died.

Laurel had tended patients of all ages, races, and both genders over the years, so she could tend an estranged husband. Or so she told herself, though her hands were shaking when she brewed a pot of Jesuit's bark tea and set it aside to steep while she treated his injuries.

She might have stripped off the tattered garments if he'd been an unconscious stranger, but with James—she couldn't. He was an intensely private man, and she of all people had no right to invade that privacy. So she inspected him limb by limb, testing that bones were intact and cleaning scrapes and cuts before moving on.

She'd known this body so well once. . . .

No! She cut off the thought and concentrated on cleaning the shallow but messy head wound that accounted for most of the bloodstains on his shirt. He was thinner than she remembered, taut muscle over bone with no softness anywhere. Working too hard, no doubt. Under his polished reserve, he'd always run on his nerves. Like a candle burning at both ends . . .

Again she cut off the thought. He'd have bruises galore, but apart from his fever, his condition was good, though he'd have a pounding headache when he awoke.

By the time she finished cleaning and treating his wounds, the Jesuit's bark was ready. She strained a cup of the bitter fluid and stirred in a generous portion of honey.

He shifted restlessly as she propped him up with pillows, then spooned tea between his lips. Though his face twisted at the taste, he must have recognized it as necessary medicine because he didn't pull away. Seeing that he was swallowing well, she held the cup to his mouth so he could drink directly.

When the cup was empty, she set it aside. She needed to light the lamps since dusk was falling. As she started to move away, he caught her hand and pulled it to his lips in a kiss that seemed to scald her fingers. She jerked away, but couldn't block the flood of memories of the night they'd met.

Daniel had often spoken of Kirkland, so she'd known that her brother's friend must be an interesting and sharply intelligent young man. But she hadn't expected his dark, riveting intensity when he found her in the music room.

She'd glanced up and was caught by the deep blue eyes that seemed to look into her very soul. When she rose to greet him, it wasn't manners that moved her but a need to move closer.

They exchanged introductions as she extended

her hand. After she gave him permission to call her Laurel, he bowed and pressed his lips on the back of her fingers, a curiously formal gesture under the circumstances.

Her pulse began to race. Kirkland fascinated her, and she seemed to have the same effect on him, though she had no idea why. She was an ordinary girl with no unusual experiences or talents. Yet when he looked at her, she felt unique and beautiful.

At his request, she played the piano more while he sat on the bench beside her and turned the pages of the scores. Though they didn't touch, he was so close that she felt the heat of his body all along her right side. When he asked her to sing, she persuaded him to join her, and their voices blended as if they'd sung together all their lives.

Neither of them wanted to say good night, so she suggested they descend to the kitchen for a midnight supper. She scrambled eggs and herbs and cheese while he made tea and toasted bread. Laurel knew basic cooking because her mother thought it was a woman's duty to understand everything in the household, but she was impressed that Lord Kirkland was not totally baffled by a kitchen.

Daringly Laurel produced a bottle of her father's best white wine to accompany the meal, and their conversation continued through the night. Kirkland encouraged her to talk about herself, and his genuine interest was intoxicating.

Kirkland in his turn told her amusing stories about the clashes between his parents. His aristocratic English father had married a strong-minded Scottish merchant's daughter for her fortune, and exchanging vows was the last time the pair had agreed on anything. Kirkland's preference for his down-to-earth Scottish relatives had resulted in his father sending him off to the Westerfield Academy after his parents separated.

Though his anecdotes were witty, Laurel could hear the pain and loneliness of the little boy he'd been. Only later did she learn that he'd revealed more of himself in a single night than he'd shown her brother in years of friendship.

Their tête-à-tête ended when the cook came yawning into the kitchen to start the day's bread baking. She laughed and shooed them away to return to their beds for the hours before the rest of the household rose. Laurel left the kitchen reluctantly, fearing that the magic of the night would vanish by morning.

But it didn't. Instead of escorting her to her room, Kirkland took a detour to the music room, where dawn's first light was brightening the chamber. Setting his hands on her shoulders, he said with quiet conviction, "Laurel, I do believe we should marry. Shall I speak with your father this morning?"

Her jaw dropped. Despite the intensity of their hours together, the idea of marriage shocked her.

This man, this brilliant young lord, wanted her for his wife?

She stammered, "I . . . I believe the correct answer is, 'Sir, this is so sudden!'"

"Yes, it is," he said softly, his gaze holding hers. "But I've never felt surer of anything in my life."

She drew a shaky breath, wanting to say yes but realizing how mad this conversation was. "Why me? Surely you've met many females who are richer, more beautiful, more knowledgeable."

"Perhaps. But as soon as I saw you, I knew you were the one I've been looking for," he said with stark honesty. "We can take all the time you want to become better acquainted. Just . . . please, don't say no. I need you."

The power of his certainty swept through her like a summer storm and found matching certainty in her soul. Though she had never believed in love at first sight, now she did. There was much they didn't know about each other, but she believed on a level of deep truth that they belonged together.

Thinking she must be mad, she hesitantly tested her conviction by standing on her toes and giving him a shy kiss. His lips were warm and firm. Intoxicating. He caught his breath and slipped his arms around her waist, returning the kiss with slow tenderness and a yearning so deep she could feel it in her bones.

From the moment they'd met, she'd known he was a passionate man. Now she discovered that she was a passionate woman. She had been kissed a few times by young men of her acquaintance, and found the process only mildly interesting.

But with James Kirkland, her body and soul caught fire. She pressed against him, her mouth opening under his with eager exploration. No wonder men and women made fools of themselves for love, she thought dizzily. She wanted to sink into him, merge into one. She wanted him to sink into her. . . .

Kirkland was the one to end the kiss, his breathing jagged as he locked his hands around her upper arms and retreated a step. "I . . . I hope that means you are at least willing to consider my proposal."

Doubts banished, she smiled up at him, happier than she'd ever been in her life. "I do believe you're right. We should marry, because I can't imagine ever feeling this way about another man."

His face lit with joy as he kissed her again. The powerful sense of rightness was irresistible and she gave herself to it willingly. They were meant to be together, she was sure of it. . . .

When Laurel snapped out of her unwelcome reverie, she realized that she had retreated halfway across the room. She was shaking and her fingers were pressed hard on her lips, as if his kisses still burned there.

If only she could hate Kirkland. But she

couldn't. Hate was not part of her nature. Instead, she had an agonizing hole in her heart because the chasm between them was too wide to be bridged.

Her parents had been startled when Laurel and Kirkland decided to marry on the basis of a single night's conversation, but they were also overjoyed at the prospect of their daughter making such a splendid match. Though the Herberts were respected members of the gentry, their branch of the family didn't possess titles or great wealth or political connections. Now their daughter would be a countess.

The Herberts invited Kirkland to stay at the house for the month until Laurel's eighteenth birthday. During that time, the two could further their acquaintance. After her birthday, if the two were still of a mind to marry, they could wed in the parish church.

Though it was sensible to take more time, nothing that happened in the following weeks made Laurel's betrothal seem like a mistake. Every day she loved James more as they laughed and talked and made music together.

He ordered books for her to read, listening to her seriously when they discussed them. One of the things she loved most was the way he respected her intelligence and encouraged her to form her own opinions.

She watched him carefully for any sign that he was regretting his hasty proposal, but she saw none. He lit up like a candle whenever he saw her, and she realized that her presence made him happy in ways he hadn't been before. She'd given up trying to understand why. She was just grateful that they pleased each other equally.

Interestingly, only Daniel, who knew Kirkland best, had doubts. Laurel laughed his concern away when her brother cautioned her that Kirkland was a complicated and not always easy man. Yes, she and her husband would have occasional disagreements. All couples did. But the love they shared was too powerful and true to ignore.

Looking back on that time of absolute certainty and joy, she knew that she'd been right about the power and truth of their love. Her tragic mistake was being too young and inexperienced to know that love wasn't always enough.

Chapter 3

Laurel's remembering ended when Kirkland moved restlessly, his face shiny with perspiration. She frowned and poured another cup of the fever tea. He needed both the remedy and the fluids. She'd treated enough patients with fever to know how unpredictable the course could be, alternating between chills and fever and, at its worst, delirium. She hoped he was receiving the remedy early enough to prevent his illness from worsening.

She propped him up on the pillows and slowly coaxed him into drinking more tea. His dark hair was matted with perspiration and needed a cut. He always wore it a little longer than fashion decreed. Though she could see fine lines of strain around his eyes, she was struck by how little his appearance had changed.

He was, what, thirty-two now? A man in the prime of life. When they'd met, he'd been twenty-one. *Young.* He was only recently down from Oxford, and had been in possession of his full inheritance for less than a year.

To her, he'd seemed like a mature man of the world, but looking back, she realized that they were barely more than children. If only they'd had the sense to wait! But with passion blazing through their veins, waiting was intolerable, and there were no barriers to prevent them from marrying.

"Damn you, you'll not get away with that!" Kirkland cried out, his voice harsh. He swung his arm, striking Laurel across her cheek and almost knocking her to the floor.

He began thrashing as if in a fight for his life. Fearing he'd fall from the examination table, she caught his shoulder. "James, stop struggling!" she said briskly. "You're safe now. I'm with you and you're safe."

He stopped thrashing and raised his head to stare at her with mad, unfocused eyes. "Laurel? Is that really you?"

She stroked his damp hair back and said soothingly, "Indeed it is, James. You are having one of your fever attacks, but you're safe here. You'll be all right."

"Oh, God, *Laurel!*" He caught her around the waist and pulled her onto the table beside him in a crushing embrace. "I had the most ghastly dreams that I'd lost you. I looked everywhere and couldn't find you." His grip tightened as he said in a hoarse whisper, "You were gone and I was so afraid. So afraid . . ."

She gasped, shocked by being held full length against his barely clothed body. She knew she should break free, but the sheer physical rightness of being in his arms paralyzed her.

Even more shocking was the raw emotion and need in his voice. When she'd left him, he'd seemed cool and uncaring, as if relieved that she'd no longer require time and attention. He'd shown no signs of pain.

Trying to control her trembling, she said, "I'm not lost; I'm right here. You need to rest and drink more Jesuit's bark tea. By morning you should be fine."

"Now that I've found you again"—he rolled over so that he was braced above her—"I'll never let you go." He kissed her with naked hunger, as if craving her very soul.

Wisdom evaporated in an instant and she kissed him back, drinking from his mouth as if she were dying and his passion was the nectar of life. All the years of weeping with loneliness and heated, frustrated dreams had made her as hungry as he.

His hands moved over her, kneading her yielding flesh as the kiss burned through the night. When he cupped her breast, heat shot straight to her loins. When he pulled up her skirts and laid his scorching hand on her bare thigh, she went half mad, every fiber of her being pulsing in response. Her legs separated and she cried out when he touched her moist, swollen flesh, desperate for the release he offered.

She scarcely noticed when he dragged off his drawers, and she was ready, more than ready, when he surged into her in the ultimate intimacy.

"Laurel, my love," he gasped, "I've missed you so much. . . ."

She needed this mating as much as he. Through the lonely years, she'd dreamed of the brief, happy months of their marriage. Though their differences had proved irreconcilable, there had been no conflict in their bed.

"Ah, God . . ." He groaned and poured himself into her, bringing on a release so shattering that she lost track of time and place, knowing only the passion that bound them together. For too long she had been empty, and now he made her whole.

She cried out and crushed herself against him, her body softening as tension flowed away, leaving peace and utter fulfillment. He also relaxed, murmuring soft, unintelligible words that she knew meant love.

She wanted this deep, treacherous sense of rightness to last forever, but she knew that it was an illusion. Society would think their coupling no sin since they were lawfully wed, yet she knew in her heart that it was wrong. She'd walked away from her husband for good reason, yet tonight, she'd weakly yielded to the damnable physical bond that still joined them. What had she been *thinking?*

She hadn't thought at all, only reacted to his touch and urgent emotions. She began to edge out from under his solid weight.

Though he was still delirious, he shifted to his

side to free her, but he caught her hand to keep her close. Rather than pull away, she took a deep breath to collect herself. Then she examined him with the eyes of experience.

Though still feverish and unaware of his surroundings, his restlessness had subsided and he was sliding into deep sleep. He'd had two fever attacks during the time they were together. The second time, they'd made love before the attack became too severe. James had been feverish but aware and passionate. Afterward he fell deeply asleep and awoke with the fever broken. As he'd kissed her good morning, he told her that she was the best remedy imaginable.

She suspected Jesuit's bark was more reliable, but her presence did seem to be good for him. Her nurse's intuition said there was a good chance that once again, James would sleep deeply and awake with the fever broken.

She couldn't undo what they had just done. She couldn't even make herself wish that it hadn't happened. But she could keep it to herself. When feverish, James had strange, wild dreams. If she acted with calm detachment, he would believe their encounter was merely one such dream.

She must clean them both and get a nightshirt on him so there would be no trace of their intimacy. When he awoke, she'd notify his servants to collect him and it would be as if this night's mad mating had never happened. James would return to his complicated world while she would continue with the work that gave her life meaning.

And she would bury her heart once again.

Laurel. Kirkland gradually rose from darkness to awareness, drifting in a sea of well-being. He'd dreamed of his wife, which wasn't unusual, but most of the time, she vanished when he took her in his arms, leaving him aching with loneliness and frustration. This time he'd had one of his rare dreams of satisfaction, and with a degree of realism that was searing.

But consciousness would not be denied. He had a large inventory of aches and pains, including a throbbing head. What had happened? And where was he?

Not a familiar place, he was sure of that, but he was reasonably comfortable, lying on a firm but well-cushioned bed with clean-smelling sheets and covers. Memory rushed back. Damn, he'd had a fever attack while walking through Bristol, and had been too weak to fend off attackers!

He recognized the scent of lavender, probably from the sheets. That must be why his thoughts of Laurel had been so vivid. He'd sometimes called her his Lavender Lady because of the scent she often wore.

Reluctantly opening his eyes, he saw a plain, light-colored ceiling. Even that small effort was tiring.

"I see you're awake." The soothing female voice came from his right, and shocked him to his marrow.

He turned his head so quickly that he felt a wave of dizziness. Laurel sat in a chair by his bed, her lap full of mending. Seeing her brought back a shocking array of sensual memories from his recent dream. Her taste, her scent, the silky warmth of her skin, the welcoming heat of her body . . .

His jaw clenched as he suppressed the passionate memories, but he couldn't suppress the reality of her presence. Even after ten years, she was achingly familiar. Her glorious bronze hair was loosely tied back and she was so beautiful his heart hurt.

But she was no longer the girl he'd married. Her openness to him and to the world had vanished, replaced by cool distance. Surely her glorious warmth couldn't be entirely gone, but it was no longer for him. His heart died a little.

Yet she was still his wife. And God help him, he still wanted her.

"I'm sorry, Laurel." His voice was a hoarse whisper. "You never wanted to see me again, yet here I am."

She set her mending in the basket by her chair. "It's hardly your fault, James. While you were suffering from fever, you were attacked by robbers not far from here. Two men who attend our chapel found you and brought you to the infirmary."

While he tried to think of what to say to his long estranged wife, he felt a soft bump on his left hip. He turned his head cautiously and found himself looking into the golden eyes of a large gray cat, which was curled up against his side. Its thumping tail was what had caught his attention.

He blinked. "Is this the gray kitten you had me fish out of the pond all those years ago?"

"Yes, it's Shadow. All grown up now. He makes himself free of the infirmary."

Kirkland scratched the cat's neck and was rewarded by a rumbling purr. "He's pretty substantial for a shadow."

"He takes a deep interest in his food dish, but he's a good fellow. Patients who come here regularly look for him." She laid a cool hand on Kirkland's forehead. "The fever is gone, but you must be thirsty. Here, drink this. It will help your throat."

She poured a drink from a stone jug into a mug, then slid an arm under his pillows and raised his head enough to hold the vessel to his lips. Her closeness was intoxicating.

Cutting off the thought, he sipped chicken broth, warm and tasty. He hated being so weak, but that was always the case after a bout of fever. It helped keep him humble.

He finished the broth, then sagged back into his pillows. His body craved more rest, but he couldn't bear to close his eyes on the miraculous sight of his wife. "How long have I been here?"

"Since yesterday evening. I managed to get several cups of Jesuit's bark tea down you and it seems to have cut off the fever quickly. More broth?" When he shook his head, she set the mug down. "I assume you have anxious servants waiting at a local inn. Tell me which one and I'll send word."

"The Ostrich." His eyes drifted shut, and he had to force them open. "Will Daniel be in later, or is he refusing to talk to me?"

"He's away for a few days on a surgical tour in Wales."

Kirkland's brows furrowed. "A surgical tour?"

"Several times a year he visits areas where there are no surgeons or physicians and provides care for those in need," she explained.

"Daniel, the saint," Kirkland murmured, unable to keep a dry note from his voice. "He was always interested in medicine and I knew he'd become a doctor, but how did he get there from studying classics and theology at Oxford?"

Laurel regarded him coolly. "He always wanted to study medicine, but my parents thought it too low an occupation. They said that if he insisted on training for a profession even though he'd inherit the estate, he should enter the church, and he was not unwilling. He didn't decide to study medicine until I left you and my parents refused to let me return home. They said I could go back to you or starve."

Kirkland winced. "I didn't know that. You should have told them I was to blame."

"I did," she said, her voice even cooler. "But you were an earl, and therefore it was my duty to accept any little eccentricities you might have. I was shameless, a disgrace to the family name, for leaving you."

Kirkland's head pounded even worse. "That's why you and Daniel chose to set up your own household?"

She nodded. "He was furious with our parents. Since you insisted on giving me a generous separation allowance, we were able to live comfortably while Daniel did his medical training." She made a gesture that included their surroundings. "When he completed his studies, we bought this house and set up the infirmary. Later, we bought the house directly behind this one and turned it into a sanctuary for women and children escaping dangerously violent men. Zion House." Her eyes narrowed. "But surely an accomplished spy like you knew all that."

"I kept track of where you lived, but no more," he said shortly. Thinking he might as well know the worst, he asked, "Does Daniel still hate me?"

She hesitated too long. "It is not in his nature to really hate. But because he's loyal to his little sister, he holds you responsible for . . . for . . ." She hesitated again.

"For ruining your life? He's right to do so." If

37

not for Kirkland, Laurel would have married a normal man and had a real home and children by now. Instead she was locked into limbo, not a maiden yet not quite a wife, sleeping alone and childless. At least, he assumed she was sleeping alone. Though he couldn't bear the thought of her with another man, he couldn't blame her if she'd found someone to warm her nights.

"You didn't ruin my life," she said calmly. "Just set it on a new course, and not necessarily a worse one. The work I do here matters, James. If I was merely a wife, my life would be narrower and shallower."

It stung that she thought a life with him would have been shallow, but at least she had moved beyond the wreckage of their marriage without bitterness. She'd always had a gift for appreciating the moment rather than longing for what she didn't have.

But though she might not hate him, an invisible wall surrounded her and made it clear that he should keep his distance. Which was easy because he didn't have the strength to walk across the room.

Though his body craved more rest, he didn't want their conversation to end. "Do you still play the piano?"

"Of course." She smiled with a touch of self-mockery. "Even serious-minded reformers like me need our pleasures. The Broadwood piano you gave me is in the music room upstairs. It was quite a challenge getting it up there."

His gaze touched her bare left hand and he wondered what she'd done with her wedding ring. "The Broadwood is a lovely instrument, but I'm surprised that you kept anything I'd given you."

"The tone is so wonderful that I couldn't bear to part with it." She cocked her head. "Do you still play? Or do you not have time?"

"I play occasionally." After Laurel left him, making music was his chief pleasure since it could be done alone and playing never failed to soothe him. He'd improved greatly over the years, but he'd never be as good as Laurel, who was truly gifted. "I'm sorry your piano is out of listening range. I'd like to hear you play again."

"I keep a small harp here in the infirmary," she said, a little hesitant. "I can play that if you like."

"I didn't know you played the harp. I'd like very much to hear it."

She set aside her mending and stood. "I'll only be a minute. Unless you need something else?"

Only her. "Music is enough. Food for the soul, you know."

She nodded agreement as she left the room. Luckily, she returned before he drifted to sleep again. The harp in her arms was small enough to carry easily and nestle in her lap when she sat again. He studied the instrument as she tuned it. "I've not seen a harp like that before."

"It belonged to an old Irish woman here in Bristol. I used to visit her every week or so. I'd take a basket of food and Mrs. Donovan would tell me wonderful stories. Because her fingers were too twisted to play the harp well, she taught me so I could play for her." Laurel's fingers rippled over the strings as she checked the tuning. The small instrument had a surprisingly deep, rich sound. "She asked me to play for her as she lay dying, and then left me the harp. It was her most treasured possession."

Kirkland had married a saint. No wonder the marriage had broken down so quickly when she realized how great a sinner he was.

But for now he had the unexpected gift of time with her. It might never come again, so he would savor every moment to create new memories for the future. And the sweetest memory of all would be that dream of intimacy that had not really happened. . . .

She began to play a haunting Irish tune, singing along in her soft, rich contralto.

The minstrel boy to the war is gone,
In the ranks of death you'll find him;
His father's sword he has girded on,
And his wild harp slung behind him. . . .

He closed his eyes, letting the music flow through him. In the liquid notes, he heard the sweet warmth that had been the essence of Laurel when they'd first met. He was glad to know that warmth still existed under her cool, controlled surface. And for these few moments, he was privileged to enjoy it once more. . . .

Chapter 4

F or a time, Laurel lost herself in the music. It was the second great passion she and her husband had shared, and playing for him eased some of the turmoil created by their swift, shocking intimacy. Thank heaven he didn't seem to realize what they'd done!

She looked up and saw that James had drifted to sleep, his breathing slow and regular. His still figure reminded her of the effigy of a Crusader knight that lay in the Herberts' village church. He had the chiseled features of a warrior, austere and haunted.

Her hands came to rest on the harp strings as she studied him, committing every detail to memory. This meeting was pure chance and wouldn't happen again.

Yet despite their fierce, unwelcome intimacy, she was glad to see him. Their separation had been an aching wound for years, but now she felt a sense of peace. The mutual attraction would likely never go away, but they had grown in very different directions. She'd learned that love wasn't enough, and apparently James had done the same.

It was full light outside, and soon the infirmary would be bustling with staff and people seeking treatment. She must send a message to Kirkland's servants at the Ostrich Inn. They would be worried. As soon as his people received the message, they'd swoop in and take him away and see that he was properly cared for.

She set the harp down and stood, but before leaving the room, she brushed her fingers lightly through his dark hair. James was the man he'd always been, only more so. She was the woman she'd always been, only more so. She would never stop caring for him, but that didn't mean she needed to see him or be with him.

Go with God, James. But go.

Kirkland was pulled from dreams of Laurel's embrace by a brisk, familiar Cockney voice. "Are you awake, sir, or shall we carry you off like a sack of potatoes?"

The voice belonged to Rhodes, who was nominally Kirkland's valet, though his sharp intelligence had him performing far more demanding duties. Today the anxiety under the brash words made Rhodes sound more like a mother hen.

Reluctantly Kirkland opened his eyes to see Rhodes frowning down at him. This room at the Herbert infirmary was flooded with light, and early morning silence had been replaced by the noises of a busy city and an active infirmary. "You are not carrying me out of here like a sack of potatoes," he said firmly.

He tried to sit up, and almost passed out from

43

dizziness. Rhodes caught him until his head steadied. "The lady said you was robbed, and then had a fever attack?"

"Fever first. Robbery after." Kirkland managed to sit up and swing his legs over the edge of the examination table. He wore only a loose sleep shirt. He tried not to think of Laurel's hands efficiently stripping him down to his skin. "Miss Herbert had Jesuit's bark. Saved me from a full fever attack."

"She's quite the lady," Rhodes said admiringly. "Your carriage is outside. If I dress you, can you walk that far?"

Kirkland considered. Fever always left him so weak he could barely move, but since this bout had been cut off early, his condition was less dire than usual. "I'll need some help, but I can make it that far."

"Then stand up so I can dress you. Sir."

Kirkland drew a deep breath, then eased himself onto his feet, swaying. He kept one hand on the examination table for balance. Rhodes had seen him through other bouts of fever and knew to bring loose, casual garments and slip-on shoes. Trying to get boots onto a man as limp as Kirkland would be an exercise in futility.

When he was decent, Kirkland sat on the edge of the table again, as tired as if he'd run ten miles. "Please ask Miss Herbert to come in at her convenience. I wish to thank her for her care."

Rhodes nodded, taking the request at face value. He hadn't entered Kirkland's service until the marriage had broken up, so he didn't know about Laurel. Because of their extended honeymoon, very few people had known about the marriage.

"Thought you'd want to thank the lady in practical form." Rhodes produced a small purse that clinked and set it next to Kirkland, then left to summon Laurel.

Kirkland straightened, trying not to look as weak as he felt. Apparently a man never got over wanting to impress an attractive woman. He ran a hand over his stubbled jaw and sighed. Impressing Laurel was already a lost cause.

As he waited, he pondered their earlier discussion. Laurel hadn't seemed angry or resentful of his presence. Was there any chance she might be willing to consider a reconciliation? Perhaps they might rebuild what had been so utterly broken.

He realized he was deluding himself when the door opened and Laurel entered. Her hair was drawn back and she wore a plain, dove gray gown that made him think of nuns. Her expression was all business, proof that he was merely one more task she needed to accomplish.

Keeping his voice equally businesslike, he said, "Thank you for caring for me. Bristol is lucky to have you and Daniel and your infirmary." He lifted the purse of coins Rhodes had left and handed it to her. "To help others."

She accepted the purse with a nod of thanks. "You're already supporting most of the infirmary through the income you settled on me when we separated, but this will be put to good use."

"I'm sure." He hesitated, wanting to say something more significant. "Though it was an accident, I'm not sorry I ended up here. It's good to know you're well and doing meaningful work."

Her expression softened. "I'm also glad to see you. I had a sense of incompleteness about our . . . relationship. Now it feels properly finished."

It was a *marriage,* not a relationship. Luckily, he was good at concealing pain. "Will you tell your brother I was here?"

She shrugged. "Not unless someone on the staff mentions to Daniel that we treated a lord while he was away and he asks me about it."

"That will spare his temper." Knowing it was time to leave, Kirkland stood, willing himself not to sway. "If you ever need my aid, don't hesitate to ask."

"That's unlikely to be necessary," she said in a cool voice.

He suspected that her real reaction was *I'll ask for your help when there are icicles in hell,* but she was too much a lady to say that. Since he might fall over if he tried to bow, he just inclined his head. "Good-bye, Laurel. And thank you."

He took one last, lingering look, committing to memory her grace and grave intelligence. His wife had been a lovely girl. Now she was a strong, quietly beautiful woman, no longer his.

Never again his.

After James left, Laurel sank into the chair beside the examination table and locked her shaking hands in her lap. Thank heaven he was gone and she'd managed not to lose her composure. It was rather shocking how deeply he still affected her.

The reverse wasn't true. He had been glad to see her, but he'd left without looking back.

Pray God the blasted man never landed in her infirmary again.

Chapter 5

Laurel's office was on the ground floor in the rear of Herbert House, and it overlooked the garden shared by the infirmary and Zion House. The evening was well advanced, so Laurel's office was quiet and she could concentrate on listing supplies that needed to be ordered. She was squinting in the lamplight when a familiar voice behind her said teasingly, "You're working late."

She spun about in her chair to see the rangy figure of her brother in the office doorway. He looked travel worn and weary, but his smile was warm.

"Daniel!" She swiftly rose to hug him. When his arms went around her, she closed her eyes and fully relaxed for the first time since Kirkland had left a fortnight before. Her kind, good-natured big brother, who had always looked out for her, even when her parents had cast her off. In his embrace, she felt safe and cared for.

Stepping back with reluctance, she said, "I didn't expect you until next week."

"With Colin Holt along to take some of the patients, I finished sooner than expected and was anxious to get home." He eyed her thoughtfully. "That was an unusually earnest hug. Problems here?"

For an instant she hesitated. If she was to tell her brother about Kirkland's unexpected sojourn in the infirmary, now was the time to do it. The moment passed as she decided to stay silent. Daniel looked tired and there was no reason that he needed to know. "Nothing unusual. One of the infant school-teachers has been ill this past week and I've been filling in there as well as doing the rest of my work. Those little ones have so much energy!"

"No wonder you're tired." Daniel slung an arm around her shoulders and steered her out the door. "But you adore them. Come along and keep me company while I find something to eat."

She smiled. "In other words, you'd like me to make my special eggs for you."

"You see through me far too easily, little sister," he said with mock ruefulness. He bent to scratch the head of Shadow, who had been keeping Laurel company in the office and would certainly continue to do so in the kitchen. "But it's sadly true that nothing will restore my energy more quickly, so I shall take advantage of your well-known charitable nature."

Laughing, she headed down the stairs with him. He really was the best brother in the world. They had the same coloring and features and long bones, so no one seeing them together ever doubted their relationship. But Daniel was much more outgoing than she was. He could talk to anyone about anything.

As they entered the kitchen, she said, "Tell me about your journey. How is the new chapel in Aberwilly faring?"

"Very well. The local landowner gave them permission to use an old house just outside the village, and the congregation has already fixed the place up and set up a school there. I performed the first wedding in their chapel since the local parish vicar doesn't approve of Methodists and won't perform weddings for them."

"It's convenient that you stayed at Oxford long enough to be ordained. How many eggs hungry are you?"

"Four. And add a couple of more for yourself. You look as if you forgot to eat."

Her brow furrowed. "I believe I did. I was working on a budget for next year and lost track of time."

Daniel unwrapped a piece of cheese and cut it into thick slices, offering one to Shadow. "Better you than me."

"Which is why I always handle the accounts. It's good that I've a knack for figuring since I'm no surgeon." She entered the pantry and collected eggs, potatoes, onions, and bacon.

"You may not be a surgeon, but you're the best nurse the infirmary has." He found a loaf of bread and a knife and began slicing. "I'll toast some bread to go with the eggs. Ale or tea?"

"Tea." Laurel cut the bacon into small pieces and

started frying it. "You thought that taking Colin on the tour would be a good test of his abilities and temperament. I gather that he proved himself?"

"He did indeed." Daniel filled the kettle with water and set it to heat. "He learns quickly and he's adaptable and willing to do what is needful rather than standing on his dignity as a physician. I've been thinking about offering him a permanent position, but I wanted to talk to you first. What do you think?"

Laurel poured her beaten eggs over the sautéed ingredients, then stirred a few times before letting the mixture quietly cook. Colin Holt had been Daniel's assistant for several months. He was a pleasant young man, and he must be a very good physician to have earned her brother's approval. "I like him, he seems capable, and if having another doctor at the infirmary means you won't have to work as hard, I'm in favor of it."

"I wouldn't mind working fewer hours," Daniel admitted.

The eggs had set, so Laurel removed the skillet from the heat and divided the dish into two pieces, sliding the lion's share onto Daniel's plate along with two slices of the bread he'd toasted and buttered. After serving herself, she sat down opposite her brother and attacked her meal. She was hungrier than she'd realized.

There was silence as they cleared their plates. When he was finished, Daniel sighed with pleasure. "That was so good. I feel restored." He poured them more tea, then spread honey on his toast. "I trust we can afford to pay Colin a decent salary?"

Laurel considered as she fed a piece of egg to the cat. "Yes, though you may need to take on a few patients who can afford to pay you well."

He shrugged. "Rich people need medical care as much as poor ones do."

"If you're not so busy, maybe you'll have time to think of taking a wife," she said, half teasing. "Surgery may be a low trade, but you're also ordained and heir to Belmond Manor. That makes you very eligible."

"I suppose someday I'll do my duty and marry to produce an heir to the family estate," he said without enthusiasm. "But there's no rush. I haven't met anyone who seemed worth disrupting both our lives for."

She frowned. "Have you been avoiding courtship because of me, Daniel?"

"Not really." He scooped Shadow onto his lap and began scratching behind the cat's ears. Shadow leaned into Daniel blissfully. "Rose was the only girl I could even imagine as my wife. After she died . . ." Daniel shrugged.

Laurel bit her lip. Laughing, golden Rose Hiller had been a neighbor and a beloved friend to both of them. Rose and Daniel had moved seamlessly from friendship into love. Though they'd not been formally betrothed, both families approved and it was understood that after he finished his studies, they would marry. Rose was maid of honor at Laurel's wedding.

Not long before Laurel's marriage shattered, Rose had died of a swift fever. She was gone before Daniel could return from Oxford. He'd been devastated.

Laurel suspected that Rose's death was much of the reason he'd decided to pursue his childhood dream of medicine rather than entering the church after his ordination. It might have also contributed to his fierce championship of his sister after she left Kirkland. He was a protector by nature, and since he'd been unable to protect Rose, he became all the more protective of other women.

Only now, when he mentioned Rose's name for the first time in years, did Laurel realize how deeply he was still affected by her death. Daniel had such a generous, loving heart. She uttered a silent prayer that someday he would find another woman whom he could love, and who would love him back as he deserved.

But she didn't speak. Instead, she stood and began to clear the table. Who was she to advise anyone about love?

Luckily the infant school teacher was well enough to work the next morning, so Laurel headed to her office to finish her budgeting. She needed to make adjustments so they could pay Colin Holt a decent salary.

She was just finishing when a light knock sounded at her door. "Come in," she called, not looking up.

She assumed it was her assistant, Betsy Rivers, who helped her most mornings, but instead an excited male voice said, "Miss Herbert?"

Colin Holt. With a smile, she rose to greet him. He was a year or two older than Laurel, but his boyish face and enthusiasm made him seem younger. "You look happy, Dr. Holt. Did my brother speak with you this morning?"

"Indeed he did!" Colin said with a grin. "I've been praying he would ask me to stay at the infirmary, and my prayers have been answered."

She offered her hand. "Congratulations! You will be a great blessing to us."

He took her hand in both of his, his expression turning serious. "You and your brother are such wonderful examples of Christian charity. I love the work I do here and the people I work with."

"I'm so glad." She tried to pull her hand away. "If you'll excuse me, I'm in the process of finding money for your salary, and I'm sure you'll agree that's a worthy goal."

Still holding her hand, he said intensely, "Miss Herbert. Laurel. Now that I have a secure position and future, I . . . I would like permission to pay my addresses to you."

Her jaw dropped. After her separation, she had consciously cultivated an air of cool reserve, and very effective it was, too. She was considered to be a natural spinster, so she'd never had to learn how to deflect unwanted advances.

Seeing her surprise, Colin said earnestly, "Surely you are not unaware of how much I admire you. You are the personification of womanly grace and goodness. Now that I am in a position to take a wife, I am eager to further our acquaintance."

Laurel yanked her hand free. Reminding herself that he didn't know her situation, she drew a deep breath before saying calmly, "I owe you an apology, Dr. Holt. Though I use the name Miss Herbert, I am . . . not free to marry. I'm sorry to have unintentionally misled you."

It was Colin's turn to be shocked. "I'm so sorry," he stammered. "I had no idea."

"The subject is not one I ever discuss." Wanting to ease the blow, she said, "Perhaps if matters were different, we would discover that we suit, but that can never be." Which wasn't true. Even if she were free, Colin would not interest her, she realized. Perhaps he might have pleased her when she was eighteen, but Kirkland had ruined her for uncomplicated men.

"I'm sorry to distress you," he said awkwardly.

"No need to apologize." She bit her lip. "I hope this doesn't change your decision about joining the infirmary permanently."

He blinked. "I . . . no, I won't change my mind. I will not find another position that so fulfills my own ideals."

"I'm glad to hear that," she said sincerely. "Daniel would be very disappointed to lose you." After a moment's hesitation, she added, "If you are seriously seeking a wife, have you noticed Miss Elizabeth Ware, who volunteers at Zion House several times a week? She watches you when you aren't looking and blushes if you turn her way."

"The pretty blond girl?" His expression brightened. "I didn't realize that she took any special notice of me. She seems very modest and ladylike."

"Yes, that's Elizabeth. She's shy but very intelligent and kind. She looks out for the youngest children and they adore her. She's the daughter of a solicitor." In other words, she would be a suitable match for a young physician.

"I must visit Zion House tomorrow to see several patients. Perhaps . . . perhaps I'll have an opportunity to speak with her." Looking happier, Colin took his leave.

Before then, Laurel would talk with Anne Wilson, the capable Zion House matron. Anne had a romantic streak and she would make sure that Colin and Elizabeth were properly introduced. The young doctor was a devout evangelical, as was Elizabeth. He would surely be happier with a sweet innocent than with Laurel.

After drafting her budget, she checked the date in her pocket book—and froze. It had been a fortnight since Kirkland's unexpected visit, and she realized that her personal body clock was off. Her cycles were more regular than most clocks, actually. Ever since she'd come to womanhood, her courses began midafternoon every fourth Monday.

Living a celibate life, she never thought much about such regularity—until now, when it was gone. Stunned, she pressed one hand to her abdomen and the other to her breast. Though she and James had shared a passionate relationship, she'd never quickened. She'd wondered if she might be barren. Then her marriage collapsed and the subject became moot. Could she be with child as a result of one brief, mad coupling?

Yes. She knew the answer in her bones as soon as the question formed in her mind. She'd learned much about childbearing during her years at the infirmary, including the fact that some women knew immediately. Now that she was no longer trying to keep her mind busy, she recognized that her body felt subtly different.

Dear God, what had she done?

Chapter 6

Shaking with shock, Laurel rose and walked into the adjacent room, where her assistant was working. Struggling to keep her voice steady, she said, "After all that work on the budget, I need some fresh air."

Betsy Rivers, who had come to Zion House as the oldest daughter of an abused wife and was now valuable in ways beyond counting, nodded with approval. " 'Tis too nice a day to waste indoors at a desk. You work too hard. Do you want me to check the supply closets to see what needs ordering?"

"Please do." Hoping her eyes didn't look too wild, Laurel headed downstairs, collecting her shawl and bonnet before she stepped blindly into the street.

What now? Her thoughts were such a jumble that she didn't realize that her long, restless strides had carried her halfway across Bristol until she found herself at the New Room, John Wesley's own chapel. The modest building was the cradle of the Methodist religious movement.

Though neither Laurel nor her brother had formally joined the Methodist church, they worked closely with the Bristol Methodists. Zion House had been set up in conjunction with a local chapel, so perhaps it was inevitable that she'd been drawn to the New Room, where she'd always found peace and clarity.

The inside was plain, in keeping with Methodist teachings, but the space was saturated with the power of faith and prayers. Wearily she subsided onto one of the long wooden pews and bowed her head to pray for guidance.

Gradually the chapel's serenity untied the knots of her anxiety. Her life might have changed forever, but it was impossible to regret having a baby when she'd always yearned for children.

The major difficulty would be telling everyone around her, since a pregnancy was not something that could be concealed. She couldn't let the world think she was bearing a child out of wedlock when she was supposedly a model of female virtue.

Daniel would be shocked and deeply disappointed. Despite his easy disposition, he might be angry with her, and much more with Kirkland.

The real question was how her husband would react. Naturally James would be pleased by the prospect of an heir. A daughter wouldn't interest him as much as a son, so he'd be unlikely to take away a female child.

Even for a son and heir, surely Kirkland would allow the boy to stay with his mother until it was time to send him to school? Laurel had to believe that her husband would be reasonable, because she couldn't bear the alternative.

When her thoughts were sorted out, Laurel gathered her shawl around her and left the New Room. The sun was low in the sky. Inner peace didn't come quickly.

As she walked through the still-bustling streets, she thought about how to proceed. Daniel must be the first person she informed. Once he recovered from his shock and disappointment, she thought he'd be happy for her. Certainly he'd love the prospect of having a niece or nephew. He was wonderful with children.

For her friends and neighbors, a simple and reasonably honest explanation would be best. She'd say that she and her long estranged husband had briefly reconciled, but it hadn't worked out so they'd separated again. All true.

Not quite ready to return home, she decided to walk by the port, which was a never-ending source of fascination. The diverse ships and sailors and babel of languages helped put her own problems into perspective.

She paused on the quay to inhale the scents that marked the meeting of sea and land, and to study the creaking forest of masts. Over the years, she'd occasionally seen a ship flying the flag of Kirkland's fleet. For the first time she wondered how often her husband came to Bristol to consult with one of his captains.

Had he thought about her when he visited the city? Surely he must have. The man was a spy, after all. He'd kept track of her ever since their separation. She still wasn't sure how she felt about that.

She was turning to head home when a plain carriage pulled up just in front of her on the quay. Two men descended and turned to drag a slender young black woman out of the vehicle. The girl was struggling frantically. "No, no!"

The burlier man slapped her hard, almost knocking her from her feet. "Shut your bawlin' mouth, girl. You're about to take a nice sea voyage with Mr. Hardwick."

Laurel's horror was instantly followed by fury. She strode toward the carriage. "Release that girl at once!"

The other man, Hardwick, was expensively dressed and had an air of arrogant authority. He drawled, "This is none of your business, madam. Violet is my property and I can do with her as I damn well please."

"No, you *cannot!*" Laurel retorted. "Let her go!"

With the men's attention turned toward Laurel, the girl managed to break loose. She bolted toward Laurel, her dark eyes terrified. "Please, ma'am, help me!"

Violet spoke with a light, musical accent, and she had the stunning, exotic beauty Laurel had seen in others of mixed race. She looked to be about twenty, and her plain, neat gray gown had been torn in her struggle to escape.

Laurel caught Violet's hand. "You're safe, my dear," she said soothingly. "These men have no right to take you away."

Eyes like ice, Hardwick barked, "I own her and I have the papers to prove it! Get out of the way if you don't want to be hurt."

Laurel stepped between the girl and her pursuers, saying in her most authoritative voice, "No one is a slave in Britain. That was decided by Lord Mansfield of the King's Bench in 1772. *Somersett versus Stewart*."

Hardwick arched his brows. "Well, aren't you the clever little thing," he sneered. "But there are two of us, and might makes right is a much older law."

"That's not a law but mere bullying," Laurel retorted. In a lower voice, she said to Violet, "We'd best leave here."

Before they could move, the burly man lunged at Violet. The girl spun out of his way, then stuck out a foot, tripping him. The man fell hard before scrambling to his feet with ugly oaths. Behind him, Hardwick whipped out a small pistol.

Laurel couldn't suppress a spurt of fear, but she kept her voice calm. "Pistols are not very accurate and a single shot will not stop us both."

"It can stop one of you," Hardwick barked as he cocked the weapon.

"Hey, there, you fellows leave Miss Herbert alone!" a voice boomed from behind.

Laurel glanced over her shoulder and saw that a crowd of dock workers had been drawn by the altercation. She recognized the speaker, a stevedore named Jeb Brown. He'd brought his wife to the infirmary when she was dangerously ill with fever.

Another stevedore stepped forward. He had a broken nose that Daniel had set after a tavern brawl. His name was Brian, if she remembered correctly. "Aye, mister. You run along now. That girl ain't a slave here."

A muttering rose from the crowd. Many had been treated at the infirmary and a few attended Daniel's chapel. They were solidly on her side and against the strangers.

Hardwick seethed on the verge of explosion, but he wasn't stupid. Grimly he uncocked the pistol and shoved it into a holster under his coat. "You win for today," he snapped. "But both you bitches had better be watching over your shoulder from now on." He stalked down the pier to a moored dinghy, his thug behind him.

Violet was shaking as she dropped to her knees in front of Laurel. "God bless you, Miss Herbert!" she said brokenly. "I was sure I was lost!"

Laurel caught the girl's hands and raised her to her feet. "You're safe now, Violet. Do you have any place to go?"

"No, but I'll find something. I'll do any work as long as I'm free."

"My brother and I run an infirmary and also Zion House, a refuge for women and children who need help. You can stay there for now. But first, we thank these men for saving us." She turned and smiled at the group of dock workers who had backed her up. "Thank you all for your good deed! Mr. Brown, is your wife well?"

"Aye, Miss Herbert, very well indeed. We're expecting a babe now." He gazed after Hardwick's dinghy. "We'll escort you ladies home to make sure you're safe."

"You are very kind." Violet brushed the tears from her eyes and smiled at her saviors. "God will bless you for what you've done."

Looking pleased with themselves, the men smiled back. Most returned to their work, but Jeb and Brian fell into step behind Laurel and Violet. Laurel said warmly to the girl, "My name is Laurel Herbert. Will you tell me about yourself?"

"I am called Violet Smith. My owner in Jamaica didn't think slaves deserved anything but the plainest of names." She glanced at Laurel fearfully. "The law you mentioned. It is true? I am free?"

"Yes, there is no tradition of slavery in England. It's generally accepted that a slave who is brought here becomes free." Since Bristol had been one of Britain's major slave-trading ports, Laurel had had occasion to learn about the subject.

Violet's smile was radiant. "Hallelujah!"

"How did you come to be here? Was that man really your master?"

Violet spat into the street. "As I said, I am from Jamaica. You can see in my face that I was fathered by a white man. His wife made him sell my mother to another plantation owner before I was even born."

Having noted how well the girl spoke, Laurel observed, "You seem to have been raised with some advantages?"

Violet nodded. "I was trained to be lady's maid to Mrs. Bertram, the new master's wife. She treated me well and brought me with her to England when she came for a visit. I have only been here a week. As I grew up, her husband came to despise me because I would not lie with him and my mistress would not let him force me. Hardwick saw me and wanted to buy me for his pleasure, and Mr. Bertram was happy to sell me."

Laurel winced. "I'm so glad I was passing by! Since you're a lady's maid, it shouldn't be hard for you to find a position. One that's away from Bristol, where you won't risk being seen by Hardwick."

Violet nodded vigorously. "Please! Any place where I can work and be safe."

Guessing the girl would feel very disoriented after the exhilaration of being free wore off, Laurel said, "It won't be easy to leave your old life behind."

The girl sighed. "My mother died not long ago, my other friends are back in Jamaica. Mrs. Bertram was a good mistress, but I can't go back to her or to Jamaica or I'll be a slave again. I will build a new life here."

"You'll do well, Violet. I know it." As they neared Herbert House, Laurel thought of how swiftly the dock workers had offered help when needed. Would they look at her the same way if they knew she was a countess? If they knew, would they be awed, or resentful? Neither reaction appealed to her.

She smiled wryly as she led Violet to Zion House and introduced her to Anne Wilson, the matron. Not only was it a blessing that Laurel had been in the right place to help the girl, but the incident had pushed her own problems away for a time.

Chapter 7

With a sigh of relief, Laurel let herself into the quiet of Herbert House. Daniel was leading a service this evening and Betsy Rivers usually took her meals across the garden in Zion House. All the Herbert servants lived there, and they came to the house daily for training in household skills so they could earn a living elsewhere.

As a result, service in the house was erratic, based on the level of training of the current servants, but in the evenings, Laurel did have privacy. Tonight supper awaited her in the kitchen, and the current cook in training was quite decent. Walking had made Laurel hungry, so after consuming a substantial meal, she took tea up to the music room. Playing the piano was as soothing as praying in the New Room chapel.

She chose the most powerful, emotional music she knew: Bach and Handel and Beethoven, interspersed with hymns and folk ballads about tragic love affairs.

She'd just finished a crashing rendition of Martin Luther's hymn "A Mighty Fortress Is Our God" when her brother's amused voice said, "Judging by what you're playing tonight, you've had a difficult day."

She wasn't ready to discuss her likely pregnancy, but the story of Violet Smith was enough to justify the music. "I was walking by the port when I ran into a horrible man called Hardwick. He and a servant were trying to force a slave girl he'd just bought out to his ship. I told him he couldn't, the good stevedores of Bristol backed me up, and she's now safe at Zion House."

Her brother stared, appalled. "Good God, Laurel, were you out of your mind? You could have been killed!"

"Someone had to do something," Laurel pointed out. "In another minute or two, Violet would have been on a dinghy heading out to the ship and a life of slavery."

"You have guardian angels lined up at your back," Daniel said, shaking his head.

"Stevedores were more useful in this case," she said lightly.

Her brother was not amused. "Interfering with a slave owner would be dangerous in any circumstances. The fact that it was Captain Hardwick is even worse. He's a notorious brute, and is probably trading in slaves even though it's illegal."

Laurel frowned. "No wonder he seemed dreadful. I shall pray that the Royal Navy catches him in the act and ends his wickedness."

"The ocean is large and the ungodly own fast sailing ships," her brother said, his voice grim.

"The illegal trade will not be ended soon, I fear."

"We can't end all the world's troubles," she said softly. "But today, one young woman was saved from slavery. Violet is an experienced lady's maid, so she'll do well."

Daniel looked thoughtful. "Perhaps she can train some of the girls at Zion House who would like to pursue that kind of work. Would Miss Smith be willing?"

"Very likely. She's grateful for being freed."

"And so she should be!" Daniel smiled at her fondly. "I know you're a certified saint, but please don't interfere with slavers unless you have stevedores at your back."

The warmth of his expression disintegrated her resolution to conceal her condition for a few more days. "Daniel," she blurted out. "I—I'm pregnant."

Her brother stared, as shocked as if she'd struck him with a club. "You're *what?*"

She could see him struggling to understand how his virtuous sister might be increasing, so she said swiftly, "I'm sorry, I should have started at the beginning. One evening when you were in Wales, Mr. Potter and Mr. Larkin from the chapel brought in a man who had been beaten and robbed and left unconscious in an alley. It was Kirkland."

Her brother's expression flattened to granite. "Kirkland! Why the devil did they bring him here?"

"He was found nearby and there was nothing to identify him, so naturally they thought of the infirmary."

A doctor to the bone, Daniel asked, "How badly was he injured?"

"No bones broken, but a number of lacerations and bruises. He was also having a fever attack, which was probably why he looked vulnerable to his attackers."

"So he was brought in here, you treated his injuries, and he ravished you," Daniel said grimly. "Or was it as much seduction as force?"

"Neither!" She paused to marshal her thoughts, unsure whether Daniel would understand. He'd loved Rose Hiller, but she didn't think he'd ever experienced the mad, consuming passion that she and James had shared. "He was out of his head from the fever. I managed to get quite a bit of Jesuit's bark tea down him and that stopped the fever before the attack was full blown. But while he was feverish . . ."

She hesitated again. "He seemed to be hallucinating about me. When I tried to calm him . . . one thing led to another."

Looking pained, Daniel said, "I don't need to know the details. So after this brief reconciliation of bodies if not souls, did he turn around and walk away? Or did you throw him out as soon as he could walk?"

"Neither," she said again. "When the fever broke

and he recovered his wits, he didn't remember what had happened." Her mouth twisted wryly. "When he woke, I was at my primmest and most virtuous, so if he did remember anything, he probably thought it was a hallucination. He told me the name of his inn, I sent word to his people to collect him, and we said polite good-byes."

Daniel's eyes narrowed. "Why didn't you tell me he'd been here?"

"It didn't seem important." She paused. "And I didn't want to upset you. I know how you feel about him."

Not commenting on that, her brother asked, "Are you sure now that you're increasing? It's very early."

"Yes, but I'm as sure as I can be. I feel . . . different." She sighed. "While we were married, I kept hoping to conceive. I was beginning to think perhaps I couldn't. It never occurred to me that one brief encounter could produce a child."

"Once is all it takes," he said acerbically. "What do you want to do? You can't deny your husband knowledge of his heir, but if you wish to keep Kirkland out of your life, you can retire to some distant place before you begin to show, have the baby quietly, and put it into Kirkland's care with a good wet nurse."

She stared at him. "Do you think I will give up my own child?"

"No, but it's the one sure way to preserve your

independence and the life you live here. If it's a boy, Kirkland will have his heir and you'll never have to see him again." Daniel shook his head. "You face a difficult choice, Laurel. I can't imagine you giving up your child completely, but keeping the baby means you will be unable to avoid him."

Her brother was right, damn him. Her jaw tightened. "I am not giving my child away to simplify my own life. I plan to tell people I have an estranged husband and we attempted reconciliation. If it's a girl, he'll have no need to see me. Even if it's a boy, Kirkland wouldn't need to be involved when the child is in the nursery. Once he starts school, it would be different, of course."

"You might find that Kirkland is more interested in his offspring than you hope," Daniel warned. "But there is no need to inform him right away. The first three months can be precarious. Perhaps the pregnancy will not hold."

Laurel pressed a hand to her belly, wishing her brother wasn't a doctor and notoriously honest. She knew from her work in the infirmary that many pregnancies failed in the early stages, but she didn't want to think about that. "I'll write Kirkland to let him know and tell him to stay away. I'll keep him informed of anything he needs to know." She swallowed. "That will not be an easy letter to write."

Daniel frowned. "Do you want me to go to London and tell him in person?"

She blinked. "You would do that? You hate Kirkland!"

"But I love you," he said calmly. "Not only do I want to make this easier for you, but I want to see what kind of man he's become."

"So you can protect me? That shouldn't be necessary. He's always been a perfect gentleman. I've often wondered if he regretted marrying an inexperienced country girl." Her smile was brittle. "He never attempted to change my mind when I left."

Daniel's frown returned. "Laurel, why *did* you leave Kirkland? You were so distraught that I never wanted to probe, but it's time you explained. Since you're going to have his child, you'll have to have some correspondence with him. Our parents thought he'd been unfaithful, but Kirkland is a stiff-necked moralist. It's hard to imagine him committing adultery under any circumstances, especially not so soon after marrying. But . . ." His voice trailed off.

She looked down and saw that her hands were locked in her lap, the knuckles white. "But what? I presume you have a theory."

"Your horrified silence suggested there might be some issue in the bedchamber." He hesitated, choosing his words. "Perhaps after six months of . . . normal marital relations, he revealed some vile

73

perversion that sent you screaming into the night."

Once she wouldn't have understood what he was implying, but after years of working in the infirmary and Zion House, she'd become almost as unshockable as her brother. "Nothing like that," she said, her voice wooden. There had never been problems in their bed. Barely able to get the words out, she whispered, "I left because . . . because I saw him murder a man."

Daniel caught his breath. "Under what circumstances? I presume he didn't kill someone at random."

"We'd just returned from our honeymoon and were settling into his London house," she said haltingly. "He was working late on his correspondence. It was almost midnight, so I went downstairs to see when he might retire."

She stared at her knotted hands, remembering her impish desire to coax her husband to their bed. It was the first time since their marriage that they hadn't retired at the same time, and she'd missed him. "I opened the door to his study and saw a man stealthily crossing the room behind him. The man was a big, muscular fellow who was roughly dressed, and he looked threatening. I'd never seen him before, so I said something like, 'James, look out!'"

She squeezed her eyes shut, as if that could obliterate what happened next from her brain. "James rose and spun around and without a word, he grabbed hold of the man and . . . and broke his neck. I could hear the bones snapping." She shuddered as she remembered the limp *deadness* of the body that crumpled down onto the Oriental carpet. "It was all over in seconds."

Daniel's face echoed her shock. "Was his life in danger?"

"It didn't seem to be. The man didn't speak and I didn't see a weapon." She swallowed convulsively. "But horrible as it was to see murder done, worse was seeing James's expression. He looked up at me, and he was . . . a stranger. A *monster*. I saw no remorse or shock. He looked . . . evil. I'd been sharing my bed with a soulless murderer." Her bed, and her body. The vile thought had made her ill. "My husband was a man I didn't know or want to know."

"I see now why you left, and why you didn't want to tell anyone." Daniel stood, expression grim. "I'll leave for London in the morning. I need to see his expression when he learns that you're increasing. And if there is any doubt in my mind about him, I won't let the devil come near you."

Chapter 8

Someday the wars with France would end, but not yet. Kirkland worked through the latest reports from his agents, trying to find the source for a certain uneasiness he felt concerning the Royal Navy. His concentration was broken when his butler, Soames, entered, probably to remind him to eat. But when he glanced up, he saw that the servant was being followed by the glowering figure of Daniel Herbert.

Soames said apologetically, "The gentleman was most insistent about seeing you, my lord."

Kirkland's first reaction was pleasure. His friends had been his family when he was growing up, and he and Daniel had been very close. Losing him at the same time he lost Laurel had made the blow even more wrenching.

But Daniel looked ready to do murder, so pleasure was immediately swamped by fear. He rose, feeling ice in his veins. "That's all right, Soames. Mr. Herbert and I are old schoolmates."

The butler nodded and withdrew. As soon as the door closed, Kirkland asked harshly, "Has something happened to Laurel?"

Daniel's brows rose. "Do you care?"

"Of course I care," Kirkland snapped, thinking that for a man of God, Daniel could be damned supercilious. "Is she ill or injured?" *Dear God, don't let her be dead!*

"In a manner of speaking." The other man's eyes narrowed. "She tells me that you were brought to the infirmary injured and feverish, and now she's with child."

The blow was even greater than the sight of Daniel. Kirkland felt as if a carriage had slammed him against a wall.

"If you ask whose it is, I will personally start breaking your bones," Daniel added caustically. "She claimed you didn't force her, but perhaps she was trying to prevent me from damaging you."

"Don't be a bloody fool," Kirkland retorted, jolted from his numbness. "While I was at the infirmary, I had a vivid fever dream which . . . must not have been a dream." He closed his eyes as the idea began to sink in. Laurel was with child. *They'd made a child together.* This changed— everything.

Warmth and wonder began to flow through him. "When I regained awareness, your sister did a magnificent job of pretending that she'd done nothing more than apply bandages and pour Jesuit's bark tea down my throat. It never occurred to me that there had been anything more between us."

"Obviously there was. She said to tell you that she's in good health and she'll inform you when the child is born. She wishes to raise it herself, but understands that if it's a boy, you'll eventually want to send him to school to be educated with other boys of his station."

"Generous of her." Mind buzzing, Kirkland headed toward the door. "I'll tell Soames to send in a supper and make up a room for you. Feel free to stay for a few days and enjoy London."

Daniel grabbed his arm. "Where are you going?"

Kirkland jerked loose. "Where the devil do you think I'm going? To my wife."

"Laurel does *not* want to see you," Daniel snapped. "She was quite clear about that. There is no need for you to travel down to Bristol."

Kirkland clamped down on his temper. "Do you think you can stop me? More than that, do you have the right to try?"

Daniel glared. "I'm her brother, and I will not see her hurt."

Kirkland glared back. "I'm her husband, and I've never raised a hand to Laurel."

Daniel's voice dropped to a menacing whisper. "Perhaps not, but when you separated, it tore Laurel's heart out."

Kirkland's mouth twisted bleakly. "*She* left *me,* if you recall. Do you think her heart was the only one damaged?"

Daniel studied him. "I was never sure. Now, I see."

"Then stay out of my way." Kirkland strode

from the study, slamming the door behind him. Laurel was his wife, and it was time and past time they talked.

After a busy day at Zion House and the infirmary, Laurel found doing accounts rather soothing. Concentration was required to make columns of figures add up—why did the British have such an absurd system of money? Surely it would be easier if there were ten pennies to a shilling and ten shillings to a pound—and the task pulled her thoughts away from wondering how Kirkland had reacted to her brother's news. She didn't think the two would have a knock-down fight, but men could be very strange.

She'd calculated how long it would take Daniel to reach London, meet with Kirkland, and return home. Tomorrow seemed the earliest possible time.

She heard male footsteps approaching her office. Hoping her brother had made exceptionally good time, she set her pen aside and turned to greet him.

Kirkland! She froze, shocked to the marrow. Dark and broad-shouldered and vividly present, he had recovered from his injuries and fever and was as compelling as when she'd first met him.

No, more so. Though she'd thought of him as a man grown when they'd met, he'd only been twenty-one. Worldly enough to sweep her off her feet, but still desperately young, just as she had been.

Now that he was neither twenty-one nor ill, she could see how the intervening years had toughened and matured him. He'd always had an air of contained force, and now he was truly formidable. Her brother had had doubts about the marriage because Kirkland was a complicated man, and he'd become more complicated with the years.

He was also vastly more sophisticated than she was. That had been true when they'd married, and was even more true now. She couldn't even guess at the things he'd seen and thought and done.

Yet his gaze was as direct as it was intense, and her spirit still responded to him because, on some deep level, they were connected. The ice in her veins vanished in a rush of heat. She should have known that he would come. Perhaps some unacknowledged part of her had even hoped that he would.

He must have read her reaction, because he halted in the doorway. "I haven't come to murder you, Laurel," he said, his voice mild.

She stood, wanting to reduce how far she had to look up to him. It would not be easy to send him away, but she must. He'd already changed her life in unexpected, painful ways. It was her task to make sure he didn't do that again.

When Kirkland had awakened from his fever in the infirmary, his awareness of Laurel had been hallucinatory, not quite real. Now he saw her with all his senses sharply alert. She was as alluring as when they'd first met, her figure graceful and her gaze direct. But her changeable blue-gray eyes were wary and she'd built a wall of reserve around herself that he could feel clear across the room. Which would make what he was going to propose even more difficult.

After the first shock of recognition, her eyes cooled to ice gray. "What an unexpected pleasure, Lord Kirkland. You made very good speed."

"You didn't expect me to come?"

"Until now, you've respected my wishes. Daniel told you I didn't wish to see you. Or did you break his neck before he could get that far?"

"Not at all," Kirkland said dryly. "I left him in possession of Kirkland House and told him to enjoy London for several days."

"Did he take you up on your most generous invitation?"

"I don't know. I left before he could reply."

Her eyes narrowed. "Have you come to say you're going to take my baby away? The law may be on your side, but I would hope for better from you."

"It's not *your* baby, Laurel," he said gently. "It's

our baby. Which is why I'm here. We need to talk."

"What if I told you the baby isn't yours?" she asked abruptly.

Every fiber of his body seemed to freeze before he said without emotion, "You are legally my wife, and I would accept the child as mine for its sake. Nor would I wish you to bear the stigma of having an illegitimate child."

"Even if the heir to your title would be another man's son?"

His mouth twisted. "When I look at my paternal relations, it's hard to make much of a case for continuing the bloodline. Was your child indeed sired by another man?"

"No," she said baldly. "Have you sired any bastards yourself?"

"Not that I know of." His mouth curved. "You're not going to drive me off until we've talked, Laurel."

"I thought it was worth a try," she said tartly. "We'd best go to the music room. We'll have privacy there."

"As you wish." He stepped back so she could move past him. She did so, her head high and lavender wafting tantalizingly in her wake.

His arm tensed involuntarily and it took all his will not to reach out and draw her into an embrace. When he'd been her patient three weeks earlier, he'd wondered if her impact on him was partly because he was weakened and vulnerable, but now he was fully fit and the sight of her undermined his hard-won control.

As Laurel moved into the anteroom, which contained a small desk and a large bookcase, a young woman entered from the other door. She brandished a sheaf of papers. "May I come in and discuss these invoices with you?" She stopped when she saw Kirkland. "Or perhaps you're still busy."

"We can go over the invoices in the morning, Betsy." Without introducing Kirkland, Laurel led the way past the girl, who watched curiously.

A flight of narrow back stairs led up to the music room. The elegant furnishings and handsome piano wouldn't have been out of place in the home of a grand lord. Which wasn't surprising, since Kirkland had bought them for his bride not long after their marriage as a gift to honor her musical talents.

After she'd left, he'd meticulously packed and shipped her family the instrument and everything else he'd given her. He'd been half mad in those days, and attending to his departed wife's possessions had been a twisted way of keeping in touch with her.

"Pray take a seat," Laurel said. "Shall I ring for refreshments?"

"I prefer not to be interrupted." Kirkland smiled humorlessly. "And it's probably best if I stand. I might end up pacing."

83

"Pace if you wish." Choosing to remain standing as well, Laurel drifted to a wing chair by the window. Her cat was stretched out on top of the seat back, so she stroked the sleek gray fur. "Though the law gives a father control over all children, there's no need for you to trouble yourself with an infant. I'll take charge of the nursery."

"I find myself oddly interested in my offspring," he said, his voice desert dry. "I have no intention of leaving you and our child alone for the next eight or ten years."

"You will *not* take my baby away from me!" Her eyes blazed. "If you try, I'll disappear to some place where you'll never find me."

"Don't underestimate my ability to find you." He caught her gaze, needing to impress her with his sincerity. "I won't take the child from you, and don't want to start a war like the one between my parents. I want for us to be husband and wife."

Chapter 9

Surely you're joking!" Laurel stared, aghast. "We can't go back to what we had. It's impossible."

There was a flicker in Kirkland's eyes, impossible to read. "No, we can't go back, but isn't ten years of estrangement enough? 'What God hath joined, let no man put asunder.' We took vows in front of God and man, Laurel. We owe it to ourselves and our child to rebuild our marriage into a form that will benefit us all."

Throat dry, she said, "The baby was an accident."

"Was it? Or could it be fate?" Kirkland regarded her with burning eyes, as dangerous as a honed blade. "When I woke after the fever broke, I thought I had dreamed of intimacy with you. Obviously I was remembering, not dreaming, but I'm not sure how accurate those memories are. I didn't force you, did I? I can't believe I would do that even out of my head with fever."

"You didn't force me. But you did strike out against some nightmare, and I was in the way."

He looked appalled. "I hit you?"

"A glancing blow only." If he hadn't been hallucinating, the night would have gone very differently. "When I tried to calm you, you recognized me as your wife so you kissed me. I could have pulled away if I wished." Her voice dropped to a whisper as she admitted, "For a few mad moments, I didn't wish that."

"We *are* still married," he pointed out. "We were drawn together by passion, so it's not surprising it still burns." Though he didn't move a muscle, the sensual tension in the room increased, making her hotly, uncomfortably aware of his nearness.

Her lips twisted. "I won't try to deny it, but passion is not enough."

"We wed too young, Laurel, and that was a large part of why our marriage splintered." There was sadness in his eyes. "We're older and wiser now. Surely we can find a way to be married that is comfortable without sharing a bed."

Warily she asked, "Could you clarify what you mean?"

"Some fashionable couples continue as loyal, affectionate friends even if they no longer live together." His smile was wry. "It will probably be easier to be friends if we're not sharing a bed."

"Youth wasn't our only problem, my lord," she said with deadly precision. "How many men have you killed since then?"

His expression blanked. "Very few, and none that didn't need killing," he said with matching precision. "Would we be having this conversation if I were a soldier instead of a laborer in the murky fields of intelligence gathering?"

It was a fair question, so she thought before replying. "I would be uncomfortable knowing you were a soldier with blood on your hands," she said slowly. "But at least I would understand. Murdering that man in front of me was very different."

She closed her eyes, wishing she could block out the horrific image. "When you looked up and saw me, your expression was monstrous. *Evil*. It revolted me to think that you were my husband. How can I allow a murderer near my child?"

He flinched, his dark blue eyes showing pain, not evil. "There were mitigating circumstances."

"What possible mitigation can there be for murder?" Her stomach knotted as she remembered her flight from her husband's house, and how he hadn't uttered a single word to stop her. "If there were good reasons, why didn't you tell me then?"

"I was as horrified as you because I didn't mean to kill the man." His face seemed carved from marble. "Despite your belief in my bloodthirsty nature, I'd never killed anyone. Not then."

"Then why did you do it? Your life didn't seem to be in danger." She realized with sharp intensity that she wanted to believe he was less ruthless than he'd seemed. "Was he carrying a weapon that I didn't see?"

"His name was Harry Moran and he was known as a hired thug and assassin. He was carrying a long and very sharp knife. But that wasn't why

I killed him." Kirkland began pacing again. "Remember that time, May 1803? The Peace of Amiens had just ended and we were once more at war with France."

"Of course I remember. We returned from our extended honeymoon because you believed that war was approaching." She tried not to think of the halcyon days of their honeymoon. It began in a lovely house on the Severn, then continued in a Scottish seaside manor where Kirkland's mother had been born. They'd had peace and laughter and solitude and more happiness than she'd imagined existed in the whole world.

As winter approached, he took her on a voyage on one of his ships. They sailed to the turquoise seas of the Caribbean, a place so magical it seemed unreal. They'd made love and slept rocked by the sea. "I was rather sorry to return to London," Laurel said, "but you had responsibilities at home and it was time to start building our new life. One can't be on honeymoon forever."

"So I learned. On that night"—he swallowed hard—"when Moran broke in, I had just read a report that my friend Wyndham had disappeared in Paris and was presumed dead when war broke out again. And it was my damned fault!"

Startled, she said, "That's nonsense! Your friend was of age. Sensible Britons had left Paris by then. What could you have done? Gone there and dragged him back?"

"That's exactly what I could and should have done," he said flatly. "I'd written Wyndham to warn him that the peace couldn't last much longer, but he was a carefree sort who'd never met a problem he couldn't talk his way out of. Until then."

"So because you were upset, you reacted more violently than you might have otherwise." She frowned, trying to understand. "How is it possible to kill a man with your bare hands by accident?"

"I'm sure Daniel told you about Kalarippayattu, the Hindu fighting technique that we all learned from Ashton?" When she nodded, he continued, "It can be very deadly. At school, we just sparred, careful to avoid doing real damage. Anyone who lost control was immediately pulled out of the sparring. But when I saw Moran and knew what he was, it released all my fury and guilt over losing Wyndham. I struck out at him, and before I realized what I was doing, he was dead."

She studied his bleak expression as she interpreted that ghastly night in a new way. "Perhaps you are not the monster you seemed then. But neither are you the man I thought I'd fallen in love with. I didn't know you contained such darkness."

"The darkness may be why I was so drawn to you," he said quietly. "You were all light. Everything that was good and true and beautiful."

"I'm no saint," she said uncomfortably. "We

married in a blind haze of desire. It would have been better if we'd never met."

"Perhaps, but marry we did. We pledged ourselves to each other, Laurel. We owe our child the chance to be a family." He held her gaze, his voice softening. "I don't want to live the rest of my life estranged from you."

She sighed. "What form do you suggest that this marriage take? I may be older and wiser now, but I'm also more set in my ways. At eighteen, all things seemed possible. Now I know better. I like my life here, I like the work I do, and it's valuable. At eighteen, I was malleable, willing to leave my family and friends without a qualm. Now I have so much more to lose."

"The work you do is important everywhere," he pointed out. "If you spend part of your time in London with me, you could start more clinics, more Zion Houses. Wealth makes many things easier. You can have two homes and move between them freely, as the mood strikes you. Our child would be able to grow up with both parents, not a permanent separation."

She bit her lip. "That might be worth risking if it was only us. But how can I raise my child near a man who can accidentally kill?"

His face turned dead white. "That never happened again. It never will."

She inhaled deeply, trying to soothe the knotted pain in her chest. "Are you sure? Those exotic

Hindu fighting skills were drilled into you until they became reflexes, or you wouldn't have killed Moran."

"Perhaps I'm uniquely evil because students at the Westerfield Academy still learn Kalarippayattu and I've never heard of anyone else doing such a thing. But I think it was a rare situation that will never be repeated. Particularly not with a child." His mouth lifted humorlessly. "Your own brother, an ordained vicar, physician, and surgeon, was very good at Kalarippayattu. Has he ever accidentally killed anyone?"

It was startling to think that Daniel might be as capable of administering swift death as Kirkland had. Then she remembered an occasion he'd mentioned in passing when he'd been attacked on the street by a pair of thieves. He'd brushed the incident off, saying that they'd quickly run away, but now she wondered if he'd used some of the same skills Kirkland had.

But Daniel was not the issue. "He hasn't, but that's not the point here. When you and I married, I trusted you completely, in all ways. That trust was broken the night you committed murder. I can't imagine being wife to a man I can't trust, and I don't know how, or even if, trust can be rebuilt."

"I don't know either," he said steadily. "But I do know that there is no chance to rebuild if we continue to live apart. Perhaps trust can grow from the mundane business of living together, even if it's only part time."

She moved to the piano and played a soft ripple of notes as she struggled to understand her panicked resistance to his proposal. Women had been leaving their homes to be with their husbands from time immemorial. She'd done it gladly when they'd first wed and she could do it again, particularly if she only lived with him part time. And he was right, she could do much good with his wealth.

Her real reasons for resisting were deeper. It wasn't just lack of trust; she liked the woman she'd become. It was all too easy to imagine losing herself in his power and intensity. "Perhaps I was braver at eighteen than I am now. Or perhaps I was so infatuated that I wasn't thinking clearly then, and now I am."

"Too much clear thinking is surely injurious to marriage," he said with wry humor. "Just remember that trying to build a bridge between us commits you to nothing but spending some time with me. If it doesn't work, you can return to Bristol whenever you wish. But I believe we should try this before the baby is born so when it arrives, we might be a couple again. Friendly. Courteous. Husband and wife. That would be better for all three of us."

She studied his handsome, formidable face. Was the passionate young man who'd loved her deeply still there? She'd thought so during the heated encounter that had brought them to this point, but perhaps that had been simply passion without love. Perhaps he was proposing reconciliation simply because it was the right thing to do.

And damnably, he was correct: attempting to reconcile *was* the right thing to do. His appeal to the sacred vows they'd taken was impossible to ignore. She had always been a woman of her word, yet in the matter of marriage, the most important vows of all, she'd failed. She had pledged herself to him for better or worse. Their vows and their child demanded they attempt to rebuild their marriage, even if it was only a shadow of what they'd once had.

"You are right that if there is to be any hope, we must spend time together," she said slowly. "And I'm right that intimacy muddles one's mind."

"Do you have a suggestion for how to proceed?"

"That we live together for—a month? Not as husband and wife, but as friends. That will give us time to become reacquainted. Perhaps trust will grow from that."

"Let's aim for three months," he suggested. "Long enough to determine whether we can share a roof amiably."

"A month," she said firmly. "We can extend the trial if it's going well. If we drive each other mad, the sooner it's over, the better."

She assumed he had a mistress, as so many men

of his rank did. Should she ask that he dismiss the woman?

No, better not to raise the subject. It would make Laurel's situation easier if he had another woman to turn to, and she was cowardly enough not to want to know about other women in his life.

"Very well, a month. We have a bargain." He offered his hand and a devastating smile. "I'm so glad, my Lavender Lady. I've missed you."

The use of the nickname was a painful reminder of what they'd lost, but she managed a smile. "I've missed you, too."

Then she made the mistake of taking his proffered hand, and the rush of emotional and physical connection was worse than any nickname.

But she suppressed her reaction. After all, she was older and wiser now.

Chapter 10

K irkland could have held Laurel's hand all night. Despite her wariness and the distance between them, touching her felt right.

When she stepped away, she left emptiness. He wanted to pull her back into an embrace, but if there was to be any hope, he must control his impatience and allow her to move at her own speed.

Laurel drifted to the other side of the piano. "I expect in your business you're very good at lying. Don't ever lie to me."

"I won't. I never have. I hope the same is true for you?"

"Do lies of omission count?" she asked.

He smiled. "If you mean your extremely prim and proper behavior when I woke up in your infirmary—no, that doesn't count. You wanted to get rid of me, so it was best not to reveal that anything had transpired between us. It would have worked if you hadn't conceived."

She swallowed hard. "I shouldn't have told you about it so soon. So many pregnancies fail in the first months."

"That would be a great sadness," he said quietly. "But even if you miscarry, we've been brought together to try again. I hadn't thought that was possible. Now, it seems necessary."

"Trying is the right thing to do," she agreed. "But that doesn't mean that I'm not as nervous as a cricket on a griddle!"

He laughed, and she laughed with him. Shared laughter must be a good omen. She asked, "What happens now?"

"We need to break the news to Daniel when he returns from London. I don't suppose he'll be enthralled by the idea." An understatement, but Daniel was a rational man and he wanted to see Laurel happy.

"The change will be good for him," she said thoughtfully. "He and I have become too comfortable. If I'm not always here to manage the household, perhaps he'll realize it's time he found a wife."

It wasn't uncommon for a brother and sister to live together, and Laurel and Daniel had always been close. But she was Kirkland's wife, dammit, and Daniel was surely good husband material if he ever bothered to look for a bride of his own. "I imagine you've made it easy for Daniel to work too hard. How long do you think it will take you to organize matters here so you can come to London?"

"Not long. Betsy Rivers, my assistant, is very capable and can manage the bills and purchasing supplies and the rest. Anne Wilson is matron of Zion House and she'll manage very well without me." Laurel smiled a little wistfully. "We'll miss each other, though. We've become good friends."

"Invite her to visit you when you're in London. I can send a carriage. I want your life to be expanded, not diminished." He thought about what should be done. "In order to support the fact that you're leaving Bristol to join a long-absent husband, do you want to introduce me to some of your friends here? I should probably call on your parents and repeat that the fault has always been mine."

"I'm not quite as forgiving as I should be for the way they behaved when I left you, but I suppose it would be best to mend the breach." She made a face. "Here at the infirmary, do you mind if I introduce you as plain Mr. Kirkland? It will be simpler if I'm not known as a countess."

Her head might believe that they should try to reconcile, but her heart still kept its distance. Concealing the thought, he said, "How fortunate that I'm one of the rare earls whose family name and title are the same. Mr. Kirkland it is."

She scooped up Shadow and settled in a chair with him in her lap. A furry chaperone. "I gather you spend most of your time in London these days?"

He seated himself on a sofa at right angles to her. Out of touching distance in order to reduce temptation. "My work requires it."

"I don't suppose you'd give up your murderous work," she said dryly.

He sighed, knowing how much that counted against him in her mind. "I can't, my lady. Much of what I do is mundane, but some matters are vital."

"What kinds of affairs?" She gestured with one hand. "Your world is so different from mine. What have you done that you consider vital?"

He thought a moment. "It's been kept secret for obvious reasons, but a few months ago, my people stopped a conspiracy to assassinate the Prince Regent and his brothers and kidnap Princess Charlotte. At one point, I killed a kidnapper who was about to shoot a woman who was risking her life to save the princess. I may regret the way I killed Moran, but I had no qualms about stopping this particular villain."

Laurel's eyes widened. "I . . . see. Such work really is vital, and I imagine you're better at it than most. Does this keep you in London almost full time? What about your estate in Scotland? Do you visit there much? It's so beautiful."

"I visit, though not often." The estate reminded him too much of the joy he'd known there with Laurel. It was easier to stay at his Edinburgh house. "I've also bought a small estate just outside London so I can get away when I need quiet. It's called Milton Manor. I think you'll like it."

"I expect I will. It's the social occasions I won't like." Her mouth twisted. "I'll never make a grand hostess who lends luster to your name."

"I don't require a grand hostess and you needn't attend any social events that don't appeal to you. I just want to be on civil terms with my wife." Wanting to reassure her, he continued, "Nor will you have to face London alone. I'll introduce you to women who might become friends. Women who care more about the less fortunate than they do about fashion. You won't be alone."

She smiled wryly. "Country mouse goes to the city. I'll try not to disgrace you."

"You won't." She'd never realized how special she was to him, how her warmth and composure made her presence a balm. Now, finally, he'd have her close again, even if it was only part time and she wouldn't be quite a wife.

He covered a yawn, suddenly exhausted now that his mission had been achieved. "Sorry, it was a long drive from London. I'll head for the Ostrich Inn now. I'm sure they can find me a room."

She glanced out the window at the night sky. "It's late. Since we've agreed to share a roof again at least some of the time, we might as well start now. You can stay in the guest room and use our stables."

Pleased that she made the offer, he said, "That would be very welcome."

"Once you're sorted out, meet me in the kitchen and I'll show you to your room."

He nodded and headed downstairs to talk to Rhodes, the only servant he'd brought with him.

The knowledge that he would be under the same roof as his wife was both wonderful and terrifying. *Dear God, don't let me ruin this again.*

He was incredibly lucky that Laurel was giving him a second chance, even if it was limited and conditional. Maybe they couldn't go back to what they'd had, but that didn't mean he couldn't hope they'd build a relationship that would take away some of the loneliness.

Laurel glanced up as Kirkland entered the kitchen. "I assumed you're hungry after your swift journey from London?"

He gave the smile that was mostly a glint in his eyes. Devilishly attractive. "Yes, but I don't expect you to feed me. You shouldn't be doing the work of a kitchen maid."

"That's a sign of the distance between our lives." She scooped steaming potato and cheese soup into two bowls and set them on the table. "We have an ever-changing roster of servants from Zion House being trained here, so I often perform tasks too menial for a countess."

He settled in the Windsor chair on the other side of the table. "Since you are a countess, by definition this work isn't menial."

"That's an eloquent rationalization." She set a platter of sliced ham and cheese and bread in the middle of the table, poured two glasses of West Country cider, and took her seat opposite. She'd forgotten to eat and hadn't realized how hungry she was. "I may be officially a countess, but I'm a working woman, not a lady. And I have the rough hands to prove it."

She held up her right hand to demonstrate, which was a mistake. He took it between both of his.

"They're beautiful hands. Strong and capable." He stroked from her wrist down over her fingers. His touch sent shivers rippling straight through her. She couldn't be losing all sense so *soon!*

She jerked her hand away. "I think we should avoid unnecessary touching."

He took a deep breath and lowered his hands. "That would be . . . wise."

She sipped a spoonful of soup, almost scalding her tongue. "This turned out well. I had some lovely cheese on hand."

He tasted the soup appreciatively. "Your culinary skills have expanded. If you don't like being a countess, you can definitely become a cook."

She smiled but shook her head. "Though working in the kitchen is soothing, I'm glad I don't have to cook all the time. Then it would be work."

"So many things are like that." He swallowed another spoonful. "The fact that you're willing to do whatever needs to be done is part of your— genuineness, for lack of a better word." His gaze caught hers. "Because I work so much in the shadows, your clarity is like a lantern in the night."

She was insane to agree to live under the same roof when he could produce shivers with words alone. Telling herself that she would become accustomed so his presence didn't unbalance her so, she said, "You're poetic and I'm practical. Eat your soup before it cools, James."

He laughed and obeyed. "Yes, my lady."

She buttered a piece of bread. "Will you return to London in the morning?"

"There are no current crises, so I can stay a few days and meet your friends and coworkers." He transferred a piece of ham to his plate. "Should we start by calling on your parents tomorrow morning?"

Laurel's stomach clenched. "I suppose we should."

"You'd rather not?" Kirkland was watching her closely.

She was startled by how upset she was at the thought of seeing her parents again. Keeping her voice neutral, she said, "It's sad to admit that since they cast me out, I haven't missed them at all. They never had much interest in me, beyond wanting me to have good manners and make a decent marriage. Dealing with them reminds me that I'm not a very good Christian."

"Forgiveness is hard," he said quietly.

"I tell myself that they're not evil. Just . . . very narrow. The only thing I've done that they really approved of was marrying you. They'd hoped for another son, and instead had me. It was a great disappointment. I suspect that my leaving you was the greatest disaster of their lives. Then to work with the poor here in Bristol . . . !" She shook her head. "Disgraceful!"

Kirkland frowned. "Would it help if we wait till Daniel returns so he can accompany us?"

She hesitated, then shook her head. "His presence would just complicate matters. Daniel has always been their pride and joy. His relation-ship with them has been somewhat strained in recent years because they don't approve of his work, or the fact that he didn't disown me, but he still sees them with some regularity."

"It's hard to admit that one isn't attached to family members." Kirkland cut his ham into neat pieces. "But the truth is the truth."

She was relieved that he accepted her unfilial thoughts so calmly. Allowing herself to hope, she said, "Now that I've accepted that I can't be the daughter they want, and they can't be the parents I want, we can at least be civil. There will never be a better time to reestablish a relationship."

He raised his cider in a toast. "Then tomorrow, we shall all practice our civility."

She lifted her glass in return, and silently prayed that all would be boringly civil the next day.

Marry in haste, repent at leisure. What a wise old saying. A pity Laurel hadn't believed it. No eighteen-year-old did. She rolled over and pounded her pillow into a more comfortable shape. Relaxing with Kirkland under her roof was difficult.

She'd gone from Miss Herbert to Lady Kirkland, then retreated into being Miss Herbert again. Now she'd be Mrs. Kirkland, at least in Bristol. But in London, she'd be Lady Kirkland, and it was an identity she'd never really come to terms with.

She reminded herself that she knew much more of the world than when she'd married. Despite her natural reserve, she could hold a conversation with anyone. Even Kirkland's friends, who probably would hate her for making him miserable.

What about the women he'd said he'd introduce her to as potential friends? Would they be his former mistresses? Or worse, current mistresses?

It didn't bear thinking about. He and she would be *civil*. That was the goal. She could be civil.

She reminded herself that she'd only be in London for a month. Then she could come home again. In the future, she might visit her husband in the city a time or two a year, but the center of her life would remain in Bristol.

She rolled onto her back as a new thought struck. She'd need a new wardrobe. Kirkland was nothing if not generous, and he'd want to drown her in dresses. She *loathed* standing still while seamstresses poked and pinned.

With a groan, she rolled over and mauled her pillow again. She could do this.

She *had* to do this.

Chapter 11

Laurel had counted herself lucky to have only a mildly unsettled stomach in the mornings, but on this day, she woke with full-fledged morning sickness. After retching helplessly into her washbasin, she wiped her face with a wet towel and wondered miserably if her illness had as much to do with visiting her parents as the fact that she was increasing. She rather hoped so because that would mean she wouldn't be so sick the next morning.

After her stomach settled, she sipped a little water. She must inform her cook that there was a husband in the house who would want breakfast. But first, she needed to dress. What should a female wear when venturing forth to visit one's difficult, long-estranged parents in the company of a fashionable and newly acknowledged husband? Demure but not dowdy, that was the ticket.

Laurel chose a simple, high-necked morning gown that she wore to chapel on Sundays. Though it wasn't fashionable, the style suited her, and the celestial blue fabric made her eyes look equally blue while her skin glowed. After pulling her hair back into a neat coil, she followed the tantalizing fragrance of baking bread to the kitchen.

As she approached the door, she heard raucous

laughter from her cook, Mrs. Wicker, a bawdy widow. Surprised, Laurel stepped into the kitchen to see that Kirkland had arrived ahead of her. He was impeccably dressed, clearly a man of fashion, and heart-stoppingly handsome, yet he managed to look entirely at home at the plain wooden table.

He was giving the short, rotund cook his full attention. That was part of his charm, she realized. When Laurel was with him, she felt as if she was the most important person in his world. Which meant that she shouldn't take that intense focus so seriously. Listening well was his nature, and surely a good trait for a spy.

The cook grinned when she saw Laurel. "There you are, Miss Laurel. Or rather, Mrs. Kirkland. Such a secret you've been keeping!" She batted Kirkland's arm cheerfully, leaving a smudge of flour on the elegant navy blue sleeve. "If I'd a husband like this one, I'd keep him in my bed!"

Laurel's gaze moved to Kirkland, whose eyes were brimming with repressed amusement. Telling herself she would not be embarrassed, she said calmly, "From what I've heard, you did exactly that with your husbands, and rumor has it that the baker from the next street is ready to become husband number four."

"You've got long ears, miss! Or Mrs., rather. Mebbe I'll wed him and mebbe not." Mrs. Wicker poured tea and slid it over the table. "You need a good breakfast before you go off to see your parents. Eggs? Beans? Ham?"

Laurel's stomach roiled at the thought. She swallowed hard. "Just tea and toast, please."

Kirkland obviously recognized her nerves, but didn't comment. He kept Mrs. Wicker laughing with his witticisms while he did full justice to a hearty breakfast.

If his parents were alive, would he be tense if he visited them? Even if he was, he'd show only that controlled, impenetrable courtesy. She must strive to do the same.

After breakfast, she donned her bonnet and stepped outside to the smart curricle Kirkland had hired for the drive. As he took her hand to help her up to the high seat, he said, "Your fingers feel like ice even through gloves. We don't have to do this if you'd rather not."

For a moment, she was powerfully tempted. *Don't be such a coward, Laurel!* If she was beginning a new life, she must be braver. She climbed up to her seat and released his hand quickly. "I truly don't want to see them, but—I should attempt to mend the breach. We're supposed to honor our father and mother, after all."

"Not all parents deserve honor," he said dryly as he climbed in and took hold of the reins. "Even so, when we get there, we need to seem relaxed with each other if we're to appear convincingly reconciled."

She deciphered that easily. "Meaning I shouldn't pull away whenever you come near me?"

"Exactly." He slanted her a glance as he set the curricle in motion. "Can you bear the usual gentlemanly courtesies from me?"

"I shall train myself not to flinch." Which would not be easy. As the curricle began to move, she added, "It's too early to mention the baby, I think."

"The news would surely please them greatly."

She did not want to tell them about it face to face. Better to impart it in a letter, where she wouldn't be immediately battered by her mother's criticism and advice. "Yes, but it would be a complication. They aren't dreadful, just . . . very narrow. They do best with simple situations."

Kirkland navigated neatly around a dray loaded with barrels that had halted in the middle of the street. Because Herbert House was close to the port, traffic was heavy, and maneuvering through the drays and carriages ended conversation. That suited Laurel.

He seemed equally comfortable with silence. The pair of bay horses pulling the curricle was lively, but Kirkland was a skilled driver who made controlling the carriage look easy. As they left the city, Laurel relaxed and began to enjoy the lovely day. She seldom got out of the city these days, and she missed the rolling hills and fresh air.

Halfway to Belmond, a question occurred to her. "Since his disappearance altered the course of our lives, did you ever learn what happened to your friend Wyndham? Or was his death one of the unsolved mysteries of war?"

Kirkland glanced at her with a rare, unreserved smile. "Amazingly, Wyndham survived. Just as the truce collapsed, he offended a French official and was thrown into solitary confinement in a private dungeon. For years, my people in France looked for proof of his fate. Earlier this year, one of my best agents followed up a lead and, through luck and skill, rescued Wyndham and brought him safely back to England."

"Good heavens!" Laurel exclaimed, shocked. "Was he even sane after ten years in solitary confinement?"

Kirkland's smile vanished. "In his own words, Wyndham was 'near as dammit to feral' when he emerged from France. But he's recovering well. He always had a happy disposition, and now he has much to be happy about."

"I'm glad," she said sincerely. "I imagine that few such stories end well."

Kirkland sighed. "We do our best. It's never enough."

How could she have forgotten about his over-developed sense of responsibility? "I realize now why you were never particularly devout. When a man thinks he's God, there's no reason to attend Sunday services."

"I beg your pardon?" he said, genuinely startled.

"You can't save everyone, James. No one can," she said ruefully as she thought of people she'd nursed at the infirmary and Zion House. "Believe me, I know."

He fell silent as he halted the curricle so a dozen cows could amble across the narrow road. "I know I can't save everyone. But I feel compelled to try."

"One must try, but we are imperfect humans," she said. "Does Presbyterian guilt from your Scottish ancestors make you torture yourself for not being perfect?"

"That's surely part of it." His voice darkened. "But . . . more a matter of atonement for my errors and the darker deeds of my work."

"The most we can ever do is our best," she said quietly. "If worry is interest paid on troubles we haven't had yet, guilt is pain wasted on what can't be changed."

"Please remind me of that regularly. I need to hear it." His glance at her was wry. "You haven't lost your ability to skewer my weaknesses and pretensions."

She laughed. "Someone needs to." Then she quickly looked away, unnerved at how they kept sliding into intimacy.

Kirkland was not surprised to find that Belmond Manor hadn't changed. As the startled but pleased old butler escorted them to Laurel's parents,

Kirkland said to Laurel under his breath, "Shall I terrorize them for you?"

Her rigid expression eased. "Tempting, but best not to do so." She took his arm. "This is going to be . . . strange."

"I can imagine." He patted her hand where it rested on his forearm. "But we needn't stay long. A brief official visit to announce our renewed civility, and then off."

Her smile was stiff, but she looked composed as the butler opened the door to the morning room and announced, "Lord and Lady Kirkland."

Their entrance produced palpable shock from the couple sitting on opposite sides of the fireplace. Kirkland was surprised at how the Herberts had aged. It wasn't only the years and the graying hair, but the lines of disapproval that had deepened in their faces.

George Herbert surged to his feet and exclaimed "Kirkland!" while his wife gasped and pressed a fist to her mouth in disbelief.

"Mr. Herbert. Mrs. Herbert." Kirkland bowed politely. His in-laws' surprise was quickly followed by pleasure, but only as their gazes locked on Kirkland. They scarcely noticed their long-lost daughter, who stood rigidly beside him.

He rested his hand in the small of Laurel's back in a deliberately intimate, possessive gesture. Her tiny flinch would have been noticeable to no one else. Voice smooth, he said, "Laurel and I have reconciled, and of course we wished to inform you of the happy news right away."

"Well, well, happy news indeed!" Herbert exclaimed. "It was very good of you to take her back after the way she behaved."

"On the contrary, it was good of her to forgive my failings," Kirkland replied with an edge in his voice. "All blame for our separation belongs to me."

"Nonsense!" Herbert said, beaming. "It's a wife's duty to obey her husband and fulfill his needs, not abandon him on a foolish whim."

As Laurel's face stiffened, Kirkland said firmly, "There was nothing whimsical about her leaving. She was fully justified."

Elizabeth Herbert frowned at her daughter. She'd been a beauty and she'd passed her looks on to her children, but her face had turned sour. "It is never a woman's place to judge her husband! I tried to raise you better than that, Laurel. I give thanks that you've finally come to your senses and Kirkland is willing to forgive your outrageous behavior!"

Kirkland felt his temper rising. Ten years earlier, he'd been so besotted by Laurel that he hadn't thought much about her parents beyond the fact that they were respectable members of the gentry and happy to give permission for their daughter to wed. Now he realized that he could have been a pox-ridden rake and they'd have encouraged the marriage, as long as their prospective son-in-law had a title and a fortune.

"As I said, I was the one in need of forgiveness. Laurel's behavior has been above reproach." Reminding himself that reconciliation was the order of the day's visit, he continued, "I look forward to resuming our acquaintance. May we sit down?"

"Of course, of course, where are my manners!" Mrs. Herbert jumped to her feet and yanked on the bellpull. "I'll order tea for us." As she resumed her seat, she hissed to Laurel, "How dare you appear with your husband in such a disgraceful gown!"

Though it was meant to be a private comment, Kirkland answered it as he took a firm grasp on Laurel's hand and drew her down beside him on the sofa. "The fault is mine, Mrs. Herbert. I asked Laurel to wear this gown because the color makes her look particularly lovely."

Mrs. Herbert bit her lip, not wanting to insult her grand son-in-law, but having trouble controlling her waspish tongue.

Clamping down on his anger, Kirkland said, "Naturally when we go up to London, Laurel can avail herself of the best modistes, which I hope will include gowns in this shade of celestial blue."

His mother-in-law's expression blazed with envy that Laurel would have access to the latest fashions, along with fury that her daughter would fail to fully appreciate her opportunities. Voice sharp, she said, "You'll need to hire yourself a good lady's maid, my girl, since you've never shown any talent for dressing well."

Laurel hadn't said a word since they'd arrived, but now she raised her head and said clearly, "I already have a maid. Violet was a West Indian slave until I rescued her from her owner."

Mrs. Herbert looked appalled. Mr. Herbert, nervous at how the conversation was going, said, "I assume you'll be living primarily in London? House of Lords and all."

Laurel's grip on Kirkland's hand tightened, but she said sweetly, "I will divide my time between London and Bristol since my work is there."

Both Herberts looked horrified. "Your place is beside your husband!" her mother exclaimed. "Surely you will no longer mingle with filthy thieves and fallen women!"

"They are all God's children, Mother," Laurel said piously. "I am merely doing my duty as a Christian."

"Bah, you're the one who poisoned your brother's mind!" her father snapped. "He would be living like a proper gentleman if you hadn't dragged him down to your level. Kirkland, you must learn to control your wife!"

Kirkland was starting to understand why Laurel hadn't missed her parents in the last ten years. He looked at her with doting warmth. "Why should I wish to eliminate those traits which make her so special? So worthy of love?"

There was no telling where the conversation might have gone if the door hadn't opened just then and two footmen entered with heavily laden silver trays. The butler had deduced that having a lord in the house meant the best available refreshments. The conversation devolved to tea and cakes and weather.

It was very, very civil.

Chapter 12

Laurel felt brittle as Kirkland assisted her into the curricle for the return to Bristol. If he said a single word, she feared she'd snap.

Perceptive as always, he was silent as he set the carriage in motion. As they turned from the long driveway into the lane that led to the main Bristol road, he said in a conversational tone, "My father used to beat me. Of course, most fathers beat their sons, but my father was particularly enthusiastic."

Jarred from her own painful thoughts, she stared at his calm, regular profile. "You never told me that."

"What young man wants to appear as a helpless victim to the girl he loves?" His strong hands reined the horses back as the curricle approached a section of deep ruts. "Nor is it amusing to talk about how one is despised by those who should care most."

She swallowed hard, understanding what he meant. "Unamusing, and . . . almost impossible. To be fair, I didn't feel despised, merely . . . unimportant. I was dutiful and well behaved, and never caused any trouble. That made me invisible, which was safe."

"Safer than attracting the critical attention of your parents?"

She looked away, her gaze resting sightlessly on the hedges that lined the road. "They didn't used to be quite so critical. I think they are disappointed in their children."

"Then they're fools." They had reached a straight section of road, so Kirkland let the horses move into a smooth canter. "I've wondered how such a traditional couple produced two such interesting and unusual offspring."

She was surprised by his comment. Daniel was interesting and unusual, but she never thought of herself that way. "My mother's father was a famous eccentric. My parents found him embarrassing, which I suspect is why they became so very, very proper." And critical of others.

"You never told me about the eccentric grandfather."

"He was never discussed because he was an embarrassment." Laurel frowned. "I'm not even sure what he did that was so embarrassing. I only met him a time or two when I was small, but I recall him as being jolly. I wish I'd known him better."

"I don't suppose your parents appreciated jollity."

Her mouth quirked humorlessly. "An understatement. Mirth is ill bred. Unladylike."

"Perhaps having an eccentric grandfather in the family tree helped you and your brother be independent and original, but it's difficult to be warm in a cold household." His swift glance was penetrating. "What is the source of your amazing warmth, Laurel? Obviously not your parents."

Her fingers clenched on the edge of the curricle. He was damnably good at identifying the aspects of her childhood that she preferred not to discuss. But his question reminded her of the good she'd known along with the bad.

"We had the most wonderful nurse," she replied. "Nan was a local girl who was educated at a dame school and wanted to be a teacher herself, so she practiced on us. She was interested in everything, so we were, too. When we outgrew the nursery, she left Belmond Manor, married a nonconformist minister, and founded an infant school."

"Lucky infants. It sounds as if she gave you a good foundation. Were there other warm, subversive influences?"

"Did I never mention the Mercers? The vicar and his wife when I was little. I practically lived at their house. They were kind and tolerant, and since they had five children, I was always welcome because I helped with the younger ones. They called me their oldest daughter." She smiled reminiscently. "They let me borrow books as well."

"They're not still in Belmond, are they? The vicar who married us was named Mr. Browne, I recall."

"When I was fifteen, Mr. Mercer inherited a nice little estate in Yorkshire and they moved away." She sighed. "I missed them dreadfully."

"So when I appeared when you were seventeen, you were lonely." He concentrated on his driving as they forded a small stream.

Lonely, and ripe to fall in love. But she would have been head over heels for Kirkland whenever and wherever they'd met. He'd been the most entrancing man she'd ever encountered. He still was. "When I turned seventeen, there was vague talk of sending me to London for a season with some of my grander relations, but nothing came of it. Such things are expensive and my mother was sure I wouldn't be a success so it would be money wasted."

"You would have been a great success," he said dispassionately. "And it would have been better for both of us if you'd been in London when I visited Belmond." His words were like a cool, smooth stiletto sliding between her ribs, but she couldn't deny the truth of them. *Marry in haste, repent at leisure.*

Her voice equally dispassionate, she said, "I'm not sure whether our meeting proves that God has a sense of humor, or that we are each other's crosses to bear."

Instead of being angry, he laughed. "That's an interesting way of looking at our marriage, my lady. I expect that we're each other's crosses, but surely we can bear them as friends. Now that we're older and wiser."

And they'd have a child to love together. She

said abruptly, "Thank you for defending me to my parents. They were delighted to see you, so it would have been easier for you to ignore their comments."

"You're my wife. It's my job to defend you, even from your own parents if necessary." He glanced over. "Didn't Daniel defend you?"

"They knew better than to be too critical of me in front of him. And once he turned ten, he was away at school much of the time."

"Which was my gain and your loss. He was a good friend to me."

"That was when I started spending more time with the Mercers." She sighed. "I really saw very little of my parents. Why do I still care so much what they think?"

She didn't expect an answer, but he said thoughtfully, "It may be nature's way of preventing children from killing their parents when the relationship proves impossible."

She blinked. "I'd think you were joking, except that I'm quite sure you're not."

"If I'd been older and stronger, I'm not sure what would have happened with my own parents. After my mother died, I told my father I wanted to live with my Scottish grandparents. He gave me the worst beating of my life." Kirkland slowed the horses as they passed through a tiny hamlet, neatly avoiding a chicken that ran into the road.

"And you wanted to kill him."

"I actually tried—you were right about my murderous tendencies. But the letter opener on his desk was dull so I didn't do much damage. Not one of my finer moments." This time, he was the one who looked brittle to the breaking point.

She laid her right hand over his left where he was gripping the reins. "Because you lost your temper so thoroughly, or because you failed to do much damage?"

"I'm not really sure. Luckily my furious attack convinced him to send me to the Westerfield Academy. He considered it punishment because it kept me away from my Scottish relations. I considered it a gift because it kept me away from him." He glanced over with a trace of humor. "The Lord truly does work in mysterious ways."

"Lady Agnes Westerfield seems to be the best thing that ever happened to her assorted boys. I hope I have a chance to meet her someday."

"You will. She comes up to Town from Kent regularly." They were entering the outskirts of Bristol and traffic was increasing, so he slowed the curricle down. "Do you really have a lady's maid that you rescued from slavery?"

She relaxed a little at his question. "Violet is a trained maid who was a slave in Jamaica, and I did prevent a revolting fellow called Captain Hardwick from carrying her off to his ship. He said he'd bought her, I quoted a legal precedent, and with the support of the local stevedores I was able to get her safely away. She's at Zion House now."

Kirkland frowned. "I've heard of this Captain Hardwick. He's a nasty piece of work and probably an illegal slave runner. I don't suppose you stopped to consider the risk you were taking?"

"Not really. There wasn't time." She arched her brows. "You needn't lecture me on my foolishness. Daniel already did."

"It's a chilling tale that could have gone badly wrong, but it didn't. Well done, my lady." He inclined his head respectfully. "So you're taking her to London?"

"I haven't yet asked her. I hadn't thought about it until my mother told me I must hire a maid. Violet might not want to go to London."

"I imagine she'll be happy to accompany you."

The afternoon traffic was heavy, so conversation ended until they arrived back at Herbert House. Kirkland stepped down and turned to help Laurel out. He held her hand a moment longer even after she was on the ground, his eyes intent.

She was acutely aware of his strength and closeness and had the absurd thought that he wanted to kiss her. She jerked her hand free.

He didn't react to her rudeness, saying only, "Would you be offended if I said that you look tired and in need of rest?"

So he wasn't interested in kissing, just worried

about her health. "You're right, it was a tiring expedition. I'll get some rest now."

He gave a nod of approval. "I must return the curricle. When will you be ready to travel up to Town?"

She considered, and realized that the sooner she moved forward, the better. "I can be ready tomorrow morning. I'll go talk to Violet."

"If she refuses, it won't be difficult to hire a good lady's maid in London."

"True, but Violet is very good, and a known quantity." And she'd rather go to London with at least one friendly face. Someone who was on her side.

Now why had she thought that? Kirkland wasn't her enemy.

But that wasn't the same thing as saying he was on her side, she realized as he bowed courteously and swung up into the curricle again.

As he drove off, she realized that she was not only exhausted but ravenous, so she headed right to the kitchen and let Mrs. Wicker feed her soup, bread, and cheese. That gave her the strength to climb up to her room. Once there, she dropped her reticule in a chair, kicked off her slippers, and settled down to nap. Pregnancy was hard work.

Shadow performed his usual cat magic of appearing to nap with her. She fell asleep with his furry body curled against her, and wondering if it had been worthwhile seeing her parents. She supposed so—but she didn't want to see them in the future without Kirkland there to defend her.

Kirkland took his time returning the curricle to the livery stable where he'd hired it, then walking back to Laurel's house. Visiting the senior Herberts had been unsettling. Not only did he hate seeing how badly they behaved to Laurel, but he now understood better why she was so reluctant to resume their marriage. With her parents as an example, it was surprising that she'd been willing to marry at all.

But he and Laurel had been saturated with blind, youthful passions which overcame experience and any claims to good judgment. Now they both knew better, yet even so, he still wanted her rather desperately.

The challenge was to persuade her to feel the same.

Chapter 13

Laurel slept for two solid hours but awoke refreshed. Time to find Violet, so she headed across the garden to Zion House. She found the girl in a corner of the common room demonstrating an elaborate formal hairstyle on one of her four students.

Seeing Laurel approach, Violet said, "Practice on each other now. Pretend you are to be presented to the queen!" Then she turned to Laurel, her expression inquiring. She wore a quietly elegant cream-colored gown that complemented her dark skin and hair. Laurel had bought the garment for her from a rag dealer, and the skill with which Violet had remade it was testimony to her ability as a lady's maid.

Laurel asked, "How are your students doing?"

"Very well. They're all keen to better themselves." Violet regarded the girls fondly. They were all neatly dressed in an echo of their teacher. "It was clever of you to buy all those old clothes from the rag shop so they can practice dressing each other."

"Those clothes also present myriad opportunities to practice mending!" Laurel studied Violet's expression. The girl had fit into Zion House easily and was well liked. She was also diligent in training future lady's maids, but there was strain around her eyes. "I expect news of my newly arrived husband has spread through both houses already?"

"Yes, Miss Laurel. Or rather, Mrs. Kirkland." Violet smiled. "We're all perishing of curiosity, of course."

"Of course," Laurel said, not offering any explanations. "Tomorrow morning I'll leave for London to spend a month or so there with Kirkland. Would you be willing to come as my lady's maid?"

The girl's dark eyes widened. "Oh yes, miss! Ma'am. I would love to leave Bristol and serve you."

Laurel cocked her head. "You don't like Bristol?"

Violet bit her lip. "Not that, but several times when I've gone out, I've been watched, I'm sure of it."

"You're very pretty and also exotic looking. Surely men always notice you?"

Violet shook her head. "That is sadly so, but this is different. As I was leaving the market yesterday, I saw a man start after me. I returned to the market and lost myself in the crowd before leaving a different way. He was dressed as a sailor and had a long, curving scar down the left side of his face." She shuddered. "I'm afraid Captain Hardwick has hired men to steal me back into slavery if they have the chance."

127

Having seen Hardwick and his cruel eyes, Laurel didn't doubt that he might have done exactly that so he could recapture the girl who had escaped him. "You should have told me! Can you be ready to go tomorrow morning?"

"I would leave this minute if it meant safety," Violet said simply. "I will go now to pack your clothing. Is mending needed? Or alterations? I could do them tonight."

Laurel made a face. "Don't worry about the mending. I think my husband will send me to a London modiste for a new wardrobe."

Violet laughed. "From your expression, I think I will enjoy that more than you."

"You're right. I shall rely on you to help me choose what is best for me rather than merely fashionable."

"You will be easy to dress, ma'am. With your height and figure and coloring you will do me much credit."

"I hope you're right," Laurel said dubiously. The real question was whether she would do her husband credit. Telling herself that modistes would be easier to face than her parents, she took her leave of Violet and went in search of Anne Wilson, the matron of Zion House.

When she found her friend in the linen closet, Anne didn't even wait for a greeting. Turning with a grin, she said, "Well, my girl! So you'll be off with your handsome husband now?"

"Does everyone here know my business?" Laurel asked with exasperation.

"Very likely." Anne, round and kind and capable, had taken refuge at Zion House after fleeing the drunken husband who had almost beaten her to death. She'd been unabashedly glad when he fell from a bridge and drowned on his way home from the pub not long after. Now she ran Zion House with strength and compassion, helping women and their children build new lives.

"I'm leaving in the morning, but I will be back," Laurel said. "Bristol will always be my home."

Anne shook her head, unconvinced. "Wait and see, my dear. You've been the soul and foundation of Zion House, but I think we've reached the point where we can survive without you now. It's time for you to tend to your own life." She smiled mischievously. "Mrs. Wicker was most impressed with your husband and she's a good judge of men."

"She should be," Laurel said tartly. "She's known enough of them. And she has a quick tongue as well."

"A quick tongue and the lightest hand with pastry in Bristol. You might want to ask her to become Herbert House's permanent cook and teacher for all kitchen arts. That would remove a major task from your shoulders."

Anne's suggestion required no thought at all. "That's an excellent idea. I'll ask her if she'd like the position."

"She's the one who suggested it to me," Anne said with a grin.

Laurel laughed and hugged her friend. "I'm going to miss everyone, but most of all, you."

Anne hugged back hard, and her eyes were bright with tears when they separated. "Whether this remains your home or not, you must come back to visit."

Remembering Kirkland's suggestion, Laurel said, "Perhaps you can visit me in London. Would you like that?"

"London!" Anne breathed, her eyes round. "That would be a fair treat! I've always wanted to see the city. But now I'll walk you out. I'm sure you've much to do."

When the two of them reached the foyer at the bottom of the stairs, a tiny girl with scorching red hair darted from a door and ran straight to Laurel, wrapping her arms around Laurel's knees. "Don't go, Miss Laurel!"

News traveled very fast indeed. Laurel scooped the little girl up. "I'm not going forever, Missy. I'll be back in a month and you'll have grown an inch, I'm sure."

Missy locked her skinny arms around Laurel's neck. "Don't *gooooooo!*"

Wryly Laurel recognized that she was being manipulated by a master. "I'm sorry, sweeting, but I must leave. I made a promise."

"Break it," Missy said firmly.

Laurel thought of her broken marriage vows and suppressed a wince. "We shouldn't break our promises, Missy."

"Promise you'll come back!" The little girl was almost five but looked more like a three-year-old because of the hunger and abuse she'd suffered until her mother took her daughter and ran away from her drunkard husband.

"I promise," Laurel said, thinking this would be one promise easy to keep.

Missy's mother, Eileen Bailey, entered the foyer. Her hair was a darker version of her daughter's red and her jaw bore a scar as a reminder of the husband she'd escaped, but now her smile was warm and genuine. "We'll be missing you, but I wish you happy in your new life."

"Thank you." With reluctance, Laurel transferred Missy's warm, active weight to her mother. Would she have a little girl of her own? She should wish for a boy so Kirkland would have his heir, but a little girl would be sweet to hold and raise.

Anne said, "I think we should hold a little going-away party for you this evening. There are many more who will want to say farewell."

"I'm not going forever!" Laurel protested again.

"Perhaps not," Anne said, "but things will change, I'm sure."

Laurel knew her friend was right. "A party, then, not too elaborate. I leave it to you to organize, but I'd like to see lots of cakes!"

As Missy squealed her approval, Laurel blew her a kiss and left. Because Daniel was away, she stopped by the infirmary before dinner. She knew she wasn't irreplaceable, but she was finding it difficult to leave the infirmary and Zion House in other hands.

Reminding herself again that she would be back in a month, she crossed the garden to Herbert House. She was surprised to see her brother in his small office outside the examination rooms.

"Daniel!" She stepped into his office. "You're just back?"

He looked up from his cluttered desk, his face like granite. "I returned half an hour ago, and was immediately informed that you're leaving for London tomorrow and that Kirkland is staying under my roof."

Suddenly exasperated, Laurel yanked the door shut behind her. "It's *my* roof, if you recall. I'm the one who bought both houses. Actually, I suppose they're both Kirkland's since a husband controls all of his wife's property. His money paid for everything we've built here."

Daniel surged to his feet, his eyes furious. "I'll move the infirmary elsewhere! Zion House is your responsibility. You can expand into this building with both of us gone."

Laurel gasped, appalled at the gap that was opening between them. "Daniel, let's not fight about this! We've always been able to settle things by talking them out. Kirkland was your friend once. Why do you act as if I'm being lured into the devil's own hellfire by attempting a degree of reconciliation?"

Daniel stared at her, and she realized how tired and travel worn he looked. Softening her voice, she said, "Let's sit down and talk like the loving brother and sister we've always been. Please?"

Daniel exhaled roughly and subsided back into his chair. "You're right. I'm sorry, Laurel. You have the right and perhaps the duty to reconcile with your husband, but you can't stop me from worrying that he'll ruin your life again." He opened the lower-left desk drawer, pulled out a bottle of brandy and a small glass, poured a stiff shot, and drank half of it straight off.

After swallowing, his expression eased. "This is why I've never formally turned Methodist. I'm not ready to give up all of my sinful ways."

"One or two drinks of brandy a month are no great sin." Laurel moved a pile of papers from the other chair to the floor so she could sit down. "Don't forget dancing. Remember how much we both enjoyed dancing when we were younger? Neither of us wanted to give that up even though we don't have many opportunities these days."

Daniel became very still, and Laurel belatedly remembered that Rose Hiller had been his favorite partner. They'd both loved dancing, and they had looked so beautiful together, moving as if they were two people sharing the same thoughts. She'd never seen Daniel look happier than when he was dancing with Rose.

He must have had similar thoughts because he tilted the glass toward her and said, "May we both have dancing days in the future."

He finished the brandy and set his glass aside. "Shall we start with you telling me how things went with Kirkland?"

"Nothing as dramatic as you're imagining." She thought a moment so she could summarize a complicated relationship quickly. "We both agree that we married too young and that we are now too different to be a conventional married couple again, but he persuaded me that for the sake of our child, we should be on friendly terms."

"How friendly, or is that none of my business?" Daniel said dryly.

"Friendly enough that our child and I would be able to move freely back and forth between Kirkland's world and my life here," she said, ignoring the implication of his words. "To begin, I'll go to London for a month. Long enough to meet some of his friends and establish a small foothold in his world. Then I'll return to my real life here. I imagine I'll visit him once or twice a year. Possibly he'll visit me in Bristol occasionally, though I'm sure it would be brief since there wouldn't be much to keep him busy."

"It's hard to imagine him living a life of leisure,"

Daniel agreed. "As hard as it is to imagine you a fashionable London lady."

"You're right about that," Laurel agreed. "But I do want to know how to fit into his world enough that his friends don't feel sorry for him for his disastrous mésalliance."

He snorted. "Anyone who thinks that is a fool."

"If his friends never met me, how could they think anything else? I'll do my best to be a modest and worthy countess." She grinned. "I think I can manage that for a few weeks. Then I'll return to Bristol and be myself again. Except for having a child, my life won't be all that different."

"I think you underestimate how much will change," Daniel said dourly. "But if you're sure you want to do this, I can't stop you."

"I'm not sure I *want* to," she said hesitantly. "But I've prayed about it, and I truly believe that attempting reconciliation is the right thing to do."

"Then there is nothing more to be said." He gave her his warm, charming smile. "You know I want only the best for you. And if that's Kirkland— well, I'll be happy for both of you."

Laurel felt something inside ease. She and Daniel had been so close for years, sharing the same goals, working side by side, that his disapproval about Kirkland had hurt. "He and I were very adult about it all. I think we can be friends and parents together."

"I hope so." Daniel's brows drew together. "I

almost forgot. Rumor has it that this morning you and Kirkland paid a visit to Belmond. How did that go?"

Her tension returned. "Our parents welcomed Kirkland and condemned me; Kirkland insisted that all blame was his and defended me, we had tea and came home."

He frowned. "How did they condemn you?"

She sighed. "I'm an undutiful wife, I've corrupted you from the gentlemanly life you should be living, and I don't know how to dress. About what I expected."

Daniel muttered a very un-vicarly word under his breath. "I'm sorry you had to deal with that, but I give Kirkland credit for defending you. I'm sure they'll be more welcoming once they get over the shock."

"One can hope," Laurel said dryly.

"They aren't the easiest of parents," he admitted. "But I'm glad you called on them. It's not good to be estranged from family."

"Which includes husbands. I shall hope that soon I'll be on good terms with everyone in my life." Feeling tired again, Laurel got to her feet. "Anne Wilson wants to have a sort of good-bye party at Zion House this evening. I hope you'll come? I think our little community will be worried if they think you and I are at odds with each other."

"Barring a medical emergency, I'll be there," he promised. "Will Kirkland attend?"

"I'm not sure. He hasn't heard about it yet, but he'll be back here soon. He did express a desire to meet my friends and coworkers."

Daniel nodded. "He and I can practice being civil to each other."

"Civility is our goal." Laurel left, hoping that her brother and her husband could become friends again. Friendship was too precious to waste.

Chapter 14

Kirkland was playing the piano softly and wondering if Laurel would appear so they could dine together, when she bustled into the music room, face flushed and her hair showing considerable independence. She looked so charming that he had to force himself not to cross the room and embrace her.

He rose, keeping the piano safely between them. "You look as if you've been very busy. If you have too much to do, we can delay another day." He liked referring to the two of them as "we."

She shook her head. "Staying longer would be an anticlimax when everyone is saying good-bye. Speaking of which, there will be an informal going-away party tonight at Zion House. Do you wish to attend?"

"Of course." He smiled a little. "Your friends need to see that I don't have horns, hooves, and a pointed tail. By the way, I heard that Daniel has returned."

"I just spoke with him, and he's also choosing civility. He'll be there tonight if he isn't called out on an emergency." She smiled ruefully. "He still has some doubts about my sanity, but he does wish us well."

"I'm glad." Hesitantly, since he wasn't used to showing emotion, he added, "I hope that someday he and I can be friends again."

"I hope so, too." She tucked a tendril of bronze hair behind her ear. Her elegant, delectable ear . . . "Violet is willing to see if she can make me fashionable in London."

He nodded. "You have countenance, which is even better than fashion, but it will be good to have a familiar face near you."

"I thought the same thing." Laurel's expression turned serious. "She thinks that Captain Hardwick has men watching her, with the goal of abducting her."

Kirkland frowned. "He's capable of that. She'll be safer in London."

"She and I can discover the city together," Laurel observed. "Shall we go down to supper, my lord? It will be a light meal because of the party. Mrs. Wicker wouldn't let me in the kitchen, so she must be making something special."

"I look forward to the gathering." He offered Laurel his arm. After a moment's hesitation, she accepted, her hand curving lightly onto his coat sleeve. He could barely feel the brush of her fingers, but even that slight touch warmed him. They were making progress—she was touching him even without an audience.

Where would they be after a month under the same roof?

After they ate, Kirkland waited for Laurel while she changed and fixed her hair. She appeared in the same celestial blue gown she'd worn to call on her parents, but someone, presumably her new maid, Violet, had cut the bodice dramatically. Too much so for Laurel, who had tucked a demure white fichu around the neckline. Even covered up, she was beautiful.

And she was wearing her wedding ring. His gaze locked onto the gold band. "I see you found your ring," he said, his throat tight.

"It was never lost," she said quietly.

He raised her left hand and kissed the gold band on her ring finger, then wondered if he'd exposed too much of himself. If she knew how he really felt, she'd bolt. Releasing her hand, he said lightly, "It's good to see it again."

"I'm not wearing gloves tonight so that everyone can see the ring and know that we really are married," she explained as she led him out into the large walled garden that joined the houses.

It was still light, so he looked around appreciatively as they followed a wide, curving flagstone path to the other house. Besides flowers and shrubs, there were vegetable and herb gardens and fruit trees espaliered against the stone walls. "The garden is handsome and also practical, I see. Your work?"

"It's the personal project of Anne Wilson, the

matron of Zion House. She puts residents to work out here. Women who have been abused find it soothing to work with plants and flowers." Laurel gestured toward the vegetable beds. "Being able to produce some of our own food is useful as well."

They paused beside a handsome wooden bench set under an arch covered with flowering vines. "I see there are places to relax and enjoy the quiet as well. Another benefit for those in need of sanctuary?"

Laurel nodded. "Violet sits out here every day for at least a few minutes. She says that she likes the freedom to just sit without worrying about being punished for not being busy."

He brushed his fingertips over the beautifully carved wood of the bench's back and arms. "Were the benches made locally? I've not seen any like them."

"One of Zion House's few male residents did the carving. He's a sailor who carved to amuse himself on long voyages," she explained. "He does beautiful work."

"How did he come to live here? I had the impression that Zion House residents were all women and children."

"He was in the navy and lost a leg in a sea battle with the French. He's one of half a dozen men, mostly former soldiers and sailors, all of them handicapped in one way or another. They live in remodeled mews on the alley that runs alongside that wall."

"Separated from the women because men can't be trusted?" Kirkland asked dryly.

"Let's say that it's wise to reduce temptation on both sides," she replied. "It's useful to have male residents. Despite their disabilities, they can do much of the heavier work, and they also serve as guards."

"Guards?" he asked, then guessed the answer. "To protect women against abusive husbands."

"Exactly. We almost had a murder here once, until one of our former soldiers stepped in. He's missing an arm, but he still knows how to be a soldier." She frowned. "Most of the females who leave here can find decent positions in service, but it's harder to find jobs for the men."

"Work is the key, isn't it?" he said thoughtfully. "It sounds as if Zion House needs to start its own businesses to provide jobs. Starting with a wood-shop."

"I've thought about doing that, but I'm not sure how to go about starting businesses and I haven't had time to learn." She glanced up through her lashes. "Start-up money would also be required."

"And you're already stretching every penny until it squeaks?" he said with amusement. "I can give you more funding, and I know a man in Birmingham who has set up several small manufactories. I think he could be persuaded to come to Bristol to help you do the same."

"That would be marvelous!" Laurel's eyes glowed.

"While you're in London, perhaps you'll have the time to research what would be suitable and successful in Bristol," he suggested. "Then you can write a proposal and we can get to work."

"I'll do that." She hesitated. "What if our reconciliation fails?"

He hated that she was even thinking of the possibility. "I'll still provide the funding and aid needed," he promised. "I like using my money to do good, Laurel. I just don't have the time to find appropriate uses. I'll leave that to you."

As they approached the sanctuary house, Kirkland heard music. "Dancing tonight? Will there be enough male partners?"

"No, but that won't stop anyone from dancing! I can't remember the last time I danced," she said wistfully.

"It will be my pleasure to partner you," he said. "That will also help us persuade your friends that we're happy together."

"That you don't have horns and hooves," she said with a smile as she took his arm in a possessive wifely way.

He opened the door and voices and music flowed around them as they stepped into the small foyer. To the left, adjoining reception rooms had been opened into a decent-sized ballroom. At the far end was an elderly piano with an elderly but skilled female pianist. Seated beside her, a grizzled man with a wooden leg played zestfully on a fiddle. Chairs were set against all the walls, most of them occupied by older women and a few men, while the center of the space seethed with children and women.

"Do all these people live here?" he asked with amazement.

Laurel scanned the room. "Many, not all. Some lived here once and now have work and homes elsewhere, but they've come back for the party. Some are volunteers who help out here regularly. Elizabeth Ware, that pretty blonde with Dr. Holt, is one." She nodded toward the left. "Violet is over there."

Kirkland followed his wife's gaze to a dark, strikingly attractive girl who dressed with ladylike restraint rather than flaunting her exotic looks. She must have learned early that it was wise not to attract male attention. A pity she hadn't been successful at that.

Someone called, "There they are!"

The music and chatter stopped dead and every head in the room swiveled toward them, including the pianist's and the fiddler's. Kirkland had confronted spies, traitors, and the Prince Regent in difficult moods, but he'd never felt so thoroughly examined. Or judged. There were children of all sizes, women of all ages, and a smattering of weathered-looking men. No Daniel, at least not yet.

Laurel's hand tightened on his arm. Raising her voice, she said, "Good evening, my friends. Allow me to introduce my husband, James Kirkland."

Kirkland offered his best smile. "It's a great pleasure to meet the friends who have become my wife's extended family."

As the crowd gave a kind of exhalation of relief and started to move again, a pleasantly authoritative woman approached. "Mr. Kirkland, welcome to Zion House. I'm Anne Wilson, matron of this establishment."

He bowed deeply. "And one of Laurel's closest friends. We discussed the possibility of your visiting us at our home in London. I do hope you'll consider it. You would be very welcome."

Her eyes sparkled, and he thought he'd made an ally. "I hope that will happen," she said. "Let me give you a tour while Laurel is busy exchanging hugs with everyone."

He glanced at his wife and saw that an older woman with ravaged features and peaceful eyes was embracing Laurel. Leaving her to her fare-wells, he followed Anne Wilson out of the ballroom. When they were in the quieter foyer, Anne said, "You don't actually have to do the tour, but I thought you might like to step away for a bit."

145

"Plus, you get an opportunity to evaluate whether I'm good enough for Laurel," he said with amusement. "The answer is that I'm not."

"It's not a matter of being good enough," Anne said thoughtfully. "More a matter of how well you suit. You're not what I would have expected in her husband."

"Which is why we separated," he said with regret. "But we are older and wiser now. At least, that's the hope. And I would like the tour. Zion House is very important to my wife, and I wish to know more about it."

She nodded approvingly. "You're wise to do so. If you asked her to choose between you and her work here—well, you might not like the results."

He suspected that she was giving him oblique advice. "I'll bear that in mind. How many people live here?"

"Usually between thirty and fifty, though in really cold weather, sometimes more. We don't like turning anyone away."

He whistled softly. "The house is large, but even so, how do you manage?"

"As best we can. The goal is keep everyone safe, and help them develop the skills to support themselves and their children as well." She led him down a short passage. "We have a nursery for the small children and an infirmary run by our own residents."

"Laurel said that you're the person who developed the garden?"

"Yes, people enjoy working there, and it's good to provide some of our own food." She led the way up a narrow service stairway. "The floors above are mostly sleeping quarters, though some rooms are used for lessons during the day."

"What kind of lessons?"

"Everything!" She chuckled. "Reading and writing for those who were never taught. Needle-work, cooking, cleaning, laundry. Sometimes music and drawing. Almost everyone has a skill they can teach, and everyone is better for learning more. Laurel set up all these programs. She's a born teacher, though she spends most of her time managing the infirmary and Zion House."

"Will they collapse without her?" he asked.

"I hope not," Anne said seriously. "Laurel has trained others in the various skills needed, but she is the heart and soul of this place. She can't really be replaced. I believe we'll manage, but it won't be easy to adjust to her absence."

Kirkland wished the matron thought there would be no problems. They might need Laurel, but so did he. "She'll be returning soon," he said. "At least that's the plan."

Anne frowned. "I wish I was sure Laurel would really be back in a month."

Kirkland wished he could be sure that she wouldn't.

Chapter 15

By the time they returned to the ballroom, Kirkland had even more respect for Laurel and what she had created here. As Anne moved away, Kirkland paused in the wide doorway, his gaze riveted on his wife. Laurel glowed with the warmth that had entranced him when they'd met.

He'd feared that he'd destroyed that quality, because he'd seen little of it since they'd met again. But tonight the kindness and acceptance that were the essence of Laurel blazed forth with a power that drew everyone in the ballroom to her. She had a gift for friendship, and it came from caring about everyone who crossed her path.

He frowned thoughtfully. Though he'd known she needed regular peace and solitude, now he recognized clearly that she also needed to be with people she enjoyed, and who enjoyed her. He must do his best to help her find new friends in London to balance the strong friendships she had here.

She held a small boy while she laughed with the group around her, and it was vividly clear that she really was the heart and soul of the community she'd created. He gritted his teeth and refused to feel guilty about taking her away. He'd found her first.

The double doors to the dining room were opened and Laurel's assistant, Betsy Rivers, emerged. "Mr. and Mrs. Kirkland, it's time to cut the cake." She grinned. "No one can eat until you've done that, so the sooner the better!"

"Heavens, we can't keep people from their supper." With a smile, Laurel returned the small boy to his mother and moved to Kirkland's side. They entered the dining room together, the rest of the guests churning behind.

The dining room's three long tables were arranged in a U shape and decorated with vases of flowers and greens from the garden. The white tablecloths were scarcely visible because of the platters of carefully arranged food. The swiftly created foods on display weren't London-elaborate or made with expensive ingredients, but Kirkland was sure the potato cakes and dressed eggs and other dishes would be delicious. Clearly everything had been made with love, which was an ingredient beyond mere money.

The centerpiece of the middle table was a magnificent bride cake with Mrs. Wicker and a round, good-natured-looking man standing behind it. Almost two feet across, the cake was iced with expensive white sugar frosting and carefully applied decorative loops of the same sweet topping.

"What a beautiful cake!" Laurel exclaimed.

"Indeed it is," Kirkland agreed as he studied the

intricate decorations. "I'm amazed you were able to produce such a splendid bride cake so quickly."

"'Tis my Harold's work," Mrs. Wicker said proudly. She patted his arm, then offered a long knife to Laurel. "I took charge of the savories, but no one makes a cake like Harold! He pieced together four smaller cakes and he's invented his own special way of decorating. 'Tisn't a finer baker in Bristol!"

As guests pressed around, Laurel cut the cake, revealing the dark, fruited interior. Fruit cake for fertility. From the scent, Kirkland guessed that good brandy was part of the recipe.

Laurel set a wedge of cake on a small plate and offered it to him. Her eyes matched the celestial blue of her gown. "Will you do the honors, my dear?"

He accepted the plate with a smile and took a bite as everyone waited for his judgment. He was perfectly prepared to praise the cake even if it tasted like sawdust, but lying wasn't necessary. The rich, spicy flavors burst in his mouth with delicious layers of flavor. His eyes widened. "I've never tasted better! Here, my lady."

He offered Laurel the rest of the cake, feeling very husbandly. She tasted it, then exclaimed, "This is better than our original bride cake! Thank you both so much."

As people applauded, Kirkland murmured, "Later, perhaps we should ask Harold if he'd like

150

to expand his bakery in partnership with Zion House."

Eyes sparkling, Laurel said, "I had the same thought." He loved that their minds were in harmony.

As Mrs. Wicker began slicing the rest of the cake, Kirkland and Laurel collected samples of all the dishes and glasses of lemonade and had a second supper. He was right—the food might be made from simple ingredients, but it was delicious.

There were no opportunities to speak privately while they ate, since there was a continual stream of people coming to speak with Laurel. They were polite but wary to Kirkland, which was reasonable enough. He said little, content to watch Laurel.

When they'd finished eating, he collected both plates and said, "I'll open the door to the garden for some fresh air."

Laurel gave him a quick smile. "We'll need that if there's dancing."

Night had fallen, but the moon was full, bathing the garden in silvery light. A lovely night for a lovely event. In just this short time, Kirkland was coming to appreciate the community Laurel and Daniel had created. His own talents were exercised on the dark side of life. His wife and her brother created light and hope for those most in need.

When he returned to the ballroom, he was

spotted by a small redheaded girl child. Her chin firmed and she marched pugnaciously across the room and stopped directly in front of him. "You're taking Miss Laurel away?"

He knelt so they were closer to the same level. "Yes, she and I are married, you know. It's usual for husband and wife to live under the same roof."

"Will you hit her?"

He blinked. "Good God, no! That would be very wrong."

She looked even more pugnacious. "Men hit women all the time."

He realized that must have been what her home was like, and his heart ached for the child and her mother. "And it's always wrong. Men are supposed to protect and cherish women and children."

Looking unconvinced, she said, "Miss Laurel belongs here with us!"

"That's why she'll return," he said seriously. "Much of her heart is here."

"Then why is she going?"

"Because I hope some of her heart is with me."

A familiar male voice said behind him, "It's a waste of energy trying to reason with Missy. She knows her own mind, and isn't about to change it."

Daniel. Feeling at a disadvantage, Kirkland got to his feet, keeping a wary eye on his brother-in-law, who looked tired and rumpled, and had traces of blood on his shirt. He must have come directly from the infirmary. "I was beginning to realize that."

Attention shifting, Missy threw her arms around Daniel's knees. "Dr. Daniel!"

Smiling, he bent and ruffled her red hair. Like his sister, Daniel had an appealing natural warmth and ease. He glanced at Kirkland and his warmth vanished, but at least he wasn't actively hostile.

Thinking he should make an overture, Kirkland said, "Anne Wilson gave me a tour of Zion House. I hadn't realized how diverse your services are."

"Laurel gets the credit. I look after people's bodies and souls. She helps them build better lives."

"Don't let Miss Laurel go, Dr. Daniel!" Missy interjected.

"It's not my place to tell her she can't go with her husband." Daniel gently pried the little girl's arms loose. "Isn't it time you were in bed, Missy?"

"No," she said firmly. Then a similarly small friend called from across the room. Missy squealed and spun away at high speed.

Kirkland shook his head in amazement. "What a terrifying amount of energy."

"When Missy arrived here, she was so frightened she wouldn't talk. Her mother was equally frightened and had a broken arm as well." Daniel nodded toward the auburn-haired woman who had taken the child's hand. "Laurel is the one who cured them of their fear so they can enjoy life again. There is no one like her."

"I suspect that your unspoken message is that saints shouldn't marry sinners," Kirkland said dryly. "It tends to tarnish the saint without improving the sinner."

"True." Daniel slanted a glance at him. "But . . . I do understand why you want to try to recapture what was between you."

"It's impossible to regain such youthful optimism," Kirkland said, his gaze on Laurel, where she held court across the room. "That doesn't mean we shouldn't try to build something of value now."

"I suggest that you not just try, but succeed," Daniel said acerbically.

Kirkland arched his brows. "Or else? I don't think you could break my neck, Daniel. As a sinner, I've had more opportunities to practice my Kalarippayattu."

"You'd be surprised what skills I need in my work," Daniel retorted. "But breaking your neck would be undignified. Far better to call the fires of heavenly wrath down on your sinner's head."

For an instant, Kirkland thought the other man meant it. Then he saw the glint of humor in his eyes. Humor had always been the wickedest thing about Daniel. They'd had a running joke that Kirkland was a sinner in contrast to Daniel's saintliness.

At Oxford, Kirkland had sampled the varied pleasures available to a young man of wealth and birth, though his dislike of losing control kept him from overindulgence. But he had indeed been a sinner compared to Daniel. Without making a public display of righteousness, his friend quietly avoided the drunkenness, womanizing, and heavy gambling that were rife around them. Likely he still did.

"Laurel said there would be dancing," Kirkland said. "Is that still one vice you'll indulge in?"

"That and the occasional brandy. It looks as if the dancing is about to begin." Daniel gave a parting nod and crossed the room to the musicians. The pianist and the fiddler smiled enthusiastically when he spoke to them, and struck up the music for a country dance. A number of the women gleefully descended on a large basket set by the piano. It contained long strips of dark cloth that could be draped or tied around their necks to mark them as male for the purposes of the dance. The lovely Violet chose one in a futile attempt to look less feminine.

It was a very long way from Almack's Assembly Rooms. Smiling, Kirkland sought out Laurel, who was flushed and laughing and irresistible.

It was time to claim his wife.

Chapter 16

At other times when Zion House had dancing, Laurel had been too busy, or felt that she really shouldn't be so frivolous. This time she tapped her foot with anticipation as the dancers formed into two sets for a reel. Young Dr. Holt had arrived and was leading out Elizabeth Ware, the pretty blond volunteer. From the way they looked at each other, they were halfway to a happy announcement. Now where was . . . ?

She jumped when Kirkland approached from the side and bowed deeply. "Dance with me, my lady?"

There he was. She realized that on some level, she'd thought it wrong to enjoy dancing with another man when she was estranged from her husband. But now her husband was here, and she intended to enjoy what she had denied herself. She offered her hand. "It will be my pleasure, sir."

He took her hand and led her to the adjacent set. As guests of honor, Laurel and Kirkland were waved to the head couple position. Daniel was in the other set with Anne Wilson for a partner, and he looked gratifyingly relaxed. There were enough dancers to make two sets of six couples each, though one giggling girl had to be pulled from a chair to even the numbers.

Once everyone was in place, an old fellow with a missing arm joined the musicians and began calling steps. It was country dancing at its most basic, and enormous fun because the participants enjoyed themselves so much.

As Kirkland linked arms with Laurel and they swung around, she remembered why dancing was so popular—it was the closest a man and a woman could be in public. She laughed with delight to feel his strong arm locked with hers, and to return his teasing smile as he gazed down at her. But she also enjoyed swinging around with sixteen-year-old Lolly, a bouncing girl who wore the strip of dark fabric that marked her as male for dancing purposes. After Lolly came Colin Holt, who now treated Laurel as a friend, not a woman he desired. Why had she deprived herself of this pleasure for so many years?

The pattern of the reel brought her and Kirkland together again and again. She loved how he entered into the mood of the occasion, smiling and talking with the other dancers. When the dance ended, he bowed deeply to her. "Thank you," he said with a lurking smile that warmed her to her marrow. "I'd like to dance every dance with you, my lady, but that would be rude. One more before the night is over?"

She shared the desire to be his partner for every dance, but this evening was for him to meet her friends and for her to say good-bye to them. "Once more. Until later, my lord." She headed to the chairs around the wall to coax one of the retired soldiers to dance with her, while Kirkland asked one of the elderly volunteers to stand up with him.

For the first time, Laurel looked forward to entering London's social world because there would be more dancing. She stood up for all the dances, including one with Violet acting as an honorary male. They laughed their way through a country dance, though Violet said reprovingly, "I altered your gown so you could show your fine figure, and now you disguise yourself with a fichu!"

Laurel rolled her eyes. "If I am to make a spectacle of myself, I'll do it in front of strangers rather than with my friends."

"Your modiste and I shall plot together in London to show you at your best," Violet warned before spinning away again. Laurel suspected that the threat wasn't idle. She and her maid would have to compromise on a neckline that was too high for Violet and too low for Laurel. Life was often the art of compromise.

By the time the fifth dance, another reel, had ended, most of the children and their mothers had gone to bed. The indefatigable Missy had hauled her patient mother out into the garden to admire the moon, and barely a crumb remained of the bride cake.

Looking over the remaining dancers, Laurel said, "Time for one last dance?"

Daniel, who looked tired but happy, said, "Laurel, Kirkland, the two of you used to do a fine minuet. Care to demonstrate for us?"

"Heavens, no!" Laurel exclaimed. "It's been years since I danced that. And we don't have the right music."

"I can play a minuet from memory," Miss Burton, the pianist, said cheerfully. She'd been a governess and a music teacher before illness had left her destitute, and her repertory of music seemed bottomless.

"Oh, please, show us!" begged Lolly. "I've always wanted to see one!"

As other voices added their encouragement, Kirkland extended his hand, his eyes encouraging. "Shall we? I expect we'll manage well enough."

She hesitated a moment longer. Unlike the jolly country dances, the minuet was a test of skill and grace, and couples were judged on how well they performed. She hadn't danced it since she'd left Kirkland.

But these were her friends, and they were here to celebrate, not judge. She clasped Kirkland's left hand. "Very well, but remember that I'm sadly out of practice!"

Miss Burton turned to her keyboard, her deft fingers sliding into the rippling notes of a selection from Handel that was often used for this dance.

Laurel's heart clenched; it was the same music as the first time she'd performed a minuet with Kirkland.

He remembered, too, she could see it in his eyes. Space cleared around them as everyone else withdrew to the walls, leaving the center of the room open. Kirkland said softly, "Begin on the count of three? One, two, *three* . . ."

On the beat they moved forward side by side, her left hand clasping his right and their outside arms held out gracefully as they glided the length of the room, gazes locked. The minuet was a more intimate dance than the bouncing reels because the partners must focus on each other.

Her feet remembered the small swift steps, and the rhythm of the music swept her along. Kirkland was a superb dancer, and she was intensely, physically aware of him. By the time they reached the end of the ballroom, she felt as if they moved as one person. She'd felt the same when they first danced.

Though she made some missteps, they didn't matter. Kirkland compensated and the dance went on. His firm clasp, the strength and precision of his movements, riveted the attention of every female in the ballroom.

He released her hand and she spun away at a diagonal, then they rejoined and again circled with clasped hands. She had the giddy thought that the minuet reflected the way they circled each other in this reconciliation. Wary. Watching. *Wanting*.

The music ended when they were near the open door to the garden and she was grateful for the soft night breeze on her heated body. Kirkland bowed, as elegant as any gentleman at court. She made a deep curtsy, wishing for the fuller, more sweeping skirts of an earlier day.

As she rose, someone called out, "Kiss 'im, Miss Laurel!"

Another voice chimed in, "Aye, kiss your husband!"

She froze, her gaze meeting Kirkland's. He looked dubious, then wryly resigned. "It's no different from meeting under the mistletoe at Christmas, my lady." He bent his head and brushed her lips with his.

No different from mistletoe . . . but she'd melted into him the one Christmas they'd been together when they'd met under mistletoe. Now, damnably, it was indeed no different. His mouth was warm, firm, beckoning her to intimacy. She would have known his touch anywhere, even in the darkest of dark nights.

His hands moved to her waist and he drew her closer until her breasts pressed against his broad chest. Mindlessly she leaned into him, eyes closed as the tip of her tongue touched his. This kiss felt so *right*. His heartbeat accelerated and she yearned for the next step of their dance.

Why had she been resisting him so hard? Yes,

he was capable of dark deeds, but surely never without reason. He was her husband, the father of her unborn child—and desire sang between them, hot and sweet. James, her husband, lover, nemesis . . .

She was jarred out of her trance by applause and cheerfully raucous comments and suggestions. The clients of Zion House were not a demure lot. Flushing, she jerked away from Kirkland.

"I didn't realize . . . mistletoe was so dangerous," he whispered under the applause. His eyes were stark. Vulnerable?

"It's poisonous, you know," she managed. She closed her eyes for a moment, centering her thoughts and emotions so that she was the Miss Laurel everyone knew.

What would happen when she and Kirkland were alone? After the dancing and that kiss, would he attempt to seduce her? And how would she respond if he did?

She was about to say her last farewell when a woman's frantic scream rose outside. An instant later it was echoed by a child's high-pitched shriek of pure terror. Even as Laurel gasped with shock, Kirkland was in motion, bolting through the open door into the garden at unbelievable speed.

Heart pounding, Laurel lifted her skirts and darted after him, almost falling down the steps into the garden. The cool, bright moonlight illuminated a frightening tableau as Eileen Bailey struggled to break free of a hulking man. She kicked him in the shins. "No! *No!* You bastard, Bailey, I'm never going back to you!"

He snarled, "Shut up, slut! You're my wife and you're comin' with me!"

A smaller man wrestled with the tiny, furious figure of Missy. Bailey barked at his companion, "Don't let the brat go, Sal! I can get fifty quid for her!"

Kirkland leaped at the second man. With one arm, he wrenched Missy from her captor's grasp. Then he smashed a knee into Sal's groin and chopped the back of the man's neck, abruptly cutting off the howls of pain.

Seeing Laurel, Kirkland thrust the child into her arms, his face grim. "Take her!" Then he charged at Bailey.

Half strangled by Missy's frantic clutching, Laurel stroked the child's back and murmured soothing words while others poured into the garden from Zion House. She could smell the stink of cheap gin on Bailey even twenty feet away. Drunkards were dangerously unpredictable, but surely Kirkland could handle him.

Bailey's eyes widened with panic at the sight of so many people. Backing away, he yanked out a wickedly gleaming knife and held the point to his wife's throat. "Get back or I'll kill 'er!"

Eileen made a strangled sound and stopped struggling, the whites of her eyes showing as she gasped with fear. Kirkland halted in his tracks and said in a clipped voice, "That's not a good idea. Release your wife and we can talk about this like sensible men."

"No! The bitch and brat are mine! Took me months to find 'em and I'm not lettin' 'em go." A thin line of blood trickled down Eileen's neck from where the blade was pressed.

Stalemate. Laurel could almost hear Kirkland's brain whirling as he considered how to get Eileen safely away from her crazed husband.

Laurel's horror turned to cold fury. Men could be very simple creatures, so perhaps she could use that. Anne Wilson stood frozen at Laurel's side, so Laurel transferred Missy to the other woman's arms. The child's hysteria had faded, but she was still shaking and tears ran down her face as she stared desperately at her helpless mother.

"Mr. Bailey." Her voice warm and soothing, Laurel took a step forward, at the same time loosening the fichu tucked into her décolletage. She'd always had an embarrassingly good figure and had learned early to conceal it if she wanted to keep men's gazes on her face rather than her breasts. Now Violet's alterations to the celestial blue gown exposed a lush expanse of curves.

"I do not allow violence at Zion House," she purred as she undulated toward him, trying to imitate the provocative motions of the prostitutes she'd seen at the port. "Please lower your knife and we'll talk."

His skittish gaze moved to her and stuck, his eyes widening as she peeled away the gauzy fichu to reveal her new, dramatically plunging neckline. She inhaled deeply and allowed the long length of white muslin to flutter sensuously in the breeze.

Mr. Bailey was indeed a simple creature. He stared at her breasts as she neared him, swallowing hard. When she was almost within touching distance, the hand holding the knife sagged away from his wife's throat.

She'd counted on Kirkland being able to take advantage of the distraction she was creating. For a moment, she feared she'd failed because her husband's gaze was also riveted on her.

But only for a moment. In the next instant he exploded forward, grabbing Bailey's wrist to wrench the knife away with one hand while he broke the man's grip on Eileen with his other hand.

The knife slashed downward, cutting at his wife and Kirkland before Eileen staggered clear of the fight, gasping and pressing her hand to her throat. Grimly Kirkland engaged with Bailey in a swift, violent struggle for possession of the knife.

Even with the bright, cool moonlight it was hard to see what was happening, but the end came swiftly when Bailey pitched backward, pawing at the knife buried in his throat. Blood spurted out, some splashing on Laurel. She stumbled backward, her anger turning to horror at the swift, deadly violence. Kirkland ordered, "Stay here with the others while I see if there's anyone else out there." Then he vanished into the shadows.

Daniel raced by Laurel as the battered Sal clambered to his feet, swearing filthily. "The brat is Bailey's!" Sal snarled indignantly. "I was just helpin' him take what's his."

"Tell that to the magistrate," Daniel growled as he gripped Sal's neck in a furious choke hold designed to stop blood to the man's brain.

After Sal went limp, Daniel moved to Eileen Bailey, steadying her with one arm. "Let me take a look at that cut." He did a swift examination by touch. "A bit messy, but not deep. Laurel, give me your scarf."

Numbly she handed it over, realizing that Daniel had immobilized Sal with the same kind of ruthless skill that Kirkland exhibited. But now he was her kind, civilized brother again. He ripped the scarf in half and used one end to gently blot away the blood that oozed from Eileen's injured throat. The other end became a light bandage.

"Missy!" Eileen said hoarsely as she scanned the onlookers. "She's all right?"

"She's fine." Anne turned the little girl in her arms so Missy and her mother could see each other. "Upset, but unhurt."

Eileen reached toward her daughter, but Anne

halted her with a raised hand. "Your gown is bloody. She might find that upsetting."

Eileen swallowed hard, then nodded. "Set her down. We can walk to the infirmary together."

Anne obeyed, and Missy darted forward to wrap her arms around Eileen's legs. "Mama," she whimpered. *"Mama!"*

"It's . . . it's all right, sweeting," her mother said, brushing her daughter's wild red curls. "We're safe now." Her gaze went to her husband's body. "Truly safe."

Daniel stood after examining Bailey. "He won't bother you again, Eileen."

Kirkland reappeared. "There was a ladder up against the outside wall and a rope falling on this side. Apparently only these two broke in."

"Your hand is bleeding," Daniel said. "Come to the infirmary so I can see to it."

Kirkland looked at his left hand, which was dark with blood. "It's nothing. Just a slash across the heel." He clumsily wrapped his handkerchief around it.

"Nonetheless." Daniel frowned at Bailey's corpse. Sal was being neatly trussed up by Ned, one of Zion House's disabled sailors, who hadn't forgotten how to tie knots. A former soldier limped out with a ragged blanket and threw it over Bailey's body.

Laurel knew she should offer to accompany Eileen to the infirmary, but her nausea was increasing. She stumbled into the shadow of the garden wall and braced one hand on it for balance.

Mrs. Wicker ordered, "The rest of you lot come along and help me clean up. There are still some ginger cakes to soothe any cases of jangled nerves." Harold by her side, she started to usher people inside.

Colin Holt said to Elizabeth, who was snug against his side, "I'll walk you home now, then call at the magistrate's on the way back to report this."

Ned, the sailor, said, "I'll keep watch over this 'un till the magistrate and 'is men get 'ere." He kicked the bound man in the ribs none too gently.

With the critical issues sorted, the crowd dissipated. Elizabeth Ware took tight hold of Colin's arm and they followed the others into Zion House.

As the garden cleared, Laurel lost her battle with nausea, folded to the damp earth, and became violently ill. She was shivering and retching up the last of the bride cake when someone knelt beside her.

Kirkland. Even ill and with her eyes closed, she knew him. A warm garment was laid gently over her shoulders. His coat, his scent. Shaking, she pulled the coat closely around her shoulders.

"Can you manage to return to the house?" he asked quietly. "I can carry you."

She'd be cradled against him. Warm and

intimate . . . She retched again, but there was nothing left in her stomach. He put his hand under her elbow, but she jerked away. After wiping her mouth with her wrist, she rose unsteadily, using the wall for support.

"Would you like water to rinse your mouth out?" There was an edge of anxiety in his voice.

Water. The thought was desperately attractive. "Please."

As he headed to Zion House, she started toward the infirmary, the coat dragged tight around her. She couldn't think beyond the horror of Bailey and his death. What next?

James Kirkland. *Husband. Lover. Nemesis.*
Killer.

Chapter 17

Kirkland caught up with Laurel halfway back to Herbert House. She accepted the tumbler of water gratefully, rinsing her mouth thoroughly before drinking. The tumbler was almost empty when she returned it with a faded, "Thank you. Now we need to take care of your hand."

He would have offered Laurel his arm for the rest of the walk through the garden, but her taut face made it clear that she was strung as tight as a drumhead. He swore silently, thinking that the ease they'd gained in the dancing had been lost again. He'd dared hope that when they were private, there would be another kiss, and perhaps more. Now she looked as if she'd shatter if he touched her.

"We need to go to an examination room so I can see your hand more clearly," Laurel said.

"It's not serious. My fingers still work." When he wiggled them as proof, he was rewarded with a vicious stab of pain. Blood was seeping through the handkerchief he'd wrapped around the injury.

"As Daniel said, 'Nonetheless.' It must be treated."

He thought about asking how she was, but wasn't sure how well his concern would be received. Instead, he said, "Distracting Bailey as you did was both clever and incredibly brave. Eileen owes you her life."

"This isn't the first time an abusive husband has come here after his wife," she said, her voice troubled. "But never with such violence. Perhaps our military men can organize a more formal guard service."

"Besides guards, both houses can be made more secure," he said. "Iron bars on ground-floor windows. Spikes on top of the garden walls. I have a man who is an expert about such measures. I'll send him here to look the houses over and see what can be done to keep the inhabitants safer." Seeing her frown, he added, "I'll cover the costs."

She glanced at him askance. "You care that much about Zion House?"

"Of course, and not just because it matters to you." He flexed his left hand again. It still hurt. "I dislike bullies. Eileen Bailey is a brave and resourceful woman to have saved herself and her daughter from that brute she married. I imagine many others like her have passed through Zion House."

"Yes, and on behalf of them all, I thank you." They'd reached Herbert House, so she opened the door and led him to one of the infirmary examination rooms. Daniel's soothing tones could be heard coming from the room next door.

Kirkland glanced around the room as Laurel lit

the lamps. Was this where he'd been treated and had his amorous encounter with his wife? He wasn't sure. His mind had been rather fuzzy at the time.

"Sit, please." Laurel directed him to a chair by the lamps for the best light, then produced a tray holding a basin, clean cloths, and various other medical supplies. She wouldn't look at him, he realized. She kept her head down as she studied the long, shallow slash that sliced neatly across the heel of his hand. Though her fingers were icy, that didn't affect her deft competence.

She still had his coat draped over her shoulders, but the way she was sitting in front of him allowed a dangerous view of her magnificent décolletage. She'd always had a splendid figure. Though it wasn't why he loved her, it had been an entrancing bonus. Since this was not a good time to be entranced, he forced himself to look away.

Laurel poured liquid from a bottle onto a cloth and began cleaning the knife slash. His hand jerked—the liquid stung like the very devil. Recognizing the distinctive scent, he said with surprise, "You clean wounds with gin?"

"Daniel once had to patch up a group of sailors after a knife fight in a gin mill by the port." She soaked a fresh piece of cloth with gin and wiped off the last of the drying blood. "When he checked later to see how they were doing, he realized that none of the many wounds inflicted that day developed any inflammation. Gin is cheap, so we use it regularly."

She still wasn't looking at him. Guessing what was wrong, he said quietly, "I'm sorry that once again I've killed a man in front of you."

"I'm very grateful that you saved Eileen and Missy," she said, still concentrating on his injured hand. "But . . . I do wonder if it was necessary to kill Bailey."

Don't ever lie to me. He'd promised her that, which meant he had to tell her the whole truth, not a partial truth that left out the difficult bits. "Perhaps it wasn't necessary," he said slowly. "But it seemed right at the time."

She looked up at him then, her eyes bleakly gray. "You could have saved Eileen without anyone dying?"

"When one is fighting a vicious brute armed with a deadly weapon, there's little time to weigh the possibilities," he said dryly. "Perhaps the knife didn't have to end up in his throat. But he was large and dangerous and mad with drink and anger. It was safer for all concerned that he not have the chance to hurt others again."

He caught her gaze, wanting her to understand. "Even if Bailey had survived, what then? Hanging? Transportation to Botany Bay, where he might brutalize other women and children? What if he managed to escape? He's the kind of man who would come after his wife and child

173

again, and next time they might be unprotected."

"So you decided to remove the threat permanently." Her voice was uninflected.

"To say I decided makes it sound too deliberate. I knew he was a murderous drunkard and a danger to the innocent." He sighed. "It's remarkably difficult to kill another living being, Laurel. But . . . I'm pragmatic."

"Ruthlessly so," she said, her voice edged.

His lips tightened. "Did you hear Bailey's comment about being able to get fifty pounds for his daughter? He probably planned to sell her to one of the brothels that specialize in small children. Missy is a pretty child and unusual looking with that bright red hair. He'd have been able to get a good price for her."

Laurel gasped, her eyes widening. "That's what he meant? How *vile!*"

"But you still are deeply disturbed that I killed the monster."

She swallowed hard. "I'm afraid so. Not that you were wrong. The problem is in me. Such violence makes me ill."

"I noticed," he murmured, trying to sound ironic and amused. "Have you reconsidered coming to London with me?"

She hesitated, and a bone-deep chill spread through him. Strange that she thought he was fearless.

"None of the reasons to attempt reconciliation

have changed," she said gravely. "We owe it to ourselves and our child to try our best to rebuild this marriage." She gave a faint, self-deprecating smile. "Not to mention that my megrims might be a result of the fact that I'm increasing. Women in my condition can behave very strangely."

His relief was almost unbearably intense. "Then we shall continue as we planned, and I shall hope never again to have to act in ways that make you ill."

"I hope so, too!" She put a light bandage on his hand, then rose. "Time for bed before I fall asleep here."

His gaze involuntarily shot to the broad examination table, which had made a fine bed on his first visit. When he jerked his gaze away, he saw Laurel's brows arch with ironic amusement, but she said only, "Can we leave an hour later than we'd planned?"

"Of course." He got to his feet. "I won't mind extra sleep, either."

He opened the door for her, and Shadow darted in and began stropping Laurel's ankles. She scooped the cat up in her arms and scratched under his chin, which produced a rumbling purr. "I'm going to miss you, Shadow cat."

"You're not bringing him with you?" Kirkland asked.

"I considered it, but he's not a young cat and it's a long journey for just a month's stay." She

175

transferred her attentions to his ears. "I shall leave him to the tender mercies of Mrs. Wicker, who dotes on him. He'll be twice this size by the time I return."

As he escorted his wife up the stairs, Kirkland wondered how many cats it would take to keep her in London.

As Kirkland left Laurel at her bedroom door, she wondered if he'd try to kiss her good night. She wasn't sure she could bear for him to touch her. Luckily, her husband merely bowed, wished her a good night's rest, and disappeared into his own bedchamber.

Laurel entered her room, Shadow draped contentedly over her shoulder. To her surprise, Violet was seated in the corner with a lamp, quietly mending stockings. "I'm not sure those are worth the effort," Laurel said as she set Shadow on her bed. "You should be getting some rest. We'll have a long day tomorrow."

"I wanted to assure myself you were well," Violet said as she set her mending into the basket beside her. "Perhaps you might want some broth to settle your stomach?"

In other words, Violet had seen her new mistress being violently ill, but was too discreet to be specific. "I just realized that I'm ravenous," Laurel said as she sank into a chair. "Broth, you say?"

Violet moved to a tray on the dressing table,

uncorked a jug, and poured gently steaming liquid into a mug. "Chicken broth and toasted bread. Delicate food after a difficult night." She set the tray on the table beside Laurel.

Laurel wrapped her cold hands around the warm mug and inhaled the rich scent of the broth. The temperature was just right for sipping. She sighed with pleasure as warmth eased through her. "You are very, very good at caring for people, Violet." She nibbled on a piece of the crisp, thin cut toast. "Have we discussed your salary yet? Anything I might have said, I'll double it."

Violet laughed but she looked pleased. "I can never repay my debt to you, but I will not refuse a salary. A woman without family or money will not fare well."

Laurel sipped more of the delicious broth. Mrs. Wicker did even the simplest things well. "What would you like for yourself in the future, Violet? Have you had time to think about that?"

The girl settled down by her work basket, her brow furrowed. "For too long, I didn't dare dream. But now . . . I want to live and die free. Perhaps someday to have a small dress shop where women who are not rich can come and I shall make garments that make them feel pretty and happy. And maybe in time I will find a man who is kind and looks at me as Mr. Kirkland looks at you."

Laurel frowned. "How does Kirkland look at me?"

"As if you are his one hope of heaven," Violet said simply.

"I . . . haven't noticed." Disturbed, Laurel finished her broth and got to her feet. "Will you help me get this gown off? I want it burned."

Violet looked shocked. "But I can get the bloodstains out! The fabric is still sound and the color is very fine on you."

Laurel looked down at herself. Celestial blue fabric and bloodstains. Not to mention a neckline cut so low that it could distract a murderous drunk. "I can't ever wear this gown again without thinking about tonight. But you're right, it would be a sin to burn it. You may have it to do with as you will. Just . . . if you make it into a gown for yourself, please don't wear it around me."

"You are generous, ma'am." Violet moved behind Laurel and began unfastening the back. "The color would not suit me, but it will be perfect for someone else."

As long as Laurel didn't have to see it again.

Chapter 18

Despite the early hour of Laurel and Kirkland's departure, friends turned out to bid them farewell. Daniel was there, of course. He gave Laurel a long hug and murmured, "You can come home whenever you want, little sister. If you need my escort, let me know and I'll be in London the next day."

"Thank you," she whispered before letting him go. "It's wrenching to leave my home of so many years."

"Another home awaits," Kirkland said as he joined them. "In time, you may come to love it equally."

"Not in London!" she retorted. "This is my home and it always will be."

"Take care of her, Kirkland." Daniel offered his hand, but the edge in his voice made his words more than routine good wishes.

"I shall." Kirkland shook Daniel's hand, his gaze level.

Not liking the way the two men were regarding each other, Laurel said, "Time we were on our way."

Kirkland nodded. "I'll have a word with the drivers."

There were two carriages, neither bearing

Kirkland's coat of arms. One would carry Laurel and Kirkland; the other had Violet, Kirkland's man Rhodes, and most of the baggage. Not that Laurel was bringing a huge amount. She would need nothing in London but her clothing, and she'd be acquiring a new wardrobe there.

Anne Wilson, Betsy Rivers, and Eileen Bailey had also gathered to see them off. When Laurel hugged Eileen, she said, "How are you after such a frightening night?"

Eileen smiled, looking more relaxed than Laurel had ever seen her. "I feel . . . very free, Miss Laurel. May God forgive me, I can't be sorry Bailey is dead."

"I think God is very forgiving in circumstances like yours," Laurel said, thinking that Kirkland's rough justice had certainly benefited Eileen. "Give my love to Missy."

After they bid each other farewell, Laurel turned and was surprised to see Violet dodge behind the lead carriage, then lean against the side, her face pale and her hands knotted in fists. Kirkland had also noticed, and he reached the girl before Laurel did. "What's wrong?" he asked.

Violet swallowed hard. "A man has been watching me, I think for Captain Hardwick. A scarred sailor. I saw him down the street."

Laurel gazed down the street, but the man was gone. Kirkland's eyes narrowed. "It's good you're leaving Bristol, Miss Smith. In London we must talk at greater length. Though it will be difficult for the man to trace you to the city, I suggest you not leave my house without a companion."

"Thank you, sir." Violet's hands unclenched. "And . . . and I have decided I will no longer be Miss Smith. The name was given to me because it was common, of no value. I was never a Smith, and I will not use that name again."

"Have you chosen another surname yet?" Laurel asked.

"Would you mind if I take the name Herbert?" the girl asked shyly. "I won't if you'd rather I didn't. But I owe you so much. This is a way to honor you."

"That is one of the loveliest things anyone has ever said to me," Laurel said warmly. "It's a pleasure to meet you, Violet Herbert!"

"Thank you so much, ma'am!" Violet gave a radiant smile. "The slave girl Violet Smith is no more."

"You should be safer in London, but a woman's first protector is herself," Kirkland said. "I know a woman who has often been in dangerous places, and she's learned how to fight well. She says most females are easy victims because they don't know how to fight back. I can ask her to teach you useful tricks for self-defense."

"I would like that very much." Violet bobbed a curtsy. "And now to London!"

As Laurel headed to her carriage, she thought

it said much about Kirkland that he lived a life where even the women knew how to kill.

Still shaken by the sight of the scarred man, Violet walked swiftly toward the carriage that would take her, Mr. Kirkland's valet, and the luggage to London. The sooner she was away from Bristol, the better.

A man emerged from the carriage and held the door for her. Youngish, brown haired, and wiry in build, he offered her a cheerful smile. "I'm Rhodes, and we'll be companions on the road to London." Then his gaze locked on her with an expression Violet was all too familiar with. He swallowed. "You're Miss Smith?"

Violet put on her most severe expression. "Miss Herbert. I have just decided to change my surname." Refusing his hand, she climbed into the carriage without aid and slid to the far end of the seat, as far from Rhodes as she could get.

He swung up beside her and closed the door behind him. As he settled onto the seat, keeping his distance, he said, "I'm sorry I gawped at you, but honestly, you can't blame a chap for being all agog at the sight of the prettiest girl in Bristol."

"Too often looking leads to touching," she said with a scowl. "I'm free now and no man will ever again lay a finger on me if I'm unwilling."

He stared at her, shocked. "That's not going to happen to you, not in Lord Kirkland's household.

He'd personally thrash any servant who bothered a woman. He's right scary when he's angry. I wouldn't do it anyhow. My mum always taught me to be nice to girls 'cause they're the weaker sex. Though I think she was wrong when it came to my sister." He offered a tentative smile.

Violet began to relax. "I'm sorry if I misjudged you. But . . . I have often been . . . offered insult." And worse.

"With looks like yours, I see why, but wrong is wrong," he said firmly. "But—you said now you're free? You weren't before?"

"I was born and raised in slavery in Jamaica," she said defiantly. "Miss Laurel freed me at great risk to herself."

"She did?" he asked, fascinated. "She looks such a sweet, soft lady."

"She is. But a lioness has soft fur, too." Remembering what he'd said earlier, she asked, "You called your master Lord Kirkland? I thought he was a Mister."

Rhodes shook his head. "He's an earl. Because his lady was shy of having her friends know she was a countess, she asked his lordship not to use the title. But since you're going to London, you need to know."

Violet swallowed. It wasn't difficult to believe Kirkland was a lord. Despite his kindness and impeccable courtesy, he radiated authority. "I didn't know how grand his household would be."

"No need to worry," he said reassuringly. "The housekeeper, Mrs. Stratton, makes sure everything is right and proper, but she's fair and good tempered. You'll rank right next to her, being Lady Kirkland's personal maid."

"The other servants won't mind that I'm . . . ?" She gestured at her café-au-lait complexion.

The valet shook his head. "Not at Kirkland House. We're quite a mix, we are. Lord Kirkland believes in giving people second chances."

"Does that include you?" Violet asked, intrigued.

"Aye." Rhodes hesitated, as if unsure how much to say. "After my da died, times were hard for my mum and sister and me. The Kirkland House cook caught me trying to steal food from the kitchen one day and took me to his lordship, who explained that I could be transported to Botany Bay if I chose to pursue a life of crime." The valet smiled reminiscently. "Scared me out of my bloomin' mind."

"How old were you?"

"Twelve. Old enough to be in big trouble for stealing. I told his lordship I'd gladly do honest work if someone would give me a job, so he did. I started out as a hall boy, but I wanted to become a valet, so his lordship had his old valet train me."

"He sounds like a good master."

"None better," Rhodes assured her. "It's a happy household and London's a grand city. You'll like living there."

She hoped he was right. "Thank you for the information, Mr. Rhodes."

"My name is Jasper, but I usually prefer just Rhodes." He smiled shyly, and she realized that he was younger than she'd thought. "On free afternoons, I can take you to visit some of the sights."

She smiled back, and thought that perhaps she would like London.

Moody swore as he watched the carriages rumble away from Herbert House. A scarred reprobate like him wouldn't get many answers if he asked where the carriages was goin', but he'd managed to get close enough to hear a thing or two.

It wasn't far to Hardwick's house. The captain kept him cooling his heels for half the morning, the bloody sod, even though Moody was his second mate. When he was finally ushered into Hardwick's office, the captain looked up impatiently. "What are you doing here, Moody? Come to report that my Violet is still hiding out in Herbert House?"

Moody felt twisted satisfaction at pricking that arrogance. "Your mort just left in a carriage. Looked like she's goin' as a maid to some lady."

Hardwick surged to his feet, swearing. "Why the devil didn't you follow her?"

"Without a horse or carriage? I'm no bloody pony," Moody retorted. "But I did get close enough to hear a name. Kirkland."

Hardwick jerked back. "Lord Kirkland?"

Moody shrugged. "All I heard was Kirkland. A dark-haired fellow who looked slick as a wet eel."

"Lord Kirkland. *Damnation!*" Hardwick sank back into his chair, his expression furious. "But at least now I know where to find my Violet."

Chapter 19

After Violet and Rhodes's carriage left, Kirkland turned to Laurel and offered his arm. "Shall we depart, my lady?"

From his expression, she guessed this was a test of whether she could bring herself to touch his fabric-covered arm. She could; the previous night's intense revulsion had passed, and this kind of casual touching was part of their attempt to reconcile. She took his arm. "It's time."

As Kirkland escorted her to their carriage, Laurel said, "The woman who knows how to fight. Could she teach me? Perhaps give lessons at Zion House as well?"

Kirkland's brows arched. "I'm sure she'd be willing. You'd want to learn such skills yourself?"

"I doubt I'll be able to fight well," she admitted. "But last night reminded me how vulnerable women are. I should at least try to learn to fight back."

Kirkland helped her into the carriage. She'd left her work bag inside earlier, but for the moment she pushed it aside and slid across the seat to make room for her husband. He settled beside her, the carriage began to roll, and her new life began.

As they rumbled through the Bristol streets, she

said, "Is the woman who teaches fighting one of your agents?"

"Yes, Hazel is a Londoner who grew up in one of the city's most dangerous neighborhoods. She had to fight to survive, and she had the intelligence and discipline to better herself. She likes helping others and making a difference." Kirkland smiled. "As do you, though in different ways."

She wondered if Hazel was one of his mistresses, then forced herself to bury the thought. It wasn't her business what he'd done during their years of separation.

Since it would be a long journey, she retrieved her work bag and pulled out her hook and a ball of soft, ivory-colored yarn. As she began a square, Kirkland asked, "What kind of handwork is that? Knitting is two needles, isn't it?"

Laurel displayed the single needle with a hook at the end. "A Belgian woman who stayed at Zion House taught several of us how to do this. She said it was called 'nun's lace' or 'crochet in the air.' Anne Wilson called it 'hooking,' and now we all do." She pulled a finished piece about four inches square from her bag and handed it to him. "This is easy to do while riding in a carriage and makes travel less boring."

He rubbed the square between his thumb and forefinger. "It's beautifully soft. How will you use it?"

"A baby blanket for an infant at Zion House.

Most of the children have so little when they arrive there." She squeezed the ball of yarn. "I like the softness of undyed wool. Since sheep come in slightly different shades, the result is subtle and rather pretty."

"Will you make one for our baby?" he asked softly.

His fingers brushed hers when he returned the square. The slight touch sent tingles through her. She tucked the square away, which gave her an excuse to avoid looking at her husband. "Surely the child of an earl should have nothing but the best."

"What could be better than a blanket made with love?"

She swallowed hard, inexplicably near tears. "Perhaps I shall make one. I'll need something to keep me busy in London."

"You can be as busy or as quiet as you choose, Laurel. As I said once, I think you'd enjoy meeting the wives of some of my friends." Kirkland opened a leather case that had been tucked in a pocket on the wall. Inside was a small lap desk, the brass corners and leather covered writing surface showing signs of heavy use.

"Can you really work in a jouncing carriage?" she asked.

"Papers tend to follow me around, so I might as well use the time when I'm traveling. Particularly since the Bristol road is one of the best in the country." He lifted the slanted lid of the desk and removed a sheaf of documents. "Reading and writing notes in pencil only. I've learned that ink and a quill can be disastrous."

"A good reason for usually wearing black, as you do," she remarked. He chuckled, then turned his attention to the papers.

"Business or spying?" she asked.

"Business." He tapped the topmost document. "All the low forms of trade that made my English relatives despise me. Besides the shipping company, I own and manage a number of properties, from estates to manufactories. Many people depend on them for their livelihoods. I have good managers, but I still need to pay attention."

She'd always liked that he was a responsible man. As she returned to hooking her squares, she realized that it was also one of the values they shared. They each took care of people, in very different ways. If she concentrated on his good points, his more dangerous traits might not upset her as much.

The weather was dry, the coach well sprung, and the road well maintained, so they made good time. Laurel found their quiet companionability oddly domestic, like the evenings they once spent together sitting beside the fire, each engaged in separate projects, but glad to be close.

After two changes of horses and a luncheon, Laurel grew sleepy. Covering a yawn with one hand, she said apologetically, "Sorry, I've been taking naps these days. An effect of being with child, I'm told."

Kirkland closed his lap desk and set it on the floor, then leaned forward and raised the padded seat of the opposite bench to reveal neatly folded blankets and pillows. "Allow me to make you comfortable."

Not wanting him to tuck her in, she leaned forward and pulled out a pillow and blanket. "I shall make a nest for myself."

The seat was well padded, and with the pillow in the angle between seat and carriage wall and a blanket over her, she was surprisingly comfortable, despite the swaying. She settled down, and retreated from her disturbing husband into sleep.

Though their wedding was mere weeks after they'd first met, each week had felt like a year. James's lightest touch or smile sparked her to yearning life. She hadn't known that passion was so powerful, so urgent. They'd been hard pressed to keep their hands off each other when they were with others. In private, they didn't even try, though they stopped well short of the final intimacy.

Now, finally, their wedding night had arrived. The senior Herberts would have preferred a grand wedding with half the county invited to see that their daughter had caught an earl, but Laurel and James hadn't wanted that. The ceremony was simple and lovely, with Daniel acting as best man.

After the wedding breakfast, the newly-weds had departed in a cloud of good wishes to a destination known only to James. Laurel was delighted to find that their honeymoon retreat was less than an hour's drive away because her new husband had rented a beautiful little estate overlooking the Severn River. Surrounded by gardens and a park, River House gave them privacy and peace for the first days of their marriage.

She'd been dazzled and a little intimidated by the idea of so much wealth that he could rent an estate as easily as most men would hire a room at an inn. But he never let her feel the disparity between their ranks. He made her feel . . . adored.

At River House, they ate a light supper before retiring to adjoining bedrooms to prepare for their wedding night. Laurel's room was filled with fragrant flowers. She sat by the dressing table and brushed her hair into a shining bronze mantle that flowed over her shoulders. As she studied her image in the mirror, she looked almost

VB   #940   05-23-2019 11:58AM
   Item(s) checked out to p11435574.

TITLE: Crash and burn
BARCODE: 3 3028 01068 6170
DUE DATE: 06-13-19

TITLE: The week before the wedding
BARCODE: 3 3028 00948 0775
DUE DATE: 06-13-19

TITLE: Forget me not
BARCODE: 3 3028 00962 9728
DUE DATE: 06-13-19

TITLE: Mercy
BARCODE: 3 3028 00869 7205
DUE DATE: 06-13-19

TITLE: Not quite a wife
BARCODE: 3 3028 01029 4785
DUE DATE: 06-13-19

Harris Branch

beautiful because she was radiant with love. Absolutely sure of her marriage and the man she would spend the rest of her life with.

She rose and paced impatiently to the window. The days were very long at this time of year and the sun was only now setting, burning a path across the vast breadth of the Severn as the river rolled down to the sea. She burned like that sun, yearning for her marriage bed so she and James would truly be husband and wife, forever and ever, amen.

When her door opened, she turned her back to the window. Her nightgown had been ordered by her mother and the long sleeves and high neck were intended to convey demure, maidenly innocence. Laurel had known better than to argue, but she'd chosen the fine white lawn fabric herself and knew the sunlight pouring through the river behind her would reveal her body in very un-demure detail.

James closed the door behind him, then halted, his gaze devouring her. He wore a long banyan robe, the dark blue fabric emphasizing the breadth of his shoulders. "You are so beautiful," he breathed. "So impossibly, perfectly beautiful."

She laughed and crossed the room

toward him. She knew her appearance to be nothing special, but when he looked at her like that, she did feel lovely. His intense blue eyes showed not only the strength and kindness that she loved, but also a vulnerability she hadn't recognized before. He needed her as she needed him.

"Tonight doesn't have to be perfect. Being together is enough. More than enough." She stepped from the sunshine and crossed the room toward where he stood in the shadows. "You're the one who is beautiful, my lord and master. If he was here, Michelangelo would beg you to model for him."

James's eyes danced. "If Michelangelo was here, I'd ask him to leave so we can have our privacy." They met in the center of the room near the foot of the vast four-poster bed.

She was tall but he was taller. He caught her hands, then bent into a kiss so that only their fingers and mouths touched. Ah, his warm, sensual mouth . . . She closed her eyes, savoring the sweet nectar of his lips. The delicious stroke of his tongue.

She drew closer until she was pressed against his lean, powerful body. After the weeks of waiting, only light layers of fabric separated them—and both of them burned.

"I've been waiting for this," she murmured. "Dreaming of you."

He stepped away, his expression strained. Puzzled, she cocked her head, trying to read his enigmatic expression. "Isn't it the virgin bride who is supposed to be nervous?"

He cupped her face with both hands. "I want this to be perfect," he said, his voice intense. "So right, so wonderful, that you'll never leave me."

"Of course I won't leave you, my one and only love. This morning I made a sacred vow to forsake all others." She brushed a featherlight kiss on his left cheek. "I can't imagine ever wanting any man but you." An equally soft kiss on his other cheek. "Perfect is a cold, lifeless concept. Who needs perfection when we have the warmth of love and passion?"

She kissed his mouth, opening her lips, dancing her tongue over his. On impulse she yanked on his sash and his robe fell open.

Whatever worries he had vanished. He caught the neckline of her demure robe with both hands and ripped the light fabric so that it tore almost to her knees. Then he embraced her so that they pressed together skin to skin, heat to heat.

She claimed his mouth again, dizzily curling her nails into his back as she melted into him, desperate for the ultimate joining. . . .

Laurel gasped as she jolted awake. Disoriented, she lifted her head. Where . . . ? When . . . ?

She'd been sleeping on James's shoulder. His arm was around her, his face only inches away. Her instinctive pleasure in his nearness was followed instantly by shock. Had he pulled her close as she slept? No, he hadn't moved, she had. Drawn to him even in her sleep.

Now her side was pressed against him, their thighs were touching, and the air was thick with sensual tension. Her chest was so tight she could barely breathe.

In his face, she saw the same desire that consumed her. He raised his hand and traced the side of her face, his fingertips warm and not quite steady. "Laurel," he whispered. "My Lavender Lady . . ."

Beautiful hands, skilled at writing or playing the piano or rousing her to madness.

Locking around a knife and slicing it into a man's throat.

She shoved violently away until she was flattened against the wall of the coach, shaken by the agonizing collision of past and present. For years, she'd suppressed all thoughts of the

196

happiness and certainty of those early days of their marriage. Now the memories were almost unbearable.

Nor was she the only one in pain. Kirkland hadn't moved a muscle, yet she knew that he felt as if she'd slapped him. Struggling to repair the damage she'd done, she said raggedly, "Sorry, it took a moment to remember where I was when I woke up. I don't usually sleep so soundly in coaches. I must have moved in my sleep? My apologies for interfering with your work."

"You didn't. I dozed a little also." He regarded her with unnerving steadiness. "You really shouldn't act as if nothing happened. You looked at me as if . . . I had horns and hooves and tail."

She drew a steadying breath. "I'm sorry. I was dreaming of . . . our wedding night. Then I woke and . . . remembered how much has happened."

"It's been less than a day since you had a close view of me killing a man," he said with cool detachment. "I wasn't sure you'd be willing to go to London with me."

She pressed a hand to her abdomen, where a tiny spark of possibility was playing merry Hades with her life. "The reasons for rebuilding our marriage haven't changed. I can't even condemn you for killing that horrible, dangerous man." The man whose blood had splashed over her. "But . . . my head and my emotions are at war."

He nodded gravely. "Head and heart have their

own truths, and too often they're opposite. As we are."

"As we are." Her mouth curved in a rueful smile. "We keep drawing together like opposite poles of magnets."

"Male and female are opposite enough without invoking magnets," he said dryly.

"The genders have some things in common," she pointed out. "The desire for home and comfort and . . . affection."

"Comfort would be good. Anything else would be an unexpected bonus." He lifted his lap desk from the floor to resume work, a clear sign the conversation was over.

Suppressing a sigh, she gazed out the window at the passing countryside. She wasn't even sure they could manage to be comfortable together. But dear God, she wanted more! And that thought moved them into dangerous territory.

Chapter 20

Kirkland had traveled from London to Bristol with absurd speed when he'd learned of Laurel's pregnancy, but their journey back to the city was a more normal two days, for which Laurel was grateful. She was even more grateful for the separate rooms in the inn where they spent the night.

There was no more drama. After she fell asleep on his shoulder and panicked when she woke, Kirkland shifted to the facing seat, which eliminated the risk of her napping and ending up wrapped around him. She did nap often, and when she was awake, she hooked enough squares for two baby blankets before she ran out of wool. When they spoke, they were very, very civil.

Given the confined quarters of the carriage, it was a relief to reach London. At least in some ways. As they moved from the country into crowded, raucous streets, Laurel began to tense. Bristol was a sizable city and a busy port, but London was in a whole different class. She could feel the weight of all the lives and strife.

"You're frowning now that we're almost home," Kirkland remarked.

"I'd forgotten just how noisy, smelly, and crowded the city is." She gazed out the carriage window. "I've only been here once before, and I didn't stay long enough to become accustomed." Since that visit had been the handful of days with Kirkland before her marriage had shattered, she didn't have many good memories of London.

"The city is overpowering for newcomers, but Samuel Johnson said that a man who was tired of London was tired of life," Kirkland observed. "Once you become better accustomed, what would you like to do beyond the normal business of living?"

Her brows arched. "Apart from compulsory visits to modistes?"

He smiled. "Apart from that. Though if you prefer, the modistes can come to you. It's one of the advantages of being a countess."

"That could be convenient," she observed. "But what I really want is music. The opera, chamber concerts, soirees. I want to hear the best musicians in England."

"You'll not hear any pianists better than you, but there is every kind of music, not to mention art and literature and lecture groups. Feasts for the mind and senses."

Until now, she'd looked on this visit as a duty, but for the first time, she felt anticipation. She hadn't had a holiday—heavens, since her honeymoon!

Though she loved her work and was proud of what she and her brother had accomplished, perhaps she was ready to sample the delights of a great city. "I want to do all those things! And also . . ." She bit her lip. "It's rather childish, but I've always wanted to visit Astley's Amphitheatre to see the stunt riders."

"I always enjoy Astley's and shall welcome an excuse to go again," he said promptly. "What else?"

She glanced out at the fashionable streets of Mayfair. If she was to spend part of her life in London, she needed more than a handsome house. "I want to make friends, because without friends, London would be a sad place. You thought that some of your friends' wives might be kindred spirits?"

"I'll arrange a dinner party a few days from now so you can judge for yourself," he replied. "As soon as you have a new gown or two made."

"For confidence? You're right, I'll need armor when meeting people who will be inclined to disapprove of me," she said wryly. "No matter how much you tell your friends that I was blameless in our separation, they'll be loyal to you and understandably suspicious of me for complicating your life."

His brow furrowed. "You may be right, but they are fair-minded people. Any doubts will vanish once they meet you. Who could not like you?"

She shook her head. "Your belief that I am special is one of your most appealing qualities, but not everyone would agree with you."

"We'll find out soon enough, but truly, I don't think you need worry." He glanced out the window. "Almost home now. We're entering Berkeley Square."

She was surprised to see that outside her window was an oval park in the center of a long city square. "This isn't the house you had before."

"That place was damp and had no good memories, so I sold it," he explained. "This house is larger and more comfortable, and the square is a pleasant place to walk."

"It looks very fashionable," she said dubiously.

"This side of the square is. One of the patronesses of Almack's, Lady Jersey, lives just over there. The other side has very nice shops, including the famous Gunter's tea shop." He smiled. "Easy walking distance."

"Lord help me," she muttered. "That doesn't mean I have to go to Almack's, does it? Not that they'd let me in since I am most certainly not fashionable!"

"I am considered very fashionable," he said peaceably, "and as my wife you'd be welcome. That doesn't mean you have to attend any of the assemblies, though."

She felt an internal twinge and pressed a hand to her abdomen. "I'm more interested in finding a good midwife. Perhaps one of your friends' wives will know one."

"My friend Major Randall's wife is a very

skilled midwife. If the Randalls are in London, you'll be able to meet her when we have that dinner."

One of his wellborn friends had married a midwife? That was unusual enough to be worthy of note, but before she could inquire further, the carriage rumbled to a halt in front of one of the town houses. After the guard opened the carriage door and lowered the steps, Kirkland stepped out and turned to offer his hand. "Welcome to your London home, Lady Kirkland."

A new house, a new start. Since she'd only be in London a month, Laurel could have endured the old house where their marriage had shattered. But she was glad she didn't have to. Feeling rumpled and not much like a countess, she took his hand and stepped down. As they entered the house, the baggage coach containing Violet and Rhodes halted behind the first coach.

Kirkland rapped the dragon's-head knocker sharply, then produced a key and opened his front door. Seeing Laurel's surprise, he explained, "I often come and go at odd hours, so I prefer not to have to wake any servants."

"Thoughtful," she commented. "As well as keeping your activities discreet."

"That, too," he agreed as he opened the door and ushered her inside.

Before the door had closed, a balding butler emerged from the depths of the house. "My lord!"

He made a swift bow. "We didn't know when you'd be returning."

"Neither did I until I left Bristol. Soames, may I present Lady Kirkland. Laurel, Soames is my extraordinarily efficient butler."

Soames was a man of military bearing and massive dignity, but his eyes almost popped before he bowed again. "Shall I assemble the staff for her ladyship to meet?"

Kirkland glanced at Laurel, then shook his head. "My wife is tired. I'll take her to her rooms so she can rest. A light supper for later, please. She can meet Mrs. Stratton and the rest of the staff in the morning. Speaking of staff, Rhodes and my wife's maid, Miss Violet Herbert are right behind us with the baggage."

"Very good, my lord."

As Laurel headed to the staircase with Kirkland, she couldn't resist saying, "Never a dull moment in Kirkland House, Soames?"

His eyes glinted. "No, my lady. And I wouldn't have it any other way."

Chapter 21

Kirkland had never believed that he and Laurel would reconcile, but even so, when he'd considered buying the Berkeley Square house, he'd thought of her. That had been particularly true when he'd walked through the mistress's suite, which overlooked the sizable garden behind the house. It had been bittersweet pleasure to imagine her gazing from the window at the flowers and plane trees of the garden, her lovely face pensive.

And now she was here. He still didn't quite believe it.

She turned with a smile. "It's a handsome house. Much nicer than the old one."

"You're free to make whatever changes you want. Painting, wallpaper, new furniture."

Her gaze swept over the serene cream walls and moldings, the accents of rose and green. "That won't be necessary. It almost seems as if you decorated the rooms to my tastes." Her glance went back to him. "Did you?"

Once again honesty was required. "Yes," he admitted. "These rooms were drab and something had to be done, so I chose colors and furnishings I thought you'd like even though I didn't expect you to ever see them."

"Life is mysterious." She turned from the window. "Your rooms are adjacent?"

He nodded. "The layout is very similar. There are connecting doors between the bedrooms and the two sitting rooms." After a moment, he added, "I can have locks put on your side if you like."

Her expressive brows arched. "Is that necessary?"

He studied her graceful figure, a perfect balance between slimness and womanly curves. "I hope not," he said honestly. "But I can't make any guarantees. You're still the most attractive woman I've ever met."

She looked away. "Is there a music room?"

"At the front of the house. This way."

Laurel's face lit up when he ushered her into the music room. "The piano looks just like my Broadwood!"

"Your instrument had the best sound of any piano I've ever heard, so I had Broadwood make another like it."

Face alight, she sat on the bench and ran exploratory fingers over the keys, producing a ripple of clear, bright notes. "I haven't played in days." She glanced up at him, her face relaxed. "Since you showed up on my doorstep. Not playing is surely bad for my temper."

"Then play for me. It will improve both of our tempers."

She needed no encouragement. Turning back to the instrument, she began the Rondeau allegro movement of Mozart's Sonata in B-flat Major, filling the room with swift, playful notes. A good omen for her mood, he thought. He settled on the sofa and closed his eyes, his tension dissolving in the rich currents of her playing.

When she finished the movement, he opened his eyes and applauded. "You're even better than you were before, Laurel. Not just technique but the feeling."

She spread the fingers of her left hand and played a low, somber chord. "There is nothing like working with people in trouble to expand one's store of feeling."

"That's part of being older and wiser, I think. Would you honor me with an encore, my lady?"

She regarded him thoughtfully. "You said you still played." She rose from the piano and gestured at it grandly. "Your turn, maestro."

"I'm not up to your standards," he said uncomfortably. He never played for others, only himself.

"This isn't a contest." A glint of humor showed in her eyes. "As your former teacher, I want to learn if you've been practicing."

He supposed that was fair. His love for music was part of what had drawn him to Laurel, who had music flowing in her veins. As a boy, he would pick out tunes on the largely unused Kirkland piano when there was no one around to hear.

When he'd revealed his passion for music to

Laurel, she'd offered lessons. He'd leaped at the opportunity to learn. She was a wonderful, patient teacher, and those lessons were among the brightest memories of their honeymoon.

As they exchanged places, he wondered what to play. Not one of the Mozart pieces that Laurel performed so brilliantly. He should choose one of his favorites. Ah, Carl Philipp Emanuel Bach. The Andante from the Sonata in G Major. He knew it well, and played it well. Usually.

He rested his hands on the keyboard for a long moment and stilled his mind in preparation. He would never be Laurel's equal as a pianist, but he didn't want to humiliate himself in front of her. As he began weaving intricate cascades of notes, Laurel sat up straight, listening with her whole body.

He hadn't played for others because for years, music had been the truest outlet for the emotions he suppressed in his daily life. But who had a better right to hear those feelings than his wife? Anger, despair, longing, hope—everything flowed from his mind to his hands and into the music.

When he finished the piece, the silence was so long that he was almost afraid to look at Laurel until she said quietly, "That was extraordinary. You've improved remarkably, my lord."

He was ridiculously relieved by her praise. Turning on the bench so he could see her, he said, "As you see, I've been practicing. I've also continued with my hobby of making new arrangements. I enjoy reducing concertos for multiple instruments into sonatas for myself."

"I'd almost forgotten, but your first arrangements were creating four-handed pieces we could play together." She rose from the sofa. "Shall we do that again?"

He'd done those first arrangements because they were a challenge, and because he liked the idea of sharing a keyboard with Laurel. Playing together had been enormous fun, and had often ended in a different kind of play. Refusing her request now would be wise—but there was a limit to his store of wisdom. "I'd like that."

He moved to the left so there was room for her on the bench. She was so close that he felt the warmth of her body. He forced his gaze to the keyboard, trying not to remember how their joint playing had ended in the past.

She began a Beethoven sonata they both loved, which was why he'd created a four-handed version. Laurel's pleasure in the result had been satisfying in a way his more worldly accomplishments had never been.

She shot him a teasing glance as her slim fingers danced across the keys. He found that he still intuitively anticipated her changes in tempo so that his playing complemented hers. It was a pleasure almost equal to kissing her.

Almost, not quite.

When they finished, she said, "That was wonderful. You must have guessed that having music here was the best way to make me feel at home in London."

"I didn't think that consciously, but I knew it was as essential to you as the air you breathe," he admitted.

"And equally essential to you." She rested her fingers soundlessly on the keys as she exhaled roughly. "You want more than to be comfortable friends for the sake of our child, don't you?"

"Yes," he said softly, matching her directness. "How could I not? We can't recapture the past, but my greatest hope is that we can find our way to be truly married again. You're the only wife I've ever wanted, Laurel."

She raised her head, her perfect profile silhouetted against the window. "You've ruined me for any other husband, James, but I don't think I can be what you want. What you deserve. My mind understands your actions, but my emotions—my sense of right and wrong—can't deal with the violence. Even if it's justified."

"You are as you are, my lady, just as I am what I am," he said with profound regret. "Perhaps spending time together will bring us together again. But I'm not counting on that."

"Perhaps when pregnancy is no longer working on my emotions, I'll be less difficult," she said with a sigh.

"Again, I'm not counting on it," he said dryly. "One's sense of right and wrong is an essential part of one's character. But I'm very grateful that you're here. If this is the closest we can be—it's a great deal better than nothing."

"James . . ." She reached out to lay her hand over his.

He jerked away. "That isn't wise, Laurel. After that music—I'm not sure that I am safe."

She yanked her hand back. "I'm sorry. I don't want to make this any more difficult than it already is."

"I know." He stood, thinking it was ironic that they could understand each other so well, yet still be separated by their essential natures. "I shall leave you to your music. I have business to attend to in my study. Until we dine, my lady?"

She stood, then sank into a sweeping court curtsy. "Until we dine, my lord." As she rose, her eyes were filled with deep sadness.

He bowed with matching courtliness, then left the room. At the moment, it was very difficult to hold on to the frail hope that she might again be his wife in every way.

Was it possible to survive without hope?

To steady her frayed nerves, Laurel played a complete Mozart sonata after Kirkland left. She liked that they could share music and talk honestly to each other.

The hard part was the abyss that lay between them. Civility and being older and wiser made it possible for them to communicate—but not to build a bridge over that damnable abyss.

As the last notes of the sonata died, she realized she was exhausted. Wearily she returned to her sumptuous bedchamber. During her time in the music room, vases of bright, fragrant flowers had magically appeared in her bedchamber to welcome the countess. Kirkland's staff was very efficient.

The open door to the dressing room revealed that Violet was efficiently unpacking Laurel's trunk. Laurel asked, "Are your quarters comfortable?"

The girl glanced up. "Oh, yes, my lady. I have a fine room all to myself in the attic as well as a chamber off this dressing room for when you need me close. The housekeeper and other staff were very welcoming because I am your personal maid." Violet placed a short stack of folded shifts in the clothespress.

Laurel subsided into a chair and removed her shoes. "My wardrobe is rather pathetic, isn't it?"

"Your clothing is suitable for a woman who runs an infirmary and a sanctuary in a provincial city," Violet said tactfully. "But the world expects more of a countess."

Laurel wrinkled her nose. "I don't want to look like a tragic mistake of Kirkland's youth, so clothing is my first priority. He says I can summon a modiste, or go out to an exclusive shop. Is one method preferable to the other? You're my expert."

Violet thought as she continued unpacking. "You should go out, I think. You need to become accustomed to London, and if you go to a shop that has partially made garments available, you should be able to walk out with a new gown. Also, there will be more samples of fabric and trimmings."

"We'll do that, then. You'll come with me, of course. You have more style in your little finger than I have in my whole body." Not bothering to remove her rumpled gown, Laurel climbed onto the bed and pulled up the folded quilt that lay across the bottom of the mattress.

"I shall be pleased to accompany you, but Lord Kirkland should come, too."

Laurel exhaled with pleasure as she relaxed. Two days in a coach, even a comfortable one, had left her very appreciative of a good mattress. "Why do we need Kirkland? I'm sure he has better things to do."

"I understand style, but I've always lived far from the centers of fashion." Violet chuckled. "Given how well he dresses, his lordship must understand fashion."

Laurel covered a yawn. "Do I want to be fashionable?"

She assumed Violet would say yes, but the

girl surprised her. "Perhaps not, but you need to understand it well enough to know what you wish to embrace or avoid."

That made sense. "Then we shall learn London and fashion together. But now I must rest. Please wake me in time to dress for dinner."

"I shall." Violet hesitated. "Forgive the impertinence, but are you increasing?"

Laurel nodded. "Yes, and a very tiring business it is!"

"Congratulations! That will affect your wardrobe, of course."

"So it will. Another subject I leave in your capable hands." Laurel pulled the quilt over her head. The bed was deliciously comfortable, and large enough for two people with room to spare. A pity to waste it on a woman who was probably born to be a spinster, and hadn't realized that in time to prevent herself from ruining a man's life.

Chapter 22

By the time Laurel joined Kirkland for dinner, the tension he'd shown in the music room had been replaced by his usual calm control. Handsome, enigmatic, and concealing mysteries beneath his polished exterior. That control made it easier to be with him, but she missed the relaxed intimacy they'd shared with the music.

As he pulled out her chair, she remarked, "This room is much more pleasant than the main dining room. One could hold a cricket match in there."

"I suspect you're right." Kirkland seated himself on the opposite side of the table and two footmen entered with trays of food and drink. "This is the breakfast room. The formal dining room is only used for company, and not always then."

As one of the footmen placed a bowl of deliciously scented soup in front of her, Laurel asked, "Do you dine in lonely splendor here?"

He shrugged. "If I'm not attending some social event, I'll usually eat at my desk in the study."

In other words, he worked much too hard. She tasted the soup, which was a rich chicken broth with herbs, rice, and shreds of chicken. She wondered if the Kirkland chef had been instructed to provide dishes that would appeal to a woman who was in the family way. She savored another spoonful. "Violet informs me that you should accompany me to the modiste because you know fashion and she only has style."

He smiled. "I'm sure she will rapidly learn what is fashionable, but I'll be happy to escort you. I presume Violet will also come?" When Laurel nodded, he continued, "Then I'll take Rhodes. As long as she might be in danger from Captain Hardwick, she shouldn't go out without protection. Rhodes is a very useful man in a fight. He'll make sure she comes to no harm."

Laurel finished her soup. "Is he rather more than the usual valet?"

After a moment of hesitation, Kirkland said, "He helps me in my work in various ways. His background has given him some useful skills."

Laurel wondered what that bland remark covered. Probably spying of various sorts. She hoped Rhodes would also be an effective bodyguard. "I presume you know the best modiste in London and nothing less than the best will do for Lady Kirkland?"

"The best is a matter of debate," he said amiably. "If there's a modiste you'd like to try, of course the choice is yours. But if you have no preference, Madame Hélier is patronized by the wives of some of my friends, and they always look very fine. I'm told she helps her clients achieve the look they want rather than imposing her own ideas."

Laurel tasted her poached sole with approval.

"Then Madame Hélier it shall be. Do I need to make an appointment to see her?"

"That would be advisable. I'll have a note sent. I imagine that tomorrow you'll want to become acquainted with the household, so perhaps the day after tomorrow?"

Laurel sighed. "That will give me time to mentally prepare for the ordeal."

Kirkland laughed. "Will you feel better about a new wardrobe if you recall that your mother will be wild with envy?"

"That's a low but gratifying thought." She sampled the cauliflower with cheese sauce. Lovely, with a hint of nutmeg. "If I am temporary mistress of the household, I need to meet your chef and possibly steal some recipes to take back to Bristol."

If he disliked her reference to the fact that she wouldn't stay, he concealed the reaction. "Mrs. Simond might not be willing to share them, but sincere admiration is the quickest way to her heart."

"My admiration will be *very* sincere!" She finished her fish. "You have a female cook? I thought Mayfair only allowed temperamental male chefs, preferably French."

"Mrs. Simond is English, but she was married to a French chef. They lived and worked together in Paris until he was executed for some alleged political failing."

Laurel frowned. "How horrible for Mrs. Simond! Not to mention a waste of a good chef. Did you find her through an agency?"

"One of my agents helped her and her two children escape to England," he explained. "She arrived with no money or references, but the agent who brought the Simonds from France knew I was in need of a cook."

"Helping Mrs. Simond was very good of you." The thinly sliced roast beef was as delicious as everything else Laurel had eaten. "Not to mention good *for* you."

"Seldom have I had a generous impulse so well rewarded. She regularly receives offers from people who dine here, but so far she has remained loyal." His eyes glinted with amusement. "I generally increase her wages to insure that."

"Whatever you're paying her, she's worth it. Your dinner parties must be very popular." The final course was cakes, nuts, and fruit, but all Laurel could manage was a single cake. A single, exquisite, cardamom-flavored almond cake.

Replete, Laurel said, "I'm tired again. I'll write a letter to Daniel to assure him I'm fine, then call it a night so that I'll be prepared to meet your household staff in the morning. They will not be enthralled by my presence."

"They will be as soon as they get to know you." Kirkland stood as she got to her feet. "Sleep well, my dear."

She hoped she would, but with her husband separated from her by only a connecting door, sleep might not happen.

Laurel had been right to say that his servants would not be enthralled, Kirkland discovered the next morning as he introduced her to his household staff. He was so glad to have her back in his life that he hadn't realized how many of the people around him felt protective on his behalf. That partisanship was demonstrated as soon as he introduced Laurel to Mrs. Stratton, the housekeeper.

Usually Mrs. Stratton was brisk but pleasant, with an easy smile. Not this morning. Her expression was flinty as she greeted her new mistress. "Good day, Lady Kirkland. Shall I summon the staff so you can meet them all at once, or do you prefer to go through the house room by room and meet them where they work?" She held up a small daybook. "I'll take notes of the changes you wish to make."

Laurel smiled and offered her hand. Even in her plain day dress, she had a quiet but unmistakable authority. "Good day, Mrs. Stratton. Naturally I wish to meet the servants, but I can do that as you guide me through the household. There's no need to take notes. Since I'll be dividing my time between London and Bristol, I intend to leave the management of Kirkland House in your experienced hands."

The housekeeper's expression thawed some-what. By the time they'd gone through half the house, she was back to her normal friendly self. Kirkland enjoyed watching his wife's charm disarm his servants. He realized he'd been foolish to worry about how well Laurel would deal with a large London household. She'd managed a larger and more complicated establishment for years, and was expert at evaluating people and problems. She not only knew the right questions to ask, but in several places she made suggestions so gracefully that Mrs. Stratton agreed without even noticing that the new mistress was making changes.

By the time they completed the tour of Kirkland House, Laurel had won respect and tentative acceptance from the entire staff. Not surprisingly, Mrs. Simond was the greatest challenge. She felt that she owed the lives of herself and her two children to Kirkland, and she would cheerfully take a carving knife to anyone who threatened him.

When Kirkland and Laurel entered the kitchen, the cook looked up with a scowl that sat oddly on her usually cheerful round face. After Kirkland introduced Laurel, the cook nodded brusquely. Her "My lady" sounded like a curse.

Undeterred, Laurel said, "Mrs. Simond, your cooking is superb! Everything from last night's soup to this morning's eggs has been masterly. Kirkland tells me that his guests often try to lure you away, so I hope you are content here. He deserves the best."

Softening a little, Mrs. Simond said, "His lordship has been that good to me, he has. He's got *my* loyalty for life." The implication was clear that Laurel had failed in the loyalty department.

Serenely ignoring the innuendo, Laurel said, "Kirkland said he generally leaves menus in your capable hands. Since that works so well, I certainly won't interfere, but I would like a tour of your domain." She smiled at the young scullery maid. "I'd also like to meet your assistants. Producing a fine meal takes many hands."

Mrs. Simond introduced the three young women who worked under her, then took Laurel and Kirkland on a tour of the pantries and the still room. Once again, Laurel's questions demonstrated her knowledge and appreciation of the work done here.

The tour was almost over when Mrs. Simond opened the door to the scullery and a furry black and white creature streaked out, bolting past Laurel and the cook with a frantic scrabbling of claws. It was a large, chunky tomcat. He ricocheted around the kitchen, but with no door open for escape, he had to settle for taking refuge in a corner under a wooden chair.

"Who's this now?" Laurel drifted toward the cat's hiding place.

"The kitchen cat," Mrs. Simond said with a

defensive glance at Kirkland. "Half wild and afraid of people, but good at getting rid of vermin."

"Every kitchen needs at least one cat. Does he have a name?" Laurel knelt, her skirts falling about her, and held out one hand as she crooned, "Aren't you the fine fellow? Do you realize how very lucky you were to have Mrs. Simond take you in?"

"I call him Badger 'cause he's black and white." Mrs. Simond regarded the cat fondly. "And because he likes burrowing under things. He's a timid fellow, for all that he's sizable. Won't let anyone touch him. He turned up in the kitchen garden half starving. I started to feed him and he came inside when the weather got cold."

"I'm sure he had a difficult life before he found you." Laurel rubbed her fingers together and the cat moved a little closer. He was mostly black, with white feet and muzzle and huge, tragic green eyes. "Will you let me pet you, Mr. Badger?"

Shy but drawn to Laurel's gentle voice, the cat emerged from under the chair and leaned heavily against her hand. He had a broad tomcat head and his left ear was ragged. When Laurel started to scratch his neck, he closed his eyes and purred rustily.

"He never did that for me!" Mrs. Simond said indignantly.

"Now that he feels safe, he's willing to be

cuddled, but because he's shy, he was waiting for you to make the first move," Laurel said. "May I pick you up, Mr. Badger?"

Carefully she slid her hands around him. Since he didn't object, she lifted him in her arms. He flattened his chin on her shoulder, purring steadily.

Laurel's face glowed above the black and white fur. "What a very fine cat, Mrs. Simond!" She moved so that the cat was within petting range of the cook.

Mrs. Simond stroked the furry head and he purred even more ecstatically. As Kirkland watched the love feast, he thought how much he and Badger had in common. Both of them wanted nothing more than to be cradled in Laurel's arms.

"You chose your feline assistant well, Mrs. Simond." Laurel gently deposited Badger on the floor. "May I come and visit him if I promise not to get in the way of your work? I miss my cat, Shadow, but he's too old to travel well."

Looking hopeful, Badger leaned against Mrs. Simond's ankle. The cook picked him up and he relaxed in her arms as he'd done with Laurel. Expression doting, Mrs. Simond said, "Of course you can visit, my lady."

Laurel and Kirkland took their leave and headed upstairs. When they were out of earshot of the kitchen, he remarked, "It's always good to charm the cook, but this is the first time I've seen a cat used for the purpose."

Laurel laughed. "Cooks and cats and kitchens always go together. Badger knows he's found himself a good berth here, and he's willing to express his appreciation."

"You were right that my household and friends would need to be won over, and you did so admirably," he said seriously. "You look . . . as if you could be happy here." Then he could have kicked himself for pushing her.

Her smile disappeared. "You have a lovely house and good people working for you, but the same could be said of a decent hotel."

He held open a door for her. "Most hotels don't have really good pianos."

Her expression eased. "There is that."

But it would take more than a cat and a piano to hold her here. He just wished he knew what would work.

Chapter 23

K irkland had five different offices, not counting the ones on his various estates or the workplaces in Scotland. There was his government office in a small, unmarked building with two cells in the basement. There was his shipping company office in the Kirkland warehouse amid London's dockyards. He shared an office with his friend Damian Mackenzie in the gambling club they co-owned, though Kirkland didn't do much of the actual work, except for the time when Mac had been officially dead.

There was also his study on the ground floor of Kirkland House, where he did the majority of his work. Lastly, a corner of his bedroom was equipped with a desk that he used when he wanted to work until he was tired enough to fall directly into his bed. That was the office he chose after Laurel retired because he could strip off his coat and cravat and boots and relax.

He was too restless to sleep, so he tried to study reports from France while quietly savoring the fact that Laurel was just on the other side of the connecting door. Since images of her sleeping in his arms—or in his arms and not sleeping— played havoc with his concentration, he decided to write some letters and later indulge in the results of some string toasting.

He'd written a dozen letters and the toasting was almost done when there was a knock on the connecting door to Laurel's suite. Surprised, he called permission to enter, and Laurel shyly entered his bedroom. She wore a plain dark robe and her bronze hair fell over one shoulder in a shining braid. He caught his breath, thinking that she had the lush, profoundly feminine beauty of a goddess—and he wanted nothing more than to worship her.

After an instant of delirious speculation, Kirkland accepted that there was nothing remotely seductive in her demeanor. Since she was followed by the soft-footed cat, Badger, he stood and said lightly, "Are you and Badger having trouble falling asleep?"

She smiled and pushed her braid back over her shoulder. "I am, though Badger has no sleeping problems. He was snoring with his head on my shoulder. I lured him to my bedroom for the company. I hope Mrs. Simond doesn't become angry with me about his fickleness."

"We all know the reputation tomcats have for visiting different beds," Kirkland observed.

"So very male," she murmured. "Actually, I'm here because I was awake and starting to feel hungry. I was about to head down to the kitchen when I noticed delicious scents coming from your room."

"String toasting is an old schoolboy custom." He gestured toward his fireplace where several apples and small, shallow pans dangled from strings in front of a fire. "Tonight is rather cold and foggy, so I decided to toast a small supper for myself. Apples are the traditional treat. I've added some small cheese melting pans."

Chuckling, she moved toward the fireplace and knelt to study what he was toasting. "Lady Agnes Westerfield never objected to her students driving nails into her mantels?"

"She knew how hungry boys are, so she made sure there were generous supplies of apples and cheese available to keep us from starving between dinner and breakfast." He smiled reminiscently. "I loved my years at the Westerfield Academy, and some of my best memories are of sitting by a fire toasting apples and building friend-ships."

"Daniel said he and you would debate theology and philosophy late into the night." Laurel rose and curled up in the wing chair that faced the fireplace, her legs tucked under her. "He never mentioned the string toasting."

"Being undignified, it was something of a schoolboy secret." Kirkland turned another wing chair to face the fireplace, keeping it far enough from Laurel's chair that he wouldn't be tempted to touch her. "But I'm far from the only grown man to still indulge. The apples aren't quite done yet, but I can offer you toasted cheddar on pilot bread, with claret to wash it down."

"What is pilot bread?"

"A simple, dry biscuit that keeps a very long time." Beside the fireplace was a square basket that contained utensils, wine, cheese, and a tin box of pilot bread. He removed a piece and handed it to Laurel. "Named for ship pilots. It hasn't a lot of flavor, but it's very common at sea because it doesn't spoil. Cheese improves it markedly."

She studied the simple square of baked biscuit. "Cheese with pilot bread, please. I think Badger will want some also." The cat had leaped onto her lap and was staring longingly at the cheese, his tail twitching.

Kirkland cut thin slices from the block of cheddar and laid them on the hearth for the cat. Then he poured melted cheddar onto the bread and handed the small plate to Laurel. "Not up to Mrs. Simond's standards, but unofficial food has its own charm."

"A very nice cheddar," she said after a bite. "Claret would go well with it."

He poured them both small glasses of wine, then settled into his chair for his own biscuits with hot cheese. He loved the quiet domesticity of sharing a fire and food with Laurel. It was the small moments like this that gave him hope for their future.

She ate several more biscuits with cheese and

sipped at her wine before saying in a low voice, "Your servants have practical reasons to accept me, but I'm worried about the dinner with your friends. When do you plan to invite them to meet me, and how large is the party likely to be?"

"In two or three days. Long enough for you to acquire suitable clothing." He made a mental count. "Five couples, if they're all in town and available."

"I trust the guest list has been carefully selected to include only people who will take a charitable view of my unwifely behavior?" she asked warily.

"The men are all friends from the Westerfield Academy, which proves they were never particularly conventional," he said reassuringly. "And none have married the sort of woman who condemns easily."

She sipped at her claret. "Have your friends known all along that you were married and abandoned? If so, they've had plenty of time to develop low opinions about me. And justly so since I was the one who left you."

"Ashton knows because he's the sort of man one can talk to when one's life falls apart." And Kirkland had fallen apart quite thoroughly when he'd told his friend what had happened. Ashton had sympathy and a grave acceptance that made it possible to reveal pain. "Mackenzie and Carmichael also know because they've worked closely with me for years."

"The others don't know you're married?" She began nervously breaking a piece of pilot bread into crumbs.

"I'm not sure about Randall, since he's spent much of his time dodging French bullets in various uncomfortable places. Wyndham wouldn't know because he was in that French dungeon. His wife, Cassie, is aware of the marriage, though none of the details." Kirkland studied Laurel's still profile. She looked less relaxed than earlier. "Prior knowledge won't matter, not after they meet you."

"You overrate my charm," Laurel said tersely. "Your male friends will probably be more accepting than their wives. Females, and I include myself in this generalization, are usually fiercely partisan where friends are concerned."

He uneasily recognized that she might be right—the wives he'd be inviting were indeed fierce on behalf of those they cared about, and they cared about Kirkland. Loyal and loving themselves, they might have trouble understanding how Laurel could abandon her marriage vows.

They would surely come around in time after they met her—even loyal friends wouldn't claim he was good husband material. But in the short term, it might be awkward for Laurel. "I promise none of them will try to scratch your eyes out."

She petted Badger, who was back on her lap. Firelight glinted off her gold wedding ring. "At least I have my attack cat to protect me."

Thinking it time for a change of subject, he said, "The apples look nicely roasted now. I usually sprinkle on sugar and cinnamon, but melted cheese would also be good."

"Sugar and cinnamon, please."

He forked a hot, juicy apple with crispy skin into a bowl, sprinkled sugar and cinnamon on top, and handed it to Laurel. "Mmmmm," she said after a bite. "No wonder schoolboys are so fond of roasted apples. This would be even better with clotted cream on top."

"Occasionally cream was available." He smiled fondly. "Food fit for the gods."

He ate his own roasted apple, the familiar flavors a soothing reminder of his school days. He was contemplating more wine when Laurel said, "You were at your desk when I came in. Do you ever stop working?"

He sighed. "Nowhere near often enough. I've been trying to cut back, though. I want to have time for my child. I've been training managers for my businesses and properties, and with the war against the French going well, my government work isn't as demanding as it once was."

"I suspect you haven't had a holiday since our honeymoon."

She was right, he realized. "After you left, there was no pleasure left in frivolity," he said dryly. "You, also, drowned yourself in work."

"That's true," she admitted. "I'm not quite sure

how to be a lady of leisure for the next month." She set Badger on the floor, then got to her feet as she covered a yawn. "But I can nap for much of the time. Gestation takes a surprising amount of energy."

He got to his feet. "I'm sure you're doing it as well as you do everything else."

Laurel hesitated before saying, "I hope so." She stepped up to him and brushed a light kiss on his cheek. "Good night, James."

Without conscious volition, his arms went around her and he pulled her close, her sweet body molding against him. In her nightgown and robe, she was all softness and warmth, with a faint scent of lavender. Warm, so warm . . .

For the space of a dozen heartbeats, she leaned into him, sighing with pleasure. Her arms slid around his waist.

His tenderness transformed into sharp, unruly heat. He bent his head for a kiss, his hand moving to cup her breast.

She stiffened, then pushed away, saying huskily, "This isn't why I came here tonight, Kirkland."

He swallowed hard and didn't reach to bring her back. "I know. But like a delicious roasted apple covered with cream, you're irresistible."

Her laughter lightened the moment. "A common apple, not one of Mrs. Simond's elegant treats. Yes, that's me." She turned and headed to the connecting door. "I think I'll be able to sleep now. Tomorrow promises to be a long and tiring day."

Badger was following her out. Kirkland looked at the cat. "I'm the one who gave you cheese, you ungrateful feline."

The cat turned and contemplated him, then trotted back into his room. Laurel smiled. "Cupboard love. I'll let you bear the weight of Mrs. Simond's jealousy if she finds out where Badger has been sleeping."

"My kitchen is supporting this beast's considerable appetite, so I might as well get some benefit." Kirkland scooped the cat into his arms and began scratching the furry neck. Badger began to knead Kirkland's chest happily.

As Laurel disappeared into her room, he set the cat on his mattress and undressed. He hoped it was a good sign that he'd managed to lure the cat to his bed.

Now if only he could do the same with his wife. . . .

Chapter 24

Madame Hélier's very exclusive salon was tucked discreetly behind Oxford Street, with only a brass plaque saying HÉLIER'S on the door leading up to the premises. As Laurel climbed the enclosed stairway, she smiled wryly at how the owner had chosen to be a floor above street level. One mustn't allow the vulgar to peer into windows.

When Kirkland ushered Laurel into the serenely tasteful showroom, she saw that the location allowed great swaths of sunlight to pour in through the wide windows. That had to be useful for choosing colors.

And there was color in abundance. The soft, neutral shades of the carpets and furnishings set off lengths of brilliant fabrics draped across two of the walls. Violet said in a low voice, "See how carefully they've chosen the display fabrics? Any woman who walks in here will see at least one color that will look splendid on her."

"You're right. Like this reddish-brown silk would become you." Laurel rubbed the fabric between two fingers to feel the sumptuous weight and texture.

"Devonshire brown." Violet gave the fabric a swift, longing look, then turned her attention to the other materials on display. "But we are here for you today, my lady. That blue silk would be lovely. Or that misty green. The gold brocade." She pointed out different lengths of rich materials.

Violet's color sense was flawless; even Laurel could see that. Laurel's gaze touched on a wide chest to one side. The massive piece of furniture had dozens of small drawers, each marked with samples of what was inside. Buttons of wood or shimmering seashell or exquisite Wedgwood china. Lengths of ribbon and lace and other trims. For the first time in her life, Laurel really understood the pure aesthetic pleasure of finery.

As Laurel and Violet enjoyed the colors and textures, Kirkland and Madame Hélier greeted each other in a friendly way. Laurel tried not to look for signs that Kirkland had expensively outfitted his mistresses at Hélier's, but saw nothing. Perhaps mistresses frequented different establishments.

After Kirkland introduced Laurel to Madame Hélier, the modiste said, "Lady Kirkland, welcome to my modest domain." Madame Hélier was a slim woman of middle years with a slight French accent, and she wore an elegant dove gray gown that displayed her talents. Her eyes were shrewd but thoughtful as she studied Laurel.

Kirkland said, "My wife needs a complete wardrobe so she will be prepared for all occasions, and it needs to be done slightly faster than is humanly possible."

As Madame Hélier laughed, Laurel said firmly, "I am not planning to have an extensive social life. I need only a morning gown and perhaps a walking dress, plus a more formal gown suitable for dinner with friends."

"She will need more," Kirkland said, his gaze slanting toward Laurel. "We have plans to attend the opera and the theater. Not to mention Astley's Amphitheatre."

"I can't wear the same gown again and again?" Laurel asked, knowing the answer.

"It would be remarked on if Lady Kirkland had only one evening gown," he said gravely. "I would be considered a neglectful and miserly husband."

She wrinkled her nose. "That wouldn't be fair to you, but too large a wardrobe seems wasteful."

"We shall begin with one each of morning, walking and dinner gowns to be created right away. More garments can be added later as needed," Madame Hélier said tactfully. "Lady Kirkland, what is your personal style? How do you wish to present yourself to the polite world?"

Laurel had never thought of her wardrobe in such terms. She didn't have a personal style, only clothing chosen for comfort and practicality so she didn't have to think about it much. "My personal style is casual to a fault. Violet, how do I want to look for the polite world?"

"Classic simplicity," her maid said without hesitation. "Timeless and flattering and dignified."

"A style not unlike Madame Hélier's," Kirkland said. "But with more color."

The Frenchwoman's brows arched. "I've never been singled out as a model for my clients." She flicked her hand at her soft gray gown. "Like the furnishings of my salon, I wish to be quietly in the background."

"But you have understated elegance," Laurel said as she admired the cut of Madame Hélier's gown. It fit perfectly and the fabric flowed around the modiste's trim figure. "I would like a similar look." She glanced at her husband. "With more color."

Kirkland smiled at her. "A riding habit will also be needed. Shoes and cloaks and all the underpinnings. Also, Violet, you have a talent for hairstyling. Would you like a session or two of tutoring by a master stylist?"

"Oh yes!" Violet's eyes rounded with excitement.

Laurel thought with amusement that being tricked out as a suitable countess might be tedious for her, but Violet was enjoying the process. There were other benefits for the girl as well since it was traditional for a lady to give discarded garments to her maid for reselling. With Kirkland insisting on outfitting his wife in high style, eventually Violet would earn enough from her mistress's castoffs to start her own shop.

"Lord Kirkland, it is time for us to take your

lady's measurements and perhaps fit a particular gown for her," Madame Hélier said. "Do you wish to wait in the gentleman's parlor, or will you be leaving now?"

"I brought some work with me, so I'll wait." He'd brought his lap desk, so he carried it with him as an assistant escorted him to a cozy side chamber. He was being asked his preference of tea, sherry, or some other beverage as he disappeared from view.

"At least my husband won't be bored," Laurel observed to Violet as they entered the fitting room behind the showroom.

"I brought a book of poetry to read to you if you need diversion, my lady. Lord Byron," Violet said. But her gaze was moving hungrily over the racks of rich, colorful fabrics. There were even more here than in the main showroom.

"It's time to remove your outer garments so we can take your measurements, Lady Kirkland." Madame Hélier gestured to a low dais. "If you will step up . . . ?"

Laurel handed her light shawl to an assistant and stepped up, but said, "I'm increasing, so my new gowns must have room to expand."

"Congratulations to you and your lordship!" The modiste looked genuinely delighted for them. "I shall make sure your new garments will look well from now right up to your time of confinement."

Laurel found that it was difficult to maintain her

distaste for the fitting process when everyone around her was so helpful and enthusiastic. Violet never did get around to reading poetry. She was too busy exploring every inch of the salon.

As Laurel's very ordinary gown was removed, she said quietly to the modiste, "That Devonshire brown silk in the showroom. Do you agree that it will suit my maid?"

"Oh yes. The color would bring out her golden skin tones."

"Add a dress length of the fabric to my order. I'm sure Violet will make a really lovely gown from it." The girl deserved something new, not a remade castoff.

Madame Hélier nodded approvingly. "It shall be done." She studied Laurel's stays and shift thoughtfully. "One of my assistants is a talented corsetiere, so we have available a supply of stays of different sizes and shapes. A fine dress requires a fine foundation. I would like you to try a set of Betty's stays."

"As long as they're comfortable," Laurel said warily.

"They will be. Once we have your measurements, Betty can make custom stays, but what is available now will do reasonably well."

With a sigh, Laurel let Betty remove her old, well broken-in stays and replace them with a new set that fit quite well and wasn't uncomfortable. She could get used to these, she decided, if she could be convinced they were of benefit.

Madam nodded approvingly when Laurel was laced up. "You must choose fabrics, and there is a draper's shop across the street if you wish a broader range of choices. But for today, I have a walking dress that should suit you."

She gestured to an assistant who disappeared into the adjoining room and returned holding a dark orange gown. "I keep a number of partially sewn garments here that can be quickly finished if a lady is in need of a new gown immediately."

Curious, Laurel asked, "Do all London modistes have so much fabric and trim and their own corsetiere?"

"No, Madame Hélier's is unique. I decided it would benefit my clients to offer as many services as possible under one roof," the French-woman explained. "I also offer swiftness without sacrificing quality." She held up the gown. "This color is called 'capucine' and will be splendid on you. Here, lift your arms so I can help you into it."

Laurel complied, and Madame Hélier dropped the gown over her head. After she tightened the lacing up the back, she did some swift pinning. "Very little work will be required to fit this to you properly. Turn and look in the mirror."

Laurel did, and her jaw dropped. She'd never worn anything like this rich, dark orange shade, and it did wonderful things for her hair and complexion. The gown was cut lower than what she usually wore, but not so low that she felt the need to reach for a fichu. There was delicate peach ribbon trim, and the garment flowed gracefully over her body, making her look simultaneously demure, dignified, and just a little provocative.

"Oh my," she breathed. "You were right about having the proper stays. How long will it take to finish this gown so I can wear it?"

"Less than an hour." Looking pleased, the modiste removed the gown and handed it to a pair of assistants to hem. "Would you like a cup of tea and perhaps some cakes while you wait? We can decide on fabrics and styles for the other garments. I also have accessories you might like."

"Tea would be very welcome." Laurel raised her voice. "Violet, I need your assistance in choosing materials and styles."

"While we are looking at samples, she can also restyle your hair." Speaking to Violet, the modiste said, "An upswept style like the one I have, yes?"

Violet nodded. "That will suit my lady very well."

Soon the round table at one side of the room was covered with tea cups, fabric samples, fashion plates, and meticulously dressed fashion dolls showing the latest styles. To her surprise, Laurel enjoyed discussing her choices with two experts.

By the time the capucine gown was ready to wear, Laurel had ordered half a dozen garments and numerous accessories, and she'd spent more of Kirkland's money than she wanted to think about. Her conscience twitched—but not as much as she'd expected.

Madame Hélier helped her into the gown, then tied a matching capucine ribbon around Laurel's throat. The final touch was to drape a magnificent patterned Indian shawl around Laurel's shoulders. The rich colors of the shawl were a perfect complement to the gown. "There, my lady! Admire yourself in that mirror, then go and show your husband how fine you can be."

Laurel studied herself in the long mirror. She looked like—a lady. Sophisticated and quietly confident and even, amazingly, fashionable. "You are a worker of wonders, madam." Head high, she left the fitting room, crossed the showroom, and opened the door to the gentleman's parlor.

Kirkland was frowning at a document, but when she entered, he looked up—and froze. In his eyes were surprise, approval, and desire. She slowly pirouetted so that he could see the whole outfit. "Behold Madame Hélier's work."

He rose, his gaze locked on her. "You look—exactly as you should. Like a lady. Like a countess. Like a woman who has accomplished important things and deserves all respect." He smiled. "You also look like a cat in a cream pot. Did you enjoy this more than you expected?"

"I did indeed." She also realized rather uneasily that she had moved from reluctant wife to a woman who wished to please her husband. She put the thought aside for future consideration. "Madame Hélier made it very easy for me and will keep the number of fittings to a minimum. She's promised a morning dress and a dinner dress for tomorrow, so I'll be ready for your friends when you invite them."

Amusement lurked in his eyes. "Just as you enjoyed this more than you expected, I hope you enjoy my friends more than you think you will."

Her animation faded. A modiste who was eager to please was very different from devoted friends who would have doubts about Kirkland's long-absent wife. But at least she would be well dressed for the interrogation.

Moody watched the passengers alight in front of Kirkland House with satisfaction. Captain Hardwick had been right that Kirkland was a bloody lord. Ah, the slave girl climbed out of the second coach. She was as hot a moll as any he'd ever seen. Even Kirkland's wife, whom Moody remembered as plain, looked worth a poke.

Wouldn't be long until the captain had his ship in London. Then it would just be a matter of grabbing the slut and sailing off with her. Moody licked his lips. After the captain was done with her, maybe he'd share.

Chapter 25

Violet was finishing her breakfast when Jasper Rhodes approached. He'd been very kind about introducing her to all the servants at Kirkland House, and she suspected that he might have worked behind the scenes to smooth her way.

But they hadn't really talked since the journey up to London. As Lord Kirkland's valet, Rhodes was one of the most important members of the household, and he seldom dined in the servants' hall. When he did, he was the object of attention from two of the young housemaids. Young, pretty, blond housemaids. Violet knew there was little age difference between her and the housemaids, but she felt ages older in experience, and sadly, she'd never be blond.

No matter. There were things she'd like to ask Rhodes, or stories he might find amusing, but she was here to work, not gossip, and lucky she was to have such a fine job. Nonetheless, she smiled when he claimed the empty chair beside her at the breakfast table.

"I've scarcely seen you, Violet, busy as we've both been," he said with a contagious smile. "But you're looking very fine. Do you like being in Kirkland House?"

There was a clean cup across the table, so she

poured him tea from the nearest pot. "Everyone has been very kind. I think you had a hand in that, so my thanks."

He shrugged and took a sip of tea. "I just said I thought you'd fit in well, and from what I hear, you have."

"Her ladyship is the best mistress I've ever had. I'd do anything for her." Which was true, but perhaps too revealing, so Violet continued, "I haven't seen much of you, though. You take your meals elsewhere?"

"Sometimes. His lordship has me doing some special work for him." Not elaborating, Rhodes asked, "What's this I hear about a self-defense class for females that will be taught in the ballroom this morning?"

"It was Lord Kirkland's idea. He knows a woman who fights well, and she's agreed to give us some basic lessons," she explained. "Every female in the household is invited to attend, from the countess on down."

Rhodes arched his brows. "Should I be afraid to ask you to go for a walk with me this afternoon since it's your half day? You may be wanting to practice your lesson on some unworthy male!"

Violet's pulse beat a little faster. "As long as you behave as a gentleman, you're safe from me. But is it allowed for us to go out together?"

"As long as we do our jobs well and act responsibly, there's no problem," Rhodes replied.

"Kirkland treats his servants like adults, not children, and those who want to learn and take on more responsibility are given the chance."

"I hope his idea becomes popular. In most households, servants are treated like something between children and thieves." And slaves were treated even worse. "But surely not all of Kirkland's servants live up to their responsibilities. What then?"

"They get one warning, and if they don't do better, they're gone." Rhodes finished his tea. "That's rare, though. Most everyone hired here appreciates their luck."

As Violet did. "Then if it won't get me discharged, I'd love to go out. We've visited some shops and every day I accompany her ladyship when she walks in the park in front of the house, but I've done no exploring on my own. I've not had the time." She sighed. "And to be honest, I've been afraid to go out alone."

"That's wise." Rhodes frowned. "I've learned more about that Captain Hardwick. He's a nasty piece of work and no mistake. But you'll be safe with me."

Having seen how dangerous Kirkland could be, it was easy to believe that his man might have some of the same abilities. Violet smiled with anticipation. "Let's hope the sun comes out by then."

"I'll put in a special order for more sunshine,"

Rhodes promised as he rose from his chair. "Till later, then. Enjoy learning how to beat up men."

Though she didn't know if she'd enjoy it, she intended to learn as much as she could. But not all men needed beating, and she was increasingly sure that Jasper Rhodes was one of the good ones.

"How did the self-defense class go?" Rhodes asked when they met in the servants' hall to go for their walk.

Violet gestured at the excitedly talking female servants who were pouring into the servants' hall. "It was wonderful! Look at how much everyone enjoyed the lesson."

"You can tell me all about it as we walk."

"I'd like to eat first." She studied a basket of fresh baked rolls that sat on a sideboard, ready to be served. "Learning how to beat off attackers gives one an appetite."

He scooped up two of the rolls and gave her one. "This should hold you until we reach Shepherd Market. It's nearby and there are good food stalls. As you see, I managed to procure sunshine for you, but I can't guarantee how long it will last."

Violet missed the sunshine of Jamaica, but she'd kill herself rather than return there to slavery. She collected her bonnet and shawl and they exited Kirkland House from the rear door, which led to the streets of mews that ran behind the grand houses of Berkeley Square. Equally grand carriages and horses were kept on the ground level of the mews, while grooms and coachmen lived in apartments above. It was a bustling place, though a girl had to watch where she stepped.

As she munched on her fresh roll, Rhodes said, "Tell me about the class." He took a bite from his own roll. "I want to know what to beware of."

"Our teacher is Hazel Wilson. I think she works for his lordship, but not here?"

Rhodes nodded. "I know Hazel. You wouldn't look at her twice in the street, but she is one very capable woman."

"She certainly is! She and Mrs. Stratton found several old feather beds in the attic and laid them out in the ballroom to cushion any falls."

"How many of the females in the household attended?"

"*All* of them!" Violet exclaimed. "Including Mrs. Stratton and her ladyship."

Rhodes's brows arched. "That's . . . disturbing that so many women felt the need to learn how to protect themselves."

"You've never been a woman, or you'd understand," Violet said tartly.

"Guilty," Rhodes said meekly. "What was Hazel able to teach in one morning?"

Violet considered how best to explain. "She said that self-defense begins in the mind. If you're out and about, be aware of what's around you. If a man makes you nervous, pay attention to the feeling and get away or prepare yourself if getting away isn't possible. If you're attacked, react immediately. Don't stand there passive as a rabbit hoping that the big bad wolf won't hurt you. Scream, kick, bite, shove. Fighting back will be enough to drive some attackers away."

"Hazel is right. What else did she teach you?" Rhodes asked.

"She said don't be afraid to get hurt, because you're apt to be hurt worse by your attacker. Since women can endure the pain of childbirth, they can endure being bruised when fighting to save themselves."

"That's good advice," Rhodes said. "If attacked, fight as hard as you can because in the terror and excitement, you probably won't feel much pain."

"What about later?"

He chuckled. "You'll feel the bruises then, but that's all right since the fight is over and you're safe again. What fighting tricks did she show you?"

"She said that learning to fight really well takes a long time, but there are simple things that any woman can do. Stick fingers in the man's eyes or throat or other soft, vulnerable spots." Violet made a V with her index and middle finger and jabbed sharply at the air. "Or bend fingers back."

She took Rhodes's hand and bent the little finger back until he yanked his hand away hastily and said, "Clever, and you don't have to be strong to do them. How did her ladyship do with the lessons?"

"Badly," Violet admitted. "She doesn't lack courage—I told you how she rescued me from a slave owner. But she found it impossible to strike another person."

He grimaced. "Truly kind, gentle people aren't good fighters. How did you do?"

Violet gave a smile that showed her teeth. "Very well. And I have the bruises to prove it."

"Good. You need to take care of yourself." Rhodes gestured at a narrow street on the left. "This leads into Shepherd Market. What would you like to eat? The meat-pie maker is one of the best in the city."

Rhodes was right; the meat pies were delicious. So was the baked jacket potato that dripped with melted butter and fresh herbs, and they washed the food down with the tangy lemonade from another stall. Shepherd Market was like a fair, with music and street performers scattered among stalls that sold food, produce, kitchen goods, and used clothing.

Violet couldn't remember when she'd had such fun. It was lovely to go out with a man she liked, and who liked her without making a nuisance of himself.

She was eyeing the gingerbread stall when Rhodes said, "Time to go. There's one more place

I want to take you on the way home. A confectioner's called Gunter's on the opposite side of Berkeley Square from Kirkland House. They make amazing fancy cakes, but they're most famous for their ices."

As they strolled back, enjoying the sunshine, she rather shyly took his arm. It was the first time she'd ever made any kind of advance to a man. He smiled and patted her hand where it rested on his arm, and did nothing to make her regret her action.

As they approached their destination, Rhodes explained, "This is a very fashionable tea shop. See all the carriages pulled up across the street by the park? The ladies eat their ices inside the carriages, their escorts lean against the railings to eat theirs, and waiters scurry back and forth across the street with orders."

Rhodes waved down a waiter who'd just delivered an order to a carriage and who was heading back into the shop. Violet couldn't hear what was said, but the waiter nodded and trotted back inside.

"The waiters are fast," Violet commented as another one darted across the street.

"Because the ices melt quickly. That's why everyone eats them right here. They'd be drinks if we tried to take them over to Kirkland House."

After a few minutes' wait, their waiter returned with their order and Rhodes paid him what Violet suspected was an extortionate amount. Rhodes gave her one of the small dishes, and Violet caught her breath when she saw that the ice was molded in the shape of a delicate pink flower. "How pretty! Let's sit on that bench behind those trees. It looks fairly private."

Rhodes agreed, and sure enough, by the time they reached the bench, the ice was starting to melt. Violet settled down in a fluff of skirts and sampled her ice with the small spoon. Her mouth filled with cold deliciousness. "This is wonderful! What's the flavor? It's not anything I recognize."

Rhodes looked at her with a smile that started deep in his eyes. "It's violet. They do several different flower flavors, and I was hoping that today they'd have violet."

Violet bit her lip, tears starting in her eyes.

Worried, Rhodes asked, "Would you rather not eat your namesake?"

She blinked back the tears. "It's just that . . . no man has ever tried to please me like this."

"I'm glad I'm the first." He scooped up a spoonful of his ice and offered it to her.

She leaned forward and licked the cold sweetness from his spoon, then offered a spoonful of her ice to him. He accepted it with pleasure.

The ices tasted even better when they exchanged them. Though the amounts were small and soon gone, Violet knew she'd never, ever forget this afternoon.

When they finished, Rhodes neatly stacked the dishes and spoons and set them on the ground below the bench. His gaze holding hers, he said seriously, "Any other girl, and I'd just try to catch a kiss. But because you are who you are, I will ask you whether you mind if I kiss you."

She caught her breath. "I am not a nice English girl."

"I know," he said softly. "That's why I find you so intriguing."

She studied his face, which she'd found very average when they'd first met. But the better she knew him, the more attractive she found his intelligent gray eyes, his laugh lines, the quiet competence he radiated.

Their shady corner under the plane trees felt very private. Private enough for a kiss. Wordlessly she leaned forward and touched her lips to his. He tasted of violet ice and kindness and tightly controlled desire.

He caught his breath, then kissed her back and she knew that her life had opened up in ways she'd never dreamed of.

She loved ices, and it was quite possible that she could come to love this man.

Captain Hardwick's schooner *Jamaica Queen* looked like any other fast cargo ship moored in the Pool of London. Nothing about the vessel proclaimed that it was a slaver, though when

253

Moody climbed aboard, he thought he smelled the faint, ineradicable stench of transported slaves.

The captain didn't make Moody wait long this time. He swung around in his chair and barked, "Have you found her?"

Moody nodded. "She lives in Kirkland House in Berkeley Square. I never seen her go out alone, but most days she and Kirkland's wife walk in the park, usually mid-afternoon. There's always a footman, but since it's fancy Mayfair, no one really expects trouble. Shouldn't be hard to grab the girl and bring 'er here."

Hardwick pursed his lips. "It would have to be timed to the tide so we could set sail right off. After all the trouble she's caused me, I want the bitch's mistress as well, so I'll need a large coach." He muttered a filthy oath. "Violet is turning into the most expensive bloody slave I ever bought."

"She's a damned fine-lookin' mort, but by the time you've had her for a few months and you're back in the Indies, you'll be bored enough to sell 'er. If she's not damaged, you'll get most of your money back."

The captain growled, "But I may want to damage her!"

Moody shrugged. Not his business what Hardwick did with his slaves. "What do you want me to do?"

"Keep watching. The more I know about their schedule, the easier this will be. When my cargo is ready and the tides are fair, we'll be ready." His tongue touched his lip. "I've waited bloody long enough!"

Chapter 26

Apart from the class in self-defense that convinced Laurel she'd better stay close to a protective man like Kirkland, Laurel had two days of lazy relaxation after visiting Madame Hélier. Kirkland was out a good deal of the days, presumably getting caught up on all the work he'd neglected in pursuit of his long-estranged wife.

That left Laurel free to sleep late, read, walk in the park in front of the house, make music, and nap. Kirkland joined her for meals and sometimes they played the piano for each other, though they didn't play together again. It was the most peaceful interval she'd had in more years than she could count.

But her holiday was over and it was almost time for the dreaded dinner party. As Laurel regarded her image in the mirror, Violet said, "This upswept style becomes you well, my lady." She twisted a tendril of hair so it fell just right onto Laurel's shoulder.

Laurel nodded agreement, but pointed out, "Perfection will vanish as soon as I leave my bedroom."

Violet smiled. "You will still look very fine and will impress the people who worry you. Now hold still while I brush a little color on your cheeks."

"I've become a painted woman," Laurel said wryly. But she had to admit that a hint of rouge made her look better, particularly when she was pale with nerves.

When Violet stepped back, Laurel stood and studied herself in the dressing table mirror. Madame Hélier's dinner gown was the same celestial blue that Kirkland had liked, but the cut and style were far superior to the dress she'd given away after the bloody death in the Zion House garden. She looked elegant in a quietly dignified way, and as close to beautiful as she could manage.

"I have a present for you, Violet. A thank-you for all your efforts to make me appear like a proper countess." Laurel had placed the Devonshire brown silk in her clothespress, so she retrieved the parcel and handed it to her maid. "I hope you enjoy this."

Violet carefully opened the wrapping, then stared at the richly colored fabric. "Oh, Miss Laurel! I've never had such a gift." She stroked the silk, tears in her eyes. "It isn't just the gift, but . . . but that you thought to give it to me."

"I'm sure you'll make the material into something truly splendid," Laurel said.

"Splendid and very, very special," Violet said softly.

A knock sounded on the connecting door. Violet brushed her eyes with her wrist, then opened the door so Kirkland could enter Laurel's room.

"Since you said you'd be wearing blue, Laurel, I have a small gift for you." He stopped in his tracks as Laurel turned to face him. "Oh my," he breathed. "You are always beautiful, but tonight you're—stunning."

She blushed. Yes, she liked pleasing him. "You look rather splendid yourself, my lord."

"Appearing like a fashionable man about town is a useful disguise." He offered her a small jewelry box, looking surprisingly shy.

She gasped when she opened the box. Inside was an elegant gold cross set with sapphires. It was accompanied by simple hoop earrings set with more sapphires. But even more important than the beauty was that it was a cross. As Violet had said, it was the thought to give such a gift that was most precious of all because, in this case, it was her husband's recognition that faith was a vital part of her life.

"How beautiful." She removed the cross from the box. The chain was a complex weave of gold links, and the sapphires flashed blue fire. "Just right with this gown. Violet, please remove my pearls." The double strand of pearls had been a gift from her parents on her sixteenth birthday and they were attractive but not particularly interesting. Tonight, she wanted to look interesting.

"I'll do it." Kirkland removed the pearls, the warm brush of his fingertips on her nape sending tingles straight to sensitive places.

Swallowing hard, she removed her pearl earrings and inserted the wires of the sapphire hoops. Then she stood very still while Kirkland fastened the cross around her throat. Mustn't think about the warm fingers heating her blood. . . .

The chain was just the right length, for the cross fell above the neckline of the gown. "Perfect." She turned to her husband. "You always know the right thing to do."

"Would that that was true," he murmured wryly. "Shall we descend? Guests will be arriving soon."

She took his proffered arm. "Forth into battle, my lord."

"Not battle," he protested. "Just a quiet dinner with friends you haven't met yet."

"I hope you're right!" As they left the room, she dismissed Violet for the evening. She guessed the girl would immediately start sketching designs for the silk.

When they stepped from Laurel's bedroom into the upstairs corridor, a burble of cheerful voices could be heard rising from downstairs.

"It sounds as if several of our guests have already arrived," Kirkland observed as they headed toward the stairs. "The Ashtons and Randalls would share a carriage since the Randalls stay at Ashton House whenever they're in London."

Ashton was a duke, Laurel recalled. "Ashton and Randall are such good friends?"

"They are. Ashton House is huge and when Randall was in the army, he was seldom in London and didn't need a full-time residence here. Ashton gave him his own suite of rooms for whenever he wants to use them."

The duke sounded generous. "Even now that both men are married?"

"Their wives, Mariah and Julia, are best friends." Kirkland smiled down at her. "You'll get it sorted out soon enough."

To Laurel, his words underlined the fact that these people knew each other very well and she was an outsider. She raised her chin. She hadn't expected this to be easy, but it was necessary if she was to move between Kirkland's house and her own. She didn't have to be best friends with any of these people. Civility would do.

As they approached the top of the steps, Kirkland said, "Now to present my friends with the surprise I promised."

Laurel stopped in her tracks, forcing him to stop also. "You didn't explain why you invited them?"

"You didn't want them to form judgments about you, so a surprise introduction seemed best."

Laurel's eyes narrowed. "This is one of those rare occasions when I understand the impulse to violence. A little push down the stairs . . ."

He grinned. "I really think this will be better because when they meet you they'll understand why I fell head over heels for you."

She rolled her eyes but stepped onto the stairs. "It's time to test your theory."

As Laurel and Kirkland descended, he patted her hand where it clasped his arm. For all the tension between them, she still found his touch comforting.

They moved into view of the people churning about the foyer. Four out of five of the couples invited had arrived. They were all good looking and intimidatingly well dressed, London's beau monde personified.

The chatter stopped and Laurel felt eight sets of curious eyes on her. "Good evening," Kirkland said, his voice carrying easily to those below. "Thank you for coming tonight to meet my wife, Laurel."

There was an audible gasp and the gazes intensified. The expressions of several of the men turned to granite, as did the face of one woman, an elegant redhead. The other guests mostly looked surprised.

Laurel and Kirkland reached the bottom of the steps and a strikingly good-looking blond man stepped forward with a smile. He was the one male who didn't look like granite, so presumably he didn't know the history. "Congratulations, Kirkland! This was unexpected. Have you just returned from Gretna Green with your lovely lady?" He bowed deeply. "It's a pleasure to meet you, Lady Kirkland."

These were Kirkland's closest friends and some

of them already knew part of the story, so Laurel would jolly well tell them the truth. "The pleasure is mutual, and will become even greater when I know who you are, sir. But we are not newly-weds." She smiled sweetly. "Kirkland and I have been married eleven years, separated for ten, and only recently have reconciled."

The blond man was briefly off balance, but he rallied quickly. "It took you a full year to realize Kirkland was impossible to live with? You must be very resilient!" he said with a laugh. "I'm Wyndham, by the way."

This was the man whose presumed death had indirectly led to Laurel leaving her husband? Wyndham seemed too light in spirit to have been imprisoned for ten years. "I'm so glad to see you whole and well," she said sincerely. "It's rather a miracle."

"Credit for that goes to my amazingly patient wife." He hooked an arm out and drew the redhead to his side. "Lady Kirkland, meet my wife Cassie. Lady Wyndham."

The redhead murmured a polite greeting. She didn't look hostile, exactly, but her gaze was sharp enough to cut steel.

Kirkland's hand came to rest on the small of Laurel's back with intimate reassurance. "Time to make our way to the drawing room. There's more space for introductions, not to mention sherry, claret, and other pleasures."

Relocating and serving drinks gave Laurel a few minutes to collect herself and study the guests. Thank heaven she'd visited Madame Hélier. If she'd been wearing one of her old gowns, she would have felt like a housemaid, and a rather shabby one at that.

Laurel hadn't much taste for alcohol, but she asked for a small sherry since it gave her something to fidget with. Kirkland brought her a glass. "Time for the introductions." He began with the Randalls, the reserved blond major and his petite brunette wife, Lady Julia. Lady Julia was the midwife, so Laurel hoped they could talk more later.

Then Kirkland escorted Laurel to a lean, dark man of middle height, mild demeanor, and striking green eyes. "Laurel, you've heard me speak of Ashton."

Kirkland had said the duke was the kind of friend one spoke to when life fell apart, and from Ashton's expression, it was clear he hadn't forgotten Kirkland's pain. For now he was withholding judgment, but Laurel suspected that Ashton would not be easily convinced that Laurel wasn't the villain of the piece.

Searching her memory, she said, "Besides the years at the Westerfield Academy, you were at Balliol College with Kirkland, weren't you?"

"Indeed we were." Ashton studied her face. "You share a strong resemblance with your brother Daniel."

Hearing her brother's name was steadying. He had been one of the Westerfield Academy students, after all. She felt less of an outsider. "So we've always been told."

"You must meet my wife." Ashton beckoned to a petite golden blonde. She joined him, tucking her hand around Ashton's arm with wifely familiarity. She was strikingly beautiful and Laurel sensed natural warmth, but like her husband, the duchess had her doubts about Kirkland's wife.

Kirkland said, "This is Mariah, sometimes known as the golden duchess."

Another golden haired woman who looked exactly like Mariah joined them. "And I'm Sarah, the poor relation," she said with a smile. "A mere golden countess."

Identical twins. Laurel's gaze moved from duchess to countess and back again. "Are the two of you often confused with each other? And when that happens, are you amused or irritated?"

The twins looked at each other and laughed. The duchess said, "It depends on the circumstances. Mostly I'm amused."

"I don't mind as long as no one tries to separate me from Rob." Sarah directed a dazzling smile at the tall, brown haired man at her side.

Her husband's handsome features seemed severe except when he gazed at his wife and his expression softened. "If anyone tried to separate us, they would fail," he said. His gaze moved back to Laurel. "I'm Kellington, Lady Kirkland. Though I've been Rob Carmichael for so long that I answer better to that."

His expression was assessing. Laurel remembered that Carmichael was another of those who knew that Kirkland had a long-estranged wife. She also suspected that he had reasons not to be fond of his title. A difficult father, perhaps.

"Do you prefer Rob, Carmichael, or Kellington?" she asked.

He smiled a little. "All three will do, in that order of preference."

"Very well, Rob." Laurel returned her attention to the twins. "I shall do my best to recognize the differences between the duchess and the countess."

Mariah asked curiously, "Based on less than five minutes of acquaintance, what differences do you see?"

During her years working in Bristol, Laurel had developed good powers of observation, but five minutes wasn't much. She scrutinized them individually. "I would say that you are more outgoing, duchess," she said slowly, "and your sister is quieter, but perhaps more confident. Lady Kellington's face is a little narrower." She studied the duchess, seeing a subtle, Madonna softness. "Have you recently become a mother?"

The sisters exchanged glances again. Sarah said, "She's very observant."

Mariah nodded. "My darling son is not quite four months old."

"In the future, I'll do my best to recognize you individually," Laurel promised, "but I'll surely make mistakes when I see one of you across a crowded room."

"As long as you at least try," Mariah said. "The most annoying people are those who just come up and ask which twin I am."

Sarah made a face. "Then they look disappointed to learn that it's just me, not the golden duchess."

"Tiresome," Laurel commented. "So sometimes you lie, because why indulge the curiosity of people who are too lazy to make the effort?"

The twins exchanged another glance. "That would be childish," Sarah said.

"And a duchess is never childish," Mariah said piously. "She is always a model of saintly decorum."

Her sister batted her lashes innocently. "As are countesses."

Their husbands broke into laughter. Rob Carmichael shook his head. "As you've probably deduced, Lady Kirkland, put Sarah and Mariah together and they're more mischief than two kittens in a sack."

The banter was interrupted by the arrival of the fifth couple, which produced a flurry of greetings. Sir Damian and Lady Kiri Mackenzie. He was a tall, broad fellow with an infectious smile while his tall, dark-haired wife was vividly attractive and had green eyes to match Ashton's. From the way Lady Kiri greeted Ashton, they were clearly brother and sister. Still more bonds within the group.

Kirkland appeared beside her. "Time for more introductions. Though you had misgivings, you're doing well, Lady Kirkland."

"No one has scratched my eyes out yet." She smiled wryly as her gaze scanned the group. "But the evening is young yet."

Chapter 27

With Kirkland at one end of the dining room table and Laurel at the other, they couldn't talk, but he could admire her smooth grace as a hostess. He knew that by nature she was reserved and rather shy, and she'd freely admitted that she was nervous about meeting so many of his friends. But she'd been raised as a lady, and in her Bristol years she'd dealt with people in all manner of different situations, including facing down a slave trader. As a result, she handled the dinner with aplomb.

When they'd finished eating, he gave Laurel a nod to convey that it was time for the ladies to withdraw and leave the gentlemen to their port. Instead, she asked the nearest footman to summon Mrs. Simond. When the cook appeared, looking wary, Laurel said warmly, "I don't think I've ever had a finer meal, Mrs. Simond. My thanks to you and your staff for your exceptional skill."

As Mrs. Simond beamed, other guests complimented dishes they'd particularly enjoyed. The cook was almost walking on air when she left the dining room.

Why had Kirkland never thought to summon Mrs. Simond to thank her? He considered himself as a fair-minded employer who paid good wages, but Laurel's public appreciation had a personal dimension that went beyond being a good employer.

Laurel had also had the tables in the main dining room rearranged so that the room felt less like a cricket pitch. She thought of things that he didn't—and that made life better for all concerned.

After Mrs. Simond retired to her kitchen, Laurel rose. "Ladies, it's time for us to withdraw so the gentlemen can solve the ills of the nation over the port."

After the wives left in a froth of bright silks and the men had reseated themselves, Mackenzie said with a grin, "I suspect the ladies' conversation will be interesting. Females are better at talking about life's more personal issues."

"Their conversation will probably be hair raising." Wyndham's glance shifted to Kirkland. "You do like your secrets, James."

"There are secrets, and there are also things one simply doesn't talk about. I'd planned to tell the world of our marriage when we returned after our long honeymoon." Kirkland poured a half glass of port, then passed the decanter to Randall on his left. "Then she left and there was no reason to mention that I had a wife." Several arched brows suggested that his friends weren't impressed with his explanation, but being friends, they wouldn't argue the point.

Friends. He scanned the faces of the men around

him. He'd known them all for over twenty years. All were intelligent, perceptive, widely experienced, had been tested in some of life's more searing fires—and all were happily married.

Since that last wasn't a state he'd achieved, maybe he should toss aside the English gentleman's stoic code and invite comments. Perhaps he'd get useful guidance. "I expect you're all keen to gossip about my situation, so feel free to speak up."

Randall said, a glint of humor in his eyes, "Gentlemen don't gossip about their friends' marriages. They analyze situations in a mature and thoughtful fashion."

Acute as always, Ashton must have sensed that Kirkland was hoping for insight. "Your wife isn't the kind of woman I would have thought you'd choose, but she's very lovely. Appealing. Enjoyable to be with." The duke frowned. "There's much more, but I'm having difficulty defining what makes her unique."

Even though Laurel had made it clear that a husband was not essential to her life, Kirkland still enjoyed being with her. Unfortunately, he was no expert at defining what made her special, either. "What kind of woman would you have guessed I'd choose?"

"I would have thought someone more like Cassie," Wyndham said. "A woman who has walked in dark places as you have. Though you can't have her. She's *mine*."

"I've come to think that a man and a woman can be too much alike." Rob Carmichael poured port and passed the decanter. "I don't think anyone can predict the right kind of partner. I never would have predicted Sarah for me." He grinned. "My imagination was nowhere near good enough."

"You look besotted," Ashton said with a smile.

"We're newlyweds so it's allowed," Rob retorted. "Though I can't imagine *not* being besotted with Sarah. She makes everything better by her mere presence."

"I think of Sarah and Mariah as the sunshine twins. If one of them walks into a room, it becomes brighter," Randall agreed. "When my uncle declared I needed a wife to secure the succession and all that nonsense, Mariah did her best to convince me that I must visit Hartley to become better acquainted with her sister."

"Lucky for me that Mariah's matchmaking failed," Rob said fervently. "I can't imagine why, when Sarah is so irresistible."

"She is lovely, charming, and amazingly intrepid," Randall agreed. "But from the moment I met Julia, I hadn't a shred of interest in any other female. I decided to stop by Hartley, not to call on Sarah and her parents, but as an excuse to see Julia since Hartley was her home, too."

"Mysterious are the ways of love." Ashton swirled the ruby red port in his glass as he pondered. "Mariah just looked right to me. She

271

filled a Mariah-shaped hole in my life that I hadn't even known was there."

Mackenzie laughed. "Whereas when I learned that Kiri was your sister, I knew immediately she was dead wrong for me. Not that the recognition did me much good."

"My sister is descended from Hindu warrior queens," Ashton pointed out with a hint of laughter in his voice. "You never had a chance to escape. Not that you seemed to have struggled very hard."

"Actually, I did try to resist," Mackenzie said seriously. "She deserved much better than a gambling house owner who was born on the wrong side of the blanket. But I'm so very glad that my resistance was futile!"

Ashton's gaze shifted to Kirkland. "Even though Laurel isn't what I would have predicted, you do seem right together. I think . . . I think it's because she seems to have depths that go down and down and down. Like you."

"You're right about the depths. I visited Daniel Herbert's home, discovered his little sister playing the piano, and was lost." Kirkland thought acerbically that Rob wasn't wrong to say that a man and a woman could be too much alike. But they could also be too different, as he and Laurel were.

"She's Daniel Herbert's sister?" Wyndham asked, startled. "We were good friends in school,

272

but for obvious reasons, I lost track of him. What is he doing now?"

"He was ordained when he finished at Oxford," Kirkland replied. "But he didn't enter the church because his true passion was for medicine. By studying very hard and probably not sleeping for several years, he acquired credentials as both physician and surgeon. He and Laurel have been operating a free infirmary in Bristol. As a change of pace from saving lives, he preaches sometimes."

Brows arched around the table. "Impressive," Wyndham said. "Though not really surprising. What part does your wife play in the infirmary?"

"Anything that needs doing. She manages the place, is an excellent nurse, and her personal project is a sanctuary called Zion House, for women and children fleeing abusive males."

"I wonder if Julia knows about Zion House," Randall said thoughtfully.

"Your lady wife has obviously not been wearing the willow during your estrangement," Ashton observed. "She's a woman of ability as well as depth."

"It sounds like she'll be hard to replace in Bristol," Rob said.

"Very true, so the current plan is for Laurel to spend part of her time in London and part in Bristol," Kirkland said.

That produced a noisy silence. None of his

friends would welcome the idea of being apart from their wives for substantial amounts of time, but they were too polite to say so. Wyndham broke the silence by saying, "Having a wife is wonderful but will complicate your life."

"She will. She has," Kirkland agreed. And he smiled ruefully.

After tea was served in the drawing room, the ladies relaxed on various chairs and sofas so they could converse casually while waiting for the gentlemen to finish their port. Lady Julia, petite, dark haired, and serene, sat on Laurel's right. Kirkland had said she was a midwife, though she didn't look like any midwife Laurel had ever seen.

The twins, equally petite but golden and laughing, shared a small sofa on the left. Lady Kiri, tall and with an exotic beauty that was different but equal to Violet's, chose a chair opposite Laurel. As she settled in, she exchanged a few teasing words with Lady Wyndham, red haired and reserved, who sat in the chair beside Lady Kiri.

The wives were as impressive as their husbands, which was saying a great deal. If there was one obvious trait shared by Kirkland's friends, male and female, it was intelligence. If Laurel knew them better, she'd doubtless add competence to the list.

Laurel's long estrangement from Kirkland was

the elephant in the room. The couples here tonight were Kirkland's closest friends and she needed to be on civil terms with them even if she'd forever be outside their magical circle of longtime friendship.

There would never be a better time to push the elephant into the middle of the circle. Laurel took a deep breath, then set aside her untouched tea cup. "All of you Westerfield wives are friends of my husband. You must be wondering about our separation and reconciliation, so ask any questions you like, no matter how blunt. I promise to answer honestly, with the understanding that what I say will remain private."

After a moment of startled silence, Lady Kiri said with amusement, "I begin to understand why Kirkland married you. If we are to be ruthlessly direct, we should set aside formality, I think. I'm Kiri, this dangerous redhead is Cassie, Lady Julia's personal name is obvious, and the twins are Mariah and Sarah. What is your Christian name?"

"Laurel." Despite her nerves, Laurel managed a smile. "I see that directness comes naturally to you, Kiri."

"It's a trait that has often been mentioned, and seldom in a complimentary way," Kiri said drolly. Turning serious, she continued, "Very well, tell us why you separated. You seem a rational woman, so I presume you had your reasons."

Julia held up a restraining hand. "A story begins

well before the crisis. It might be more useful to start with how you met and married. And I'd like to learn what you were doing in the years of your separation so I'll know more of who you are now."

"We met in the usual sort of way. Kirkland and my brother Daniel were good friends from the Westerfield Academy and Oxford. My brother brought Kirkland home for a visit and Kirkland discovered me playing the piano, which entranced him because of his passion for music." Laurel's mouth twisted. "If I'd been doing anything else, such as embroidering or working in the garden, he'd probably not have noticed me."

Cassie's brows arched. "Kirkland has a passion for music? I had no idea and I've known him longer than anyone else here."

A little surprised, Laurel said, "Music is his greatest pleasure, I think. He loves listening, and he plays the piano extremely well himself. We often played four handed."

"He kept both you and the music secret." Kiri's green eyes narrowed. "One can only wonder what other large secrets he has."

Anything to do with his work would be a secret, but Laurel wouldn't mention that, since she was unsure what the other women knew. "To return to the tale, he liked my piano playing, we were both young, and it was . . . love at first sight."

"So often that means lust as first sight," Mariah

276

remarked. "But they can end up being the same thing. How old were you?"

"Seventeen. We married a few weeks later."

"Your parents didn't think you should wait longer?" Sarah said, startled. "I admit that Rob and I had a very short courtship, but I was twenty-six and he's thirty-one and the courtship was . . . intense. Surely it would have been advisable to take the time to become better acquainted?"

"My parents were not the sort to risk losing a wealthy earl as a son-in-law," Laurel said dryly. She could see from her guests' expressions that they understood the implications of that remark. "But to be fair, we were both mad to marry. After the wedding, we had a wonderful long honey-moon in Scotland and the West Indies. Then we came to London to settle into normal life." She swallowed hard as she thought about what had happened next.

Seeing Laurel's discomfort, Mariah said, "We can return to the subject of the separation later. What have you been doing more recently? Not, I think, embroidering in your parents' parlor."

The duchess was observant. Laurel replied, "I've been working with my brother at his free infirmary in Bristol. I also created a refuge for women and children who have fled violent husbands." Laurel looked around the circle with a touch of defiance. "It has not been a ladylike existence."

Julia blinked. "Is your sanctuary Zion House?"

"You've heard of us?" Laurel asked with surprise.

An odd smile played around Julia's lips. "Last year, you were visited by a pair of women who asked to study what you have achieved because they wished to establish similar refuges in other cities."

"Yes, they were directors of the Sisters Foundation and they've been working with the Methodists," Laurel said. "Since then, they've started refuges in three other cities, and are planning more in the future. I'm surprised you've heard of Zion House."

Julia chuckled. "I'm the founder of the Sisters Foundation."

"And I'm a patroness," Mariah added. "We chose to work with the Methodists because they were already involved in social welfare and improving the lot of women."

"I had no idea that the founders were from the highest ranks of society," Laurel said, fascinated.

"Being a duke's daughter doesn't mean one is always safe from abusive men," Julia said with desert dryness. "My directors said they offered you a grant to help your work, but you told them you were sufficiently well funded and they should use the money to start new refuges."

Though Laurel could have found a good use for the two hundred pounds offered by the women from the Sisters Foundation, starting a new refuge in another city seemed like a better use of the grant. "Zion House is funded by the money Kirkland settled on me for my support," she explained. "He was very generous. Enough so to pay for Daniel's infirmary and Zion House both."

Cassie sat bolt upright in her chair. "I want to contribute to your foundation, Julia. The cause is one I support wholeheartedly."

Her voice suggested that she knew something of male abuse, but it also implied something else. Laurel scanned the faces of the other women. "I was vaguely assuming that all of you knew each other well, rather like Kirkland's school friends know each other, but that's not true, is it?"

"Definitely not," Mariah said. "Julia and I have known each other about three years since we lived in the same small town, Hartley, but I only met Kiri after I met Adam. Cassie I've met in the last fortnight." She smiled at her sister. "And though Sarah and I are twins, we weren't raised together. We only found each other about a year ago."

"Which is why we sometimes indulge in twin silliness," Sarah said with a chuckle. "We have so many years to catch up on."

"So I am less of an outsider than I expected," Laurel said.

"If you thought we're a tight little group that hisses at everyone else, you're wrong," Kiri said with a laugh. "But enough of the digressions. Why did you and Kirkland separate if you were so much in love?"

"We had just returned to London after a lengthy honeymoon, and Kirkland was about to send notices to the newspapers to announce our marriage since few people knew of it." Laurel dropped her gaze to her cooling tea. Though she had invited questions, the separation was still difficult to discuss. "Then . . . a man broke into our house, and I saw Kirkland kill him with his bare hands. Swift, brutal, and efficient. I . . . I was horrified to discover that my husband was a dangerous stranger. I left the next morning."

After a shaken silence, Julia said, "That would be deeply upsetting. But surely it was self-defense?"

Laurel sighed. "At the time, the killing seemed wholly unnecessary. When we reconciled, Kirkland explained some mitigating factors, but still."

"Violence is too often a fact of life," Cassie said slowly. "For a sheltered and very young wife, it would be particularly horrifying. Only monsters kill for pleasure, or for no reason at all. But sometimes, killing cannot be avoided."

"My mind knows that. My emotions have much more trouble with the lethal reality." Laurel swallowed hard. "The night before we left Bristol to come here, not even a week ago, he once again killed a man in front of me. It was completely justified because his action saved the life of a woman who was very nearly murdered by her husband. And yet . . . and yet the sight of his violence made me ill."

"Even though he saved a life?" Kiri frowned, trying to understand.

"We are what we are," Julia said. "For someone who is a healer by nature, violence is particularly dreadful. As a midwife, I understand this." She paused, then said deliberately, "I once killed a man. It was an accident, but the death still haunts me."

Kiri's green eyes rounded. "How dreadful! What happened?"

"My first husband was beating me," Julia said, her voice flat. "I shoved him as I tried to escape, and his skull smashed into the fireplace."

Her words created a horrified silence until Sarah said tautly, "I have also killed. Not that long ago, and not by accident."

"What happened?" Julia asked in a gentle voice.

Sarah swallowed convulsively. "Evil men planned to slaughter a party of girls and women, including my young stepdaughter. The men deserved to die. I regret nothing. But dear God, the nightmares!" Tears showed in her eyes.

Mariah slid across the sofa and put her arm around her sister's shoulders. "Thank heaven Rob is there when you have nightmares," she said softly.

"Thank heaven indeed," Sarah whispered.

Stunned, Laurel said, "I know that much of my

life I was sheltered, but is murderous violence common and I've just been lucky not to see more?"

Cassie sighed. "Mercifully, it's not common. But since we are being ruthlessly honest with each other, I have killed, and more than once. I have no regrets and no nightmares about my actions." She bit her lip. "My nightmares are of the people I couldn't save. But my life is not common. For many years, I was an agent moving between England and France. It was a long madness, and I'm glad that it's over."

So Cassie had been an agent. Putting the pieces together, Laurel said, "Kirkland mentioned that you were the one wife here who knew he was married. Since we're being ruthlessly honest, I shall ask this. Were you one of Kirkland's lovers? Did he tell you he had a wife over his pillow?"

Cassie looked startled before her face eased into a smile. "It was over a pillow, but not the way you think. Kirkland had a bad fever attack. You know about them?"

When Laurel nodded, Cassie continued, "His condition was very dangerous and he couldn't be left alone. Those of us who sat with him had to be trustworthy in case his ravings revealed any of his many secrets. In one of his deliriums, he spoke of his wife in heated but very complimentary terms."

She smiled impishly. "I won't deny that I found him attractive and if he had made advances, I would have considered it. But he never did. I'm sure he thought it would be bad policy to become involved with one of his agents, and of course he was right." She caught Laurel's gaze. "I swear that I was not his mistress."

"No, you weren't the lover of Laurel's husband," Sarah said coolly. "You were the lover of *my* husband."

Chapter 28

Without moving a muscle, Cassie came alive with dangerous alertness, as if uncertain whether Sarah might attack. She looked very like Kirkland had when he was killing Bailey, Laurel realized. The room pulsed with tension as the other women watched Cassie and Sarah. Mariah was frowning.

Voice soft, Cassie said, "Yes, we were lovers on and off for years. I thought of him as my best friend. I didn't realize that he thought of me differently until I met Grey and discovered—hope."

"Hope?" Sarah's brows arched.

Cassie rose and moved restlessly around the room. There was a curve to her abdomen that suggested the middle months of pregnancy. "Rob and I had both lost so much that we had little to give to each other except . . . some kindness on the rare occasions we were together. Between his work and mine, that wasn't often."

"Rob referred to you as a companion who dealt with danger, as he did," Sarah said, her gaze following Cassie. "He thought someday the two of you would be able to settle down together."

"In a cottage by the sea," Cassie murmured. "But since I never expected to survive the wars, I had no plans for the future." She turned to face Sarah. "Despite all he suffered in prison, Grey has a . . . a brightness of spirit that changed me even when I didn't believe we could have a future. I think you do the same for Rob. You give him a lightness and warmth that I could never have managed."

"Yes, and he gives me the steadiness I need." Sarah met the other woman's gaze. "Thank you for the kindness you gave Rob when he needed it, Cassie." She grinned. "And thank you for being fool enough to let him go!"

Visibly relaxing, Cassie returned to her chair. "I'm glad you're being so civilized! I was worried you might try to scratch my eyes out."

Sarah laughed. "I doubt I could if I tried. Not that I would try. You are part of what made Rob who he is, and I love who he is."

Laurel had been watching the other two women with fascination. "I was so worried about meeting you all, even though Kirkland said I shouldn't be. But he was right. You are remarkable." She smiled a little. "I rather thought it would be my eyes that would be scratched out for leaving Kirkland."

"No one can judge the truth of another marriage," Kiri said seriously. "That said, you are the one who opened the door to all this ruthless honesty, but you have not completed your story. We know why you left Kirkland, but what has brought you back together again?"

Laurel had asked for this, hadn't she? "Kirkland was in Bristol meeting with the captain of one of his ships. When he left the port, he suffered a fever episode and then was assaulted by two thieves. He was brought unconscious to our infirmary. My brother was away and I was the only one available to treat him."

"That must have been quite a moment when you discovered the identity of your patient!" Mariah exclaimed.

"An understatement of massive proportions," Laurel said fervently. "His injuries weren't too serious, but he was feverish. After I patched him up, I dosed him with Jesuit's bark tea and that reduced the severity of the fever attack." Her hands clenched. The next part was where it became difficult.

When Laurel's silence stretched, Kiri said, "Please, we are perishing of curiosity! Though perhaps I can guess what happened next."

Blushing violently, Laurel said, "Attraction . . . had never been a problem. He was delirious, I caught him to prevent a fall, and . . . I leave the rest to your imaginations."

"And we all have vivid imaginations!" Sarah exclaimed. "So the next morning you decided to reconcile?"

"You overrate my honesty," Laurel said ruefully. "Kirkland was out of his head and had no recollection of what we'd done. I was horrified by my temporary madness, so in the morning I pretended that nothing had happened. We said civil farewells and I thought that was that. Then"—her hand went to her abdomen—"I found I could not pretend that nothing had happened."

"So you're with child!" Julia said. "I wondered. You have the look. That is certainly an excellent reason to put the past behind so you can build a future together."

"But I don't know how to do that!" Laurel looked at the other women pleadingly. "Of course I had to tell Kirkland, but I wanted to quietly raise the child in Bristol. As busy as he is, I couldn't imagine he'd be very interested, particularly if it's a girl, but he *is* interested. He persuaded me that even if we didn't fully reconcile, we must become friendly again. Enough that our child can move back and forth between our households. That made sense, so I agreed to come to London for occasional visits. I know he wants more, but whenever I think about that . . ." Her voice choked off.

"You see him breaking a man's neck," Cassie said quietly.

Laurel swallowed hard. "I can't stop caring, but he is not the man I thought I was marrying. We are too different. We always will be."

"You should think less about the death of villains at Kirkland's hands and more about the vows you took," Julia said with unexpected tartness. "For better or worse, Laurel. Of course you didn't know everything about the man you married. No one ever can. Marriage is a leap into the unknown, holding the hand of the person you have pledged yourself to. Remember that he doesn't know all about you, either. Because you loved, you promised. You must try harder to keep that promise."

Laurel jerked back at the uncompromising words. Before she could think of what to reply, Sarah mused, "I wonder why he didn't come after you when you left. He's not a man to give up easily."

"He never gives up," Kiri agreed. "Not *ever*. Yet he let you walk away."

Through numb lips, Laurel said haltingly, "Very well, since we're being honest—I thought he let me go so easily because he didn't want me. The honeymoon was glorious and he'd talked about holding a grand ball to announce the marriage to everyone in London. But I think that when we arrived here, he realized I was just a provincial girl of no great charm or wit or beauty. After I left, he was free to live as he chose."

"You underestimate yourself," Mariah said with compassion. "He certainly seems to want you now."

Laurel shrugged. "Now that he's older, he must be concerned about getting an heir, and for as long as I live, I'm the only possible source of an heir.

288

He can't divorce me for adultery since I haven't lain with another man, so yes, he wishes to reconcile."

Cassie shook her head. "You also underestimate Kirkland's stern Presbyterian conscience. I'd wager half my fortune that he felt profoundly guilty for killing even if his victim was a villain. He might have thought your leaving was the punishment he deserved. Now he's getting a second chance, and he's trying to rebuild what was broken. I saw the way he looked at you. There is no question that he wants you as his wife."

"The real question is what you'll do about that." Julia bit her lip. "I speak from experience about vows. My life was being threatened by my former father-in-law, who thought of me as the murderer of his only son. Even though we scarcely knew each other, Randall offered marriage as the best way to protect me. I was reluctant, and for the first months I had one foot out the door, ready to bolt. It wasn't until I closed that door and committed myself to the vows I'd made that our marriage became real."

Laurel stared at her interlocked fingers, which were white with tension. "You're right. It is perhaps understandable why I left him. I was very young, and very horrified. But now . . . I am a woman grown, and I have seen how complicated the world is. I . . . I must do better than I have. I *will* do better. I just . . . have to figure out how."

The silence was broken by Sarah. "I don't know if I should speak up when I've been married the shortest time of anyone here," she said hesitantly. "But it seems to me that physical intimacy strengthens all the other bonds of marriage. The emotional intimacy, the trust, the commitment. Without that physical intimacy, it might be impossible to accept the aspects of Kirkland's nature that shock you. You said that your head accepts his actions but your emotions won't. Perhaps you should give your emotions more reason to trust him."

"In other words," Kiri said irrepressibly, "return to your husband's bed and everything may sort itself out."

A wave of heat passed through Laurel. Kirkland might not remember that mad coupling at the infirmary, but she most certainly did. Suspecting her face was scarlet, she said, "I'll have to have a serious talk with my conscience. Is it right that doing something so pleasurable should dissolve my moral objections to murder?"

"Don't think of it that way," Cassie said seriously. "Yes, you have a visceral abhorrence of violence, but there are different kinds of violence, and Kirkland has restricted himself to the more honorable kind. If you strengthen your bond with him, perhaps you will no longer be ruled by your revulsion."

Could rekindling the fierce passion Laurel and

Kirkland had shared change her to the point that she could accept her husband's dark side? Laurel bit her lip. Certainly passion would change the shape of their marriage, and that might be for the better. "I shall have to think about that. You might well be right."

"Or she might be wrong." Mariah had a private smile. "But it is worth thinking about. Mating in all senses of the word does change everything."

Laurel surveyed her companions. "I thought that my estranged marriage was an elephant in the room, so I should shove the beast into the middle where it could be acknowledged and dealt with. I think that has happened."

"I think that elephant has been sliced into cutlets and grilled over a fire," Kiri said with a laugh. "Having ridden elephants, I can say that is no small feat you have achieved. I commend your courage, Laurel."

"Thank you," Laurel said shyly. "I'm very glad we've—banished the elephant together." As she looked around the circle of women, she realized they could all become friends—and were well on the way to achieving that.

The drawing room door opened and the gentlemen ambled in, all of them gravitating toward their wives. Except Kirkland, who entered the room last, his expression contained and impossible to read.

"Have we interrupted anything hair raising?"

Mackenzie asked with a grin. "When I thought of the six of you in one room with a teapot, I found myself alarmed by the possibilities."

Kiri caught his hand and drew him to her side. "And well you should be! We have vanquished an elephant. What, pray, did you gentlemen discuss over your port?"

"Nothing the least bit interesting," her husband said promptly. "Affairs of state. Very tedious."

Wyndham chuckled as he bent to brush a kiss on his wife's head. "Don't believe a word he says."

Cassie smiled up at him, her face coming alive. "Did you know that Kirkland is an accomplished pianist and a lover of all things musical? I didn't."

"I didn't, either," Wyndham said, surprised.

Mariah covered a yawn. "I wish to make an early night of it, but it's been a remarkably fine evening. Thank you, Lord and Lady Kirkland."

"I also want to return to my daughter," Julia said thoughtfully, "but I was hoping that perhaps we might have a brief recital? Laurel also plays the piano, and I suspect she is very good. She says you often played four-handed pieces."

Laurel's gaze shot to Kirkland. After a barely noticeable pause, he said, "Laurel plays superbly, so I don't see why not. Unless you're too tired, my dear?"

"Never too tired for music." She rose with a smile and a mild inner curse aimed at Julia, who was creating a situation to draw Laurel and her husband together. It wasn't a bad impulse, but too soon! Laurel had so much to think about.

But Kirkland was smiling and ushering her toward the stairs. "Shall we do something from Vivaldi's *Four Seasons*? That was always a favorite of ours."

" 'Primavera,' " she said. " 'Spring.' " The season of growth and rebirth, and may it symbolize what she was going to attempt.

"That's always been my favorite of the concertos," he said. "A good end to a good evening."

The music room had enough seats for all the guests, though there were none to spare. As two footmen lighted lamps, Laurel settled on the piano bench and flexed her hands, then ran her fingers lightly over the keys in the lilting bars of a serenade her nurse had sung to her when she was a child. As always, music calmed her.

The bench creaked as Kirkland sat down on her left. She felt the warmth of his body teasing her nerves. *Don't think of him as a murderer, but as a brave man who does what is necessary no matter what the cost to himself. The man you vowed to love and cherish, for better or worse.*

Because you loved, you promised. You must try harder to keep that promise.

Try harder.

She stilled her hands and glanced over as Kirkland readied himself, his long, elegant fingers stroking out a progression of deep chords. At seventeen, she'd thought him the handsomest man she'd ever met. Years and pain had given him the finely drawn beauty of a medieval saint.

If he'd married a woman who could have accepted him as he was, there wouldn't be such pain in his face. He'd be a happier man if he'd never met her.

And if she'd never met him? She couldn't imagine what her life would be like. Simpler but narrower. Less rich.

Try harder.

When he was settled, he gave a nod and they began, the swift notes dancing from their fingertips. The first movement vibrated with life. When she made swift little soprano improvisations with her right hand, Kirkland grinned and did matching improvisation in the bass notes with his left hand. Unlike when they'd played several days earlier, she didn't resist the way their rhythms matched.

Once the side of her left hand grazed his fingers and a shock went through her. He didn't seem to notice, but she'd taught him to be wary of her. To be separate.

Try harder.

She gave herself to the joy and fulfillment of the music. When they ended the concerto, she allowed the notes to fade. Then on impulse she began to sing one of the songs they'd loved to sing together as she softly played the accompaniment.

Drink to me only with thine eyes,
And I will pledge with mine.

After a startled instant, Kirkland joined in on the next lines, his gaze holding hers.

Or leave a kiss within the cup
And I'll not ask for wine.

At first his rich baritone was rusty, as if he'd not sung for years, but by the next stanza, their voices were blending as if they'd never stopped singing together. She forgot their audience, forgot their long estrangement. All that mattered was James, and the mesmerizing passion that had bound them from the first.

When they finished the song, she remembered where they were and blushed for the intimacy of what they'd revealed. She glanced at their audience, and saw that Kirkland's friends were staring as if he'd grown a second head.

Then the room filled with applause. It sounded like many more than ten people clapping. Someone, Wyndham or Mackenzie, cried, "Encore, encore!"

When the applause ended, Ashton said, "You've been holding out on us, Kirkland! I had no idea you were so musically gifted."

Laurel and Kirkland turned toward each other, laughing. "We make beautiful music together!" she exclaimed.

"Indeed we do," he said, but she saw that he was withdrawing. Maintaining the distance she'd put between them.

When they rose from the polished bench, she extended her hand. "My lord?"

"My lady." He took her hand and they took their bows. His hand felt right in hers. Strong. Steady.

And as she looked over their audience, Lady Julia Randall nodded approvingly.

Their guests left, and Laurel's energy departed with them. Physically drained but mind whirling, Laurel said to Kirkland, "You were right. Your friends' wives are an impressive lot, and no eyes were scratched out."

"That's good." He cocked his head. "But what was that about an elephant?"

She laughed, then hastily covered a yawn. "I'll explain another time. For now, I'm exhausted."

"I imagine you'll sleep well now that you're no longer worried about meeting my friends."

"That worry is removed," she assured him. But as she headed to her bedroom, she doubted she'd sleep easily. She had far too much to think about.

For too long, Laurel tossed restlessly as she pondered what the Westerfield Wives had said. It was certainly possible that becoming Kirkland's wife again in all ways would change her so that she could better accept that his lethal abilities were not a crime but a dangerous gift.

But she might *not* change enough to be able to deal with his possible violence, and if, God forbid, she saw him kill again, she might shatter. Surely that would be worse for both of them than the present uneasy truce.

It didn't help to know that passion was a powerful enough lure to distort her judgment. A woman could delude herself about anything if it meant she could lie with a man like Kirkland. . . .

With nothing resolved, Laurel finally fell into restless slumber, only to be jerked awake when she heard a low, despairing cry. After she blinked awake, it took her a moment to realize that she was in Kirkland House, and the distressing sound came from the other side of the door that connected to Kirkland's bedroom.

She sat bolt upright, listening hard. Another cry, barely audible, but unmistakably despairing. She slid from the bed and darted barefoot to the door. The knob turned easily under her hand and she moved soundlessly into his room. It was dimly illuminated by a lamp turned very low. Kirkland moved restlessly in the bed, his eyes closed. His face and shoulders were bare and sheened with sweat.

Worried that he was suffering a fever attack, she moved to the side of the bed and laid a hand on his forehead. Though his chest was heaving and he was in distress, he didn't feel feverish.

He jerked away from her hand and mumbled something unintelligible. Hoping he wouldn't use some lethal fighting trick, she shook his shoulder gently to pull him back from whatever dark place held him.

"James, wake up, you're having a nightmare," she said soothingly as she wondered what dark dreams haunted his nights.

Chapter 29

"Y ou're having a nightmare."

The warm, familiar voice pulled him from the horror of falling through darkness, anguished and forever alone. Beside him, Laurel was a pale shape standing at the head of his bed, her hand resting on his shoulder.

"Laurel." Driven by pure instinct, he rolled over and wrapped his arms around her waist, then dragged her onto the bed with him. "Laurel," he said again, his voice rasping. "Sorry . . . to have woken you."

If he'd been more rational, he would have expected her to pull away, but instead she settled back on his pillows and drew him close, his head on her shoulder and her warm arms cradling him. He closed his eyes, shaking, wondering if this embrace was a cruel, taunting dream. If so, he hoped it never ended.

"I do enough nursing to be a light sleeper, so I wake easily," Laurel said, her voice soothing as warm chocolate. Her hands caressed the taut muscles of his back, releasing some of the iron strain. "Do you have nightmares often?"

"I don't know because I'm asleep then." His ragged attempt at lightness was undercut by the fact that he was still shaking. He buried his face between her neck and shoulder, feeling that he'd gone from hell to heaven. Lavender and the uniquely Laurel scent that he would recognize anywhere.

One of her warm, strong hands kneaded the back of his neck. It felt unbelievably wonderful. She murmured, "Do you remember what haunts your sleep?"

He couldn't bring himself to describe the endless falling through dark, lonely despair that was the worst of his nightmares. Even thinking about that made him feel too vulnerable. But he was not short of other nightmares. "The mistakes I've made. The lives my mistakes have taken." He swallowed convulsively and tried to slow his breathing. "The knowledge of my appalling effrontery for making the decisions that cause such damage."

"It's never easy to deal in questions of life and death." Her voice was soft in his ear. "Bad enough for a doctor like Daniel, who struggles against injury and disease, but that's a relatively straight-forward business. It must be far worse to send people into danger. You take on those respon-sibilities because someone must. At least you have a conscience. If anyone must deal in life and death, I'm glad it's someone like you."

He sighed roughly into the thick braid of her hair. "No doubt you're right, but it would be a lot easier if I didn't have a conscience. Or better yet, if I always know what is the right thing to do."

"Infallibility is reserved for the Almighty." She rested her cheek against the top of his head. "You've surely made mistakes. Who hasn't? But you've also done things right. You saved Princess Charlotte from kidnapping and the royal family and others from assassination. You rescued your friend Wyndham from imprisonment long after anyone else would have given up on him. You were responsible for bringing Mrs. Simond and her children out of France. Surely those things balance the mistakes."

He shrugged. "Most of the work was done by my colleagues. They're a rare lot, and they deserve the credit."

"In other words, your Presbyterian conscience says that if something goes wrong it's your fault, and if something goes right, the credit goes to others?"

He laughed a little. "That's how it works." Of its own volition, his hand stroked down her waist and over her hip. He made the hand stop, but couldn't force himself to remove it entirely.

Needing talk for distraction, he said, "In the case of Mrs. Simond and her two children, the heroine was Cassie. The Lady Wyndham you met tonight. She was one of my best agents for years and I miss her skills, yet I regularly thank God that she decided it was time to retire from spying."

"Why did she decide to do that after so many years?" Laurel asked.

"Because of Wyndham. They are each other's salvation." Kirkland smiled into the darkness. "That was an outcome I never could have predicted, yet when I see them together, it's clearly so right."

"Now she has someone to live for. And another someone on the way, if I'm interpreting her figure correctly." Laurel's fingers drifted through the hair at the back of Kirkland's neck, sending him into full, throbbing arousal.

"You are. Wyndham is equal parts ecstatic and terrified." Kirkland shifted his position so she wouldn't notice his erection, because once she did, she'd leave, and he couldn't bear that. Holding her was too precious to risk. Dear *God*, but she smelled wonderful!

Laurel chuckled. "From what I've seen, happiness and terror are normal for a man about to become a father. That was the case with you, wasn't it?"

"No," he said softly. "I was entirely happy when I learned of it."

After too long a silence, she said, "I suppose the terror was mine."

He suppressed the pain her words caused. "No happiness at all?"

"Oh, yes, I've always wanted a child and had given up hope of having one." She laughed ruefully. "But the circumstances are certainly complicated!"

He couldn't deny that. But he didn't miss the bleak years of shutting down his emotions and concentrating all his time and energy on his secret government work and his public role as earl and shipping magnate and all the other responsibilities he'd taken on to give himself a reason to get out of bed every morning.

Speaking of complications . . . He was lying on his right side with his head pillowed on Laurel's left shoulder. And while his thoughts wandered, his left hand, his traitorous left hand, had caressed up her torso and was now coming to rest on her right breast. She'd always had beautiful breasts that were surprisingly full given her slim height. The past ten years had made them even more lush.

Carefully, since he'd heard a woman's breasts became extra sensitive during pregnancy, he thumbed her nipple. It immediately became rigid and Laurel gasped.

He forced his hand to become still. "This is where you say this isn't what you came for, after which you take a polite leave."

She laid her hand over his, where it rested on her breast. "Actually, I . . . I did come for this, James, though it wouldn't have happened tonight if not for your nightmare."

He froze, wondering if he was delusional again. "Perhaps . . . you might clarify your meaning?"

Because the night was warm, he wore only a pair of drawers, so he felt the heat of her palm as her hand glided down his torso. Then her questing fingers slid under the waist of his drawers and clasped him firmly. Lightning blazed through his veins. Every fiber of his body was on fire and he briefly forgot how to breathe.

"Is that clear enough?" she asked with a mixture of shyness and laughter.

"Dear God, Laurel!" he groaned as he remembered speech again. "Are you sure of what you're doing? Because if you don't leave *right now,* I don't think I'll be able to stop." Even now he wasn't sure, but his last ragged shred of honor needed to hear that she had no doubts that could turn into agonized regrets.

She took a deep breath. "I know I'm opening Pandora's box, but I'm sure that I want to. My fears and reservations have kept us in limbo. It's time to move forward, though I don't know if I'm sending us to heaven or hell." She squeezed him with her warm hand and his last shreds of rationality disintegrated.

"Maybe I'll be in hell tomorrow, but this is certainly heaven now," he breathed. Knowing he'd last only moments if he allowed her to continue, he removed her hand and rolled above her, pinning her wrists beside her head as he leaned into a kiss.

Her mouth and lips were softly welcoming, her tongue a serenade. This was how they'd kissed when they were newly wed and overflowing with passion. He was drunk with the taste of her, with the yielding female flesh beneath him.

Even more, he was drunk on her warmth, the endless, life-giving warmth that was why he'd fallen in love with her. Though he'd persuaded her to attempt a modest reconciliation for the sake of their child, she'd retreated behind emotional barriers. Now those barriers were gone, revealing the essence of the woman he loved.

Impatiently he tugged off his drawers. He wanted to see, touch, taste all of her, so he sat back on his heels, studying her in the dim light. Their wedding night had been a journey of discovery. Tonight was a rediscovery of what the years apart had wrought. She was no longer an innocent, but a woman who had dealt with the rougher side of life, and who had dedicated herself to a vital, sometimes dangerous calling. Yet she was still Laurel, with all the world's warmth in her face.

"Why are you so far away?" she asked with a teasing smile.

Voice thick, he replied, "Since I didn't really experience our encounter at your infirmary, I don't want to miss a single precious moment this time."

Her taste in nightgowns hadn't changed. This one was even plainer than what she'd worn on their wedding night, a simple garment of white cotton with a high neck and long sleeves and no decoration. It deserved the same fate.

He took hold of the gown's neck and tore the

garment from neckline to bottom hem, which was harder to do than it looked. The controlled ferocity of his action relieved some of his churning emotion. Better yet, it revealed the luxuriant female curves that had been concealed by the garment.

She smiled up like a sensual Madonna. "You're very hard on nightgowns."

"Two in eleven years isn't so terribly destructive," he said, smiling back. The smile faded. "You are so beautiful. So impossibly, painfully beautiful."

"We'll have no pain tonight," she said firmly. "Only pleasure as simple and unshadowed as when we made love in the captain's cabin of your ship while sailing on turquoise seas."

"The *Lavender Lady*. She's the sweetest ship I've ever sailed." The schooner was the first vessel he'd commissioned for the small shipping company he'd inherited from a Scottish uncle. It had been almost complete and ready to launch when he married Laurel. The vessel was as sleek and lovely as his new bride, so he'd changed the name and had Laurel christen it.

He'd planned to have a new figurehead carved, one that looked more like Laurel, but before he could, she'd left him. He'd changed the name of the ship because it seemed bad luck to name it for a woman who would never return.

The thought caused pain, and she'd forbidden pain tonight. He stretched over her again, bare skin to bare skin, acutely aware of all the erotic differences in firmness and texture between male and female. Supporting enough of his weight that he didn't crush her, he began kissing his way downward.

Because of Laurel's natural reserve and bone-deep dignity, he'd been surprised after their marriage to discover that she had an equally natural, unashamed sensuality. She was an elegant lady and an earthy nymph wrapped in one irresistible package.

The pulse in her slender throat beat its rhythm under his lips. He worshipped her magnificent breasts with tongue and mouth as she gasped and arched her back. Her breasts were so luscious that he could scarcely bear to leave them, but he was impatient to rediscover all the other long-remembered delights. He was intoxicated by her taste, her texture, the rippling responsiveness of her body.

When he savored the tender arc of her abdomen, he left a special kiss for the seed of new life that was hidden within. Their child, conceived by chance and so doubly a miracle.

When his questing lips reached the sweet heat and moisture between her thighs, he discovered that she still loved the most intimate of kisses. As he delicately lapped the tender folds, she began thrashing out of control. "James! *James!*"

Her fingers dug into his scalp and her thighs

crushed around him as she cried out wordlessly. As her muscles and breathing relaxed, he rested his head on her stomach, the hammering of her blood beneath his cheek echoing his own pounding heart.

He felt vastly pleased with himself. Pleasuring her was almost as intense as receiving pleasure himself. Laurel had always been the most generous of lovers. He'd had to teach her to accept as well as give.

"Oh my . . ." she breathed as she slid her fingers into his hair. "Here I intended to make up for all I've denied you, and instead you've enraptured me. I'd almost forgotten how wonderful it is to be with you."

Smiling, he cupped his hand over her most secret parts. "If you need another reminder . . ."

She gasped, then rolled away. "Perhaps later. But now, my lord, it's your turn." Gently she pushed him onto his back, touching him in profoundly interesting ways in the process.

By the time he settled into the pillows, he was breathing hard. His gaze locked on her lovely, intent face as she bent over him, contemplating where to begin. Her hair had come undone from its soft braid and spilled over her shoulders and her ripe breasts. "It's a pagan thought," he said unsteadily, "but you are the very model for Aphrodite. Infinitely desirable and bringing blessings to worshipful mankind."

Laughing eyes peered out from her tumbling bronze hair. "Not mankind. Only you, my very patient husband." She caught a handful of her long hair and brushed it over him, stroking down his torso to his groin.

He ground out, *"Not. Patient. Now!"*

Her laughter turned wicked before she bent and let her skilled, sensual mouth follow the teasing trail of her hair. When her lips reached his throbbing erection, he thought he'd go mad. She'd lost none of the uninhibited expertise that he remembered.

She took her time, bringing him to the brink, then slowing down to prolong the firestorm of desire. When he could endure no more, he gasped, "Enough!"

In one swift movement, he rolled her onto her back, then positioned himself between her legs so that his heated flesh could slide along her moist, equally heated cleft. She moaned and clawed her nails into his back as he aroused her to desperate need.

When he could endure no more, he buried himself in the intoxicating depths of her body. The explosion of sensation seared his senses. How had he lived without this fierce intimacy? Could he survive without it if she left him again?

Furiously he banished all thoughts of the past and future. Nothing mattered but his wife and the glorious present.

Culmination was only a dozen urgent thrusts away. As he shattered, she convulsed around him and they melded into one spirit, one mind, one passion.

Every fiber of his body vibrated as his frantic blood slowed to normal. He rolled onto his side and pulled Laurel close against him. She was here now, and it was impossible to imagine them ever separating again. Even though passion was for the moment burned out, the warmth of her spirit still embraced him. When she decided to lower her defenses, she'd opened herself completely.

Again he wondered how he'd lived without her life-giving warmth, and whether he could survive if she left him again.

Don't think such things. She was his wife and they were pledged to each other, now and forever, amen.

And because he didn't quite believe that, he held her close and refused to think about the morning.

Chapter 30

Laurel lay in James's arms, her arm around his waist and her head on his shoulder. She loved his beautiful, strong, lean body; loved that they'd regained the intimacy of lying naked together without inhibition. Everything between them was so right that it was almost as if the years of separation had never happened. How could she have left him? *Why?*

Immediately the horrific image of those beautiful hands snapping a man's neck knotted her stomach with sick horror. She'd been so appalled, so anguished, that she couldn't imagine letting him touch her, so she'd had no choice but to leave him. Even now the memories choked her breathing.

But emotions faded with time. What she felt now was more the memory of horror than the harrowing pain of the original emotion. Also, she now knew that the intruder had carried a knife and might have taken James's life. Self-defense wasn't murder.

And yet . . . "All those years ago—why didn't you try to stop me from leaving?"

His stroking hand stilled. "Because I killed a man and hadn't meant to," he said flatly. "Losing what I valued most seemed like a suitable punishment for my sins."

So Cassie had been right. Even though Cassie and Kirkland hadn't been lovers, the woman knew him very well.

He deserved equal honesty. Laurel forced herself to say, "I thought that when we arrived in London, you realized I was ill-suited to be a countess, so you made no attempt to change my mind because you didn't want me anymore."

He sucked his breath in, shocked. "How could you have ever thought that?"

"We had been on our honeymoon for a year, visiting your scattered properties, never meeting any of your friends." Laurel moistened her lips. "After we separated, I wondered if you felt that I'd never fit into your world."

His face paled. "I was young and very selfish. You were the best thing that ever happened to me, and I didn't want to share you with anyone or anything. I knew I'd have to when we returned to normal life, so I kept us away for as long as possible."

She swallowed hard. "I wish I'd known that."

"Would it have made a difference if you had?" He began stroking her back again. "Would you have stayed if I'd asked? Pleaded? Begged?"

"I . . . don't know." She considered. "My revulsion was too powerful, I think. Time has dimmed the horror. Plus, in my work, I've seen a wide range of life's rawness and cruelty. I'm much harder to shock now. But then . . ." She shook her head.

"So it probably wouldn't have made any difference if I'd tried to change your mind." He exhaled. "I'm glad to know that, because I've often wondered if letting you walk away was the right thing to do."

"It was," she said, regretting the pain they'd both endured. "Devastating, but right."

"In that case, I have a question for you, though I probably shouldn't ask. But needing to understand is my besetting sin." He smiled. "One of them, anyhow. What changed your mind about . . . marital intimacy?"

"The wives of your friends," she said wryly. "Remember the elephant mentioned earlier? I knew they'd all be madly curious about our separation and reconciliation. It was like an unacknowledged elephant in the room. So when we retired to take tea, I told them to ask whatever questions they liked. They asked, and I answered. I didn't speak of private things, of course, but I told them enough that they could understand."

"Good lord," he said, amusement in his voice. "Mackenzie was right. You were having hair-raising conversations."

"I've never experienced anything like it! But as we talked, I learned about them as they learned about me. While they understood why I left you and didn't condemn the girl I was then, it was pointed out that I am no longer eighteen and it's time I took my marriage vows more seriously."

She swallowed hard. "I think of myself as a woman of my word, so it was difficult to be reminded how badly I've failed to keep those vows. I'm sorry, James. I'm trying to do better."

"For which I'm incredibly grateful," he said fervently. "But don't be too hard on yourself, Laurel. Having strong moral objections to murder is a legitimate value that conflicts with those vows."

"I thought so at the time. But one of the ladies suggested that by denying physical intimacy, I was . . . unbalancing the scales. The deeper my bond with you, the more I should be able to accept the aspects of your character that are most opposed to my own." She paused. "It's a good theory."

"Theory is all very well," he said in a voice that was not as light as he probably intended, "but do you think it will work out in practice?"

She tightened her arm around his waist. "I certainly hope so!" she said wryly. "If you can refrain from killing anyone in front of me, all should be well."

He sighed. "I'll do my best."

"There's one other thing," she said in a small voice. "I understand that you've had mistresses. I can't expect otherwise when I wasn't fulfilling my wifely obligations. But . . . I hope you will dismiss whoever holds that position now."

"I hate to shatter your belief," he said softly, "but

there is no mistress, nor has there been one. Since we've married, it's only been you."

She jerked away from him and pulled herself up on one elbow so she could stare into his face. "What? Why not? No one, even me, would blame you for seeking satisfaction elsewhere when I failed to uphold my end of the marriage."

"Did you have lovers?" he countered.

"Of course not!"

"Why not?"

"Those vows I mentioned earlier. To forsake all others, keeping only unto you," she said, trying to make out his expression in the dim light.

"Do you think a man is any less capable of keeping his vows than a woman?" he asked. "You're a deeply passionate woman, Laurel, yet you held to yours."

She bit her lip as she thought about it. "I thought men were different. That celibacy is almost impossible."

"A lot of males promote that belief, but it's not true. Mind you, it wasn't easy!" He laughed suddenly. "Celibacy has been very good for my work."

"As it has been for mine!" She tried to absorb the enormity of what he'd said. No mistresses in all the years of their separation. He had kept to his vows just as she had. It had never occurred to her that he would do so, but the knowledge lifted a weight that she hadn't realized she carried. "I'm so glad that I no longer have to pretend I'm not upset by the thought of you lying with other women. I didn't think I had a right to resent it if you had other bedmates, but I *hated* the idea!"

His arm tightened around her. "Just as I hated the idea that you might have lovers. I suppose it was a form of superstition to hope that if I honored my vows, you would, too."

"I'm so very glad we both did." That knowledge strengthened her closeness to him. "I thought that Cassie might have been your mistress. It was a relief when she said the only pillow talk she heard from you was during a bout of fever."

He made a face. "Believe me, the situation was profoundly unromantic. Cassie and I are friends with a great deal of shared history and trust, but never more."

After a hesitation, he continued, "Not that I didn't find her attractive, but even if I'd made a habit of taking mistresses, I wouldn't have become involved with Cassie. My agents are committed to our work and they know the risks. Even so, it's hellishly difficult to send them into certain danger. To send a woman who'd shared my bed would be . . . unbearable. That was another reason to avoid temptation."

"Whatever your reasons, I'm grateful for the result." She closed her eyes, content as she hadn't been in ten years, and uttered a silent prayer of thanks.

With one hand, he began a gentle massage of the back of her neck that made her feel even more relaxed, if that was possible. "When we arrived in London, you said you hoped to make friends here," he said thoughtfully. "Do you think any of the women you met tonight have that potential?"

"They're a rather intimidating group," she replied, "but they were also intelligent and compassionate. I liked them all, particularly Lady Julia. Do you think she'd mind if I called on her?"

"I'm sure she'd be pleased to see you. Ashton House, where she and Randall stay when they're in town, isn't far from here."

"I'll send her a note in the morning to see if there's a convenient time for me to visit." She chuckled. "I'm trying to get used to having footmen at my beck and call."

"Think of them not as a luxury, but as men in need of a job who are now well employed."

She came alert. "I just realized. A number of your male servants are soldiers who were injured in the line of duty, aren't they? Not the matched sets of footmen that I've heard are common in great houses."

"Yes, several were soldiers, but since I have a shipping company, I have sailors also. It's best not to confuse the two," he said with a laugh.

She was half asleep when he said hesitantly, "Will you consider spending more of your time in London rather than merely visiting now and then?

I know your roots in Bristol are deep, but surely we can find a balance so we will be together most of the time. I often need to be in London, but we can have another home in Bristol. I've been training Rhodes to handle more of the spying work, which means I'll be less busy than I was. More time to spend with you."

She blinked. She hadn't thought that far ahead yet, but he was right. Tonight had changed everything. They were no longer two people who happened to be married but lived separate lives. They were a couple who should be—*wanted* to be—together.

When she'd come to London, she'd been adamant about returning home to Bristol in a month, but the definition of "home" had changed. Now home meant where James was, and it sounded as if he wanted to be with her as much as she wanted to be with him. Shockingly wonderful marital relations had that effect. "If we're both willing to compromise, we can work it out. And I think we're both willing."

"I feel very willing indeed," he murmured as his stroking hand moved down her back under the covers. "I've been thinking Shakespeare tonight."

She laughed. "I hope it's not 'I do desire we may be better strangers!' "

"No, that was your motto," he replied, unperturbed. "I was thinking more along the lines of 'She makes hungry where most she satisfies.' " He cupped her breast, his thumb teasing her nipple into swift hardness.

"In other words, you're hungry again?" She drifted her hand down his torso and found that he was, indeed, hungry again.

"I've been starving for ten years," he whispered.

"So have I." She rolled into him, unable to get enough of his touch, his taste. " 'He makes hungry where most he satisfies,' " she breathed, and those were the last words either of them said until they were both, once again, satisfied.

Chapter 31

Kirkland might have thought it was another vivid dream, but when he woke up to the dawn, Laurel was in his arms, her glossy hair half covering her lovely face. His wife. The mother of his child. His one and only love. The sheer rightness of her presence made him feel whole as he had only been in the brief months after their marriage.

As newlyweds, there had been no shadows on their love. They'd gone through their long honeymoon without a single argument. Thinking back, it was like a long, perfectly executed piano duet. Perhaps if they'd learned then how to disagree, the marriage might not have shattered so thoroughly.

Now they'd both been tempered by life. They'd recommitted to their vows, so they should be able to resolve future disagreements without falling apart. All he had to do was refrain from killing someone in front of his wife. Surely he could manage that.

Laurel shifted a little in his arms, moving onto her back. Her eyes opened sleepily and she gave him a smile as purely loving as when they'd been honeymooners. "I'm so very glad to be here," she murmured.

"Back where you belong." He kissed her temple. "Alas, I must be out and about for much of the day. Do you have plans, or will you stay in bed all day and think of ways to drive me mad?"

"No need to do that," she said demurely as her hand moved down his body in a very undemure way. "It's quite easy to drive you mad. Advance planning isn't required."

He gasped as her hand reached its goal and arousal blazed through him. "It's true. Men are such simple creatures."

"Only in this one area," she said rather tartly. "But if you were simple in all ways, you'd be boring." She pushed herself up on one arm and gazed down at him thoughtfully. "I do believe that I shall have my wicked way with you. I would advise complete surrender."

"You have conquered me, my lady." He rolled onto his back. "Do with me as you will."

She smiled mischievously. "I intend to."

As she leaned down into a kiss, he closed his eyes to better savor the joy of surrender. She was a woman who loved to give, and he could think of nothing better than allowing her to do so.

Laurel dozed again after Kirkland reluctantly left their bed so he could attend to business. As her husband left, Badger entered the room, circled three times by Laurel's pillow, then settled with his head on her shoulder. He wasn't as good a bedmate as Kirkland, but in his own softly purring way, he was very fine.

After Laurel finally rose, bathed, and breakfasted, she sent Lady Julia a note to ask what might be a convenient time to call. The response was swift. Laurel was playing the piano when she received Lady Julia's invitation to join her that morning for a visit and luncheon. Laurel sent an equally swift acceptance and headed for her wardrobe.

Violet was in the dressing room pressing more of Madame Hélier's newly delivered garments, so Laurel announced, "I need a gown for a quiet private visit with the daughter of a duke who is also a midwife. What would you suggest?"

"A lady who is well born, yet down to earth." Violet's brows drew together for a moment. Then she gave a decisive nod. "This morning gown, my lady."

She removed a garment from the wardrobe. The gray was a warm, misty shade, subtle and interesting. "It's not ostentatious, but the cut is elegant enough that if a duke strolls in, you need not be ashamed of your appearance. Wear it with your French shawl that blends shades of blue and gray and green, along with the dark gray bonnet with the peacock feather trim."

"Perfect!" Laurel stroked the soft, rich fabric of the gown. "I shall grow very lazy letting you always choose what I wear, but you do it so much better than I."

Violet laughed. "It is my job to make you look beautiful as you have not allowed yourself to look before."

"With such a talent for flattery, the shop you own someday will be very successful!" As Violet laid out the gown and accessories, Laurel added, "You're looking especially happy this morning. Any particular reason?"

Violet blushed, her café au lait complexion darkening. "After breakfast Mr. Rhodes asked me to take a walk with him on my next half day. We did the same last week and it was . . . very enjoyable."

Laurel arched her brows. This was the first she'd heard of a budding relationship, but because Kirkland trusted and respected Rhodes, Violet should be safe with him. The girl's glow when she mentioned his name proved that she was overcoming her wariness, at least with Rhodes.

"Now that I'm settling in," Laurel said, "I should take more walks around the neighborhood, too. What did you particularly enjoy? Other than the company."

Violet blushed again and disguised it by reaching into the clothespress for the charming dark gray bonnet she'd suggested. "Shepherd Market is quite near here and it was lovely, like a fair. Music and jugglers and a woman who makes the best meat pies in London, according to Mr. Rhodes."

"That sounds like a perfect excursion. I'll ask Kirkland to take me there." Laurel raised her arms so Violet could drop the gray gown over her head. "Did you go anywhere else? I know there are fashionable houses to the west and fashionable shops to the east, but I've been so lazy that I've made no attempt to explore."

"Just across Berkeley Square is a tea shop and confectioner that Mr. Rhodes said is famous. It's called Gunter's and they serve the most delicious ices. Mr. Rhodes bought me one, but I think they're too dear for a poor servant girl." Violet batted her long black lashes innocently.

Laurel laughed, delighted that the girl was revealing such playfulness. Violet had been so quiet and anxious when she first came to Zion House. "In other words, when we walk in the park, your long-suffering mistress should buy you an ice."

"Exactly. As well as one for yourself, of course. You will not regret it."

"We'll do that next time we walk in the park." Laurel studied her image in the mirror. Once again, Violet was right. The combination of blues and warm grays suited Laurel very well and emphasized the changeable colors of her eyes.

As she wrapped the shawl around her shoulders, Laurel said, "Now we're off to Ashton House. I'll be there for several hours so you might want to take something to amuse yourself. Do you enjoy handwork?"

"Like embroidery? Not really, and I'm caught up on the mending." Violet broke into a smile. "Did you know that his lordship has a collection of books just for servants? Stories and travelers' tales and sermons and texts on subjects like doing accounts. If we want to borrow one, all we have to do is sign it out with Mrs. Stratton. Since arriving in London, I read one whole book and I'm on my second now. Do you mind if I read while I wait for you?"

"Not at all! I'm a great believer in reading. What is your current book?"

"*Robinson Crusoe.*" Violet chuckled. "It is a tale of adventure set on a tropical island that is not much like Jamaica, but the author has a good imagination. It's most enjoyable."

As she pulled on her gloves, Laurel realized that Zion House could use a similar lending library. She'd see that one was added.

She was also warmed by the recognition that Kirkland shared her desire to help people better themselves. As he'd said, much of his time was spent on his spying and business responsibilities, but he'd still taken the time to create an exemplary household with customs that showed respect for all who dwelled within.

If her husband could refrain from killing people when she was present, they should have a long and happy future together.

・・・

Violet's jaw dropped when the Kirkland carriage drove through the gates of Ashton House. "It's huge! Like a royal palace."

Laurel was equally impressed. "Kirkland told me it's the largest private home in London, but that didn't prepare me for the reality." No wonder Ashton didn't mind having the Randalls stay with him. He could probably fit the entire Westerfield Academy in one wing and not notice.

Ashton House was equally imposing inside, with sweeping staircases, high molded ceilings, and an impeccably trained staff. Violet was led off to the servants' hall while Laurel was escorted upstairs by the butler.

It was a relief to be welcomed to the Randalls' rooms by a smiling Lady Julia. Petite, dark haired, and serene, she looked exactly as one might expect of a high-born woman who had become a skilled and compassionate midwife.

"Are you properly intimidated by Ashton House?" Julia asked laughingly as she opened the door to admit her guest.

Laurel chuckled. "I thought that Kirkland House was imposing, but I now realize that we're paupers."

"You can see why Ashton was happy to grant my husband his own suite of rooms for as long as Randall wants them." Julia gestured for Laurel to sit in a comfortable grouping of chairs and a sofa.

"When Randall was in the army and seldom stayed in London, he didn't need his own place, and now we all like the arrangement so much that Randall and I are impossible to dislodge." She grinned. "Particularly since Ashton assigned us several more rooms after our marriage and the baby."

"It's nice that this space is used rather than sitting empty," Laurel said as she settled into a wing chair. "My first thought when we entered the grounds was, 'Good heavens!' My second thought was to wonder how many women and children could be housed here if it became another sanctuary like Zion House."

"A woman after my own heart!" Julia settled in the sofa opposite Laurel and tucked her feet up under her. "I don't think Ashton is ready to give up his home, but he and Mariah have been very generous to the Sisters Foundation. I have all kinds of questions to ask you. Do you mind if Mariah joins us later? She's interested, too."

"Not at all. I want to get to know her better. I'd also love to meet your daughter, and I gather Mariah has recently had a baby also?"

"Yes, her Richard is only about five weeks older than my Anne-Marie." Julia smiled. "Naturally we want to show our babies off, and all you have to do in return is say how beautiful they are."

"That will be easy. All babies are beautiful." Laurel rested one hand on her belly, wondering if she dared discuss her recurring fear that she wouldn't be able to carry this pregnancy to completion. But there was no point in mentioning that, since if Laurel was right, there was nothing Julia could do anyhow. "Could you recommend a good midwife? I'm not sure if this baby will be born here or in Bristol, but I thought I should have an expert on hand in both locations. I haven't talked to a midwife yet, but it seems as if I should."

"It's good to think ahead," Julia agreed. "We won't be in London long enough for you to become a patient of mine, but I can give you several recommendations here in the city. If you have questions to ask now, feel free. You're not far along, I think?"

"Almost two months." Laurel could give the exact date and even the exact hour if that was requested. "It's so early I haven't wanted to speak much about it."

"I presume you've had symptoms. Would you care to discuss them?"

"Some sickness in the morning." She remembered the visit to her parents. "That's not usually too bad unless I must do something I don't want to later in the day."

"That does happen," Julia said with wry amusement. "What else?"

Delighted to talk to someone who understood and was interested, Laurel explained what her body was doing and received useful information about what to expect in the coming months. They were just finishing their discussion when Major Randall and a boy around thirteen or so entered the sitting room from the private rooms beyond.

The major smiled at Laurel. "Welcome to my humble quarters, Lady Kirkland. You see the straits former officers are reduced to." He waved a hand that took in the airy chamber and sumptuous furnishings.

Laurel laughed. "My heart is wrung by your plight, Major."

Humor lurking in his eyes, he said, "Your sympathy is appreciated. May I present Benjamin Thomas Randall? Benjamin, this is Lady Kirkland."

Benjamin bowed politely, but his curious expression suggested that he was interested to meet Lord Kirkland's wife. After the introductions, Randall said, "We are off to indulge in masculine pursuits like riding and perhaps visiting Tattersall's." He brushed a kiss on his wife's hair before he headed to the door. "I expect the two of you will have half of Britain's social problems sorted out by the time we return."

Julia laughed. "We'll do our best." She caught Benjamin's hand as he passed and gave it a quick squeeze. "Please don't bring a pony home from Tattersall's. I'm not sure our rooms have space for one."

"I suppose not," Benjamin said with feigned

regret. He kissed Julia's cheek, then followed Major Randall out.

After the door closed, Laurel said, "Randall's son? He's an engaging lad."

"Benjamin's father was Alex's cousin, but he's ours now." Julia smiled fondly. "He's a student at the Westerfield Academy."

"I hope to meet Lady Agnes Westerfield someday. She must be the most amazing woman."

"She is, and I'm sure you'll meet her soon." The reply came from Mariah as she entered the sitting room with a warm smile. "It's so nice to see you again now that the elephant has been dismissed!" She brandished notebook and pencil. "And now to work."

As the duchess plumped down on the sofa, Julia said, "When my foundation directors visited you at Zion House, you were starting some job-training programs for your residents. How have you gone about it and what is proving successful?"

"We concentrate on practical skills like cleaning, cooking, baby nursing, and for women with more education, subjects like keeping accounts. Most of our teachers are residents so the classes vary, but we're developing formal plans of study to assure that the students learn all the skills necessary," Laurel explained. "After that, they serve an apprenticeship in homes of local people who support the program."

That kicked off an animated discussion that

carried the three women through the next hours, including shared ideas, laughter, and an excellent luncheon. By the time she left, Laurel knew she had two new friends who were kindred spirits. She must invite Anne Wilson up from Bristol so all of them could meet together. As matron of Zion House, Anne had practical experience of the day-to-day details. Perhaps she could be persuaded to write a guide for matrons of other refuges.

Heavens, Laurel hadn't even broached the subject of security, or their plans to start small businesses. She'd met both of Kirkland's experts and been impressed. Both men were now in Bristol, one making Zion House safer, the other starting a woodshop.

As Violet joined her and they waited for their carriage, Laurel asked her maid, "How did you and *Robinson Crusoe* do?"

"I read some, but I also talked with the maids of the duchess and Lady Julia. We exchanged some recipes." Violet smiled. "I was also well fed."

"A good day for both of us." An idea struck Laurel. "The afternoon is pleasant, so I'll have the coachman take us to Gunter's for ices and we can walk home across the park."

"I shall be most happy to assist you with the ices, my lady." Violet's words were prim but her eyes sparkled.

The carriage arrived and Laurel was assisted in by a footman. As she settled inside, she smiled with satisfaction. There was nothing like making friends to reconcile oneself with living in a new place.

Laurel had sometimes had ices, but they were a rare and expensive treat because of the difficulty of obtaining sufficient ice and the complexity of the production. Visiting Gunter's was almost as much a treat for her as for Violet.

After her first taste of her orange flower ice, she sighed with pleasure. "You were right, Violet. This is exquisite. We must end all our walks here."

Violet smiled happily over her cinnamon-flavored ice. "I shall be honored to accompany you every time."

Despite making her bites small, Laurel's ice was gone too soon, and it would be undignified for a countess to lick the dish. Could a pregnant woman justify wolfing down one or two more? Though the thought appealed, she didn't think she was capable of letting herself be so undisciplined.

But she could certainly become a regular patron since Gunter's was so close. "I must speak with Mr. Gunter about supplying ices to Kirkland House when we entertain. They should be able to pack them in an ice-filled chest so they'll last a few hours."

"I'm sure they'll be able to accommodate you for a suitably outrageous price."

Money did have its uses. Not only ices, but this

lovely park right in front of Kirkland House, where Laurel could so easily stretch her legs and breathe fresh air.

As she and Violet strolled into the square, the Kirkland footman jumped from the carriage to escort them home while the coachman took the carriage around to the stables. Laurel was getting used to having so many servants. It was easy now that she knew them as individuals.

She circled one of the great plane trees, thinking that she was having a splendid day, and the best was yet to come. She gave a very private smile, and estimated the number of hours it would be until she and her husband could go to bed.

Chapter 32

In the week since Laurel and Kirkland had gone from sharing a roof to sharing a bed, they'd started to shape their lives into a new pattern that suited them both. Usually they would have a leisurely breakfast where they laughed and discussed interesting stories from the newspapers. Then Kirkland would go about his work, usually leaving the house, while Laurel would consult with Mrs. Stratton about household affairs. The housekeeper no longer felt threatened by her new mistress since Laurel seldom interfered.

Laurel had better things to do. In Bristol, she'd been busy from dawn to dark, but now she worked on a larger scale. Lady Julia had put her on the board of the Sisters Foundation, and along with Mariah and Kiri, they were developing plans to expand the network of shelters. She missed working directly with the women and children, but her present work would benefit many more people.

London was starting to feel more like home. Under the terms of their original reconciliation, she'd planned to visit London occasionally and spend the bulk of her time in Bristol. Now the balance was reversed. She would visit Bristol to see friends and her brother and also to check that the infirmary and Zion House ran smoothly, but her presence would be needed less and less.

As Laurel and Violet prepared for their afternoon walk, Laurel wondered how long this magical phase of her marriage would last. After the child was born, there would be many changes. But the elements—time with her husband and meaningful work for both of them—were now in place.

When they stepped out of the house into Berkeley Square, Violet looked at the sky doubtfully. "It looks like rain soon, my lady."

"Very true, but this is England. If we only ventured out in sunshine, we'd never get any exercise," Laurel said briskly. "And we would also have many fewer ices."

"True, and that would be very sad," Violet agreed.

"Martin, best bring an umbrella," Laurel said to the wiry former sailor turned footman who was escorting them today. Violet had told Laurel that escorting the countess on her daily walk was such a coveted task that the men took turns, largely because Laurel always bought ices for the escorts as well as for herself and Violet.

Ices were expensive, but she enjoyed spending Kirkland's money in ways that brought such pleasure. He'd certainly brought pleasure to her every night for the week since they'd become lovers again. It would be more proper to say that they had resumed marital relations, but "becoming lovers" did a better job of capturing the flavor of their wickedly passionate nights.

Besides establishing more refuges, the Sisters Foundation wanted to expand their training programs. Too often a woman stayed with a brutal man because she feared she and her children would starve if she left. These women needed to acquire skills to support themselves.

Sketching out training programs had given Laurel an idea. As she and her maid started around the park, she asked, "Violet, how would you feel about writing a short book about the skills required of a lady's maid?"

Violet stopped in her tracks, her eyes widening to saucer size. "I could never write a book!" she gasped.

"Of course you can. It would just be a matter of writing down what a good lady's maid needs to be able to do, and how to do it. Rather like the classes you were teaching at Zion House. Clothing, hair, making creams and lotions and cosmetics, and the rest. I realize it's taken you years to develop these skills, but you were good at explaining how to do each task. The first use of the book would be a guide for women at refuges like Zion House, but I believe that it could find a broader audience."

Violet resumed walking, but she bit her lip. "I have learned to speak and read well, but I do not write so well."

"That's not a problem. I can work with you. We'll call it a pamphlet if that sounds less alarming." Laurel smiled. "Wouldn't it be splendid to have a book with your name on it? You can dedicate it to me and people will know that you are the personal maid of a countess. A countess who needs a great deal of help to look respectable!"

That made Violet laugh, and as they walked around the park, the girl began listing the topics such a book would need to cover. Even though the sky was darkening, Laurel was in no rush to go inside, because the more Violet talked and expanded on her ideas, the more she believed she really could write a book.

Laurel and Violet and the ever-patient Martin circled and crisscrossed the oval park. Because of the threatening rain, the square was almost empty, but that didn't matter. Violet was bubbling with ideas. As they neared Gunter's for their end-of-walk treat, Laurel said, "About your recipes for cosmetics. Are you willing to share all of them? Or most of them?"

Violet pursed her lips as she thought. "Most I will share. There are a few I would rather keep secret."

"There's a good title for you. *Secrets of a Lady's Maid*," Laurel suggested, half serious and half teasing. "As long as people don't expect naughty stories!"

Several carriages were pulled up opposite

Gunter's, including a huge travel coach, but there were no open vehicles and only a handful of customers were in the shop. As always, Laurel and her companions ate their ices outside. The first drops of rain began to fall as they finished the treats, and a cold wind swept across the park.

"Time to go home," Laurel said. Kirkland would probably be there since he'd planned to invite several friends over for a meeting of some sort. She hoped the meeting wouldn't be long. If his friends were gone, perhaps she could persuade him into an afternoon nap. Being with child gave so many good excuses to go to bed.

The Duke of Ashton was the first to arrive. As he shook Kirkland's hand, he said, "You're looking remarkably well, and I don't suppose it's hard to guess the reason."

Kirkland laughed. "It's been the best week of my life, Ash. Laurel and I get along so well that it's difficult to remember all those years of separation."

"I'm glad for you," Ashton said sincerely. "Mariah said to thank you for bringing her a new friend. Now what is this mysterious meeting you've called?"

"I've invited Randall and Carmichael, so I'll explain it all at once."

A gleam in his eyes, Ashton said, "Since they're coming also, I'll wait before I tell you how my latest infernal machine is doing."

"Your new steamship? I trust it hasn't exploded."

Ashton grinned. "Be fair. The only time one exploded was attempted murder."

Before Kirkland could ask another question, Randall was announced. As he handed his hat to the butler, he said, "You have competition for your wife's affections, Kirkland. Benjamin fell halfway in love with her when she played the piano for us."

"I can hardly blame him, since I did the same," Kirkland said mildly.

Rob Carmichael entered last. He'd spent time as a sailor and had a keen weather sense, so he announced, "There's a squall coming. Literally. And perhaps there's a metaphorical squall in the area since you asked us to meet with you, Kirkland?"

"Yes," Kirkland said as he ushered his friends into his study. "I've asked you here because there's a large issue I've not paid much attention to, and I'd like your thoughts and perhaps your influence if we decide to chart a strategy for the future."

"What's the issue?" Randall asked as he settled into a comfortable chair.

"The illegal slave trade. Ash, you probably know most about the subject. You aligned yourself with the abolitionists as soon as you took your seat in the House of Lords and threw your considerable weight behind the legislation that banned the slave trade. It's been what, six years since the bill was passed?"

Ashton nodded. "Yes, and it was a major victory. But not a final solution, of course. There is still much to be done. What has brought about this interest on your part? I would have thought defeating Napoleon would be enough to keep you busy."

Kirkland grimaced. "Heaven knows that's true. But I was reminded by Laurel's maid that there are other pressing issues. Violet was born a slave in Jamaica and trained as a lady's maid. Her mistress brought her to England for a visit. Violet is an intelligent, thoroughly decent young woman with a passion to grow and learn, but unluckily, in England she was sold to a certain Captain Hardwick, who became obsessed with her."

"I've seen the girl leaving Ashton House with your wife," Ashton said. "Very striking, unfortunately for her."

Carmichael frowned. "Hardwick is a thorough-going villain. Did Lady Kirkland buy the girl's freedom?"

"No, Laurel came across Hardwick and a couple of his men at the port of Bristol trying to force Violet out to Hardwick's ship. Laurel cited legal precedent and took Violet away from him with the help of some friendly stevedores who backed her up."

There was a stunned silence before Randall said,

"It didn't occur to your lady wife that taking a slave away from a vicious brute might be dangerous?"

"Probably not." Kirkland still winced when he thought how badly her intervention might have gone. "She saw a girl in desperate straits and couldn't *not* help."

"I'm starting to understand your mutual attraction better," Randall said acerbically. "You're both mad martyrs who will do what is right even if it kills you."

"That's probably true, though I'm much more devious than Laurel," Kirkland said ruefully. "There's more to Violet's story. Hardwick set one of his men to watching the girl, probably in hope of taking her back. That's one reason Laurel brought Violet to London, where she should be safe."

Randall spoke again. "So the plight of this one girl you know has made you start thinking about all the unfortunates you don't know?"

"Exactly. I'd been vaguely aware of Hardwick, but after I learned how he was stalking Violet, I decided to investigate him further."

"There have been credible rumors that he is involved in the illegal slave trade," Rob Carmichael said. "Have you confirmed that?"

Kirkland nodded. "My valet, Rhodes, is in charge of the investigation. I've been training him to take on some of my intelligence work, and he shows real talent. Now that you've gone and married, Rob, I can't count on you to handle everything if I drop dead."

His friend grinned. "Sorry about that," he said, not sounding sorry at all. "Rhodes combines a rather unremarkable appearance with a very clever mind, and he grew up in the dockland area, didn't he?"

"Exactly. He's first rate at finding information and putting the pieces together, which is what the job requires. I'll have to find a new valet soon, which will be a nuisance, but it's easier to find good servants than good spymasters."

"What are your goals?" Randall asked. "To bring down Hardwick and in the process protect Violet and others who might be threatened by him?"

"That would be just the start," Kirkland said. "The larger issue is to increase the resources of the Royal Navy's West Africa Squadron so they can do more to stop illegal slave ships on the Middle Passage between Africa and the new world. I'm not sure how that would be done. It will probably require an act of Parliament."

"The ocean is large, the squadron currently has only three or four ships, and there are those who feel the Royal Navy should be concentrating on the war in Europe." Ashton frowned. "Not to mention that there are men who still make a great deal of money from slavery, and they will not want to see the illegal trade stopped."

"All true, and Hardwick is such a man. This must be a long-term project. The European wars should be over in a year or two, which will free up resources," Kirkland replied. "It's time to start planning for the future."

"If Parliament becomes involved in the next few years, you and Ash and Rob all have seats in the Lords and can vote to raise appropriations, but I'm a mere commoner for the foreseeable future," Randall said. "I don't know if I can do much to help."

"Lord Daventry is one of those peers whose vote is always hard to predict. As his heir presumptive, you have some influence with him, don't you? Any chance he might be persuaded to support an increase in funding and resources for the squadron?"

Randall considered. "My uncle hasn't much use for my opinion, but the project is one he might be inclined to support if it comes before the Lords. The best way to influence him would be to have Julia talk to Lady Daventry. They've been thick as thieves ever since Julia delivered her ladyship's baby."

"Is Wyndham still thinking about becoming a Member of Parliament?" Ashton asked. "I should think he would be a solid supporter of antislavery measures."

"Yes, just as his father will support such measures in the Lords," Kirkland said. "Wyndham and Cassie have returned to Summerhill, but before they left, he told me that he's now able to tolerate crowds again, even a crowd of politicians, so he'll take a seat next year after one of his father's MPs retires."

"It sounds like you'll be able to marshal quite a bit of support," Rob observed. "Have you asked Violet what she knows? If she spent much time with Hardwick, she might have picked up information about his activities."

"That's a good thought. I'll ask her to come down now, and Laurel as well. Since Bristol was a major port for ships in the trade to deliver cargo from the Indies, she might have some useful information."

A footman had entered to light lamps since the sky had darkened, so Kirkland asked him to request that Lady Kirkland and her maid join them in the study. "I shall inquire, my lord," the footman said. "But her ladyship and maid have gone out for their afternoon walk in Berkeley Square, and I believe they haven't returned yet."

"Find out, please," Kirkland said tersely. The footman left, accompanied by a flash of lightning and a crash of thunder that followed almost instantly. Rain began pounding down and the sky was almost full dark.

"You predicted that squall right, Rob." Restlessly Kirkland rose and lit the lamps himself. He was getting the itchy feeling that something dire was about to happen, and he'd learned that such feelings were usually right. They were also too damned general to be of any use other than to make his nerves twang like piano strings.

By the time he'd lit the last of the lamps, the footman had returned. "Her ladyship and her maid are still out, my lord. But they generally frequent Gunter's at the end of their walk, so doubtless they are waiting out the storm there."

"A footman accompanied them?" Kirkland asked.

"Yes, sir, 'twas Martin today."

Kirkland's feeling of disquiet intensified. But it couldn't have anything to do with Laurel. The park in the middle of the square wasn't large enough to get lost.

"No reason to worry," Randall said. "Gunter's would be a rather pleasant place to be caught during a storm."

Unable to explain his concern, Kirkland said, "I'm sure you're right. I just hope that Laurel didn't get drenched. She has reason to . . . take extra care of herself."

"If that means what I think, congratulations!" Ashton said with a wide smile.

"It's early yet, so we haven't wanted to talk about it." The storm was so noisy that Kirkland had to raise his voice.

The other men chimed in with more congratulations and best wishes while Kirkland stared out the window. He'd sent Rhodes to the docklands to gather information and his valet might be the person who had run into trouble. Kirkland didn't want anything to happen to Rhodes, but God help him, better Rhodes than Laurel.

The rain was beginning to slacken a little when the door to the study opened and Rhodes appeared, saturated and dripping on the expensive carpet. "Sir, I'm sorry to interrupt you, but I learned that Captain Hardwick's flagship, the *Jamaica Queen*, is moored in the Pool of London."

Kirkland felt an internal twang that confirmed his worry was connected to Hardwick. "I thought he never came to London. All his operations are out of Bristol."

"That's been true in the past, sir, but he's in London now. I heard he's preparing to set sail on this evening's tide." Rhodes grimaced. "Maybe the weather will change his mind. Until he's gone, I think it best to keep extra guards on your lady and Miss Violet."

Lightning sent searing light through the study and the accompanying thunderbolt was instantaneous. As the house shook and the lamplight swayed crazily, Kirkland couldn't help thinking that the thunder sounded exactly like the crack of doom.

Laurel and her servants were just starting back across the park when the skies split with lightning and the rain began pounding down as if they were under a waterfall. Violet exclaimed, "This is like rain in Jamaica!"

Kirkland House was visible on the other side of the park, but the rain was turning the ground into mud and the plane trees were lashing violently. "Back to Gunter's!" Laurel ordered as water streamed over her bonnet. "It's much closer."

As Martin opened the umbrella, a gust of wind caught the canopy and blew it into Laurel and Violet. Panting apologies, Martin struggled to get the umbrella under control.

Unable to see anything, Laurel tried to bat the umbrella out of her way—and in that moment, she was grabbed from behind. An instant of shock was followed by memories of the self-defense class. She tried to slam her elbow back into her attacker, but with no effect.

Violet screamed and Laurel saw that she had also been grabbed, by a burly man with a scarred face just like the one Violet had described seeing in Bristol. Martin shouted for help as he leaped at the nearest attacker, then pitched to the ground when a third man bashed the footman in the head with a club.

Laurel learned that fear made it easier to fight back in a real attack than in a class, but nothing she did helped, and no one heard their cries amidst the howling of the storm. She and Violet were bundled into the large coach—and waiting there was the evilly grinning Captain Hardwick.

Chapter 33

Face grim, Kirkland strode from the study toward the foyer of the house. "I believe that I'll go across to Gunter's to make sure that Laurel is all right."

"I'll go with you," Rob said, frowning.

It was still raining hard and Soames, the butler, appeared with Kirkland's great coat when he realized his master was going out. As Kirkland impatiently pulled the coat on, someone began weakly striking the front door.

This was it, the dire thing Kirkland had been expecting. He jerked open the door and a blood-stained figure staggered inside before crumpling to the floor. Martin, the footman who had been escorting Laurel and Violet.

Snapping into cool emergency mode, Kirkland knelt beside the man as blood and rainwater spread in a scarlet pool across the pale marble floor. "Soames, call a surgeon!"

Someone pressed a handkerchief into Kirkland's hand and he blotted around the head wound. It was bleeding freely but didn't seem deep. *If Laurel was here, she would know how to treat this.*

Pain lanced through him, making it difficult to breathe. *Don't think about Laurel, not yet.*

"Martin," he said in a calm voice, "can you tell me what happened?"

Martin's eyes opened and he blinked dazedly. "So . . . bloody sorry, my lord," he rasped. "Right in front of Gunter's. It was pouring rain. Three men jumped out of a bloody big travel coach. Grabbed her ladyship and Violet. Tried to stop them, but one bashed me . . . with a club."

It was a miracle Martin's skull hadn't been crushed. "Brave of you to make it across the park after that. How long ago was the attack?"

Martin frowned. "Not . . . long. Bloody rain was full force then."

The storm was easing now, so not long. Ten or fifteen minutes, depending on how long it had taken Martin to stagger across the park. Wise of him to come here, where Kirkland would do something, rather than go into Gunter's, where there would be no useful aid. "Did you notice what the coach looked like?"

"Dark. Full team of horses. Not matched, but strong beasts. Off wheeler had white socks." Martin made a raw sound like a sob. "I failed you, my lord. Didn't . . . keep your lady safe."

"With three of them and only you, you were lucky to escape with your life." Soames and Mrs. Stratton and a maid had returned with blankets and towels to make Martin more comfortable. Kirkland got to his feet. "Rest now, Martin. You did well."

The fault lay with Kirkland, for not anticipating how much of a threat Hardwick was. *Laurel. Kidnapped by a murderous brute. She might be dead already.*

He almost blacked out from fear and fury at himself for not keeping her safe. *How could he live in a world where Laurel was gone and it was his own bloody-bedamned fault?*

Ashton put a hand on his shoulder and said quietly, "James. *Breathe.*"

Sanity returned and Kirkland shoved his fear into a box buried deep inside, where it was only a faint wail of anguish. *Don't think of Laurel, only about the problem of stopping an evil man.* "Soames, send someone across the park to Gunter's to see if there's any evidence on the ground or if anyone saw anything that might be useful."

"I'll go," Rob said. "It won't take long to see if there's anything helpful."

Kirkland nodded his thanks. Having spent years as a Bow Street Runner, Rob would be thorough and fast.

He drew a deep breath. What next? "My best guess is that Hardwick is taking them to his ship, but I'm not sure how good my judgment is at the moment. Does anyone think Hardwick would take them anywhere other than his ship?"

On the verge of going out the door, Rob paused to say, "He's a man of the sea. From what Rhodes said, he almost never sails into London. He must have come here to retrieve Violet and maybe get revenge on Lady Kirkland as well. He'll go to his ship." He gave a swift, dangerous smile. "Don't go after them without me."

"I'm in, too," Randall said. "Ashton?"

The duke's brows rose. "Of course."

Kirkland swallowed hard. One couldn't ask for better friends. He glanced at Rhodes. "You agree that Hardwick is most likely heading to the *Jamaica Queen*?"

"Yes, sir. Like Lord Kellington said, the sea is Hardwick's home. He has a house in Bristol, but he's not there much. In London he's staying on his ship. From what I learned, he's anxious to get away to Africa, so he'll sail as soon as possible." Rhodes's voice broke. "And the bloody bastard has Violet and your lady!"

"He may have them, but he won't keep them," Kirkland said grimly. "He probably timed his kidnapping so that he'd catch the tide quickly. What time would that be?" Because of his shipping company, he always tracked the tides in the back of his mind. "About seven o'clock this evening, I think?"

"A little earlier, but close to that," Ashton replied.

Kirkland's gaze returned to Rhodes. "Where is his ship moored?"

"Billingsgate, just east of London Bridge. I'll draw a map." Rhodes pulled paper and pencil from an inside pocket. There was writing on one side, but he flipped it over, flattened the paper on a table, and began sketching out the harbor area that stretched east from the bridge.

"What do you need us to do?" Randall asked. "If we're right about his destination, we should be able to catch him at the river if not before."

"I've five good horses in my stables, so we ride after them. There are several routes, but two are most likely," Kirkland said. "If we split into two groups, one might catch up with the coach, but we can't count on that."

"I'm going, too," Rhodes said, his expression stark.

Kirkland remembered what Laurel had said about Violet and Rhodes. Luckily, the man was a decent rider. "Of course. Did anyone come by horseback?"

"I did," Randall replied. "My horse is fresh and up for a chase."

"I came by carriage," Ashton said. "I assume you want to enlist some of the veterans of your household to follow those of us on horseback?"

Kirkland nodded. "Exactly. Most of them aren't skilled riders so we'd need the carriages even if we had more mounts, but Jones in my stables was a cavalryman. He can ride with Rob and me. Randall, Ashton, Rhodes, you'll go together. I figure two coaches of men to follow. Soames, organize that while I unlock my gun closet."

Soames's elegant butler's bearing vanished and he straightened like the army master sergeant he'd once been. "Yes, sir!"

Rob returned a quarter hour later with no useful new data. By then, Kirkland had armed and organized his troops. Every man in the household had volunteered to help rescue their lady. Martin wanted to come, but he could barely stand.

They gathered by the mews. Kirkland swung up onto his horse, his face grim. Laurel hadn't wanted to see her husband kill another man in front of her, but when he caught up with Hardwick, the bastard was a dead man.

His slow gaze moved over the nearly two dozen men assembled. There hadn't been time to change, so they were a motley crew. Ashton, calmly lethal on horseback, wearing a pair of boots borrowed from Kirkland. Alex Randall, a steely-eyed veteran of any number of battles and skirmishes. Rob Carmichael, who had fought in dark and dangerous places. His servants, all of them veterans and used to discipline. They would do for a task like the one before them. They would have to.

"We all know what needs to be done," Kirkland said tersely. "First and foremost, we must get the women back safely, and I damn well expect you to do it without getting killed yourself. Good luck to you all. We'll rendezvous on the riverbank in Billingsgate if neither group catches Hardwick first."

He gathered his reins. "Now, my friends, keep your powder dry and *ride*."

Hardwick's coach was jammed with four large men and the two women. It had taken off as soon as the doors were closed, throwing the occupants off balance. Violet managed to land a kick on one man's knee that made him yelp, but it took only a few moments for the abductors to truss up their captives. Their wrists were bound together in front of them, then their ankles tied so they couldn't run even if they could escape the coach.

Violet had tried to scream for help and Hardwick slapped a heavy hand over her mouth. "Save your screams for later," he growled. "You can scream as much as you want after we set sail. Moody, give me one of the gags."

The scar-faced man handed over a worn handkerchief, but it took both him and Hardwick to gag Violet. Laurel had given up struggling since she was hopeless at fighting, and her efforts were futile when she was surrounded by burly men.

The coach rocked perilously as it thundered through the London streets, splashing through massive puddles. The motion, plus the fact that their captors stank, made Laurel sick to her stomach. When Moody tried to gag her, she bit his fingers. He swore and jerked his hand away.

The coach lurched around another corner, tilting so far to the right that Laurel thought they'd pitch over. The vehicle managed to avoid crashing, but nausea overcame her and she vomited in Moody's lap.

"Filthy slut!" he roared as he pulled his fist back to strike her.

"Don't damage her, Moody," Hardwick snapped. "Just gag her, and be more careful about it."

Laurel jerked her head away from Moody when he tried to gag her again. "My husband will come after us," she snapped. "Then you will all be very, very sorry."

Hardwick laughed at her. "Maybe he will, if he ever figures out what happened. But that's not bloody likely. Your footman's dead in the rain and no one saw what happened. We'll be at sea before your fancy fribble husband even knows you're gone. He'll probably think you ran off with a lover."

Damnably, he was half right. Kirkland was not the fashionable fribble Hardwick believed him to be, but it would take time for Laurel and Violet's absence to be noted, longer still before the kidnapping could be puzzled out. Hardwick had been known to be a threat in Bristol, but how long would it take for Kirkland to realize the man had followed Violet to London?

She shuddered at the thought of what had happened to Martin. He hadn't had a chance against Hardwick and his thugs, but he'd tried, and that had cost him his life.

Moody ordered one of the other men to hold Laurel's head and this time he managed to gag her despite her attempts to jerk away. The sour taste of vomit was trapped in her mouth and it was hard to breathe.

She fought rising panic by closing her eyes and consciously slowing her breathing. Inhale slowly. Exhale slowly. *Breathe!* Kirkland was the most resourceful man she'd ever met, and he had abilities and connections beyond anything Hardwick could imagine.

There was nothing she could do but pray. She was experienced with prayers of gratitude and thanks, prayers for help and for healing. She'd prayed less than usual in the last week because she'd been so busy and happy, though she'd offered a heartfelt prayer of thanks when she and Kirkland had attended the parish church together on Sunday.

Now she prayed for strength, endurance, and calm. Succumbing to her terror would help nothing.

With Laurel jammed between Moody and another of Hardwick's men in the rear facing seat, Hardwick was free to pull Violet onto his lap. She struggled and made frantic sounds behind her gag, but she was helpless.

Hardwick laughed at her resistance. "If this coach wasn't so bloody crowded, I'd shag you here, but you won't have to wait long. Make yourself comfortable." He wrapped his arms around her, squeezing her breasts as he did.

Violet was rigid, her dark eyes a whirlpool of anguish, fury, and despair above the gag. Laurel caught her gaze and tried to send what support she could. *Be strong. Have faith. While we are alive, there is hope.*

Violet couldn't have known Laurel's exact thoughts, but her expression calmed. As long as they were alive, there was hope.

Laurel closed her eyes and prayed for a miracle.

Chapter 34

Laurel hadn't been in London long enough to travel beyond the West End, but she knew the port and docks were well to the east. It was a long ride across London. She felt increasingly ill. Lucky there wasn't anything left in her stomach.

Violet was limp as a cloth doll. Eventually Hardwick tired of holding her, so he squeezed her into the narrow gap between himself and one of his ruffians. Laurel guessed that the girl had mentally withdrawn as far as possible from her present circumstances.

The storm had blown over, leaving heavy gray skies and spatterings of rain. The coach slowed as traffic increased, and at one point they were stopped for long minutes by an accident. The captain swore and drummed his fingers on his thigh as he stared out the window. Since he didn't fear pursuit, there must be another reason for his impatience. Catching the tide, perhaps?

Finally the coach lurched to a halt. Laurel heard the shrieks of gulls and smelled the various scents created where land met water. Once more fear threatened to engulf her, because if she and Violet were taken out to sea, they were doomed.

Hardwick opened the coach door and jumped down. Outside Laurel could see the river, and it was crowded with ships. Some were moored at piers, others away from the shore, and everywhere smaller boats scurried in all directions.

"Wrap 'em up and bring 'em to the dinghy," Hardwick ordered. His men produced two coarse, crumpled sacks and a pair of ragged blankets. One of the dusty sacks was pulled over Laurel's head and an old blanket wrapped around her and tied. The blanket wasn't tied very tightly, but it trapped her bound hands close to her throat. Hardwick didn't want it to be obvious that he was carrying captives out to his ship.

Laurel was tossed over someone's shoulder and carried out into the open air. It was acutely uncomfortable, and dear God, she prayed that the cramps in her stomach didn't mean what she feared they did!

She was dumped unceremoniously on a curved wooden surface with water sloshing around her. A dinghy. Violet was dropped beside her. Laurel wished she could give a comforting hug, but she could barely breathe, much less hug a friend.

Then she realized that her hands were high enough that she was able to tug the gag down and no one would notice since she had the sack over her head. She dragged it from her mouth and sucked down great gulps of air. There was so much noise around the docks that there wasn't much point in shouting for help, but at least she could breathe.

Another thought struck her. Concealed under her morning gown was the sapphire studded cross Kirkland had given her, and which she'd been wearing daily. Today it was concealed under her morning gown. Though the cross didn't have any sharp edges, it was metal and hard. Perhaps it might have some use as a tool.

Underneath the loose sack, she managed to grasp the cross and break the slender chain with a hard jerk. There was comfort in holding the symbol of her faith, and also in the knowledge that it had been a gift from the husband she loved.

A hoarse voice shouted, "Cap'n, there are half a dozen men galloping this way! Comin' straight at us!"

Hardwick's "Shove off!" was followed by language so filthy she didn't understand most of the words, but his snarled, "How'd the bastard get here so fast?" was clear.

Kirkland! She was sure of it.

The dinghy lurched away from shore, rocking nauseatingly. Water splashed over her as oars squealed in their locks from the swift rowing.

She clasped hope as hard as she clasped her cross. Even though Hardwick had a head start, he still had to sail downriver all the way to the North Sea. Kirkland had a chance of catching up—and given the odds he'd already overcome, she wanted to believe he'd succeed this time, too.

She swallowed hard as she realized that it would be more difficult, and far more dangerous, to assault a ship at sea rather than a coach. Kirkland and the men with him would risk death if they tried. And if they were winning, Hardwick would probably kill his prisoners before he'd surrender them. *Dear God, please don't let James be killed trying to rescue me!*

To bury the frightening thought, she tested the bonds around her wrists. The line wasn't heavy and there was some stretch, possibly because it had been saturated by the sloshing water while she was lying on the bottom of the dinghy.

She turned her cross and began sawing the long end against the line. It was damnably uncomfortable and there was no chance of really cutting through, but with the rubbing of the metal, the line did seem to be stretching and loosening.

All too soon the dinghy reached the ship, the hull scraping as the vessel was secured. "Take this 'un!" a voice barked.

Rough hands grabbed Laurel and tossed upward. For a ghastly moment she hung in midair, knowing that if she fell into the river she'd drown. Then she was jerked as other hands caught her upper arms and she was dragged onto the deck like a just-caught fish.

As she lay there, bruised, wet, and shivering with cold, Violet was deposited beside her. Hardwick's voice barked from above. "Lock these two sluts in my cabin while we cast off. We'll just barely catch the tide."

Another voice—Moody?—said, "At least those fellows coming after us are trapped for hours until the tide rises again."

Laurel didn't know much about sailing, but that didn't sound good. Putting her faith in God and Kirkland, she went to work on her bonds again. If nothing else, the activity distracted her from how wretched and terrified she was.

Several minutes passed before she was again lifted and draped over a sailor's shoulder. As she was carried along, his bony shoulder ground into her abdomen, making her feel even more miserable.

She was lowered belowdecks, passed from one set of hands to another. Carried along a narrow passage where her head and feet banged into the walls. Through a door into a more open space. The man carrying her asked, "Where should we put 'em?"

Another man laughed coarsely. "On the cap'n's bed, of course. He'll probably want to take 'em both right away. After that, who knows? I think 'e wants to keep the nigger for himself, but maybe he'll let the rest of us have the blonde."

"She really a countess?" the man carrying Laurel asked.

"So they say. Doesn't matter, they all have the same thing under their skirts." More coarse laughter.

A soft thump, then Laurel was dumped on the bed with Violet between her and the wall. The men left. A lock clicked. For long moments Laurel just lay there, grateful for the relative comfort of the bed and Violet's warmth, though now it was impossible to ignore all the aches and bruises and her general feeling of sickness.

On the deck above, there were shouted orders, the creaking of wood, the snapping of canvas as sails were unfurled. She supposed they'd have at least a little time before Hardwick returned to his cabin. Softly she said, "Violet, because my hands are up by my face, I was able to pull my gag off. Can you do that?"

Violet shifted and it sounded like she was struggling with her gag before she exclaimed, "Hardwick tied this *tight!*" She exhaled roughly. "But I can breathe now."

Laurel was grateful that Moody hadn't tied her gag more tightly. He didn't take her seriously as a threat, which was certainly justified.

"You heard just before we left the shore that horsemen were charging toward Hardwick? It was Kirkland, I'm sure of it."

"But he's on the shore and we're sailing away." Violet's voice was almost a sob. "It's too late. There's nothing he can do."

"It sounds like he had friends with him, and believe me, he can do a great deal."

"Not enough," Violet said tightly.

"Don't underestimate my husband." The sack over Laurel's head was loose and the rope that secured the blanket around her was lightly tied, only intended to keep the blanket in place. The rope was loose enough that she was able to push her arms straight up, which dragged the sack off her head. She exhaled with pleasure. There was nothing like being blinded for a while to make oneself appreciate sight.

Though her wrists were tied, she was able to swing herself to a sitting position on the edge of the bed. She looked around the cabin. Hardwick didn't stint himself. The furniture was polished mahogany and rich Turkey carpets were underfoot. At the foot of the bed, a gleaming brass tube stood on a tripod, the large end by a porthole. A telescope.

"Are you sitting up?" Violet asked.

"Yes, I was able to get the sack off over my head. I'm looking around for anything that might help us get free."

Unfortunately, since it was a ship's cabin, everything was tightly secured. There was no convenient penknife lying on the built-in desk.

But her wrist bonds definitely seemed loose. The sawing with her cross had stretched the rope. She relaxed her left hand as much as she could and tried to wriggle it out of the looped line. It took time, scraped skin, and several words she almost never used, but finally she pulled her left hand free.

As she tore off her other bonds, she said, "Hallelujah! My hands are free, Violet. Now to get that sack off your head and untie you."

Kirkland reined in his sweaty horse and stared at the dinghy tied onto the *Jamaica Queen*. Dear God, those two long bundles being hauled aboard had to be Laurel and Violet, and *he couldn't do a damned thing!*

"Jesus Christ and all angels," he breathed, not sure if it was a prayer or a curse. "I wonder which of these ships I can most quickly hire to take us after Hardwick."

"The tide will be against us soon," Rob said, his flat voice not concealing his suppressed fury. "It will be difficult to pursue them until the water rises again."

"Not necessarily," Ashton said, his voice lethally cool. "Kirkland, remember that just before the others arrived we talked briefly about my latest infernal machine? I didn't get a chance to say that my new steamship, *Britannia*, just arrived from Glasgow at the end of her sea trials. She's docked less than a quarter mile downriver, and her draft is shallow enough to travel the Thames even at low tide. I was going to invite you all for a test ride this week."

A steamship! Kirkland's head whipped around. "It can follow quickly?"

"It can. It will." Ashton gathered the reins of his

weary mount. Behind them, one of the following carriages rumbled to a stop, and the second carriage wasn't far behind. "There's only a skeleton crew on board at the moment, but with your men here to help, we can catch those bastards."

Kirkland couldn't remember if he'd ever heard Ashton swear before. He'd be swearing more himself if he knew stronger curse words. "Lead on, Ashton, and thank God for infernal machines."

"Incidentally," Ashton said, "you may think you recognize the *Britannia*'s captain, but really, you don't."

Kirkland arched his brows, wondering what mystery was involved. But no matter. As long as Ashton trusted his captain, that was good enough.

The *Britannia* looked squat and odd among the tall-masted sailing ships, with stubby stacks and a wheel on her stern, but to Kirkland she was the most beautiful vessel he'd ever seen. The steamship was moored to a pier rather than anchored out in the river, so a gangplank was laid down when a lookout spotted Ashton approaching.

The duke led the way aboard. He was as sodden and muddy as the rest of them, but his voice crackled with command when he said, "Gordon, we're going in pursuit of a kidnapper right *now*. I trust the boilers are warm?"

"They are," the captain said tersely. A lean man with white blond hair and tanned skin, he froze when he saw who was behind Ashton.

Kirkland did indeed recognize him, and he was sure Rob and Randall did as well. The captain, then not called Gordon, was probably the only student who Lady Agnes Westerfield would consider a failure. Kirkland would love to know how "Gordon" had come to work for Ashton, but at the moment, that wasn't important. All that mattered was that he was competent.

"One of the two women kidnapped is my wife, Captain Gordon," Kirkland said, "so I will be forever grateful if you help us bring them safely home."

Gordon relaxed when he saw that his new identity was accepted. "We can be off in twenty minutes."

"Make it ten," Ashton said. "Is McCarran aboard?"

"No, he's taking shore leave."

"Then I'm chief engineer." Ashton stripped off his exquisitely tailored coat. "The men behind me can be assigned to whatever tasks are needed. A few were sailors and most are experienced in combat. If we can overtake the *Jamaica Queen* before she reaches the sea, we have a fighting chance of saving Lady Kirkland and her maid."

"Give me enough speed from the engines and we'll catch the bastards," Gordon said gruffly. "As soon as we're off, I'll have the grappling hooks brought up."

The captain turned to Kirkland's men as the

handful of *Britannia*'s crew prepared to cast off. "Which of you have sailing experience?" Half a dozen men, including Rob Carmichael, raised their hands. "Then we'll be getting busy now!"

As Gordon snapped orders, Kirkland said to Randall, "Since this is turning into a military operation, you'll be in command of the assault when the time comes. I assume the plan is to roar down the Thames at full speed, pull up alongside the *Jamaica Queen* and lock the ships together with grappling hooks, then board before they figure out what's happening?"

Randall nodded. "There's no way they'll be able to overlook the fact that a steamship is overtaking them, but other steamers have been running trials on the Thames. We'll probably have regular steam packet service in the next few years. Hardwick won't have reason to believe we're after him until we pull alongside and hook on."

"I wouldn't think they'd be able to load and fire the cannon quickly, but surely they'll have guns on board."

"Yes, but they'd be secured in a weapons locker. Most ship captains are justly wary of letting sailors have easy access to weapons," Rob Carmichael said as he joined them. "Gordon doesn't need me as a deckhand since he has enough skilled labor, so I can help with the strategizing, to the extent that can be done."

The steam engines began pounding and the

Britannia pulled away from the pier and began chugging downstream. The great wheel on the stern churned powerfully through the dark water as the captain piloted his way out of the Pool of London.

Kirkland said, "How do you feel about leading a boarding squad when we catch up with the *Jamaica Queen*, Rob?"

"It sounds like a wonderful antidote to the quiet life of an impoverished country gentleman," his friend replied, a wicked gleam in his eyes.

"I thought you were managing to repair your broken inheritance?" Randall said.

"Actually, we're doing fine," Rob said reassuringly. "The mortgages are under control, Ashton gave me some of the best breeding stock in Britain, and some investments I made in India are worth more than expected." He grinned. "I only feel impoverished compared to Ashton and Kirkland."

"If the life of a country gentleman becomes too tedious, you can come back to work for me," Kirkland suggested.

"No, thank you! Agriculture is proving to be more interesting than I expected." Rob's voice turned hard. "But I'm quite ready to administer some justice. Men like Hardwick deserve to be exterminated."

"He will be," Kirkland said tersely.

The *Britannia* had cleared the Pool of London

and was moving more swiftly as she headed eastward toward the mouth of the Thames. If they could maintain this speed, they should catch up with the *Jamaica Queen* well before the sailing ship reached the North Sea. "Randall, is it a fair assumption that Hardwick's men won't have time to get weapons and be ready to shoot when we board?"

"Probably, though never stake your life on 'fair assumptions,'" Randall warned. "What we can ensure is that our men are armed and ready when we board, so we'll have the advantage. Now it's time to look at the grappling hooks and weaponry."

Kirkland and Rob Carmichael accompanied Randall. Kirkland had never fought in a pitched battle before, but he didn't need that experience to know that it was always better to be prepared for as many contingencies as possible.

Be strong, Laurel! I'm coming to take you home.

Chapter 35

E very creak of the ship made Laurel stare fearfully at the cabin door to see if Captain Hardwick was returning to his cabin, but so far there had been no sign of him. The busy river must require the captain to be on deck until traffic thinned out.

As Laurel released Violet, she asked, "Are you hurt? There's blood in your hair."

"Bruised, but nothing broken, I think," Violet whispered. "My head and my ankle hurt the most."

"Lie still while I examine you."

"Lying still is what I can do best," Violet said with a gallant attempt at humor. She relaxed and closed her eyes while Laurel did a swift inventory.

Though the girl had been knocked around more than Laurel, there didn't seem to be serious damage. Violet's ankle was badly sprained, not broken, so she wouldn't be able to move quickly if they had a chance of escape, but binding it would help.

Looking for bandages, Laurel found a drawer containing expensive, carefully folded linens. Monogrammed handkerchiefs served to blot the sluggish bleeding from Violet's grazed scalp. Two cravats gave support to the girl's swelling ankle.

"Rest now," Laurel said as she tied off the cravats. "I'm going to see if I can block the door so Hardwick will have trouble getting in. If Kirkland is coming after us, any extra time will improve our chances of escaping alive."

Violet opened her eyes, showing the strain of not crying out from pain when her ankle was bound. "See if you can find any weapons."

"I don't know how to load or fire a gun," Laurel cautioned.

Violet gave a smile that showed her teeth. "I can. Or a knife. I know how to gut a pig, and Hardwick is a swine."

Laurel firmly repressed her squeamishness. "I'll see what I can find."

Almost all the furniture was built into the cabin so nothing could be moved in front of the door. She tried searching his desk, but most of the drawers were locked. The top drawer did contain a pencil as well as writing paper, so she jammed the pencil into the door lock in the hope that would make it difficult for Hardwick to enter.

His clothespress contained a long wool robe that helped warm her up again. Though she loathed the idea of wearing a garment of Hardwick's, warm was warm. She tucked blankets around Violet, who had dozed off, her face pale.

Laurel was exhausted and would have liked to sleep also, but she couldn't bear to be vulnerable when Hardwick returned. She tucked her sapphire cross into her bodice to keep it safe, then paced the cabin, looking for anything that might be used as a weapon.

The telescope? She removed it from its cradle consideringly, but it was too heavy and clumsy to be an effective club. The only other loose objects were too light to be of use. Even the swiveling desk chair was bolted down.

How long would it take Kirkland to hire a ship to pursue the *Jamaica Queen*? At least a couple of hours, and then there was the matter of the tides. She wasn't sure how long it would take to sail from London to the open sea, but she had the sick feeling that it would be too long for her and Violet.

So she paced the cabin, and prayed.

It was full dark now, with enough light from the stars and a waxing moon to see other boats on the river. With night, there wasn't much other traffic.

Kirkland stood in the *Britannia*'s bow, straining his eyes for the first glimpse of the *Jamaica Queen*. Rhodes stood to his left, tight lipped and silent. Rob Carmichael and Randall were to the right, equally watchful but more relaxed. Randall in particular looked as he must have before battle. Calm, focused, and ready for anything.

Ashton had yet to emerge from the engine room, where he was squeezing the maximum possible speed out of the engines short of blowing up the ship. Kirkland had visited his friend in the small, fiercely hot room. Ash was having the time of his life. He'd always had a very un-ducal passion for mechanical devices, and never had that skill been more vital.

"There's our quarry." Rob pointed. "Just before the river bends. She's fast, but we're faster."

"Much faster." Randall uncoiled from the railing. "Time to muster our troops so they're armed and ready. Captain Gordon is going to blow that horrific horn of his as if we're just passing the *Jamaica Queen*. Then we'll ram the *Queen*, lock on, and board her. Our main deck is a couple of feet higher, which is an advantage. It's always better to have the high ground."

"I'll go belowdecks to find the captives as quickly as I can," Kirkland said. "I'm guessing they're in one of the cabins, most likely Hardwick's."

"I'll go with you," Rhodes said, his voice hard.

"I'll follow once the main deck is secured," Rob said. "With luck, we can move fast enough to do this without much bloodshed."

"I don't care if we kill them all!" Rhodes spat out. "The bloody bastards are slavers as well as kidnappers."

"You've never killed a man, have you, Rhodes?" Randall's voice was soft.

"No," Rhodes admitted, "but I'm ready to tonight."

"It's harder to kill than you might think,"

Randall continued in that same low voice. "So concentrate your murderous impulses on those who deserve it the most."

Despite the soft tone, there was something in Randall's words that cut to the bone. Rhodes drew a deep breath. "I know you're right, sir. But if I can corner Hardwick or that scar-faced devil who was stalking Violet, I'll damn well make them pay for what they've done."

"You may have to fight Kirkland for the honor," Randall said dryly. "But believe me when I say that it's best to concentrate on achieving our mission rather than dwelling on revenge. Too much emotion can be dangerous in battle." He moved off to prepare his troops, Rob Carmichael by his side.

"I'm understanding better what it takes to be a soldier," Rhodes said to Kirkland.

"It's going to be an educational night all around," Kirkland agreed.

"You've been doing this sort of thing for years, haven't you, sir?"

"Not full-fledged assaults like this, but there have been dangerous situations." Kirkland's mouth tightened. Never had the personal stakes been as high as tonight.

Rhodes gazed at the *Jamaica Queen*, which they were fast overtaking. "Educational indeed. By dawn, I'll be wiser or dead."

Kirkland hoped neither of them would be dead. But death was a very real possibility. There was no question that he would sacrifice his life to save Laurel's. He just hoped he didn't have to.

Captain Gordon did a flawless job of bringing the *Britannia* alongside the *Jamaica Queen*, then slamming it into the port side of the other vessel. They crashed with an impact that probably knocked half the men on the sailing ship off their feet, but neither vessel was damaged to the point of taking water.

Kirkland and his men were waiting and braced for impact. The sound of the crash was still reverberating when Randall bellowed, *"NOW!"*

Grappling hooks flew through air, propelled by the men with sailing experience. Rob Carmichael was among them, and he hooked into the sailing ship's rigging with his first cast.

In moments, enough hooks had caught to lock the two vessels together. Soames, who was such a dignified butler, had explained that screaming unnerved the enemy, so the boarding party catapulted over the railing with howls that could curdle a man's blood.

Though Kirkland was known for his reserve, he found himself shouting, *"For Laurel!"* like a berserker as he vaulted down to the *Jamaica Queen*'s deck beside Randall. Killing wasn't his first choice, but he had a pistol in one hand and a dagger at his side, along with the skill to kill with his bare hands if necessary.

They caught the *Jamaica Queen* totally unawares. Sailors boiled out of the hatches onto the main deck and were rounded up by some of Kirkland's men who were armed with shotguns that could tear large, messy holes in anyone who resisted.

A few fought, and fought hard. Randall charged full force into a skirmish and took two men down immediately while Rob protected his friend's back and brought down a man who was coming at Randall with a knife.

Cursing the darkness, Kirkland scanned the battle. Where the devil was Hardwick? Shouldn't he be up here leading his men? Maybe he was and Kirkland just couldn't find him.

The scar-faced man! Kirkland spotted him amidships. Probably an officer since he was shouting orders and trying to rally his sailors. He would know where the captives were being held.

Kirkland raced across the deck, dodging skirmishing sailors until he reached Scar Face, who was shouting orders with his back against the main mast. Kirkland used the single shot in his pistol to put a bullet through the man's shoulder.

Scar Face spun and fell to the deck, screaming with pain. Kirkland planted a boot in the middle of his chest and held the tip of the dagger to his throat. "The women! Where are they?"

Scar Face spat. Kirkland drew an inch long slice

across the devil's throat. *"Where are they?* Tell me and you won't die just yet."

Face white in contrast to his blood, Scar Face gasped, "Captain's cabin, one deck down in the stern."

Kirkland was preparing to club the side of Scar Face's head with the butt of his empty pistol when Rhodes appeared, a line of blood on his forehead.

"You *bastard!*" Rhodes snarled. "This is for what you did to Violet!" Gripping his pistol in both hands, he shot Scar Face in the head at point-blank range.

"Congratulations," Kirkland said dryly as he swiftly reloaded his pistol. "You can now say you've killed a man."

Rhodes stood over the body of his victim, staring at the blood and blasted bone. Fury had turned to sick horror. He was indeed having an educational night.

Rhodes would recover in time, but Kirkland wasn't about to wait for that to happen. Reloaded pistol in hand, he turned toward the stern hatch that would take him down to the captain's quarters—and found one of Hardwick's men aiming a pistol at his head from barely six feet away.

Kirkland was about to hurl himself to one side and hope that the pistol ball wouldn't hit any lethal area when a shot rang out and his attacker crumpled. Blood sprayed from his temple and he was dead before he hit the deck.

Kirkland had heard the sharp crack of a rifle, so he spun around, looking for the source. Captain Gordon stood on the deck of the *Britannia*, almost obscured by the cloud of smoke belched out by his rifle. The weapon was clamped upright between his knees as he swiftly reloaded.

As the smoke cleared, their gazes met. Kirkland gave a fierce nod of acknowledgment and thanks. Gordon inclined his head ironically. Everything that had been between them in the past vanished, no longer important.

Then Kirkland headed toward the rear hatch that would bring him down by the captain's cabin, and prayed that his wife was still safe.

Laurel had lit a lamp when it became dark. She'd also found a flask with a small amount of excellent brandy. She gave most to Violet to dull the pain, but took a couple of swigs herself. For the first time, she had some empathy for men who drank too much.

She was pacing around the cabin once again when a shocking crash rocked the ship and pitched her to the floor. As the swinging lantern sent wild shadows splashing across the cabin, she looked up at the portholes. Good heavens, another ship was crunched against the left side of the *Jamaica Queen*! Grinding against it, in fact, with deep, ominous groans.

Kirkland. She couldn't imagine how he'd done

it, but somehow he'd found a ship and followed faster than was humanly possible.

As shouting and shots sounded above, Violet was jarred awake. Looking composed after her rest, she pushed herself to a sitting position. "What's happening?"

"Kirkland has caught up with us and has a crew boarding like pirates." More grinding sounds from the friction between the ships. "I don't know how on earth he did it, but he did."

Violet's eyes glinted with fierce satisfaction. "You warned them he would come. And I am sure my Jasper is with him."

Laurel nodded agreement. "Hardwick isn't the sort to listen to a woman. The more fool he."

Violet's knuckles whitened on the edge of the bed as she swung her legs over the side and carefully stood. "My ankle is . . . better. If we must run, I can run."

"God willing, we can stay safely inside here until the fighting is over."

The shouting and shots above were dying down. The battle must almost be over. Then the door rattled and a key scraped futilely in the lock. Hardwick was trying to enter the cabin. Laurel froze, her gaze riveted on the door.

The pencil jamming worked! Vicious oaths scalded the air on the other side of the door. Laurel held her breath. The lock wouldn't have to hold for much longer. . . .

Boom! The door rattled from a thunderous kick. *Boom! Boom! BOOM!* The door lock shattered and the door swung inward. Hardwick charged into his cabin like a rampaging bull, flinging the useless door shut behind him.

For an instant he stared at his captives. "Stupid sailors! I just said to lock you in, not untie you. But no matter. Since you can walk, it will save me time as I escape this rattrap." He crossed the cabin to the desk in three long strides.

The captain did something to the desk and there was a loud click as the drawers unlocked. He yanked a pair of pistols from the bottom drawer.

Laurel bit her lip, wishing she'd been able to figure out the desk lock. She doubted she could shoot a man, but Violet would have fewer qualms.

As Hardwick checked the loading of his weapons, he snarled, "You bitches are going to be my hostages to get out of here. If I have guns to your heads, they'll let me go off in a dinghy."

His gaze locked onto Violet. "Haven't got time to shag you, but I'm bloody well going to have a sample." Leaving one pistol on the desk, he strode toward the bed and grabbed Violet's hand. "Feel what's waiting for you, slut!"

He was pulling her hand toward his crotch when she jerked free and caught hold of his little finger. Eyes blazing, she bent the finger backward with vicious force.

Hardwick pulled back, screaming with shock and pain. *"Damn you!"*

Face feral, Violet hissed, "You're the one who will be damned to hell for eternity, you vile swine!"

As Hardwick struck her with a heavy hand, the lockless door swung open so hard it smashed into the wall. "It's all over now, Hardwick!"

Kirkland's voice was lethally cold as he charged through the doorway, his gaze scanning the cabin. When he saw Laurel, desperate relief blazed in his eyes.

In that instant when Kirkland's attention was on Laurel, Hardwick spun around and raised his cocked pistol, taking dead aim at Kirkland.

Noooo! As panic screamed through Laurel, the action slowed to a hallucinatory speed. Operating on frantic instinct, she grabbed the heavy brass telescope from its stand as if it weighed no more than a broom handle and smashed it into the back of Hardwick's head with every iota of strength she possessed.

She could feel his bones break under the impact of her blow. Hardwick made a single strangled sound before pitching over on his side. His pistol discharged into the ceiling with a deafening boom in the confined space.

Then there was silence except for the low grinding of the ships. Laurel stared aghast at Hardwick, knowing that no one could survive with his neck bent at that angle.

She had killed a man. Laurel Herbert, known for her gentleness, kindness, and cowardly inability to wring a chicken's neck, who had broken her sacred vows and walked away when her husband killed, was herself a murderer.

She began shaking and her knees started to buckle. Then strong, warm arms embraced her, holding her safe. "Dear *God,* Laurel," Kirkland breathed, his words an anguished prayer of relief. "I was so afraid that I'd lost you forever!"

She buried her face against him, still shaking. As if at a great distance, she heard another man enter. Rhodes called out, "Violet!"

Violet cried, "Jasper!" Laurel heard the sound of two people coming together, heard sobs and ragged prayers of thanks, but she couldn't move to save her life.

She'd saved her husband's life—and incinerated her soul.

Chapter 36

B ecause Kirkland and his friends had discussed the possibilities, cleaning up after capturing the *Jamaica Queen* was surprisingly swift. They'd achieved the best of all possible outcomes. Both women were safe and had suffered no serious physical damage. Kirkland was sure there was some mental and emotional damage, but Laurel and Violet were strong women. They had survived, and they would heal.

Several men from the *Britannia* had been wounded, but none of the injuries were serious. The *Jamaica Queen* had suffered many more casualties, with four deaths: Hardwick; Scar Face, who turned out to be a second mate named Moody; the sailor shot by Captain Gordon; and a brute of a sail maker who made the fatal mistake of trying to stab Rob Carmichael with a huge marlinespike.

Hardwick's first mate claimed that he'd known nothing about the kidnapping in advance. He'd been appalled to learn that two women, one of them gently born, had been abducted, and he'd planned to secretly help them escape in a dinghy before the Thames emptied into the sea. Kirkland judged him as a liar and a weasel, but his earnest desire to change sides made him useful.

Rob Carmichael and Randall stayed on the *Jamaica Queen* with enough of Kirkland's men to ensure that the surviving members of Hardwick's crew would behave. They'd sail the ship back to London.

Kirkland, Rhodes, their ladies, and the Kirkland House men who'd been injured returned to London on the *Britannia*. With Ashton in the engine room and Captain Gordon at the helm, they steamed back to the city at a speed only slightly less than what they'd maintained on the chase downstream. Ashton was very pleased with the performance of his new steamship.

Kirkland spent most of the return trip with Laurel, lying on the bunk in a cabin and holding her in his arms. She seemed numb with shock and barely aware of him. Kirkland wasn't in the habit of praying, but he sent up fervent prayers that she would recover swiftly from all she'd endured.

But the disasters weren't over. When Kirkland and Laurel arrived home in late morning, Laurel closed her eyes and pressed her hand to her belly, a spasm of pain twisting her face. "Please," she whispered, "ask Lady Julia to come as soon as she can."

Dear God, what if she was miscarrying? The thought made him ill, but Kirkland guessed that after all that she endured in the last day, it wasn't surprising. "I'll bring her right away," he promised, "but first we need to get you to your bed."

When he scooped her up in his arms, he saw two or three tiny drops of scarlet blood on the foyer's marble floor. His heart twisted beyond grief.

With most of the male servants not yet returned, it was a housemaid who appeared when he called out. Tersely he said, "Send Mrs. Stratton up to Lady Kirkland's rooms immediately." Then he carried his wife up the long stairs, each step pounding like a lead weight on his brain.

He hated to leave her, but he could bring Julia most quickly. Plus, he needed to reassure Mariah as well as Lady Julia that their husbands were all right.

By the time he laid Laurel on her bed, Mrs. Stratton was there, her expression aghast. "Poor sweet lady! We'll take care of her."

Kirkland brushed a kiss on Laurel's pale cheek, then headed out to the mews, not bothering to change his muddy clothing. He would have hitched the horses to his chaise himself, but the one groom who hadn't gone after Laurel because he'd lost a leg in the army insisted on doing it for him. Kirkland leaned against the stable wall, so tired that he was in the numb state that lay beyond exhaustion.

Luckily, it was a short drive to Ashton House. As soon as he was admitted, Mariah, Julia, and Sarah came flying down the sweeping staircase along with Randall's foster son, Benjamin, and Rob's daughter, Bree.

"Our mission was a complete success," Kirkland said quickly, realizing he should have known his friends' families would gather here for mutual support. "Your menfolk are unhurt, and they made it possible to rescue Laurel and Violet."

As Benjamin whooped with relief and Bree hugged Sarah, Mariah said fervently, "Thank heaven! What happened?"

"The kidnapper, Hardwick, got them onto his ship and was sailing down the Thames," Kirkland explained. "But Ashton's steamship, the *Britannia*, was moored nearby, so we went in pursuit. With Ashton ruining his clothes in the engine room, we made record speed. We overtook and boarded the kidnappers' ship, ably led by Rob and Randall. No serious casualties on our side."

"When will they be home?" Mariah asked.

"Ashton will be here quite soon. He brought us back on the *Britannia*, but he had to shut the boilers down or some such before he could leave the boat." To Julia, Kirkland said, "Randall will be home later today, probably this evening. He and Rob are bringing back the sailing ship with prisoners." He exhaled roughly. "I am fortunate in my friends."

"You've more than earned that, James," Julia said quietly as she wrapped an arm around Benjamin's shoulders. "Given everything Alex has survived, I shouldn't have been worried, but it's hard not to. How is Laurel doing?"

Every muscle in Kirkland's body tensed. "I think . . . I think she's miscarrying. She sent me to get you. Do I need to call in a physician as well?"

Her face compassionate, Lady Julia said, "Not unless there are complications, which is unlikely this early in the pregnancy. I'll go upstairs for my midwife bag and we can leave right away."

As Lady Julia moved swiftly up the stairs, Sarah said softly, "I'm so sorry, Kirkland. If there's anything I can do . . ."

He closed his eyes, knowing there was nothing that could be done for the child that would never be. "Thank you. As long as Laurel is all right . . ." His voice trailed off.

"She will be," Mariah said firmly. "Julia is probably the best midwife in England. She saved my life when Richard was born. But you, sir, also need some saving. Or at the very least, a long rest." Her nose wrinkled. "And a bath!"

He smiled a little at that. Trust Mariah to bring a bit of light into a dark day. "I fully intend to sleep the clock around once I know Laurel is all right."

"See that you do," she ordered.

Lady Julia was already gliding downstairs, one hand on the railing and the other holding a sizable tapestry bag. He took it from her and led the way out to the chaise.

When they reached Kirkland House, he returned

the chaise while Lady Julia went inside immediately. By the time he returned to Laurel, Lady
Julia was able to meet him outside the bedroom
with a diagnosis.

"It's as expected," Julia said quietly. "It was far
too early to know if it would have been a boy or a
girl. As miscarriages go, this one was fairly easy
physically, if that's any comfort. Laurel is doing
well, but very, very tired. She just wants to sleep.
She said that you were to do the same."

"Can I sleep with her? Just . . . to hold her?"

Julia shook her head. "You both need deep,
uncomplicated rest. Someone will stay with her.
She'll be tired for a few days, but she should be
back to normal within a fortnight." Julia hesitated,
then added, "Physically, anyhow. She's had a
difficult time of it. I know I don't have to tell you
to be gentle with her."

His mouth twisted humorlessly. "I shall do my
clumsy male best. I assume there's no reason I
can't see her, just to be sure she's all right?"

"Go ahead, but quietly. She's sleeping now."

He opened the door to her bedroom and saw that,
rather unexpectedly, Mrs. Simond was the one
sitting with Laurel. But they had become good
friends, and Badger had followed along. The cat
lay sleeping at Laurel's side. She'd be happy to see
him when she woke.

He moved silently to her bedside and saw that
she'd been cleaned up and put into a nightgown

with her lovely bronze hair in a braid. She lay peacefully, looking very young. He kissed her hair with gossamer lightness. "Sleep well, my love."

When he headed out to his own room, he realized that he couldn't remember when he'd last eaten. But the numbness that wrapped body and soul had also numbed his appetite. Sleep first. There'd be time enough to eat when he awoke.

He barely managed to get his boots off. Rhodes-the-valet would have been upset by their condition, but Rhodes-the-lover probably wasn't thinking about much beyond the fact that he had Violet safely back.

Kirkland stripped off his coat, which was ruined, and his cravat, whose condition didn't interest him in the least. Then he crawled into bed, wrapped his arms around a pillow as a poor substitute for Laurel, and slept the clock around—despite recurring nightmares of losing his wife beyond recall.

It was barely dawn when Laurel woke the next morning. She lay in bed and watched the shape of the canopy become more visible in the lightening room. Physically, she felt fairly well. The cramping was gone, and while she had bruises all over her body, when she considered what her condition would have been on the *Jamaica Queen*, she felt amazing.

Except . . . she rested her hand on her belly,

which no longer contained that bright spark of possibility. She felt hollow. Worthless. She'd failed her husband and herself.

And she'd killed a man. Not in cold blood, and not without cause. But she would remember the crunching bones when the heavy telescope smashed into her victim for as long as she lived.

Wanting to obliterate the memory, she sat up in bed and looked around the familiar room. Mrs. Stratton was asleep on the most comfortable chair. Everyone had taken such good care of her. And yet . . .

With sudden desperation, she wanted to go home. Not this grand house which belonged to Lady Kirkland, but home to Bristol to her brother and her friends and her plain, practical clothing. Lady Kirkland, after all, had failed in the first duty of a peeress, which was to produce an heir. She didn't deserve this grand house.

Quietly, so as not to wake the housekeeper, she rose and tiptoed into her dressing room. It took only a few minutes to don one of her simple old gowns and to throw a few items into a bag. Most of her life was back in Bristol, after all.

She slung the bag over her shoulder and headed downstairs and out to the mews. The household would be waking soon, and the stables were already stirring. The grooms were awake and drinking strong tea, grooming horses, and telling each other stories of their grand adventure of rescuing her ladyship and the pretty lady's maid.

The grooms fell silent when they saw her approaching. She managed a smile, though it didn't feel real. "I owe you more than I can ever say. Thank you."

They smiled and shuffled and looked very proud of themselves, as they deserved to. Addressing the head groom, she said, "Could you hitch up the travel coach? I'm going home to Bristol."

"Will his lordship be coming with you, my lady?" the groom asked doubtfully.

She shook her head. "No, he has a great deal to do here before he can go anywhere. Being a pirate in the Thames requires a fair amount of explanation."

They laughed at that, then went to hitch the horses to the travel coach. In here as in all ways, Kirkland had made her life so easy.

Such a pity that she hadn't done the same for him.

Chapter 37

When Kirkland awoke after the longest sleep of his life, he realized that his brief career as a marine boarding an enemy vessel had involved a lot more bangs and bruises than he'd realized. He rang for hot water to bathe, wondering who would appear. Rhodes and Violet had both been given a week off to recover. Rhodes intended to take Violet to meet his mother and sister and then show her some of the sights of London, since she'd not been able to travel freely about the city.

While waiting for the hot water to arrive—he really needed to upgrade the plumbing; what he'd seen at Rob Carmichael's house had been worth duplicating—he crossed to Laurel's room. The bed was empty and neatly made up, so she was up and about. She must be feeling better.

As he turned to leave, he saw her sapphire cross sitting on the dressing table. The chain was missing. He wondered what happened to it, but it was no great matter. Chains were easily replaced.

He took the cross to his room, where the hot water was arriving, and Yarrow, one of the footmen who aspired to become a valet, was waiting to shave him. This was a good chance to assess the fellow's skills, since Rhodes would be moving into Kirkland's intelligence office soon. Apart from his initial shock after killing Moody, he'd acquitted himself well under dangerous conditions.

Washed, shaved, and dressed in clean clothing, Kirkland felt like, if not a new man, at least a man in good functioning condition. He also realized that he was ravenous, and the quickest way to be fed was to head right to the source.

As he entered the kitchen, Mrs. Simond looked up and beamed. If he wasn't her employer, she might have hugged him. "There you are, my lord, and right hungry, I'm sure! Shall I make up a skillet of eggs and sausage and potatoes the way you like it?"

"That would be splendid, along with toast and preserves and something hot to drink." As the cook ordered one of her assistants to take care of tea and toast, he settled into a Windsor chair by the deal table, feeling deeply content.

Badger leaped onto his lap and settled down with a purr, leaving white hair on Kirkland's dark coat and black hair on his white shirt with a complete lack of discrimination. As Kirkland scratched the broad feline head, he asked, "Do you know where Lady Kirkland is at the moment?"

"Oh, she must be halfway to Bristol by now," the cook said cheerfully. "You slept a very long time, my lord, and no surprise, such a hero as you are!

The stories the men brought back about how you rescued her ladyship and young Violet!"

His hand froze on Badger's head. Laurel was gone. She'd left him again and he knew this wasn't a simple visit to see her brother. Once again their marriage had broken.

No, it was Laurel who was broken. As anguish flooded through him, he felt equally broken.

Breathe! He was lucky that a body eventually remembered to do so. Belatedly responding to Mrs. Simond, he said, "I had a great deal of help from my friends."

"Aye, and you're all heroes." She set a steaming mug of tea in front of him, along with a plate of fresh toast and little pots of preserves and honey. "With maybe some divine intervention, I say."

He took a deep swallow of scalding tea, feeling it curl through him with heat and energy. "You may be right. The Duke of Ashton has been developing better steamships for years, but having one nearby and ready to go was truly a miracle."

He needed another miracle. As he ate Mrs. Simond's hot, hearty breakfast, his mind began to clear. Once before he'd let Laurel run away and made no attempt to stop her, but not this time. Then he'd been too aware of his failings. He hadn't believed that he deserved love and happiness.

Though he had all those failings and more, he'd come to realize that if only those without flaws deserved happiness, the world would be a bleak place indeed. He thought of his closest friends and the remarkable women they'd married. In no case had building a lasting marriage been easy, but those friends had proved it could be done.

Laurel had changed, he had changed, the situation had changed. They need not make the same mistakes again.

It wasn't too late in the day to set off for Bristol. But before he left, he would pay a call on Lady Julia Randall.

Laurel found it comforting to sleep in her own bed again with Shadow lying beside her. Even more comforting had been her big brother's welcoming embrace. His first question after she'd buried herself in his arms was, "What has Kirkland done?"

"Nothing," she whispered. "Nothing at all."

Her voice ragged, she told her brother the bare bones of the story. She could feel his pain when he heard of the miscarriage, but with the wisdom learned in years of medical practice, he didn't offer soothing platitudes. Instead he invited Anne Wilson to put Laurel to bed, then gave his sister the solitude she craved.

She slept the sleep of utter exhaustion through the night and most of the next day. Now night had fallen again and she could sleep no more. She supposed she should be hungry, but she had no appetite.

She supposed she should cry, but she had no tears.

Music. Only music might express the wordless anguish of her soul.

> Music alone with sudden charms can bind
> The wand'ring sense, and calm the
> troubled mind.

That was William Congreve, she thought. She had the wandering senses, and certainly the troubled mind. She lit a lamp, then made her way to the music room.

But she feared that on this night, even music wouldn't be enough to soothe her troubled mind.

Chapter 38

Kirkland arrived in Bristol after dark. It was almost too late to call on anyone, even a family member. But to hell with manners—he wasn't going to wait a moment longer than necessary to see Laurel.

He waited so long after wielding Herbert House's knocker that he nearly gave up. Then Daniel opened the door, his face weary and his shirt spattered with dried blood.

Daniel's brows arched when he saw who was on his doorstep. "I've been wondering if you'd come." He moved back so Kirkland could enter the small foyer.

"I'm not making the same mistake I did before." Tiredly Kirkland stepped inside. "Are you going to castigate me for bringing pain and trouble on your sister's head?"

"I expect you're doing quite enough self-castigation without my help," Daniel said gravely. "I'm deeply sorry for your loss, James."

"It's a loss for all of us." Daniel had always loved children and would have delighted in a niece or nephew. Kirkland forced himself not to think of that. "Are you going to be a protective big brother and refuse to let me see Laurel? I don't advise it."

"It's not my place to interfere in your marriage." Daniel hesitated, then added with painful honesty, "I've recognized that my motives have been less than pure. Yes, you're a complicated devil and not necessarily whom I would have chosen for my sister's husband, but you're her choice, which is all that matters."

"For which I've never stopped thanking God. Laurel has been the greatest blessing of my life." Kirkland wished that she could say the same of him, but he was no one's blessing.

"When she went to London with you, her absence left a large hole in my life." Daniel's mouth twisted. "She's been my best friend and partner for years, but it's not fair to her. She deserves so much more than an absent-minded, overworked brother."

Kirkland shook his head. "Don't regret what you've built here together. Laurel certainly doesn't. You gave her love and support when your parents turned her away, not to mention the chance to use her abilities as few women can."

"Yes, but I think her true home is with you." Daniel smiled self-mockingly. "I'll have to find the time to make some friends."

"We were good friends once, Daniel," Kirkland said quietly. "When Laurel left me, it was doubly painful because I lost you at the same time. Is there any chance we can be friends again?"

Daniel became very still. "I've never found

anyone who was so good at discussing theology and philosophy."

"And disagreeing with you half the time." Kirkland smiled and offered a hand. "I believe I still owe you a letter rebutting your foolish opinions of Adam Smith and his *Wealth of Nations*."

Daniel's face eased into a real smile and he took Kirkland's hand. "You're still wrong, you know."

"Prove it!"

Daniel laughed and released Kirkland's hand. "I'll start mustering my arguments. But for now—follow the music." He opened the door that led into the house and a mournful tune drifted down from the music room.

Kirkland took a deep breath. "Wish me luck."

"I'm wishing you both luck. Or to be precise, I'm praying for you." Daniel inclined his head, then returned to whatever he'd been doing.

Kirkland climbed the stairs and quietly opened the door to the music room. Laurel sat on the bench with her skirts spilling about her and a flickering lamp sitting on the Broadwood. She glanced up, her expression bleak. Unsurprised and uninterested in his arrival, she turned back to the instrument.

Kirkland sat on the bench beside her, but kept distance between them since she didn't look as if she wanted to be touched. She seemed frighteningly withdrawn, and he didn't know how to reach her.

He began with the music, since that was an integral part of their marriage. "I love Gregorian chant and you play it beautifully, but it's melancholy."

"It suits my mood." Her long fingers stroked out a haunting melody of loss.

Since that was a dead end, he asked the question that mattered the most. "Do you plan on returning to London, or is this intended to be a permanent move?"

"I don't know," she said softly. "I don't know anything except that I have failed as a wife and as a woman. I have miscarried my salvation."

Her palpable pain sliced through him like a blade. Though he doubted words could lance such grief, he had to try. "I talked with Lady Julia before I left London. She says that many conceptions, perhaps as many as one in four or five, end in early miscarriage. Perhaps even more. There was nothing unusual about this one. Julia thought it would have happened even if you hadn't been abducted by Hardwick."

"She can't know that. No one can." Laurel finished the chant she'd been playing and let her fingers walk slowly up and down the keyboard. The result wasn't music. Just sad, lonely notes.

Trying again, Kirkland said, "Julia thinks there's no reason to believe you can't have a child in the future."

"She told me the same thing," Laurel said, her voice dull. "But given that I didn't conceive in

401

the first year of marriage and now I've lost this child, I don't seem to be very good material for motherhood." More lonely plunking notes.

He swallowed hard. "A marriage is more than procreation."

"Yes, there's inheritance as well." Her hands stilled on the keyboard. "I've been thinking. It wouldn't be difficult to arrange apparent adultery on my part so you could divorce me and find a more fertile wife."

He stared at her. "What an *appalling* idea! Divorce is . . . unthinkable. Remember those vows we've discussed? For better or worse, as long as we both shall live."

Her voice profoundly sad, she asked, "Even if I can't give you an heir?"

"*Bedamned* to having an heir to the title!" he exploded. "I don't care about the bloody title! All I care about is you. Would you like to raise a child? Several children? There are always babies in need of homes. Any child we raise will be ours in every way that matters."

Finally she looked at him. "You wouldn't mind that?"

"Not at all." He laid his hand over hers where it rested on the keyboard, his fingers striking a deep chord. "As long as I have you, Laurel. As my wife in all ways. We've worked to rebuild our marriage, and I think we've done a decent job of it. Don't give up now."

She swallowed convulsively. "I . . . don't know how to go on."

"Hour by hour. Day by day. In time, going forward becomes easier." His voice turned wry. "I certainly didn't spend ten years celibate so I could find another woman! The night we met, I knew I'd love you as long as I lived. I told myself the thought was absurd, but it was God's own truth. You are my soul, Laurel. Without you, I'm a hollow man with nothing in my life but responsibility." His hand tightened on hers. "I want more than that."

Her detachment shattered and she jerked her hand away from him. "I'm a murderer, James! I killed Hardwick without a single instant's thought." Her voice choked. "I feel as if . . . as if losing the baby is punishment for my sins."

The power of guilt; he knew it well. "That's rubbish," he said flatly. "Would you rather have let Hardwick kill me? I'm vain enough to think my life is worth more than his. I certainly hope you think it is!"

"Of course I'm glad to have saved you! But does that make me any less of a sinner? *Thou shalt not kill*." She buried her face in her hands, her shoulders shaking. "Perhaps I could have stopped him without using so much force."

His voice softened. "When vicious men are waving loaded pistols around, it's best to err on the side of force. Trust your instincts, my lady. You did what was necessary."

"It isn't just that I killed a man, though that's bad enough," she whispered. "I put you and your friends in mortal danger. I don't know how I can live with myself. "

"We managed to rescue you and Violet with no serious casualties," Kirkland said. "But even if we hadn't been so lucky, every man who came with me knew the risks. To act is to accept the consequences of that action, and all of them did. Doing the right thing often means taking risks."

She swallowed hard. "I'm glad there were no other casualties, but I'm responsible for the death of Martin. He was just doing his job, and they killed him right in front of me! He never had a chance." Her eyes closed briefly. "Did you know that he and one of the housemaids had been planning to marry? And now he's dead."

Glad that he could offer some good news, Kirkland said, "Actually, Martin is alive and reasonably well. After they carried you and Violet off, he staggered across the park and fell bleeding at my feet with the news of the abduction. He behaved admirably, and I intend to see that he is well rewarded, along with my other servants who went so far above and beyond their duty."

Her head snapped up. "Martin isn't dead? Thank *God!*"

"You need to do more than thank God, Laurel." Kirkland pulled her sapphire cross from an inside pocket. It had a delicate new golden chain. He pressed it into her hand, then wrapped an arm around her shoulders and pulled her close to his side.

Softly he continued, "You need to ask God for forgiveness. That's His job, isn't it? To forgive imperfect humankind. You are quick to forgive others and offer them kindness. Do the same for yourself." He couldn't keep the catch out of his voice. "*Please.* Because I can't bear to lose you again."

For an instant she stiffened and he feared that she would pull away. Then she opened her hand and stared at the cross. The sapphires sparkled in the lamplight with a clear Madonna blue.

Turning her face into his shoulder, she began to weep great, tearing sobs of loss and anguish. He wrapped his other arm around her and drew her closer to his heart.

Her agonized tears would have been unendurable, except that finally she'd turned to him.

Laurel felt as if the pain would tear her apart. With stark clarity, she recognized that she'd never fully accepted that James could love her because she had never loved herself. No matter how hard she'd tried, she'd never been quite good enough for her parents, and that deep belief in her own unworthiness had shaped her life.

Laurel Herbert, the doctor's saintly sister, had been considered a paragon of faith in her community. Giving love had come easily to her, so she gave to everyone around, both for the pleasure of giving and as a way to compensate for her unworthiness.

Yet she had never been fully able to accept love, except perhaps from her brother, who had been raised under the same roof. She had wanted to give James a child as the ultimate gift, for nothing less would be a sufficient return for all he'd given her. Having the prospect of a child, then failing, was devastating.

Knowing herself to be unworthy, she'd never dared ask for forgiveness. The faith she had tried to keep at the center of her life was as weak and flawed as the rest of her.

And yet—James loved her anyhow. His words, his voice, the tenderness of his embrace made it impossible not to believe. She realized that beyond the passion and music they shared, on a deep level beyond words they were the same: flawed, imperfect beings who yearned for love and doubted they were worthy of it.

Where there was love, there was grace and mercy and forgiveness. With her tears ruining her husband's shirt, she began to pray for the ability to forgive herself. For acceptance of her failings, for the strength to do better, and for the ability to give James the joy he deserved.

A pinprick of golden light formed in the center of the despair that enveloped her. She caught her breath at that break in the darkness. When she reached for the light with her heart, it expanded through her, growing into brilliant currents of warmth and forgiveness that illuminated every dark corner of her tarnished soul.

Her tears faded as she contemplated this new inner landscape. Yes, she'd miscarried the child she'd longed for and the pain was deep, but it was a grief that had been born by women from time immemorial.

She had killed a man and that was not something she would ever forget, yet committing lethal violence had been the right choice when the alternative was seeing her beloved killed before her very eyes. She had brought Hardwick's danger into the lives of her husband and his friends, but she couldn't have walked away from a desperately struggling Violet that day in Bristol.

To act was to accept the consequences of one's actions. She had done the right thing by rescuing Violet, and though the consequences had been terrifying, in the end right had prevailed. For that, she gave profound thanks.

She lifted her tearstained face and looked into the fathomless blue depths of her husband's eyes, which had seen so much. "Have I mentioned lately how much I love you? You are not only stronger, richer, and better looking than I am, but wiser. I don't know if I'll ever understand why you love me, but from this day forth I won't question it. I'll just accept your love as the greatest gift of my life."

"You don't know why? Because of your warmth, my lady," he said as a smile illuminated his face, dissolving his pain and yearning. "The endless, blessed warmth that surrounds you wherever you go. Your presence makes everyone around you feel better and happier." His smile turned rueful. "The intensity of my love is a mark of how very much my cold, dark soul needs that warmth."

"Then it will be my pleasure to warm you day and night." The new lightness in her soul allowed her to add teasingly, "Warming your nights will have to wait a bit, but not long, I promise you."

She tilted her head back and gave him a kiss that was a promise of forever. "We'll make enough warmth together to light all the nights of our lives."

He kissed her back, his strong arms enfolding her. "For better or worse, as long as we both shall live. You're all I ever wanted, my love."

And it was enough. *He* was enough. For always.

Epilogue

London

The house was filled with music. Kirkland smiled as he entered his home, Laurel's rich piano performance floating sweetly down the stairs. Since the servants enjoyed hearing her play, she'd taken to leaving the door of the music room open so the sound carried through the house.

The first thing Kirkland did was hand his hat to Soames, now a butler again, though the older man admitted he'd enjoyed his brief return to his military days. Then Kirkland followed the music.

He paused in the doorway of the music room. He always loved watching Laurel, and never more than when she was creating magic at the piano. Today she wore a bright gown in shades of violet and rose, the silk shining as the folds spilled around her. She was surely the loveliest creature on God's earth.

Sensing his presence, she looked up and gave the smile that was special for him, the one filled with endless warmth and love and understanding.

In the month since they'd returned from Bristol, their marriage had entered a new phase. Passion was banked as they hadn't yet resumed marital intimacy. Both of them, especially Laurel, wanted to put some time between the disasters that had almost shattered their marriage and the future they were building. At night they shared a bed and talked, holding hands and wearing nightclothes because bare skin was altogether too tempting.

Through talk their mutual understanding deepened. He spoke of the mistakes he'd made, the successes, and the damnable occasions when there was no good solution.

Laurel haltingly revealed how she'd spent a lifetime being good, yet feeling deep inside that she could never be good enough. And when they ran out of words, they slept, always touching even as they shifted and turned throughout the night.

Laurel looked so lovely that Kirkland couldn't help but hope that soon there would be enough space between their past and their future that they could resume their physical intimacy. But he'd wait as long as it took for his wife to be fully restored and ready. He'd waited ten years, after all.

He smiled as he crossed the room. "Your favorite Mozart Allegro and even Vivace. You must be feeling happy, my lady."

"I am!" She caught his hand and pulled him to the piano bench beside her. "An understatement, James. Come sit with me so we can play together."

He did, and the magic of their sharing a keyboard was a good metaphor for how much else they shared now that she'd fully opened her heart. After they finished a favorite Vivaldi piece,

Laurel turned to him, her changeable eyes shining.

"Lady Julia visited earlier today, and we had a most interesting discussion," she said rather shyly. "I told her that despite the miscarriage, I still felt pregnant, which made no sense. Then I started to expand. You might have noticed?"

His brows arched. "I haven't seen enough of you to be aware of that."

Laurel blushed. "Because we've not been entirely—marital in the last month, it seemed impossible that I could be pregnant again, and the other possibilities were somewhat alarming. So she examined me, and said I'm not pregnant *again,* but *still!*"

He stared at her. "You didn't miscarry?"

"I did, but Julia said that she's heard of cases like mine, where there was an early miscarriage but a continuing pregnancy." Laurel caught his hand and pressed it to her belly, which did indeed have a fuller curve. "Her theory is that there might potentially have been twins, but one wasn't strong enough to survive. So it was lost. In such a case, the stronger child survives and is born normal and healthy. Julia said that seems to be *exactly* what has happened with me!"

He stared at her, not quite able to believe. And yet this felt true and real. "I thought we'd already had our share of miracles."

She closed her eyes as she held his hand against her. "When I first realized I was pregnant, I was shocked and amazed and delighted, but felt . . . tentative. As if something wasn't quite right. When I miscarried, it seemed almost inevitable." Her eyes opened. "But this feels *right*. I still mourn the lost child, but the fact that there is another, stronger child truly is a miracle."

He wrapped his arms around her, feeling the warmth and female strength that gave his life meaning. "Blessed be," he whispered. "I'm tempted to pick you up and whirl you around, but I don't dare because I can't risk hurting you. So I'll kiss you instead." Which he did, with passion, thoroughness, and joy.

When the kiss ended so they could indulge in breathing, Laurel rose and caught his hands as she began to sing as she had once before.

> Drink to me only with thine eyes,
> And I will pledge with mine;

He stood and joined in the song, his gaze on hers. This time his voice was no longer rusty, and it blended tenderly with her lush contralto.

> Or leave a kiss within the cup
> And I'll not ask for wine.
> The thirst that from the soul doth rise
> Doth ask a drink divine;
> But might I of Jove's nectar sip,
> I would not change for thine.

When they finished the second verse, Laurel said shyly, "I asked Julia some other questions. I won't break, my love. And don't we have something wonderful to celebrate?"

Clamping down on unruly hope, he asked, "You're sure about the not breaking part?"

Her smile turned wicked and she tugged him toward the bedroom. "Julia says that generally speaking, when women are increasing, they act in one of two ways. They either don't want to be touched, or they want to be touched all the time. Guess which type I am!"

Laughing, he stopped resisting and let her tow him toward their bedroom. "Have I mentioned lately how much I love you?"

"Not since you left this morning." She looked back over her shoulder with a smile that could light up London on the darkest day of winter. "I love you, too, James. Even more than yesterday, but not as much as tomorrow."

They were in their bedroom now, so he closed the door and took her into his arms. The future would have sorrow as well as joy because sorrow was part of life. But he knew now that nothing, *nothing,* could separate them again. The bonds between them had been forged in fire for all eternity.

And today—today there was joy.

Author's notes:

For the record, I did not invent the Vanishing Twin Syndrome for plot purposes. The syndrome was mentioned to me by an author friend who is an RN of many years of experience. I started researching, and found a Web site of posts from women who experienced an early loss, then went on to have a healthy baby. Modern technology makes the process more understandable, but I think a wise midwife might have been able to deduce that this happened even in the days before ultrasound.

The slave trade was banned by the British Parliament and the American Congress in 1807. In 1808, the Royal Navy established the West Africa Squadron to stop illegal slavers by patrolling the coast of West Africa. Though the squadron started with two small ships, at the height of its efforts it employed a sixth of all naval vessels.

Starting in 1820, the United States Navy began to join with the British to suppress the trade. The West Africa Squadron captured about 1,600 slave ships and freed around 150,000 Africans in the years between 1808 and 1860, so there must have been people like Kirkland supporting their efforts.

Regular steamboat services started on the

Thames in London in 1815, so Ashton wasn't the only one testing steamboats at that time.

I'm quite sure that Violet Herbert Rhodes completed her book, *The Secrets of a Lady's Maid*, and that it became a bestseller!

Center Point Large Print
600 Brooks Road / PO Box 1
Thorndike, ME 04986-0001 USA

(207) 568-3717

**US & Canada:
1 800 929-9108**
www.centerpointlargeprint.com